BRIANAG

THE BLOOD QUEEN CHRONICLES

DAVID H. MILLAR

TITLES BY DAVID H. MILLAR

CELTIC HISTORICAL FANTASY/FICTION

The Conall Series

Conall: The Place of Blood: Rinn-Iru
Conall II: The Raven's Flight: Eitilt an Fhiaigh Dhuibh
Conall III: The Sisters: Na Deirfiúracha
Conall IV: A Brace of Eagles: Snaidhm Iolar
Conall V: Retribution: Díoltas

The Dog Roses Series

The Dog Roses: Na Feirdhriseacha
The Dog Roses: Resolution

The Blood Queen Series

The Blood Queen: A 'Bhanrigh Fuil
Brianag: The Blood Queen Chronicles

Brianag:
The Blood Queen Chronicles
DAVID H. MILLAR

Brianag: The Blood Queen Chronicles is a work of fiction. Apart from obviously historical figures and places, all names, characters, and incidents are either the product of the author's imagination or are used fictitiously. Any resemblance to actual persons, living or dead, establishments, events, or locales is entirely coincidental.

Copyright © 2025 by David H. Millar. All rights reserved.

No part of this book may be reproduced or transmitted in any form or by any means, electronic or mechanical, including photocopy, recording, or any information and storage retrieval system now known or to be invented, without permission in writing from the publisher, except by a reviewer who wishes to quote brief passages in connection with a review written for inclusion in a magazine, newspaper, blog, or broadcast.

A Wee Publishing Company, LLC
HOUSTON, TX, USA
http://www.aweepublishingco.com

Paperback ISBN: 979-8-9865756-7-4
eBook ISBN: 979-8-9865756-8-1
Library of Congress Control Number: 2025905189

A Wee Publishing Company, LLC, Houston, TX

To Ethan. Welcome.

ACKNOWLEDGEMENTS

The process of writing, publishing, and marketing novels is a team sport. Often, it is arduous, especially when I am faced with a blank page for days, weeks or months—and sometimes it is inspiring. A good sense of humour and a bottle of Irish whiskey within reach are essential.

I have always appreciated the international cast that comprises Team Millar. Thanks to my editors, Kahina Necaise and Naomi Muntz from The Fabled Planet, my cover designer and internal formatter, Ida Jansson, Amygdala Design, and my cartographer, Dewi Hargreaves.

Last but certainly not least, thank you to my beta readers: authors Judith Fullerton, Jolie A. Reynolds and Brendan Sullivan, and Lauren Millar and Susan Robitaille.

CONTENTS

CHARACTER NAME PRONUNCIATIONS

The tongue of my homeland, Gaelic, is not an easy language to learn. That said, neither are the dialects used in Cornwell's Saxon Stories, Tolkien's Lord of the Rings or Martin's Game of Thrones.

I have tended, whenever possible, to use ancient Gaelic (Irish and Scottish) names, which sometimes does not equate with modern Gaelic. My advice is to read the novel with a glass of Irish or Scottish whiskey in hand. Furthermore, to increase the pain of my readers in the United States, the story is written in British English!

To ease your pain, I have provided a guide to the most frequently used names in the novel. I hope it adds to your enjoyment of the tale. That said, pronounce the words however gives you the most pleasure. That is what I generally do!

IRISH GAELIC NAMES

Aoife Ni Cináed (**EE-fa** nee KIN-awd)

Áine (**AWN-ya**)

Ardghal Sgiathdubh (**ARD-ul** SKEE-a-DOO)

Brion Ó Cathasaigh (**BREE-un** o KAS-akh)

Caoimhe (**KEE-va**)

Cassán Mac Brion (**KAS-awn** mak BREE-un)

Conall Mac Gabhann (**KON-ul** mak GAWN)

Cú Sídhe (**KOO SHEE**)

Daghdha (**DAG-da**)

Draighean (**DRYNE**)

Éile (**AYL yeh**)

Fearghal Ruadh (**FER-ul** ROO-uh)

Íar Mac Dedad (**EER** mak DAY-da)

Íde (**EE-deh**)

Leannán-Sídhe (**LA-nawn** SHEE)

Medb (**MAY-ve**)

Mongfhionn (**MUNN-yung**)

The Mórrígan (**Moe-rig-gAHn**)

Neamhain Ni Fearghal (**NYAV-in** nee FER-ul)

Oghma (**OGG-mah**)

Sorchae Ni Íar (**SUR-a-ka** nee EER)

Torcán Ó Dubhghaill (**TURK-awn** o DOO-l)

SCOTTISH GAELIC NAMES

Beira (**BAY-ruh**)

Brianag Ni Brion (**BREE-uh-NAK** nee BREE-un)

Cè Mac Drostan (**KEE mak** DROST-an)

Conn (**KON**)

Dolidh (**DOL-ee**)

Drostan Ruadh (**DROST-an** ROO-ag)

Earc (**ERK**)

Eimhir Nic Finnean (**AY-veer** nahk FIN-yan)

Ealasaid Nic Finnean (**YAHL-uh-sek** nakh FIN-yan)

Giosail (**GEE-sil**)

Finnean Mac Sèitheach (**FIN-yan mak** SHAY-ke)

Fionn Mac Drostan (**FYOON** mak DROST-an)

Gràinne Ni Fearghal (**GRAN-YUH** nee FER-ul)

Luag (**LOO ak**)

Malmhìn (**MAL-uh-veen**)

Mòrag Nic Artair (**MOR-ak** nak ASH-ter)

Mùirne Nic Amodocus (**MOORN-a** nahk Amodocus)

Niall (**NEE-ull**)

Ròs Nic Cassán (**ROES** nahk KAS-awn)

Seonag Nic Drostan (**SHO-nahk** nak DROST-an)

Sidheag (**SHEE-ak**)

Teàrlag Nic an t-Sionnaich (**CHAR-lak** nak an-CHUN-ich)

NON-GAELIC NAMES

Amodocus (Thracian)

Heilasa (Thracian)

Thrax (Thracian)

Pytheas (Greek)

N
NA DAOINE-CAIT
Loch nan Clàr
Càrn Liath
Cùil Daothail
Loch Eireachd
A' Chrìon Làraich
Dùn Athad
Dùn Brion
SLEAGH
ABHAINN DUBH
LINNE FOIRTHE
Northern Albu

CHAPTER 1

The slave bowed, walked across the wooden floor, and set a wooden platter on the side table. Without turning around, Gràinne Ni Fearghal, the Blood Queen, Ruler of the Na Daoine Tùrsach and High Queen of the Eastern Tribes, knew what the plate held—a bloody, still-warm human heart. She had been served the same dish every full moon for the past decade.

The ritual was one of the details omitted from her conversations with the spirit of the original *A Bhanrigh Fuil*—Blood Queen. Yet if Gràinne had known, would it have stopped her? *How else could I have saved Brianag?* So far, battles and the sacrifices of those about to cross the veil sustained the supply of hearts. Yet when the conflicts ended through victory or exhaustion, what then?

If she stopped the practice, she would die. It was that simple. Good or evil, everything has a consequence. What would happen to her hand-fast partner, Amodocus, or her children, Brianag, Heilasa, and the twins? A single ruby tear rolled down Gràinne's cheek.

She missed Brianag. *Why will she not talk to me?* Gràinne's shoulders slumped. *Can I blame her?* Another droplet escaped from her eyes. *Will I ever hold her in my arms? Has she changed? What does she look like?* Imprinted on Gràinne's mind was Brianag's furious, savage face before she was chained and dragged away by her grandmother, the demigoddess Mongfhionn of the *Aes Sídhe*.

Anger and frustration made Gràinne stamp her feet on the wooden slats. A miasma of red leached from her body and her eyes became blood red, as did her nails and the curling ribbons of power swathing her body. As Gràinne reached for the heart, tendrils of the red mist preceded her. When they touched the heart, she felt power drawn from the blood. She steeled herself and bit into the organ. As she chewed the muscle, she gagged on the meat and the thick blood that slithered down her gullet.

It still revolts me. That must be a good sign. "Please, Goddess, allow me some relief," she pleaded. There was no answer, as there had been none for ten summers. "What did I do to make you ignore me? What do you want of me, *bitseach*—bitch?"

You may think it justified, but I will only tolerate disrespect for a short time, Gràinne Ni Fearghal. Even from one imbued with ancient powers. Stop thinking as a human or you will go mad. You inherited the mantle of A 'Bhanrigh Fuil, of the Ancients. Your spirit is older than the Tuatha Dé. Accept it. You will need it, or many will die.

"I am neither god nor demigod. I live in the human world, as do my partner and children, and those I rule over. I am a person who bleeds, and hurts, and I count time in cycles of the moon, not thousands of years," railed Gràinne.

Stop whining, child! The Goddess's tone was sharp, like a whip.

Gràinne was instantly furious but soon smiled. The Goddess had re-established communication. *But why now?*

***

Gràinne wiped her lips on the red cloth accompanying the wooden platter, walked to the chamber door, and roared, "Burn the salver and cloth!" There was no need to shout. The slave, Giosail, stood a respectful five paces from the room's entrance.

Giosail was a *bana-phrionnsa*—princess—and the youngest daughter of the king of the Na Daoine Smeurta, a minor north-eastern coastal tribe commonly known as The Smeared. Because of her father's arrogance, they had stubbornly resisted Gràinne's entreaties. His posturing was vain and futile, and the clann was defeated. The warriors who had not died in battle were executed, along with every male over the age of fourteen summers.

Only women and young children were spared. Still, it was debatable whether enslavement was better than death. Giosail's servitude to the Blood Queen began when she was eight summers old. She had faithfully served Gràinne since her clann's demise and was now seventeen summers.

The young woman was wise for someone of her years and knew Gràinne's tantrum helped her recover from the awful ritual. She dropped her head, expecting Gràinne to stride past. Thus, she was startled when Gràinne stopped and calloused fingertips lifted her chin. Giosail's blue eyes met the *bhanrigh's* ruby gaze without flinching.

"I'm sorry," whispered Gràinne. The apology was unnecessary but made Giosail's heart smile, and she prayed to the Goddess for mercy for the queen. No one deserved to suffer so much. "If you were free, Giosail, would you continue to serve me? Your presence comforts me." Gràinne's voice was gentle yet held great pain.

"I would be honoured, my queen."

Another bellow echoed off the timber walls of the royal crannag. "Giosail is a free person and my personal aide from this moment." Gràinne turned to another servant. "See that Giosail has better accommodation and clothes."

She strode past a grinning Amodocus. "What?"

The burly Thracian hugged Gràinne until her ribs cried out for mercy. "You're a good person, my love."

"Tell that to Brianag."

"She knows."

* * *

The Goddess was furious, although not at Gràinne. No, she was proud of the Blood Queen's strength, and through all her travails Gràinne had remained faithful. *She will have her reward… but not yet.*

Rather, the Goddess's wrath was directed at the squabbling siblings of Drostan Ruadh. Seonag should have grasped Drostan's dying command, seized, and secured the throne. Instead, they warred among themselves. *I have direr problems to address, and the Forest People's stupidity is a distraction jeopardising more than their tribe. I will not forget.*

CHAPTER 2

The Halls of the Aes Sídhe

My mother and I saved the bitches from Sidheag. Does that not afford me some credit or a lessening of the guilt they wish to lay on my shoulders? Brianag knew Mongfhionn, the powerful Sídhe, and her grandma, loved her, but how long would that last? The demigoddesses of the Aes Sídhe were not known for moderation or patience.

Her gaze swept across the vast Great Hall. Its crystal walls glittered as if bathed in sunlight, creating a myriad of rainbows. Brianag felt the sun's warm rays, but it was an illusion. There was no burning to darken her skin. Her golden glow from a childhood spent in Southern Gaul and the Great Sea was a distant memory. In its place was a smoky white hue. Still, it could justifiably be claimed the skin tone perfectly complemented her long auburn hair. Therefore, it accentuated Brianag's undoubted beauty.

My body came from Sidheag's blood. Am I as false as my surroundings and the whores of the Aes Sídhe? Whose daughter am I? The bitch who kidnapped me to force my mother to serve her or the one who birthed and nurtured me? One created a monster, the other became the Blood Queen to save me. The choice should be simple. Why isn't it?

A small cohort of the Aes Sídhe loved Brianag. A larger minority were kind or apathetic to her. The remainder distrusted, hated, or sought to use Brianag. Over and above that, the demigods feared her. *Why? How could I possibly be a threat?* Brianag grinned. *A pain in the arse, yes, but do I deserve notoriety?*

Still, Brianag's thoughts were disingenuous. The Aes Sídhe had good cause to either dread or worship her, and she knew it. To them, she was Sidheag reincarnated… but much more powerful.

***

Another thought diverted Brianag's attention. She had met only one of the rulers of the Aes Sídhe—the Nine. They were the nine Womb-Born sons and daughters of the Mother Crone of the Tuatha Dé—the ancestors of the Aes Sídhe. Based on her observations, Brianag concluded the Nine either encouraged or were indifferent to the wider community's hostility towards her. In this, Brianag could not have been more wrong.

She snorted. *The Nine? It should be the Eight.* The fiercest of the Womb-Born and their Battle Queen—The Mórrígan—had not been seen for a thousand years. *I applaud her for fleeing this pit of humourless vipers. I will do likewise as soon as I'm ready.* To voice the thought made Brianag tremble and so she kept silent.

Time was meaningless to the Aes Sídhe. Hence, Brianag did not know how long she had been their guest. Was it counted in cycles of the moon or in decades? Still, there was safety and comfort in her bejewelled cage. Everyone she knew might be dead and this was her home. *Please, no. Goddess.* How would her return be received? Would it be as violent as her departure? An emerald tear rolled down her cheek. *Is it too late for me?*

As for the Goddess, she kept her counsel to herself. And Serendipity had been bound from interfering in Brianag's life—until now.

***

Brianag's vision travelled beyond the chamber and the Mound known as Coria to view the *Land of Immensity*, which the Tuatha Dé immodestly named their domain. There were four huge cities, or Mounds, in the Land of Immensity. A few island kingdoms rose from the seas surrounding the land but were inhabited by outcasts. *Will that be my fate?* All were cloaked in swirling mists and darkness that even her gifts could not penetrate.

To the far north was a great island of snow-capped, red mountains and caves—the *Island of the Wind-Born.* The latter were also known as Dragons. The kingdom was connected by a single, narrow bridge to the Land of Immensity. Brianag had never met or seen a serpent and was sceptical of their existence.

Never mind dragons. Does this place exist? Is it a grand illusion—a mass hallucination? The beauty of the Halls of the Aes Sídhe was painfully flawless. Like gazing too long at a field of fresh snow, it burned the eyes. The climate was perpetually temperate. There was no rain, snow, or storms— unless there was a fight, but, alas, they were rare. *If this is the Afterlife, you can keep it, Goddess. It is boring. My punishment is a prison of boundless luxury but remains a cage.*

Each demigod was millennia old. Yet they were long-lived, not immortal. Only the Goddess deserved that title. All appeared impossibly beautiful and not older than forty summers. Many were vain and chose younger facades. Still, all could change their age and body with a thought.

The Tuatha Dé were barren, which was of great concern to the Nine. There were, and would never exceed, forty-four thousand, four hundred and forty-four members of the race. The number was a mystery to Brianag, but she concluded it was a punishment of the Goddess. *What was their sin?* The Womb-Born knew the population would inevitably decline and they would vanish, if over hundreds of millennia. Children born from sex with races beyond the Land of Immensity were the only exception to the rule. Thus, the Aes Sídhe envied the humans' ability to procreate.

Artistic talent was admired by the Tuatha Dé above all other abilities and guaranteed a high position in their society. The demigods allayed the monotony of their existence by creating artistic masterpieces that would never be seen beyond their domain, or they vied for power and influence. Yet the latter had a ceiling in the form of the Womb-Born.

There were occasional internecine battles, but what is the point when the options of serious injury or death are removed? Only weapons made from iron could kill a sídhe, and these were banned from the Mounds.

***

Man's ancestors, the Sons of Mil, had defeated the Tuatha Dé. A treaty was negotiated, forbidding the Aes Sídhe from waging war on humans. It also banished them to the Mounds.

Currently, an influential faction within the Aes Sídhe, including some of the Womb-Born, thought it was time to revisit that surrender. What would they risk if they chose to confront the humans—obliteration? Would a glorious battle and defeat be worse than their current circumstances—inevitable extinction?

A clever loophole in the Treaty gave the Aes Sídhe free movement between the Land of Immensity and the Land of Man. Yet only a small group, such as Draighean, Medb, and Mongfhionn, who were intimate with the humans visited the realm regularly. The taint of humanity on them prompted snide looks and sniggers from their sisters and the Womb-Born but also fear and envy. Bonding with men and women bestowed two unforeseen advantages to that band—it enhanced their powers and restored their fertility. The latter was reason enough for the Tuatha Dé to consider war.

Paradoxically, the standing of Brianag's grandma, the sídhe Mongfhionn, rose and she became the de facto leader of the Aes Sídhe. Many disliked her, most distrusted her, and a few hated her. There were always rumours of a challenge, but the practicalities of that meant a battle to the death. Tradition decreed such a contest must occur in the land of the humans, and no sídhe was foolish enough to defy Mongfhionn on what was considered her home territory.

Where are the men? The famed heroes of the Tuatha Dé? Brianag sniggered at her random thought. Perhaps they became tired of the bitches and moved elsewhere? *Who could blame them? Who would want to rut the frigid bitches?* Brianag chuckled at the startled looks of the nearest gaggle of sídhe. Brianag guarded her thoughts jealously and rarely permitted access. The ability infuriated the Aes Sídhe and gave Brianag great pleasure—and a crucial advantage.

⁎⁎⁎

Brianag wondered if it had been one sunset or ten thousand since her grandma had dragged her in chains through Coria's gates. She had stopped counting after a thousand false sunsets. The Aes Sídhe were vain creatures and Coria had an embarrassment of mirrors. Hence, Brianag knew she had aged. She sensed time had slowed for her, but she could not tell by how much. Looking positively, she was finally comfortable with the curvaceous shape and sensuality Sidheag bequeathed her.

Am I as long-lived as the sídhe? How old does my mother look? Would I recognise her? Does she think about me? Brianag's lip trembled, and she murmured, "Mother." The word brought fear, trepidation, and a feeling of emptiness. She knew Gràinne had sacrificed her soul for her. Yet it was only recently Brianag finally understood this. *She deserted me. It was her fault.* The bellyaching that occasionally surfaced sounded hollow, selfish, and pitiful. *Am I still an adolescent—a child of fifteen summers? Have I not matured?*

Whether she had grown or developed was a question in the eyes of every sídhe she passed, including the Womb-Born. With few exceptions, the demigods were wary of Brianag. They measured her growth by whether they could control her. With each false sunset, they acknowledged the futility of the task. Thus, they remained angry, frustrated… and fearful of her.

"Why? It's not my fault I'm like this. One of your own did this to me!" she screamed. Emerald-green talons snapped into view; the green sheath that wrapped her body shimmered and became one with her skin. Her eyes blackened, and her mouth filled with needle teeth. She opened it into a garish smile. The nearest sídhe recoiled. Was this the day Brianag would cast off her restraints, and the carnage begin? How would they stop her? Could they?

"Have I not behaved as well as could be expected of any adolescent torn from those who loved her?" she shouted. Her infrequent outbursts gave a fleeting look into Brianag's thoughts and reminded the Aes Sídhe they could not see into her head unless she permitted it.

Brianag whispered, "Thanks," to Sidheag for an immensely useful gift. It was only a murmur. Despite seeing Sidheag encased in molten iron and hearing her terrible screaming, she remained unconvinced of the creature's destruction. Brianag's belief was shared by many sídhe who either held the same opinion or wished it were true. She knew this because she had read their minds. Before her resurrection in the cold waters of a loch in Northern Albu, Sidheag had survived for many centuries as a thought, a whisper, and a formless wraith. Could molten iron destroy any of these?

* * *

Brianag inhaled, regaining control of her physical form and thoughts. She was vastly better at that now. *Perhaps I have one thing to thank the Aes Sídhe for.* She smiled at the trio who walked towards her. Still, Brianag had reservations concerning their leader—her grandma.

She remembered, as if it were only a sunset ago, the blow from Mongfhionn's oak staff that laid her out cold on Dùn Brion's stone ramparts. She rubbed her wrists and recalled how the chains binding her burned her skin. *Why does iron burn me? What am I?*

While only the memory of the links remained, Brianag still bore the star-shaped shadow of the staff's imprint on her forehead. The Sídhe liked to leave mementoes as lessons. Brianag could not hold back a grin. Her head had shattered her grandma's ancient weapon into a thousand splinters.

I was only fifteen! Her mind screamed, and those around her recoiled again. Heat flared in Brianag's cheeks, and her hands became fists. The anger of the adolescent lashed out. This time, the deep sadness in her grandma's eyes as she approached tempered it. The heat of Brianag's anger diminished from boiling to tepid water.

The second group member was a sídhe more striking than Mongfhionn—a feat few came close to achieving. Tall, black-cloaked, and with hair as black as night, only the thin, braided red highlights and full red lips gave colour to a porcelain-white face. Yet, Draighean, or Blackthorn—for that was her name—seemed deeply troubled and very angry, but not because of Brianag. *That's a change.*

Brianag's unreserved smile was for the final member, Neamhain. Her friend was a summer younger than Brianag and was, in every way, her mother's daughter. The willowy adolescent frame had transformed into one that rivalled Mongfhionn's. Like her ma, long strawberry-blonde hair, which flared like a halo around her oval face in a breeze, crowned her head.

As a child, Neamhain's favourite activity was finding a high vantage point. With her friend, Sorchae, and her hands stretched upwards, Neamhain would scream into the wind. A precocious talent, at ten summers her ululations sent shivers down the spines of nearby adults. Now, they had the same effect… on the Aes Sídhe.

During Brianag's abduction by Sidheag, Neamhain brought light and sanctuary into her seemingly bottomless pit of despair. Only she had never let Brianag down or betrayed her. She stood resolute at Brianag's side, wept with her, and staunchly defended her through thick and thin. *I will destroy any who seek to harm you.*

Neamhain was closer than a sister but was torn between loyalty to Brianag and her mother. Neamhain's startled look and the furious chatter among the Aes Sídhe made Brianag mutter, "Shite!" *I must not lose control.* That would give the Aes Sídhe the evidence or excuse they needed to destroy her. Brianag smirked. *Could they terminate me?* It would not just be her they would confront, but Mongfhionn, Neamhain, and possibly Draighean and Medb.

In her mind, she heard her grandma's chiding: *Hubris, granddaughter. I need to leave the Land of Immensity.*

✳✳✳

"Is it your intent to forever seek revenge on those you deem to have caused you harm?" asked Neamhain. Given the question's source,

Brianag was taken aback. Neamhain usually had a more subtle approach. Open-mouthed, Brianag could do little other than make gasping noises, like a fish tossed onto a riverbank.

"Given that Sidheag has been dealt with, and your father, Brion, died trying to save you, then your only remaining targets appear to be those who love you." Again, Brianag made sputtering sounds. "In which case, you have succeeded, for both of our mothers are miserable. Perhaps, having tortured them, you intend to release them through death."

Why now, Neamhain? What do you know? What does my grandma know?

The young sídhe held Brianag's gaze. "That might be considered merciful. Yet if you do, then add me to your list. I will not stand by and see you destroy our mothers. Yours is my sister, by adoption. It will break my heart, Brianag, but I *will* fight you, and more than likely, you will end me." Neamhain sighed. "Is that what you want? To be alone… forever?"

"You have spoken to my mother?"

"Of course I have, Brianag, and do not pretend to be ignorant. Her powers are older and darker than the Aes Sídhe. Like us, she does not need physical contact to communicate… *and neither do you.*"

"How is she?"

"Grow up and stop being a self-centred bitseach. Ask her yourself!" snapped Neamhain before adding, "Irreversibly changed, I fear." Brianag fought to stem the tears demanding to be released at the sadness in Neamhain's voice.

"It's my fault." Brianag quashed the nascent sob that threatened her composure. *I cannot show weakness in these Halls.*

"Yes, it is." Again, Neamhain's directness shocked Brianag. "You're not the only one with challenges to resolve."

What is going on? What am I missing?

Neamhain's tone softened. "She has no regrets. However, I wish she had fewer sorrows and an occasional hug from a daughter she loves unconditionally. You have never met or held Heilasa, Brianag. She is nine summers old and has never met her sister, although your ma has told her about you. The twins have no memory of you."

Brianag did not know whether to laugh or cry. Instead, she chose anger. "I have been here ten years." Brianag spoke slowly, emphasising each word. She had done the calculation. Neamhain coloured as if guilty of disclosing a great secret. Ten years to a demigod has less meaning than a breath.

A cough drew them from their musings, and they turned to face Mongfhionn. The sídhe did not look happy.

✶✶✶

"We need to talk," said Mongfhionn. Never were four words spoken so ominously. "Cloak us, Brianag."

Brianag's eyes opened wide. "What do you mean, Grandma?" Brianag's feigned innocence failed miserably.

"Do not test me, child. I am not as oblivious to your considerable talents as you would like me to be. *Nor are you immune to mine.* If you consider me an enemy, you should know my powers better." Mongfhionn held Brianag's gaze until she sighed and surrendered.

"Yes, Grandma."

To those watching, nothing changed. The trio continued their conversation. There was even the sound of scolding and protesting to bolster their assumptions. It was an illusion. In a fleeting moment, Brianag constructed a sanctuary no sídhe could break through. Perhaps it might even fool the Womb-Born.

"The Womb-Born and the Aes Sídhe continue to be troubled about your powers and presence…"

"Even you, Grandma?" Brianag's lip quivered.

"Do not interrupt me, child. My concern is not about your powers, but how you use them. I am very proud you have learned to manage them. You have achieved an incredible feat in a very short time." Brianag's face glowed at Mongfhionn's praise. It was short-lived.

"Paradoxically, it has also made you much more dangerous in the eyes of the Aes Sídhe. Your continued presence in the Mounds will lead

13

to rifts among the sídhe and potential rebellion. A large section views you as the natural, and more powerful, successor to Sidheag. That creature had protectors, even among the Womb-Born, and still has many adherents. The Nine cannot permit that."

"No!" This time, both Brianag and Neamhain responded.

"It is time for you to go home, Brianag. The question is how." Brianag's and Neamhain's eyes looked as if they might burst from their sockets. "The Womb-Born have met and quarrelled… *about you*," said the Sídhe. "Leannán-Sídhe, who claims to be Sidheag's creator and mother, wants to avenge her daughter.

"For all her many flaws, Sidheag was a sídhe, and the Womb-Born look dimly on anyone destroying any of the Tuatha Dé, even if it was justified. Leannán has a pet called the Cú Sídhe, whom she proposes to use to track and kill you."

"The Hag, no, Ma! Will she prevail over the Womb-Born?" asked Neamhain, fearful of the answer.

"Leannán is a seductress, although that does not fully describe her talents." Mongfhionn sighed. "She only needs one of the Womb-Born to agree. Áine, Queen of the Bright Ones, is one of the Nine and Leannán's mother. Hence, inevitably, Leannán will get her way." Exasperated, Mongfhionn ground her teeth. "To the Nine, this has a delightful symmetry. Either Leannán and the Cú Sídhe will be destroyed, or you will. No matter which, the Womb-Born win."

"Who or what is the Cú Sídhe?" asked Brianag.

"A man and a beast you never want to meet," replied Mongfhionn, staring at Brianag. "Be honest with me. Can you slip from this realm without being detected? You must have considered escaping your 'gilded cage'." Brianag blushed. Her grandma had abilities she had not considered.

"I think so…"

"I am going with Brianag."

"No!" This time the riposte was from Brianag and Mongfhionn.

"I did not desert my sister when Sidheag ensnared her. I will not abandon her to Leannán or the Cú Sídhe." The set of Neamhain's jaw shouted she would not be dissuaded. Then she said, "You know the prophecy, Ma. It is time for me to face it."

Mongfhionn's shoulders slumped, and Brianag looked curiously at Neamhain. "How can I help?" asked Mongfhionn.

CHAPTER 3

Northern Albu—Gràinne's Crannag at Loch nan Clàr

Sorchae Ni Íar had a promise to fulfil. Anyone who understood her character knew nothing would prevent her from keeping it. Standing on the deck of the leading trireme, she gripped the rail and shivered. "How will I get used to this weather?" she grumbled.

The autumnal festival of Lugnasad had just been celebrated, and a golden sun lingered in the sky. Yet without her heavy cloak, she would freeze. As for the continual mizzle, the less said, the better. Ardghal Sgiathdubh, Sorchae's shield-man, stood alongside her. The veteran of many campaigns laughed. "Lazing about, half-naked, on the Great Sea's beaches with rich young princes and princesses has made you soft. You need to toughen up." The giveaway was the deep dimples in Ardghal's weather-beaten cheeks. The veteran warrior's eyes twinkled, and his lips could barely restrain a smile.

"*Tuilí*—bastard!" retorted Sorchae before releasing a great belly laugh. Among Clann Ui Flaithimh, Sorchae's reputation as a warrior, who had little time for frivolity, was uncontested. Many justifiably claimed her fighting talents eclipsed those of Mòrag Nic Artair, her mentor and adopted aunt. Sorchae was not to be trifled with.

Sorchae's aunt was a queen of Clann Ui Flaithimh. However, by blood, Mòrag was also Bhanrigh of the Aos an Fhithich—the Ravens— upon whose lands Sorchae would shortly step. Her arrival was not a coincidence. Mòrag had no desire to return to her native land. Yet following her brother Blàr's death at the Battle of Cùil Daothail, she had a duty to ensure the tribe thrived and was ruled by someone she trusted. Mòrag had offered Sorchae a challenge she found impossible to refuse.

***

Four warships, triremes, glided into the sheltered bay and crunched onto the pebble-and-shingle beach. One hundred riders and two hundred horses disembarked. The latter showed their joy by churning the sea into a froth. According to Pytheas, the Greek explorer and merchant who owned the vessels, if they rode north-west after breaking their fast, they would reach their destination by *meán lae*—midday.

A cry from above caught Sorchae's attention, and she saw a great golden eagle dip and soar. Once more, the bird opened its mouth, but this time, the sound seemed like a child's laughter. "Thanks for the welcome, Goddess," murmured Sorchae.

The Goddess smiled. Sorchae had a special place in her heart because she was a fighter from before her birth. She was conceived by a murderess driven insane from the pox and executed by her brother and Sorchae's adopted father. Sorchae never knew her da, and never would. It was no loss. He was one of her ma's victims and likely the one who infected her. The child fought for life in the womb and, as she grew, let nothing dishearten or defeat her.

***

Gràinne shivered as she traversed the wooden bridge between the royal accommodations and the separate edifice that housed the Great Hall, the armoury, and additional guest quarters. The two buildings sat one hundred paces apart and two hundred strides from Loch nan Clàr's shoreline. A wide ribbon of pines protected the lake's pebble beach. Beyond that, towering, snow-capped mountains were the crannags' guardians.

My crannag is much better than a rock-and-stone dùn—fort. I do not need ditches planted with stakes or war machines to protect my walls. Even when frozen, the water protects me. Gràinne smiled, soothed by the gentle lapping of wavelets against the foundational piles and jetties, and the fragrance of pine trees carried on a friendly breeze. In a cycle of the moon, a crust of ice would form on the surface; in two cycles, the loch would be frozen solid, covered in waist-deep snow and assailed by bone-numbing winds. Such was the weather of Northern Albu's eastern domains.

The heavy wolf's-fur cloak draped across Gràinne's shoulders, and the sheepskin boots, were unnecessary and the shivering an affectation. She was immune to the cold. Gràinne huffed. It was the only practical benefit of being A 'Bhanrìgh Fuil. She feigned vulnerability to lessen others' nervousness. However, the boots' fleecy lining on her toes was a luxury she would never surrender.

***

"Has everyone arrived?" asked Gràinne.

Amodocus, Gràinne's partner and battle commander, dipped his head. His homeland was the mountains of Thracia, which could get very cold. Aptly, the giant of a man was swathed in a bearskin. "All, apart from Cassán Mac Brion and Eimhir. Dùn Brion remains besieged by Cè, the youngest of Seonag Nic Drostan's brothers. Fionn and Cè are the last of the brothers, likely because they are the best warriors of that nest of vipers."

"Cè is the clever one. What madness makes him adopt such a strategy? Dùn Brion is practically impregnable. The only way to capture it would be to starve the fort's garrisons, and neither Fionn nor Cè has the patience for a prolonged siege." Gràinne shook her head. "Cè's actions make no sense and only weakens the brothers."

Amodocus spat over the rail and into the water. He shook his head. "It only weakens one brother—Cè. I, too, thought he had more sense." The burly Thracian sighed. "The war with Seonag has been at an impasse for three summers. The pretenders' treasuries are depleted, and they need victories to satisfy their supporters." The Thracian rubbed a whiskered chin. "I think a weakened Cè is what Fionn wants. I doubt he wants to share the Forest People's throne."

"This war needs to end, Amodocus. However, I doubt they would appreciate me taking a more active role." Gràinne chuckled. "Although that would probably unite the Forest People—against the Eastern Tribes."

"How much longer can you avoid taking a side? Seonag is your best friend. How would you feel if you were in need, and she did not come to your aid? Consider the consequences of Fionn as king of the Forest People. You know as soon as his arse is on the throne, he will declare war on the Eastern Tribes. It's his nature. We already bleed from the drop in trade between the Forest People and the Eastern Tribes."

Amodocus paused. "Have you studied the southern border and the tribes across the Linne Foirthe? They have no love for the Lowlands and Highlands and have warred against us before. The reports of ships being built to transport warriors across the estuary increase with each cycle of the moon. Cassán and the Na Mèadaidh are the bulwark of the North. They would be swept away because Fionn would not come to their aid, and we would be too late."

"Have you any good news?" asked Gràinne.

"Yes. For the first time in history, the Eastern Tribes are united under a fearsome High Queen. We should not waste the opportunity to help a friend and secure our future."

Gràinne did not dispute Amodocus' argument. Yet his criticism of her procrastination stung, and she wanted to stomp off in an unqueenly huff. Fortunately, they had reached the door of the second crannag.

✶✶✶

Twenty sat around the High Table, but only five were significant—six if Cathbad, the newly appointed leader of Northern Albu's druids, was included. By all accounts, he was a fair arbiter, and no one challenged his knowledge of the Law. Still, Cathbad had a challenging task in this part of Northern Albu.

Until Gràinne and her allies destroyed them, the priests of the Na Daoine Tùrsach, under the thrall of Sidheag, were known for blood sacrifices, cannibalism, and the rampant debauchery of young girls. The clerics' despicable ministries had left few families untouched. Rightly or wrongly, among the Eastern Tribes, few distinguished between Sidheag's priests and the druids. Thus, many looked at Cathbad with suspicion.

The others around the table were minor *righrean*—kings—or influential chieftains. All had come to an accommodation with Gràinne and accepted her as High Queen. It was not Gràinne's way to use assassins or agents. She stood with her army and fought toe to toe with her enemies. Those who opposed her died in battle.

As of the meeting in the Great Hall, only a few islands in the extreme north-east remained beyond Gràinne's purview. Their remoteness likely meant they were uninformed or, more probably, did not care about the tribulations of the mainland. Their foes were the harsh weather, stormy seas, and inhospitable lands.

Gràinne scratched her chin. The Na Daoine Cait—the Cait People—were another exception to her conquests. It was rare that Gràinne thought about the small, isolated tribe, although it continued to puzzle her why she had never conquered it. She snorted. *Conquered it. I have never set eyes on one person from the tribe.* Gràinne wisely deduced the Cait People were protected—but by whom and for what purpose? *Perhaps, one day, I will find out.*

Following two summers of Gràinne's rule, battles between the tribes had diminished to minor skirmishes. The traditional raids on neighbours for cattle and young women resumed. It was an accord under Gràinne's terms, but it was peace. Many resented the Blood Queen's rule, but few challenged it. No one wanted to face her battle chariots or Amodocus' heavy cavalry.

Gràinne hosted the seasonal meeting in the Great Hall. The topics discussed were officially about cooperation and the economic prosperity of the eastern clanns. However, the war in the West dominated recent agendas. Those who submitted to Gràinne's leadership wanted assurances, but the queen knew if she was guided by Amodocus, she might be challenged.

She smiled. *When did that ever give me concern?*

***

Seonag Nic Drostan and her ma, Teàrlag Nic an t-Sionnaich, were in animated discussion. Seonag's father Drostan Ruadh's dying command was that Seonag should succeed him and rule the Forest People. Her brothers disagreed. Thus, for ten summers, the siblings had waged a bitter tribal war, and the Forest People's throne remained unoccupied.

Both women thought the meetings were a waste of time. Their priorities were defeating the remaining brothers and reuniting the tribe. The Forest People remained the most populous tribe and traditionally were the mediators of disputes and guarantors of peace in Northern Albu. Currently, they were as divided as the rebellious clanns they once controlled.

Teàrlag scowled at Gràinne. Seonag's *àrd-chomhairleach*—chief counsellor—did not trust the Blood Queen. Indeed, she had advocated for the eradication of the Na Daoine Tùrsach and its queen. Teàrlag's opinion had not changed. However, political expediency forced her to accept Seonag's view that a divided Forest People could not fight wars on two fronts.

Seonag was conflicted about her relationship with Gràinne. Until Amodocus' arrival, she had considered Gràinne a rival for the late king of Dùn Brion's affection. In a curious twist of fate, Gràinne became the friend who helped her in turbulent times and a warrior who fought by her side. Seonag loved the "old" Gràinne as a sister, but she was not as sure about the Blood Queen. She sighed. Time or war would tell.

She glanced at her ma. A frown lit on Seonag's face, and her brow furrowed. In the beginning, Teàrlag advocated destroying her sons because they had disregarded Drostan's dying command. However, recently, Teàrlag had mysteriously softened her position, suggesting an accommodation between Seonag and her two remaining brothers should be considered. *Over my dead body, Mother.*

***

Numbed by the drone of meaningless conversations, Gràinne forced her eyelids to remain open and her brain from succumbing to sleep. The babble ceased when the doors of the crannag swung open. The queen's head snapped up, and she stared at the entranceway. A chorus of "Shut the bloody doors!" rose as a brisk easterly wind stole the building's warmth. Positively, it also cleared the fug of minds deadened by the tedium.

Sorchae and Ardghal stepped across the threshold.

"That's interesting," remarked Amodocus.

At Gràinne's raised eyebrow, he pointed to the young woman. "Her skin colour says that she is not from here. Yet the raven feather on the thin braid of red hair points to an uncommon familiarity with the Ravens' traditions. Furthermore, her arse-length, black hair is braided as if ready for a fight, not a *céilí*." Amodocus chuckled. "I thought I carried an impressive array of weapons, but her weapons belt outclasses mine."

Gràinne rose as Sorchae strode towards the High Table. Both actions succeeded in quieting the hum of conversations. "This is a private meeting of kings and queens. You are not invited, if only because no one knows you. However, we are not inhospitable. Please wait in the royal crannag." She pointed to Giosail. "My aide will take care of you and ensure that you and your shield-man have food and drinks."

Sorchae stopped five paces from the table and bowed deeply. When she straightened, Sorchae smiled pleasantly. "Thank the Goddess. I'm in the right place, and my timing is perfect." She grinned. "I have no wish to correct you, my lady; however, we have met—in Lugudunon. I was Brianag's friend, and as a child you bounced me on your knee. Still, that was a long time ago."

Arms wide apart, Sorchae spun around and laughed. "I am not offended. I have changed considerably." Laughter rippled around those seated, for the young woman's demeanour was infectious. "I am Sorchae Ni Íar of Clann Ui Flaithimh and the daughter of Rí Íar Mac Dedad, whom I believe you know well. My father sends his regards."

"Welcome, Sorchae Ni Íar. I look forward to hearing news from Lugudunon… *after* this meeting." Gràinne's demeanour began to soften until Sorchae shook her head.

The young warrior inhaled deeply, knowing her next words would receive a less congenial reaction. She took a few steps closer to the table, bowed, and placed a seal on the table before Gràinne. "On the authority of Mòrag Nic Artair, Bhanrigh of the Ravens, I am commanded to succeed her as the Bhanrigh of the Ravens."

Sorchae pointed to the ring. "That is Mòrag's seal. Pytheas, whom I believe you know well and respect, will bear witness to its authenticity, and my declaration and claim. However, he sails for Ériu in a half-cycle of the moon, so please be quick."

The silence that descended on the gathering and the rumbling that subsequently ascended was expected. Yet Sorchae had not finished. "All alliances agreed in Mòrag's absence are suspended until I have reviewed them." The new Queen of the Ravens paused to let her news sink in before adding, "I am sure any challenges adjusting to the new situation can be resolved. We are reasonable people, are we not?"

Sorchae's belly rumbled loudly. "Apologies, I have travelled a long way, and my warriors and I are starving. Perhaps, while we enjoy your hospitality, those I do not know would introduce themselves. I would also appreciate an update on the People of the Ravens. Finally, I wish to familiarise myself with my kingdom while the weather permits. Perhaps you will recommend a guide."

"Niall is the King of the Ravens, appointed by common consent after the death of Blàr Mac Artair at the Battle of Cùil Daothail," snapped Gràinne. Her day had started badly and gone downhill with breathtaking rapidity. *I have better things to do than this.*

"Appointed by who?" asked Sorchae with infuriating innocence. "I am sorry, my lady. Niall may be very competent, and he and I will discuss his future role under *my* reign. However, he can only be a *tànaiste*—caretaker. He is certainly not the *rìgh*. That said, he will make an excellent and knowledgeable guide."

Sorchae paused, lifted a pottery jug from a nearby table, poured cool water into a cup, and took a sip. "According to the Law, what you have done in good faith does not supersede the wishes of the blood descendant of Artair Mac Artair."

She inclined her head to Cathbad. "Do not take my word, my lady. Please ask the druid or consult with as many Brehons as you wish. They will not tell you otherwise… unless bribed. *I* am the Bhanrigh of the Ravens. I will be delighted to meet anyone who wishes to challenge me in battle."

"What army supports your claim? You have fifty riders."

Sorchae's blue-green eyes narrowed. "Do I need an army when the Law is on my side?" She looked at Cathbad again. "*He* will confirm that the Druidic Council of Albu will not allow the Fénechas to be so easily dismissed." Sorchae's calm mien and twinkling eyes made Gràinne wary.

"Also, your scouts have misled you, my lady. I have one hundred heavily armed riders. Fifty remain in the forest. It will only take one to reach Pytheas' ships with the message each one carries." Sorchae paused as if making a calculation.

"My aunt loves her dùn and lifestyle in Gaul. By my reckoning, an irate Mòrag and her equally angry hand-fast partner, Torcán, whom I believe you also know, should arrive here by the festival of Bealtaine. Their armies and likely a substantial portion of Clann Ui Flaithimh's shield-wall will undoubtedly accompany them. Is that what you want? A war with your former friends, including one who once rescued you from certain death?"

Loud guffaws from Amodocus and Teàrlag broke the silence before pandemonium broke out around the table. "I like her," said Amodocus. Gràinne glared at her hand-fast partner. "She would make a formidable *fidchell* player."

The meeting was on the cusp of descending into mayhem when the crannag's doors crashed open again. "*Rut the Hag's bony arse! Who is it now?*" bellowed Gràinne. Amodocus shrugged. A tedious meeting had transformed into something much more entertaining and intriguing.

At a first glance, Gràinne thought the figure with the black staff and distinctive grey cloak was her mother, the Sídhe, Mongfhionn. She rose with a broad smile of relief. The halo of blonde hair swirling around the figure's head seemed to confirm her impression, until the corona settled.

"Neamhain!"

However, Gràinne's reaction was eclipsed when Sorchae screamed, *"Neamhain!"*, ran towards the door, and flung herself at the young sídhe, almost bowling her over. In doing so, she exposed the tall figure who followed in Neamhain's wake.

Long fingers reached up and threw the emerald-green hood back. A mass of waist-length auburn tresses was released as Brianag stepped forward. From across the room, mother and daughter gazed into each other's eyes. Brianag bowed respectfully. "Greetings, Mother. It has been a long time." The soft hiss of swords drawn from wool-lined scabbards was the immediate reaction of those gathered. Many remembered Brianag's association with Sidheag. In response, Brianag laughed and stretched out her arms. "Can a daughter not visit her ma?"

Brianag's cloak fell to the floor, and she stood sheathed in a translucent, emerald-green chiton that left nothing to the imagination. Still, most eyes were locked on Brianag's obsidian eyes and long green talons. "Please put your blades away. You will not last a moment if you confront a powerful sídhe and one who is more formidable than a sídhe."

"Hubris, Brianag," whispered Neamhain. Still, her blackthorn staff pointed forward. Sword in hand, and wondering what her friend had become, Sorchae took a position to guard Brianag's left flank.

Brianag spoke through gritted teeth. "They started it, Neamhain. I hoped to be welcomed, not attacked." Brianag's talons retracted, and her eyes reclaimed their original green hue. Only a primal sensuality radiated from her, and perhaps that was the more threatening.

"You look well, Ma. Indeed, you appear to have got younger since we last met."

"*This meeting is over!*" roared Gràinne. Then she pointed to Brianag, Neamhain, and Sorchae. "You three, in my crannag. *Now!*"

CHAPTER 4

The Land of Immensity—Oileán Dubh

The Tuatha Dé were complex and powerful, yet their solution to unacceptable behaviour was bizarrely simplistic: exile. The community recoiled at the suggestion that some members were irredeemable and deserved annihilation. Indeed, the limit on their population negated the latter. Thus, the Womb-Born banished those who threatened the status quo.

However, the rationale that miscreants would reflect on the reason for their antisocial behaviour, become enlightened, and mend their ways in exile was deeply flawed. The mischief-makers' twisted minds and isolation generated anger, resentment, and a thirst for vengeance. Hence the errant demigods bided their time for an opportunity. Given their longevity, the moment was inevitable.

Oileán Dubh—Black Island—was the home of the Leannán-Sídhe and her pet, the Cú Sídhe. The location lived up to its name, atmospherically and physically. The landscape and the tall fortress at its centre were built of black basalt. Even the fine sand on its beaches was black lava. Obsidian and black diamonds, opals, onyx, tourmalines, and pearls provided relief and decorative flourishes.

Leannán was conceived by Áine, an original member of the Womb-Born, in an era when the Tuatha Dé were still fertile. Leannán's notoriety, which eventually led to her banishment to the island of Oileán Dubh, was to be known as the mother-creator of Sidheag. No one knew the name of Sidheag's father or, indeed, if he ever lived. If he existed, it was unlikely he would ever volunteer that information, since exile would be his reward.

On the island, Leannán favoured black lace and delicate silk mourning garments. Painted black nails and lips complemented her raiment. Leannán's preferred hair was as black as a raven's feather, although, like all sídhe, she could change it at will. Perfectly camouflaged in her stronghold, only Leannán's porcelain-pale skin stood out from the darkness. However, she mitigated that with gloves, long sleeves, and veils.

Like all the Aes Sídhe, Leannán was beautiful and ageless. In the beginning, her chosen vocation as an artisan and patron of the arts was commendable. Like her mother, Leannán's creations were highly praised and valued by the Womb-Born and the wider Aes Sídhe community. And, like her mother, she was held up as an example.

The cause of Leannán's corruption remained a mystery and a source of perpetual gossip among the Aes Sídhe. Many declared the reason was simple—the Goddess had cursed her. Yet what was Leannán's offence? After her fall from grace, Leannán became faceless, ironically adding to her mystery. The choice also propagated the common perception that pride was her downfall.

A novelty among the sídhe, when Leannán walked among humans, her face changed to adopt her lovers'—men or women's—dreams of their perfect partner. Yet victim or prey were better descriptions than suitor, for none survived the affair. She could also choose which persona she allowed others to see. Leannán was a powerful enchantress whose aura few could resist. She was a blood drinker like Sidheag, although more controlled. Hence, she was more dangerous.

Many said, with good cause, that Oileán Dubh was alive. Leannán was a formidable witch and the island had absorbed her essence for millennia. It was a cloak that shrouded, protected, and warned her of intrusions. If she willed it, the island would repel uninvited guests. Hence Leannán's surprise to be faced by her mother. She growled and swore to find the gap in her defences.

"Don't bother, daughter. You may be one of the most powerful witches among the Aes Sídhe, but your abilities pale compared to one of the Womb-Born's."

Leannán dipped her head. "Yes, Mother." Two words had never been infused with so much venom. If the progeny of the Womb-Born ever had familial feelings towards their mothers, the emotion had dissipated aeons ago. The feeling was mutual, so any communication was infrequent and based on need.

Both Áine and Leannán wanted Brianag destroyed. Leannán blamed Brianag, and sought justice, for Sidheag's death. Áine's rationale was more arcane and frustratingly beyond Leannán's reach.

"You have permission from the Womb-Born to travel to the land of the humans. There, you will seek and kill Brianag and all who participated in Sidheag's destruction."

"Thank you, Mother."

"Thank me by proving you can accomplish this task. Succeed, and your exile will cease. Fail, and I will end you. I will not be embarrassed before my brothers and sisters."

✳✳✳

Leannán's sole companion on the island was another outcast, the Cú Sídhe. The beast originated in the dark, furious mists of the time preceding the Womb-Born. He was the last of his kind and a reminder of an era the Aes Sídhe preferred to forget. Deemed too violent to walk among them he was exiled.

In human form, the Cú Sídhe, also known as the Hound, was a tall, muscular, and handsome man. He was vain, although less narcissistic than Leannán. His face had an oval shape with a square jawline, and the eyes were a striking shade of luminous amber. When he smiled, it seemed he had too many canines. Like a wolfhound's, his jaw had the strength to snap thigh bones. A lustrous blue-black mane hung loose in tresses that tapped his arse as he paced the chamber like a caged animal.

The Cú Sídhe had a soft fleece of black hair covering his torso and legs, with a fist-sized white patch on his chest breaking the pattern. He had a dense but short, trimmed beard.

Oileán Dubh's Great Hall was cavernous. Still, its walls made the Cú Sídhe feel claustrophobic. His pace lengthened as his anxiety rose. Yet Leannán had summoned him, and he could not refuse her invitation. He breathed easier as he heard the door open and watched her enter.

Anxiety dissipated and was replaced by wariness. The hair on the back of his neck stiffened. Leannán was a powerful witch, and he would enjoy killing her once he uncovered how she had bound him to her. Paradoxically, as Leannán approached her pet, her senses were also on high alert. She knew he hated her. Thus, neither of the island's residents trusted or had any affection for the other.

"We have a mission among the humans," she said. The Hound instantly smiled, and then his eyes became suspicious. Leannán chuckled and shook her head. "This time, we have the approval of the Womb-Born."

The Hound's smile became more expansive, and Leannán's mien became guarded. She knew that time away from her island and the Halls of the Aes Sídhe would slowly degrade her sorcery and weaken her hold over the Cú Sídhe.

CHAPTER 5

Dùn Brion

"Seonag promised us warriors to lift the siege. Where are they?" asked Cassán Mac Brion, Righ of the Na Mèadaidh. "Do you expect my people to fight *your* war without support?" Cassán scratched his shaven head in frustration and then brushed dry skin flakes from his shoulders. Beside him, a stoic, expressionless Earc Ruadh, Seonag's battle commander, said nothing.

Cassán gazed around the surrounding landscape and watched the latest assault by the rebel forces of the Forest People. Under Cè's orders, they made another attempt to scale the crag and the fort that perched on it. They looked like ants but were less successful in their endeavours than the productive insects. He listened unsympathetically to the screams of those who lost their handholds and whose bodies were broken on the rocks.

Those who reached the base of the towering grey stone walls of Dùn Brion were met with deluges of boiling oil, pitch, and water. It was a nasty way to die, but much worse if the besieger lived. The ballistae were silent, apart from the machines on the southern wall. The latter rained iron on any who approached the main gateway via the long, gentle incline of the crag's tail.

This time, his stronghold had been under siege for a half-cycle of the moon. As with the previous attempts, Cassán never seriously thought Dùn Brion was in danger of falling. There were cliffs on all sides, except the south, and the fort was built of stone.

However, once again, the garrison was trapped. Hence, there was a rising and understandable disgruntlement inside Dùn Brion. Many of Cassán's warriors had farms, and their families worked the fertile lands on either side of the Sleagh mountain range. It was harvesting time, but the fields lay unworked. The warriors on the ramparts could see the fires of burning farmsteads at night and the black smoke of corn fields curling skywards at sunrise.

Lives were sacrificed and livelihoods ruined, for a fight that made no sense to most. Why was it their conflict? Families fleeing the ashes of their homes could not enter the dùn because of the siege. Those who escaped the pillaging and raping crossed the Abhainn Dubh river to seek shelter in the pine forests south-west of Dùn Brion. Early snow flurries presaged a hard winter, and Cassán knew many would die if the siege was not lifted.

"This civil war within the Forest People has endured for ten summers. It is past time for Seonag to reach an accommodation with her brothers," said Cassán.

"That would be a mistake," said Earc, annoyed at Cassán's bluntness, which he perceived as interfering in the Forest People's politics. The man's brogue was as thick as Cassán had ever heard, except maybe Gràinne's. Earc hailed from a clan that originated in A' Chrìon Làraich, a stronghold in the forest's south-western region. Its people were fiercely loyal to Drostan and now to Seonag.

A head taller than Cassán, Earc had a shock of red hair, and piercing blue eyes. A mass of freckles covered his face, torso, and limbs—thus, he was well-named. His whiplike body belied his strength, and the web of scars testified to his battle experience.

"How so?" asked Cassán.

"We would make a bad future enemy."

Cassán sighed. Every conversation he had with Earc confirmed his dislike of the man. *If only you were my enemy.* Earc was not a king, and kings sometimes had to make terrible choices and decisions. "What threat is there from an enemy that tears itself apart?" Earc scowled at the insult yet had no riposte to Cassán's words. "How many Forest People will be left after this war? The glorious and prosperous days of Drostan passed with his death and are unlikely to return. Seonag has battled her brothers for ten summers. How long will this go on? Ten more summers?"

Earc's lips curled into a sneer. "There were six brothers, and now there are two."

"Fionn's assassins killed two, not Seonag… *or you*. Look over the walls. Cè's army, not Fionn's, is broken on Dùn Brion's walls. Fionn will murder a weakened Cè and combine both forces. Seonag will be vastly outnumbered and forced to flee, likely to *my* fortress." Cassán held Earc's eyes without flinching.

"When you leave, take this message to Seonag. My advice is to come to an agreement with Cè and Fionn. Another ten summers of war, she will either have no Forest People to rule, or she will be dead."

As Earc turned, Cassán dipped his head, and several burly warriors grabbed the emissary. His struggles were futile and ceased when Cassán laid the cold edge of a knife against his throat. "Threaten me again, and I will have you thrown from these ramparts. My fortresses are stronger than A 'Chrìon Làraich. More than that, family ties will place the Blood Queen and the Eastern Tribes on my side. Gràinne's ma is a sídhe, and her daughter, Brianag, is my sister. Do the Forest People want *that* war?"

Cassán nodded, and his guards released Earc. "You may leave. Inform Seonag you are not welcome in Dùn Brion… or I will."

"You don't like him, do you?" asked Cassán's shield-man.

"He's an arsehole with an over-inflated sense of his own importance." Cassán sighed and signalled the battlefield. "I wish my father had not been killed. Seonag and he were made for each other. By now they would be King and Queen of the Forest People and the Na Mèadaidh. Instead, she ruts eejits like Earc, who see her cot as a path to the throne."

The shield-man dipped his head and turned to walk away. A hand on his shoulder stopped him. "If any of what I said becomes gossip, you will lose your head." The genuine hurt in the veteran's eyes told Cassán he had been insulted. *Now who's the arsehole?*

* * *

Mumbled curses accompanied Earc's humiliating descent of the parapet's stone steps, but Cassán's attention had turned to Eimhir. His handfast partner gazed over the western wall. He could feel her anger even at this distance. *Who is it directed at?* There was nothing he could do or say to take the pain of betrayal away.

Eimhir's people brought him the information, knowing what would happen and what he had to do. Exasperated, Cassán slapped the stone crenulation and began the longest walk of his life to Eimhir's side. He cursed Eimhir's sister, Ealasaid, and the daughters who had cut their mother's throat, albeit to avenge their father. Cassán ground his teeth, remembering the unanimous advice of their friends. They had counselled Eimhir and him not to trust the mother-killers. Yet he and Eimhir stubbornly ignored the warnings and adopted the girls to raise as their own.

Now, his ears rang with the screaming of his nieces as they were dragged up the steps to the western rampart. Bewitched by stories of how they were the rightful heirs to the throne of the Na Mèadaidh, like their mother, they chose to chase a mirage. Seduced by the weasel words of Seonag's brothers, they took a treasonous path.

However, the young women were poor shadows of their ma. Their skills were untested and their plotting amateurish. Thus, they were readily detected and observed. When they were caught opening the small exit gate on the northern wall, it sealed their fate. Ironically, it was the same gateway Ealasaid and they had used to escape Dùn Brion ten summers past.

They were no longer children. Cassán had no room to pardon or reduce their sentence because it was a time of war. Any show of partiality would cause the people and garrison to revolt. A garrison weakened by internal strife and riven by family loyalties would have presented Cè with his opportunity.

Faced with Cassán, the young women shrieked, alternately cursing Cassán and pleading for Eimhir to come to their aid. Their aunt could not, for her hands were bound as if by chains. The Brehons had spoken, and the sentence was pronounced. "I am sorry it came to this," said Cassán. "You enjoyed a privileged life and spurned it. Worse, you betrayed your aunt."

He stood resolute as they cursed and spat on him. A curt nod, and brawny warriors grabbed the nieces and dragged them to the parapet's edge. "The sentence is death."

The screams of "No!" seemed endless, yet lasted moments as they were thrown from the western walls. Only when their bodies were dashed on the rocks below did the shrieking end. In his mind, Cassán continued to hear them begging for mercy as they fell. *What else could I do?* Hang them. Stake them. Cut their throats. Gut and quarter them. There were no good options.

Now, they joined the ghosts of their grandfather, Finnean Mac Sèitheach's family on the Sleagh. Perhaps they would find peace. It was better than the Goddess's judgment and the Otherworld. Cassán sighed long and mournfully and took Eimhir's hand, and together they trudged their way to the steps to the courtyard.

CHAPTER 6

The Royal Crannag, Loch nan Clàr

Brianag stopped at the entrance to the royal crannag and shook her head. She peered closely at the door and the timbers of the building, smiled, and shook her head again.

"What's wrong? Your ma won't bite you," said Neamhain.

"That's open to debate but the royal crannag certainly will. Look closely. The runes carved into the timbers of the Great Hall made me tingle and itch." She pointed to the symbols on the door. "These, however, are much stronger and their origin is ancient. They will not let us pass without permission. The Hag, Neamhain! My ma's a witch."

A cackle from inside the crannag appeared to confirm Brianag's observations. "You have permission to enter," shouted Gràinne, a little testily. "Although sometimes the runes think on their own and have a wicked sense of humour."

***

"Shite! Am I the only 'normal' one in the room? Where did Brianag get that body?" murmured Sorchae, somewhat enviously. Yet that was a measure of the young woman's modesty. Broad, muscled, yet softly curved shoulders from weapons training tapered down to a narrow waist and hips that swayed provocatively as she walked. Full, teardrop-shaped breasts would not disgrace her, even if measured against Brianag or her aunt, Mòrag.

A vivacious nature supported Sorchae's physical attractiveness, ensuring she was never short of admirers. That said, it clashed with a discriminating palate, which drastically reduced the number of lovers. Few could ever measure up to her adopted father, Íar, who was also the brother of her deeply flawed and tragic mother. She sighed. Mòrag constantly warned Sorchae of setting impossible standards. Worse, so had her da.

She looked at Neamhain and saw a graceful and powerful sídhe. Yet Sorchae instinctively knew her friend was struggling with something beneath the composed veneer. Sorchae smiled. She also knew Neamhain's delight at seeing her was honest. They would share secrets when the time was right.

As for the mother and daughter, tension crackled between Gràinne and Brianag. Sorchae felt she could reach out and touch the angst. Both glared at each other with unnatural eyes. Curling rivers of crimson and pine green constantly flowed over bodies tensed for battle. Red and green talons replaced nails. Tendrils of their auras flickered like snakes' tongues. The runes flared. Neither would ever back down. It was their curse.

Yet Sorchae looked beyond the outward postures. She saw two people who had suffered terribly and struggled with how they should act after many summers of separation. She would have wept for their pain, but that was not what they needed. Therefore, instead of offering empathy, she rebuked them. "For the Hag's sake, hug each other. It's what you both want—*and need.*"

"You may have a future as a sídhe, Sorchae," murmured Neamhain appreciatively.

The heat in the room subsided from volcanic to simmering and finally to a gentle warmth. Gràinne's shoulders slumped under the burden of ten summers as the Blood Queen and the estrangement from her firstborn. The adolescent in Brianag fled, and she looked at Gràinne through a daughter's eyes and sobbed. "What am I, Ma?"

"You are my daughter, Brianag. That is all that matters," said Gràinne. Closing the few paces between them seemed the longest journey Gràinne had ever taken, even with Brianag meeting her midway. Waterfalls of tears accompanied rib-cracking embraces.

Neamhain touched Sorchae's arm. "We should not intrude on this moment."

It was doubtful whether Brianag or Gràinne saw them exit or heard the door close. Outside the private chamber stood Amodocus. He had diplomatically remained separate from the females and now levered himself from the doorpost.

"Thank you, Sorchae. I am in your debt."

****

The hugs ceased reluctantly, and the tears ran dry, although that was temporary. A dam built over a decade cannot be emptied in a sunset. Next came the awkward silence of a mother wanting to understand and find common ground with her daughter. The last time they met was on the parapet of Dùn Brion. Brianag had threatened to kill her, and if it would have saved her daughter, Gràinne would have let her.

"I was only fifteen, Ma. Sidheag twisted my mind. I was not strong enough to resist her totally."

Gràinne started when Brianag answered her unspoken thought. "We need to establish boundaries, Brianag," chided Gràinne. "You and I can see into each other's minds, but should we?" Gràinne chuckled. It sounded like a spring burbling out of the earth and seemed strange and new to her. "Yet I sense you could shut your mind to me instantly—and to much more powerful beings than me."

"I am so sorry, Ma." A single tear rolled down Brianag's cheek. It was green and sparkled like an emerald. "If only I'd known what saving me would do to you and how it continues to burden you. I was a stupid bitseach. *I* should have died."

"*Never!*"

Brianag's eyes widened at the vehemence of her ma's tone. In a softer voice, Gràinne said, "You will understand when you have children." Gràinne grasped Brianag's hand and guided her to a wooden bench strewn with furs. "We must talk of sober matters. That you and Neamhain arrived at the same time is curious, but not surprising. She has always stood with you. However, Sorchae's arrival is beyond coincidence. Did your grandmother plan this?"

Brianag shook her head. "No, although she counselled us to leave the Land of Immensity speedily."

Gràinne's eyebrow lifted. "Then I see the hand of the Goddess in this. She paid me an unexpected visit a few sunsets ago. That was surprising since she has been absent for a decade." Gràinne's eyes sharpened. "It means a wagonload of horse shite is coming our way. Am I right?" Brianag nodded. "Is this something we should discuss with your friends present?" Another dip of Brianag's head, and Gràinne called out. "Everyone, please return, and that includes Amodocus."

She followed a gentle squeeze of Brianag's hand with an impish smile. "Whatever trials may be imminent. We will meet them together. However…" Brianag's eyes widened. "…after our meeting, you have a duty to perform. It may be the greatest trial you have ever faced or ever will." Gràinne's ruby eyes sparkled mischievously at Brianag's disconcerted expression. "You have two sisters and a brother to meet. Prepare yourself for an exhausting evening."

✷✷✷

A short time later, Giosail entered the room and was surprised to find three young women seated at the table with the queen. They appeared as young as she was, perhaps a few summers older. *Who are they?* Giosail had heard rumours of new arrivals but had been busy with her duties and, as was her habit, she took little notice of gossip.

She directed the servants where to set the food and refreshments, bowed, and was about to follow them from the room when Gràinne stopped her. "Stay a moment, Giosail. This is my daughter, Brianag, and her friends, Neamhain and Sorchae." To the trio, Gràinne said, "Giosail is my aide and has been a loyal friend under difficult circumstances—for her and me. It would please me if you became friends."

It was unclear who was the more surprised at Gràinne's request, but Sorchae was the first to recover. She stood and inspected Giosail with enough intensity to make the young princess blush. "Are you battle-trained?" Giosail shook her head. "If we are to become friends"—she looked at Gràinne—"and with the Bhanrigh's permission, we will need to train you quickly in weapons and fighting." Sorchae grinned. "None of us enjoy quiet lives."

As a flustered and excited Giosail exited the room and the door closed, Gràinne said, "She is a faithful servant trusted with my secrets and was once a princess of one of the remote tribes. I wish her to become one again. Your helping her achieve this will be appreciated." Gràinne exhaled slowly. She looked at Sorchae.

"I knew Mòrag well. She is not stupid, and that speaks well of you. It also means there is much more to you than meets the eye." This time, Sorchae blushed. "Later, there will be time to talk long about old friends and new challenges, but first"—Gràinne's gaze fell on Brianag and Neamhain— "which of you would like to explain why you fled the Halls of the Aes Sídhe?"

Amodocus responded with a loud slap of his hand on muscled thighs and a roar of laughter. "It was getting quite boring around here until now."

***

The meeting ended, and a solemn-faced group exited the Royal Crannag and stepped onto the connecting bridge. However, soon, the excited chatter of friends estranged since childhood overwhelmed sobriety. As with those who love each other, it was only a short period before it seemed as if they had never parted. Still, each was not blind to the battles ahead and revealed willingly or not.

Gràinne's hand on Sorchae's shoulder caused her to fall behind. "You have had a glimpse of our lives and are astute enough to realise none of us can be described as 'normal'. Neamhain is and will remain a faithful friend to Brianag, but she is a sídhe. I hope you become the rock that keeps Brianag grounded—and sane. My daughter has suffered much. Also, having lived with the Aes Sídhe, she is unaccustomed to human company and comportment."

The party was midway across the causeway when the door to the Great Hall opened, and Niall stepped across its threshold. The thick wolf's fur on his shoulders made the stocky veteran appear huge, and he was dressed for battle. His expression seemed neither angry nor happy.

"He would be an intimidating fidchell player," murmured Sorchae.

"I'll handle this," said Gràinne and made to step ahead of Sorchae. Sorchae's firm hand on the queen's arm stopped her progress.

"With respect, my lady, I precipitated this. It is my problem to resolve," said Sorchae. She strode towards Niall, and he matched her step for step until they stood several paces apart. He looked over Sorchae's shoulder to Gràinne and dipped his head. "In your absence, my queen, I have consulted with Cathbad and the Ravens' chieftains. We are of one accord." The group tensed.

"Sorchae Ni Íar will not be challenged. Several of the older chieftains, who knew Artair, recognised the royal seal. Sorchae is acknowledged as the Bhanrigh of the Ravens." With a grunt, Niall dropped to one knee and held out his axe. "You have my oath, and those of the Ravens' chieftains, if you accept it."

To everyone's surprise, Sorchae laughed loudly. "Thank the Goddess. Ardghal and I are horse fighters; I need someone I can trust to command the Ravens' spears. I happily accept your oath, but please stand. It's too bloody cold to be on your knees."

A question occurred to Sorchae. She dipped her head to Niall's ear and whispered, "How many warriors do I have?" She had one word to his reply: "Shite!"

***

"That is a frightening alliance," said Teàrlag as Gràinne's group took their seats at the High Table. "By his demeanour, Niall is comfortable with whatever has been decided, and that is equally troubling."

"With the powers of Brianag, Gràinne, and Neamhain, let's hope they remain on our side," responded Seonag. "Each day the Forest People fight, the Eastern Tribes grow stronger. Their numbers increase while ours shrink."

The meeting of queens, kings, and chieftains resumed as the sun hovered above the western horizon. A swarm of slaves and servants lit hundreds of rush torches and encouraged the firepits into life with logs of pinewood and peat bricks. The fragrances of the latter combined to overwhelm the strong smell of the rushlights.

Since the crannag was built of wood, fires of any size were always dangerous. Thus, each firepit had a foundation of flat stones and was surrounded by a small, circular wall of rocks. Slaves and servants kept a close watch on the firepits and torches.

Gràinne sat on an ornately carved throne and observed the consternation of those seated on the opposite side of the long High Table. She stood, and the hum of anxious conversations diminished to a murmur. "Many of you have travelled far to attend this assembly. I apologise for the unforeseen disruption to our proceedings. At least it has not been as boring as our usual gatherings." A ripple of laughter flowed along the guests.

"I will keep this part of our conversation short. Following this meeting, there will be a feast where you can greet and get to know those who arrived earlier. It will be a family-oriented celebration. Everyone is invited, but I will not take any offence if any cannot attend.

"More formal introductions are in order. I will be as brief as protocol allows." More laughter trickled through those gathered. *Let's see how long their humour lasts.* Gràinne touched Brianag's left shoulder and whispered in her ear, "Please stand… and behave yourself." The almost instant *Ma!* in her head made her eyes mist over.

"This is my daughter, Brianag Ni Brion. She has returned from the Mounds of the Aes Sídhe to be reunited with her family. Amodocus and I welcome her homecoming, as I am sure you will." The babble of conversations signified a rising anxiety in the room. Hence, Gràinne moved on quickly, tapping Sorchae's right shoulder. Her seat scraped on the wooden boards as she stood.

"I was thoughtless in my initial reaction to Sorchae. She is a childhood friend of Brianag and Neamhain, and as she reminded me, I had not seen her since she was a wee'un. I have apologised for being a poor host. The Ravens and the Eastern Tribes have reached an accord. Sorchae Ni Íar is confirmed as Bhanrigh of the Ravens."

As the hubbub of conversations grew, Gràinne said, "Niall supports this decision. He and the nobles of the Ravens have given their oath to Sorchae. The Leader of the Druidic Council has also given his blessing. There will be *no* further discussion on this matter."

Next, Gràinne turned to Neamhain. Like most of the Aes Sídhe, she stood and now stepped forward from behind the throne.

"This is my sister, Neamhain." Gràinne paused to emphasise the announcement. "She is the daughter of the Sídhe, Mongfhionn, who is my mother. By happenstance, Neamhain is also a childhood friend of Brianag and Sorchae." A pin dropping in the Great Hall would have sounded like a rack of weapons crashing to the floor. "The Lady Neamhain is like her mother in many ways. It is a family trait that neither is to be trifled with nor underestimated."

"Coincidence, my arse," muttered Seonag. "At best, this bears the mark of Mongfhionn all over it... or worse, the Goddess."

"Before we begin the festivities, I have one closing announcement. As some of you will have deduced from her name, Brianag is the daughter of Brion Ó Cathasaigh, the former Righ of Na Mèadaidh, who sadly crossed the veil ten summers ago. Thus, she is the sister of Cassán Mac Brion." Mutters of "Shite!" and "The Hag's arse!" were the congregation's response.

"In two sunsets, Brianag, Neamhain, and Sorchae, along with Amodocus and several hundred riders, will travel to Dún Brion. Their mission is to help Cassán break the siege of his beleaguered fort. Sorchae has agreed a division of Ravens' spears will follow them under Niall's command." The audience's response divided between cheers of approval and rumblings of interference.

"This should have been discussed with the Forest People," said Seonag, rising from her seat.

"This is something I have neglected and should have done much sooner, Seonag. I count Cassán as my family. Do *you* not wish to see Dún Brion relieved from your brothers' assault?" asked Gràinne. "This war is not of Cassán's and Eimhir's making, nor is it the Na Mèadaidh's fight. Dún Brion and Dún Athad have not been overrun only because of their walls and locations. So far, Teàrlag and you have promised warriors but sent emissaries."

Gràinne's gaze held Seonag's. "Choose, Seonag, Bhanrigh-in-waiting of the Forest People. Are we on the same side or not? All warriors from the Forest People who join us will be very welcome."

Dumbfounded and embarrassed, Seonag sat down. Teàrlag fumed at her daughter's treatment. Still, even she could hardly blame a sister for wanting to help her brother.

"I greatly underestimated your talent as a fidchell player, Ma," whispered Brianag.

"Maybe, but I hope I have not alienated a friend."

***

As the noise of multiple conversations rose and fell, Seonag turned to Teàrlag. "How many warriors do I have within the sound of a bell?"

Teàrlag considered the question for a few moments. "There is a division of around one thousand warriors, less than a thousand paces from here." At Seonag's raised eyebrow, she said, "There is always that number who shadow you. It is not enough to attack this crannag."

Seonag looked incredulously at her ma. "That would never be my intention. You will inform Gràinne that they will accompany the Ravens' warband."

"You will be defenceless. I cannot not allow this."

"It was an order, not a request, Mother." Teàrlag flinched at Seonag's anger. "Your tactics have embarrassed me before my friend and the Eastern Tribes. I will not permit the Forest People to be accused of abandoning our allies."

Seonag paused. "Ask Gràinne to send a rider to Earc in A' Chrìon Làraich. He is to return to Dùn Brion. This time, not as an ambassador, but to command our warriors. After this meeting, you and I will return to A' Chrìon Làraich and review our failing strategy. Are my orders clear?"

****

Later that evening, amid the revelries, the doors of the Great Hall opened to allow Giosail to enter. Gràinne's and Amodocus' children accompanied her. The girls were named Heilasa and Mùirne, and the boy's given name was Thrax. All were nervous, yet that was because of their excitement. It was rare for them to be permitted to attend important feasts.

Giosail was equally anxious because she wore the garments of a princess and had been commanded to sit at the High Table. It was the first time she had been recognised as a bana-phrionnsa in ten summers, and the implications were as worrying as they were exciting.

As the trio of siblings approached the High Table, they saw Brianag sitting beside their mother. Their pace slowed, and their mien became wary. "The Hag!" muttered Brianag. She had never seen her siblings before and needed to figure out what to do… fast. This was worse than an audience with the Aes Sídhe. At least there, she had anger as a defence.

"Meet them halfway," whispered Gràinne. "They do not know you, either. Defend and love them; you will never have more loyal champions."

When they were a few paces apart, Heilasa stared at Brianag and said, "Wow! Will I be as beautiful as you?"

Brianag dropped to one knee, opened her arms, and shook her head. "No, you won't…" Heilasa's disappointment was fleeting before Brianag continued, "… because you are already much more beautiful than I will ever be." Screams and tears of joy flowed as brother and sisters hugged each other.

"We have a gift for you, Brianag." Thrax offered up a circlet of purple violets and placed it on his sister's head. When more tears streamed down Brianag's cheeks, a curious Mùirne reached out, plucked a tear, and said, "Your tears are beautiful, like little liquid emeralds."

Brianag observed Thrax's perturbed face and wondered if she had offended him. With all the seriousness of a child, he looked at his three sisters and then at Amodocus and Gràinne before solemnly pronouncing, "I need a brother." The cheers and banging of wooden tables suggested that those present agreed with him.

***

Just wait until they get to know the "real" you.

The voice in her head startled Brianag. It had been many summers since she heard the voice of Sidheag, yet it was instantly recognisable.

You owe me a debt, Brianag. The time to satisfy it is here.

I am not afraid of you, bitseach.

Good.

CHAPTER 7

Dùn Brion's Domain

The stalemate began three summers ago and showed no sign of breaking. The toll of the dead on both sides continued to rise, as did the unease of the Forest People's chieftains and nobles. Sieges and long battles were atypical for hot-headed Gaels. Traditionally, they fought with fire in their breasts and beer in their bellies. They won, lost, or were bribed to go away.

Fionn and Cè knew the impasse with Seonag was fertile ground for malcontents. Rumours of other chieftains who saw none of the siblings as having proven their case to rule the Forest People grew. Soon the leaching of support on both sides rose to become a peril as great as losing battles.

Under their father's rule, the Forest People's nobility had become prosperous. With the war, the tribe's wealth, built over generations, declined, ceased, and regressed in just ten summers. Rumblings of discontent from the civilian population became open calls for change. Merchant traders from the Great Sea, such as Pytheas, assessed the risk, re-evaluated the opportunity, drastically reduced the frequency of their visits, and increased their prices. Prosperity faded.

Slaves, taken in battle and sold for gold, became the only stable currency. Nevertheless, Cè Mac Drostan was not stupid. He knew that poverty and selling their people into slavery divided the Forest People more and drove them into the hands of other warlords. On the fringes of the main contest, independent warband leaders offered protection and carved out territories with little resistance from Cè, Fionn, Seonag, or the people.

To complicate matters, for the first time in many generations, under Gràinne, the Eastern Tribes were united. How long would it be before the Blood Queen looked beyond her friendship with Seonag and viewed a weakened Forest People as an opportunity to expand her kingdom?

Cè sat around a campfire with his chieftains to break their fast. He knew the siege of Dùn Brion was a waste of time and warriors, but had agreed to the assault primarily to end his brother's constant fulminating. That was a piss-poor reason, and he knew it. Cè slurped a thin, tepid soup of oatmeal and berries. Most of it spilt onto his ginger beard, and he swore, but only because the spillage reminded him his beard was a straggly disappointment. *I should scrape the bloody thing.*

He slapped bony knees, stood, and grimaced at the sound of his joints cracking. *The Hag, I'm only thirty summers. Perhaps the best reason for me to conquer Dùn Brion is to have a roof over my head and a warm cot.* He looked at his council and spoke. Cè's voice had a deep richness, contrasting with his wiry frame. "Find me a way out of this slaughter. We cannot afford to keep butting our heads against Dùn Brion's walls like demented goats. We are losing too many warriors, and that only benefits my brother."

∗∗∗

It was a pleasant *meadhan-latha*—midday. Winds always swept Dùn Brion's ramparts, but Cassán thought they seemed less aggressive. Above the stronghold, an amber-gold sun held court on a bed of fluffy clouds. Its light added highlights to the landscape's autumnal canvas.

While the pines remained steadfastly green, random clusters of alder, birch, and ash added splashes of russet and orange. On the Sleagh, heather and gorse painted its plateau in hues of purple and yellow. Closer to the fort, rocks and grass splashed with blood blended with the seasonal palette. Only the broken bodies disrupted nature's harmony.

There was evidence of an early frost. Mostly it was between the couple on the walkway. Perhaps it was inevitable the execution of their adopted daughters had strained their relationship. Eimhir knew she was wrong to assign any blame to Cassán for the deaths of her nieces. After all, it was she who, through intermediaries, laid the evidence of their treason before him. But blood was blood, and she needed an outlet for her grief.

Eimhir was not a cold and callous murderer like her sister, Ealasaid. Yet even Ealasaid could not bring herself to kill her daughters. For that mercy, she paid with her life when her daughters cut her throat to avenge their father's bloody death. *If not discovered, would they have done the same to Cassán and me?* The resounding "Yes!" made her shoulders slump. The blame was hers. She had failed the young women—and Cassán.

She looked at the forlorn figure of Cassán. His issue was no longer the girls. His male brain had cast that aside soon after Eimhir and he watched the girls' funeral pyre reduced to ash. No, Cassán grappled with the tension between them. *We need a distraction to force us together.* Eimhir knew the thought was cowardice, hypocrisy, and procrastination at its finest. She growled, and Cassán looked curiously at her. She shrugged and gave him a wan smile. His response was warmer, and she felt her heart begin to defrost.

Cassán was worried, and not just about Eimhir. Like his father, he cared deeply for his people. While those inside the fort were as safe as possible in such times, the civilians outside its walls suffered. On still nights, the garrison heard the cries of mothers and the wailing of babies and children. The fort's atmosphere became increasingly anxious and fearful. There was always the danger of foolish, if understandable, behaviour. Could Cassán stop a determined effort by fathers, brothers, sisters, and uncles to rescue their families? How many would he have to kill to stem such acts of desperation?

Cè was a canny leader who would not waste the opportunity of a divided garrison. He only needed the gates opened briefly and had almost achieved that with Eimhir's nieces. Cassán sighed loudly, and Eimhir knew his thoughts. She turned to face him and put on a brave face. "We will find a way through our troubles."

***

"What's our plan, Neamhain?" asked Brianag. She enjoyed the touch of heather on her bare feet and its delicate fragrance. The shrub's constant decay and renewal made the experience sweeter. She could not recall if the meadows of the Aes Sídhe were scented. They probably were, but the absence of rebirth made them unremarkable. Similarly, the Aes Sídhe's artistic endeavours were incomplete because there was nothing imperfect to judge them by.

The two friends stood on the highest peak of the Sleagh, assessing Dùn Brion's defences and the attackers who surged from the north-eastern forests. "I can slaughter them. They are human, not sídhe." To Brianag, the prospect of being free to kill *and* being on the "good" side was intoxicating. Brianag grinned and her voice held equal measures of anticipation and excitement.

Neamhain knew Brianag's claim was justified, but she dismissed it with a roll of her eyes and a firm shake of her head. "I was thinking of a more indirect approach." The disappointment in Brianag's eyes made Neamhain chuckle. "You know we cannot make our presence obvious," she chastised. "That would alert Leannán and the Cú Sídhe. Keeping them on the margins is our best strategy until we have a viable plan to end that pair. Our priority must be to protect the people and stronghold until Amodocus and Sorchae arrive in five sunsets. Once they are here, their activities will shield us."

"Very disappointing, Neamhain." Brianag's eyes glistened mischievously. "If boringly sensible."

"I can feel your devious mind examining options to circumvent my intent, Brianag. What are you thinking?"

"What if a wild animal killed Cè and his chieftains—perhaps a wolf?" asked Brianag. "We are surrounded by forests and mountains teaming with bears and wolves. Our enemy's demise would be seen as unfortunate, but natural, deaths." Innocence bloomed in Brianag's words.

The offer tempted Neamhain, but she sighed and said, "No, Brianag, I have seen your wolf, and it is anything but natural or indigenous to Northern Albu." She paused. "However,"—Brianag's eyes lit up—"we should keep it as an option." Neamhain pursed her lips.

"What?" asked Brianag.

"Our biggest challenge may be the residents of Dùn Brion. You did not leave on the best terms with Cassán. They may doubt our sincerity and spurn any offer of help."

"Brion was my father, too, Neamhain. Sidheag deprived me of the chance to know my father. My loss was greater than Cassán's. He squandered seventeen summers being a fat wastrel. I didn't get the opportunity to disappoint my da." The hard edge in Brianag's tone abated and her lips lifted into a smile. "Besides, who's to say *I* should not be the Bhanrigh of the Na Mèadaidh? Before Sidheag got her hands on me, I beat Cassán in a duel and spared his life. With my talents, he and any who supported him would be at my mercy in a future contest."

Neamhain's alarmed demeanour made Brianag laugh. "It was idle *craic*, Neamhain. A challenge to Cassán's throne is more likely to come from Sorchae. They share the same mother." Brianag paused, and her words took on a hard edge again. "Why would I covet a stone fortress when I can lay waste to the Land of Immensity?"

"No," said Neamhain. Her voice was faint, and her heartbeat raced.

***

A slight shimmering of displaced air followed by the scents of jasmine and rose oil were the garrison's only warning. "Neamhain, do you miss riding a horse when travelling great distances? I do. I think I understand why Grandma still rides her black mare." Neamhain chuckled. Brianag had pitched her voice perfectly to alert those manning the ramparts to the duo's presence.

The garrison's reaction was instant and predictable. The warriors unsheathed axes, hefted spears, and put arrows to bowstrings. "Perhaps we should have sent a messenger ahead of us," said Brianag through gritted teeth. "The hostility irks me." As the iron edges and tips came closer, Brianag unclasped her cloak and laid it with exaggerated deliberation on the wall's crenulation. When she turned to face those who threatened them, Brianag's auburn hair flared in the wind, and her body shimmered green. Neamhain's hand on her arm stopped the progression from going further.

"If you permit us, we are here to help," said Neamhain. She threw back her hood and released a cloud of blonde hair. Neamhain's strawberry highlights were styled in narrow braids, and as the wind blew, they flickered like tongues of fire. Her eyes narrowed and darkened as the circle of iron surrounding them came closer. "It is never prudent to threaten a sídhe. Sheath your weapons…"

Neamhain's command echoed off the fort's stone walls. Then she hissed like a mountain *lincse*—lynx, "…or I will relieve you of them *and* your lives."

"Neamhain," whispered Brianag.

"I'm sorry, Brianag, but I am a sídhe, and we are not known for our forbearance. Besides, the lack of hospitality pisses me off, too."

"Put your weapons away and return to your posts," bellowed Cassán as he and Eimhir pushed their way through the circle of warriors. "We have enough problems without antagonising a sídhe and whatever my sister may be."

"Thank you, brother." Oozing charm, Brianag looked at Eimhir and smiled. "And one I think of as my sister. Perhaps we could retire to a suitable chamber and discuss how we might help you." Wary of how reasonable Brianag sounded, Cassán dipped his head.

***

As Eimhir and he sat down, Cassán asked, "Do they teach you in Aes Sídhe school that standing intimidates humans?" He should have said it with a smile or a wink. Puzzled at the question, Brianag looked at

Neamhain. Then she did something that no abomination or demigod had a right to do. She giggled. Neamhain quickly joined her. Cassán's cough returned the duo to a semblance of normality.

"Frankly, until now, I've never thought about it. The Aes Sídhe stand as naturally as men and women sit, except when we pretend to sleep. If it troubles you, we will sit, even if it makes *us* uncomfortable." Neamhain's emphasis did not go unnoticed.

However, Brianag, after ruminating on Cassán's question, decided she had been insulted. Her eyes intensified to forest green and then black. The atmosphere in the chamber crackled with tension, and the curling designs on Brianag's skin flowed. Only the tapping of her talons on the oak table broke the silence that descended.

Cassán studied Brianag, and his Adam's apple bobbled up and down. He recalled being tossed across the room by her ma as if he weighed no more than a feather. "Do something," hissed Eimhir. "It is not your fault, but you have obviously hit a raw nerve. The Aes Sídhe are often sensitive about things we consider unimportant or humorous." Cassán opened his mouth to speak, but Brianag beat him to it.

"'*Humans*'! Do you deliberately insult us? Neamhain bleeds like you. My mother bleeds like you. I bleed like you. See…" The green talon was a blur as it sliced along the inside of Brianag's lower arm. She held her forearm over the table; blood welled from the gash and splashed the table. "Should I cut you to compare our lifebloods?"

Neamhain placed a hand on Brianag's arm and said, "Sister."

Brianag shrugged it aside. "We are not welcome among the 'humans' and should leave, Neamhain. There are greater challenges, and they don't want our help. Let them slaughter each other. Let the mothers, babies, and children die in the forests. The animals will be thankful for the bounty before winter arrives, and Finnean's ghost will once again have a tribe to rule."

A chair scraping the stone floor halted Brianag as she turned to leave. She whirled about to face an attacker, but only Eimhir stood before her. The bhanrìgh flinched at Brianag's terrifying appearance but held her ground. "I apologise. It is a poor excuse, but the ashes in the courtyard are what remains of my nieces and our adopted daughters. They were convicted of treason and executed earlier."

Eimhir sobbed, and her tears joined with Brianag's blood on the table. "Cassán's and my relationship is strained by grief. Neither of us is thinking straight, but I know him better than anyone. He made a bad jest, that is all. No insult was intended."

"The mother-killers?" Brianag asked. Eimhir flinched but dipped her head. "The Aes Sídhe and humans have more in common than they realise. They, too, hold on to things that should be cast off." Brianag took Eimhir's hand. The talons had retracted, the sigils were calm, and the cut on her arm had vanished. Brianag's eyes regained their natural green hue. "I grieve for your loss. Blood is blood."

"I, too, am sorry for my behaviour, Brianag… and Neamhain. You would think that after ten summers, I would have learned to be less of an arsehole rather than a bigger one." Cassán held out his hand. "Brothers and sisters should be thankful for each other's company." Brianag ignored the offer but, in a blur of movement, was in front of Cassán.

"Some fine control would be good," gasped Cassán as Brianag crushed him in her arms.

"Have you not learned Brianag is not known for her subtlety?" said Neamhain, and everyone laughed.

✳✳✳

"Will you fight with us?" asked Cassán.

The shake of Neamhain's head was disappointing, but Cassán maintained a neutral demeanour. "Some complicating factors mean our immediate help needs to be more indirect." Brianag snorted, and Neamhain smiled. "However, with your consent, Brianag will go to the forest and help protect the vulnerable. I will remain in Dùn Brion and see what trouble I can design to make life miserable for those who attack you."

Cassán nodded and smiled at Brianag. "Thank you. Dùn Brion's garrison will very much appreciate that. My warriors do not fear battle or death but worry constantly about their families. Your presence will foster goodwill within the Na Mèadaidh."

"I will need a few well-recognised people to accompany me. Not to guide me but to assure the people I'm on their side," said Brianag. "We have found our presence causes conflict." Cassán winced and dipped his head. "I think together, we should be able to hold things for five or six sunsets." Neamhain smiled and dipped her head in agreement.

"I'm curious. Why five sunsets?" asked Eimhir.

"Oh, did we forget to mention that Amodocus and several hundred horse warriors departed from Gràinne's crannag a sunset past? They ride for Dùn Brion." Cassán clapped his hands in glee and relief. A cough brought his attention back to Brianag. "One thousand each of the Ravens and Seonag's army also march towards Dùn Brion, but they will take a half-cycle of the moon to arrive." Brianag's eyes twinkled impishly. "The new Bhanrigh of the Ravens, Sorchae Ni Íar, leads the riders."

Cassán expressed surprise that the Ravens had a new queen but did not recognise her name. "She's your sister, eejit," said Brianag. "I'm sure you will have a lot of catching up to do."

"No…" said Cassán and slumped back in his seat. "I never knew I had a sister… apart from you. Our father never told me, and my mother was executed when I was seven summers."

"Sorchae was adopted by your ma's brother, Íar, and taken to Gaul along with Conall's army," said Brianag. "It's understandable you know nothing of her." Brianag looked at Neamhain, puzzled.

"What?" asked Neamhain.

"Since Cassán is my brother, does that make Sorchae my sister? Our family confuses me, Neamhain."

"It is not Neamhain. It is Aunt Neamhain to you, young lady. Show some respect." The room dissolved into tears and peals of laughter.

CHAPTER 8

Loch Eireachd—Fionn's Camp

Fionn Mac Drostan was considered by many as a man of limited intellect with sadistic tendencies. The latter was certainly true—he was brutal in all aspects of his personal and public life. As for his lack of intelligence, Fionn had a predator's cunning. Allied with his physical strength, this had propelled him to his position as one of the two remaining sons of Drostan Ruadh.

Credible rumours suggested two siblings were assassinated, if not by Fionn's hand, then certainly at his command. To his way of thinking, his remaining brother, Cè, was as much of an obstacle to him succeeding his father as Seonag and the easier one to eliminate. If Fionn admired any of his kin, it was Seonag whom he conceded was a formidable opponent. Indeed, if she were more ruthless, he would be dead. Fionn had no such weakness and fully intended to remove his remaining brother and sister by whatever means necessary.

Fionn stood a head taller than most of his warriors. An unruly shock of red hair and a bushy red beard concealed most of his head. Thick slabs of blue-veined muscles sculpted his limbs and torso. He trundled like a bear and like that beast was deceptively fast. Fionn was like his father in appearance, but did not inherit the king's bearing or charisma.

As his father, Fionn had one eye. The other he lost in a rash attack on his sister's camp in the early days of the war. An axe blade had carved a path from his brow to his jawline. Fionn was lucky to escape the blow with his life. Yet he bore the thick, raised scar, which left a hairless track down his face, with pride.

In Fionn's mind, the Goddess had blessed and marked him for greater triumphs. The Goddess, and his mother, Teàrlag, who had wielded the axe, disputed Fionn's conclusion. Yet, perhaps disagreeing with Teàrlag's intent, the Goddess permitted the blade to scar but not cleave Fionn's face in two.

Thus, the Goddess could have ended the sibling wars before the pretenders gained momentum or the tribe suffered significant casualties. Why she did not was a source of concern to the Aes Sídhe, who wondered what game the Goddess played.

＊

Fionn watched the young woman walk across the camp towards him and smiled in anticipation. As she came closer, he admired the bluish-purple bruises on her cheeks and arms. He knew there were fist and boot marks on her torso, especially on her breasts and belly. The bruising looked livid against her milk-white skin.

That she had amazingly short recovery times did not cause Fionn to ponder why. He saw it as a gift from the Goddess that allowed him to indulge his darker sadistic inclinations. She was his perfect woman, and one he had previously violated and punished in his dreams.

She was smaller than Fionn, although not by much, which was good. Fionn would not abide a woman whose eyes looked down on him. Long blonde hair with copper tones flowed freely over slender shoulders to tap her bottom. That his vision of perfection bore the mirror image of his sister's face never entered Fionn's mind or caused him to question its meaning or origin.

Fionn scratched his balls and leered, barely stopping drool from wetting his beard. She had an excellent *tòn*—arse—with firm, round cheeks, which were just beyond the ability of his calloused hands to cover. To establish his dominance, he mounted and rutted her without ceremony or permission at their first meeting. That he did this in daylight and before his warriors did not concern him… or Leannán.

As for his fighters, they cheered and shouted lewd comments and instructions for more perverted behaviour. They had witnessed the same scene many times previously. However, this time was different; in Leannán, each saw a male or female whose face, body, and age mirrored the objects of their lusts. They wanted to hear the victim broken, crying and begging for mercy, which they did… at least in their minds.

Fionn's intent was to possess, own, and use Leannán until bored with her. Then, he would give her to his men. Sadly, Fionn mistook who was dominant. He did not notice the mysterious bites from needle-sharp teeth or the spots of hardened blood on his nape and back. Thus, he never connected these to her remarkable healing powers or his light-headedness and momentary loss of strength after she departed.

***

Later, in the cool mountain cave chosen as her refuge, Leannán groomed herself like a cat with a long, pink tongue. She smiled at men's gullibility. *How did they ever conquer us?*

The taste of Fionn's blood lingered in Leannán's mouth. She loved its saltiness, if not the metallic harshness. Blood was the only source of iron that did not harm the Aes Sídhe. Leannán pondered that for a few moments and then shrugged. It was of no consequence, and she laughed. *Why would I not like blood? Did I not infect Sidheag with my appetite?*

Yet, Leannán, as had other blood drinkers, failed to follow the trail of crumbs from consumption to consequence. The blood she drew from Fionn's veins put him under her enchantment but also forged a link between them that only death would sunder. Worse, it initiated a perpetual craving she could never satisfy among the Aes Sídhe, and which would only grow.

Soft moans drew Leannán's attention to the array of men and women hanging like butchered cattle from the thick roots of the cavern's ceiling. Their cries showed they were still alive. They were of differing ages, although none were over forty summers. Older blood carried the taint of death in it. Like wine, the crimson liquid dripped into pottery amphorae for storage. They would keep her sated… for a little while. Then she would hunt again.

Leannán wondered what progress the Hound made. She had decided they should split up, with her concentrating on Fionn's camp and army and her pet scouting Cè's camp. She had warned him to keep his beast under control. Hence, the howl carried by a west wind made her exclaim, "Shite!" At least it was a single bark. Three would bring too much attention on them so early in the game.

✳✳✳

It was exhilarating to be far from the island. Hence, the Hound's senses were quickly overwhelmed, and his brain became confused. For a time, the many opportunities to feed and rut paralysed him. In the domain of the Aes Sídhe, neither had been available since the genocidal war which obliterated his tribe.

In his head, he heard Leannán urging caution and knew he had a job to do. He ignored her. *The bitseach can wait for a few sunsets.* That he could rebel against her command gave him hope. Perhaps in the Land of the Humans, he could break free. The idea of violating and devouring Leannán sent his pulse racing and made him drool.

Evil is often attractive and desirable. The Hound cut an imposing picture in his human form, and he radiated a toxic yet appealing aura of devilment and sensuality. He breathed a taste of the forbidden into the air. It was an effective lure, yet the Hound was careful and had a predator's instinct for survival. Thus, he kept to the margins of Cè's sprawling encampment, skirting the tents of the families and camp followers.

A broad smile of perfect, if unusually pointed, teeth completed the Hound's package of temptations. A roguish wink and an artful nod towards the forest were enough to tempt the girl to set aside the drudgery of her daily chores. She was not a virgin—few were—but unlike the men in the camp, the Hound wooed her, and she followed him.

Once beyond the thick, verdant undergrowth of the wildwood, he led her by the hand to a small clearing. A fallen tree at the centre of the glade seemed perfectly placed, and he guided his prey towards it. She examined his face. The open mouth appeared to have too many canine teeth, and his eyes glowed unnaturally amber. When she ran her fingers through the hair covering his chest, it was as soft as fur.

The absence of animal noises or birdsongs in this part of the forest sent trickles of fear along her spine, but the danger was upon her before she could flee. Pushed against the bole, he ripped her threadbare *léine* effortlessly and tossed it aside.

Laid across the stump, she felt a breeze on her raised arse. The position was not unknown to her. In her limited experience, most men preferred it. Still, she was disappointed because she had hoped he was different. The rough bark abraded her belly like clothes on a washing board, and she cried out as slivers of skin were torn from her. The dense trees surrounding the clearing connived to mute her protests.

He licked between her shoulder blades, the valley between her arse cheeks, her *anas*, and her *pit*. His tongue was long and wet. It had thousands of minute barbs, which were delightfully rough on her skin. Irresistibly aroused, her fear subsided. She surrendered and moaned, "Yes."

Numerous nibbles and bites between her thighs and on her arse drew more sighs of pleasure. Her pit honey flowed. She heard him lap it up and loved the sound. He was much more experienced than her usual lovers. She wanted more and ground against his hardness. It was warm but felt misshapen, and much bigger than she had experienced. Her heartbeat synchronised with its pulse. Fear transformed into wanton lust, and she begged him to penetrate her.

The Hound's hand between her shoulder blades was much too strong for her to put up any resistance, even if she had wanted to. The girl felt his hot, panting breath on her neck. She cringed at the drool that splashed her back and imagined a much heavier mass pressed on her torso and arse.

The beguiled screamed at the awful pain and force of the rutting. It was a lesson learned too late. Mercifully, after a few thrusts, the Goddess stopped the girl's heart and called the *bean-sìth* to guide her spirit to a better place. Thus, she was spared the true horror of her abuse and did not feel the teeth that savagely tore her apart and feasted on her tender flesh. Neither did she lose her soul for the Cú Sídhe was a soul-eater.

The Goddess cursed the beast from the Aes Sídhe's dark past, and the abominations created by their foolish ambitions. She swore to make them pay and smiled menacingly. Was Brianag the weapon she had waited for?

∗∗∗

On the ramparts of Dùn Brion, Brianag heard the howl, looked at Neamhain, and blurted, "The Hag, Neamhain! He's here, and so must she be."

"He's usually a silent hunter until he kills. The availability of prey must have overwhelmed his control. Shite!"

"Who's here?" asked Cassán.

The young women started at his voice. *We need to be more careful about our words, Brianag. And I think we need to bank lots of goodwill to counter what will be a nasty surprise for Cassán. Your mission is critical in that respect.* The dip in Brianag's head was invisible to any but a sídhe.

"Please bear with us, Cassán. I promise we will talk about that when the others arrive. However, our current priority must be the safety of your people in the forest. Have you chosen Brianag's guides?" asked Neamhain.

Cassán smiled crookedly. "You are as adept at diverting conversations as your mother, Neamhain, but you are right." He looked at Brianag. "At dawn, two will wait for you at the eastern gate. Cè's warriors will likely block your way. Is that a problem? I can assemble a shield-wall if you need a path cleared."

"Thanks, brother, but that will not be required," responded Brianag before descending the stone treads to the yard. Cassán shook his head. His sister's graceful steps bore the hallmarks of a young woman going to her first céili, not to battle.

"She has exceptional gifts, which bring her deep anxieties," said Neamhain. "Try to understand, but *never* underestimate her."

***

I had hoped to embrace nieces and nephews, brother. If you need help in that area, I have some healing abilities. Cassán scowled at the voice in his head yet was unsure what disturbed him more: Brianag's knowledge, her offer, or that her voice was as clear as if she stood before him. He tried to be mad at the giggling that followed her, but it held no malice.

"Maybe we should take Brianag up on her offer," said Eimhir.

"Bloody interfering women," growled Cassán before he stomped off.

CHAPTER 9

The Forests South-West of Dùn Brion

Two waited for Brianag at Dùn Brion's Eastern Gate. The exit's designation was misleading, as the stronghold lay on a north-west to south-east axis. However, the need for brevity overruled precision in its naming. Brianag thought the female looked about the same age as her. The man was handsome, not pretty but rugged, and about five summers older. The young woman appeared displeased; the man was downright angry. *Not volunteers, then.*

Brianag knew the girl was too young to have fought in the Sidheag Wars. However, the man would have been about eighteen summers. *Did he lose friends or family? Did I kill any of them?* Brianag sighed. *I killed many people. Most deserved it, but some were good. What can I do about that now?* She walked barefoot across the courtyard, barely leaving an impression in the mud.

Dùn Brion, like most significant forts, had a smaller egress adjacent to the main entrance. There was no sense in opening and closing the fort's massive oak gates when only a few people and horses needed to enter or exit. Brianag smiled confidently at the duo.

The man responded with a curt nod towards the smaller exit where four warriors stood ready to open the gate. They were supported by a score of fighters, in case something went severely wrong. "They will open the gate and slam it shut as soon as our feet cross the threshold. There will be no return except to retrieve our bodies if the wolves have not dragged them away," said the male. The timbre of his voice was pleasant, but not the scowl on his face.

The young woman glowered at her companion. Brianag was disappointed. *His face has character, but he's an arsehole.* "You appear to have little confidence in your ability as a warrior." She looked up to where Cassán watched from the walkway. "Should I ask the king to replace you with a more experienced warrior who is not quite so fearful?"

The man's eyes widened at the insult, yet instead of keeping his thoughts to himself, he blundered forward. "I have no fear of dying alongside comrades, but not at the side of an Abomination."

"The Hag's tits!" exclaimed the female warrior. "Do you want to start this now? Like her or not, she's our only hope of getting out of the mission alive. Do you want to explain your objections to the king? *She* is his sister." The young woman poked the man's chest angrily. "This is war, and we're soldiers. We can die fighting at her side or be staked for cowardice." The young woman's voice stung like a wasp; the man flinched, and his face reddened.

"Anyone who does not fear dying is a fool," said Brianag. "However, even if your fighting skills are lacking, you will be safe… at least until I am hungry." Beads of sweat appeared on the man's brow. "Did the king not tell you? We *Abominations* need snacks to maintain our energy. No? How remiss of my brother."

The man lost two shades of colour; the girl, being more observant, appreciated Brianag's humour and tittered. Both recoiled when Brianag grinned, and they glimpsed the mouthful of needle teeth.

Be good, Brianag.

Now would be a good time, Neamhain. Rolling peals of thunder and lightning dancing along the horizon preceded the staccato drumming of hail the size of small crab apples on stone and wood. Shrieks of agony rose from besiegers and defenders alike. Some in the dùn were too slow to take cover.

"Stay within arm's length if you want to live. Step beyond my protection, and I hope you have been steadfast in your sacrifices to the Goddess." Brianag dipped her head to the gate's guards, and the oak door swung open.

＊

The dirt track from Dùn Brion's gates was a thousand steps long and sloped gently downwards. Brianag felt her companions' anxiety rise steeply with each step taken from the gateway. She could hardly blame them. Although in no danger, they constantly and reflexively flinched as they walked through a slavering mass of spear- and blade-wielding war-riors who slashed at them, albeit without consequence.

Brianag was delighted with her latest talent—the ability to create il-lusions. She had discovered it by accident in a game of hide-and-seek with Neamhain and honed the skill in the Halls of the Aes Sídhe. Yet until Neamhain and she escaped from the Mounds, it had been a game, and another way to annoy the Aes Sídhe.

Their flight had been successful. Or had it? *Were we allowed to flee to facilitate Leannán's mission? Are we pawns of the Womb-Born?* Brianag shook her head and muttered, "I have no time for conspiracies." She sensed the frustration of the mob surrounding them and their rising apprehen-sion. To them, the trio was a mirage. An undulating bubble of displaced air marked their progress. Whispers of *"Bana-bhuidseach*—witch!" grew louder.

Brianag felt her companions wince, and knew their confidence leached away with each step taken. She had no time to explain that they were in a different space, and the enemy attacked an illusion. Instead, she said, "Stay tight to me and hold your nerve. I have no time to stop and retrieve you." A sídhe could have spoken the words, but as a speech to inspire confidence, it fell well short.

The young woman turned to the man and hissed, "Keep up. You will not leave me with her."

Brianag chuckled. She liked this one. As for the man, she did not care if the arsehole lived or died. Still, she heaved a sigh of relief as they neared the end of the track. The enemy had thinned out to small groups of ten or more fighters, with no inkling of what had happened near the gateway or who was in their midst.

"We will be at the end of the path soon, and I will drop the cloak. There will be straggling groups of Cè's warriors. You have a choice. Fight or stand aside and let me deal with them. Your worst option is to get in my way."

"You haven't been around humans for a while, have you? Your motivational skills need work," remarked the man.

For the first time, Brianag warmed to the man. "If you are to die at my side, I should know your names."

The man rolled his eyes. "What kind of being are you?"

"If I knew, I would tell you. However, it is safe to assume I am the first and, if the Goddess is merciful, the last of my kind," said Brianag. "I did not ask for this 'gift'. I was fifteen summers when Sidheag slaughtered my friends, including one whom I might have loved, and abducted me.

"She fed me her blood to keep me from freezing to death in the Highlands, but it changed me. My ma sacrificed herself and became the Blood Queen to save me…" Brianag's voice trailed off.

The man reddened at his ignorance and the deep sadness in Brianag's voice. "I apologise for my lack of understanding and am sorry if I caused you pain. I am known as Luag."

"My name is Malmhìn," said the girl. "I hope we don't die too soon. I'm starving." All three laughed; the veil was lifted, and the clash of steel became real.

* * *

Eimhir and Cassán stood on either side of Neamhain on the eastern walls. The young sídhe frowned. Her quandary was convincing the besiegers to abandon the attack without alerting Leannán or the Hound.

Among the Aes Sídhe, the inheritance of familial traits and talents was mainly arbitrary, and not by design. However, Neamhain shared her ma's talent for commanding the weather. Hence, the ominous grey skies laden with rainclouds were perfect. Yet when she lifted her hands and began to sing, her presence would be evident to any sídhe and definitely to one of Leannán's longevity. She stamped tiny feet in frustration.

Cassán laughed. "Your father, Fearghal, was a great warrior, but I have heard that he, too, lacked patience in situations like this. Can we help?"

Neamhain shook her head. "Unfortunately not. I need a song to camouflage mine. It is not a criticism of your worth or skills, but I need someone with a special talent. Are there any witches in Dùn Brion or nearby?"

"No. A smattering of covens are scattered throughout Northern Albu, and there are strong rumours of one on the Sleagh. However, they keep to themselves." Cassán blushed and cleared his throat. "Frankly, they hide from us. They make us nervous and we are not friendly towards them." His smile was rueful. "And yet, we host a sídhe and whatever my sister is. I think the Goddess wishes us to change."

Resigned to revealing herself to Leannán, Neamhain dropped her cloak and chiton and raised her arms. In the silence that fell, a raven's feather hitting the walkway would have been deafening. "Like mother, like daughter," whispered Cassán to Eimhir. Neamhain was as naked as the day she was born and unapologetic.

They watched her mouth open and her muscles tense as the song rose from within. The curling sigils on her body and face, fed on the energy in the skies, became darker, and began to flow. Yet when they heard the song, it was carried on an easterly wind and was not Neamhain's voice. The young sídhe smiled, and tears flowed down her cheeks.

✳✳✳

"Whoa," said Sorchae, gently pulling on the reins and bringing her chestnut mare to a halt. She acknowledged Amodocus' quizzical look. "Neamhain needs my help." *How did I know that?* The cry of a golden eagle in the sky above her was a clue, but she had no time to decipher it.

Sorchae dipped her head towards a nearby grassy hillock. "This should not take long. Let our riders rest and eat."

If Amodocus considered it odd that Sorchae knew Neamhain needed assistance, he showed no sign. *I'm the hand-fast partner of the Blood Queen. Strange is normal.*

Sorchae's long sigh became a faint white mist in the chilly morning air. "I'm going to freeze my arse off," she grumbled as she dropped her armour and clothing to the grass. Neamhain, she, and sometimes Brianag had stood on similar mounds or huge rocks as children. Hands raised, they shouted into the wind. As they grew older, the shouts became songs, and clothing became an unnecessary distraction.

Neamhain had a natural talent and unnatural power. Given who her ma was, it was unsurprising. Sorchae was simply observant, although that is a vastly underestimated talent. She watched her friend's mannerisms and listened carefully to every tone and inflexion in Neamhain's voice.

Only the Goddess discerned the change as Sorchae practised daily alongside her friend. Her song evolved until it was no longer a copy and became one unique to her. As she lifted her arms, Sorchae murmured, "I'm rusty. Forgive me, Neamhain." Yet the song that flowed from her lips was pure and potent.

In the sky above Sorchae, the magnificent eagle screeched the Goddess's approval and commanded the breeze to carry the refrain to Dùn Brion. On the ramparts, Neamhain whispered, "Thank you." She smiled. "You and I will talk about this when we meet, Sorchae."

Camouflaged by Sorchae's song, Neamhain's refrain ascended. Thunder growled, and lightning struck the land. Hail the size of small rocks and freezing rain crashed down on Cè's warriors.

Bloodied by the ferocity of the onslaught, many turned and ran to the eastern forest. The unlucky were those who had partially climbed the cliffs or managed to establish foot- and handholds on Dùn Brion's walls. Freezing rain made the surfaces treacherous. Many left nails frozen in the walls before they fell, shrieking, to die on the rocks below. The few who survived the fall were too broken to fight again… ever.

∗∗∗

In her forest cave, Leannán was fearful, then irritated, and finally dismissive. Whose voice sang the new refrain? Had she an unknown enemy? It was time to visit the idiot, Fionn. Maybe he knew something.

∗∗∗

When the trio emerged from Brianag's cloak, a warband of thirty warriors confronted them. "Rut the Hag!" exclaimed Malmhìn, pulling her axe from the leather loop on her back. Luag, mirroring her intent, unsheathed his sword and brought his shield across his chest. The group's sudden appearance confused the enemy momentarily before their chieftain shouted, "*Ionnsaigh*—Attack!"

Luag and Malmhìn reacted quickly but were several paces behind Brianag. Her movement was elegant, deceptively fast, and terrifying. In a breath, she was in the face of the warband's leader. The chieftain leered at the young woman's breasts. Brianag shook her head. *Men are so easily distracted.*

When the chieftain gazed into the depths of Brianag's obsidian eyes, he saw his death. He blanched at the rows of needle teeth and had only a moment to appreciate the razor-sharp, forest-green talons. With one hand, Brianag ripped out his throat, and with the other, she shredded his chest.

A bloody mist enveloped Brianag as she moved forward, biting and slashing. Her arms and hands moved like flails threshing corn in an unceasing and furious blur. A predator, she slaughtered by instinct and without compassion. She left heads and limbs strewn over the grass, as if her ma's war chariot had driven a bloody path through the band. Battle cries and curses became screams and shrieks and, finally, whimpers for mercy. Yet all Brianag had to give was death.

Luag observed the gore-soaked Brianag as she turned. His stomach lurched at the strings of flesh hanging from her nails and teeth. "Keep your axe ready, Malmhìn. She may not know whether we are an enemy or a friend."

"Given what we witnessed, do you think our weapons will help us or just piss her off?"

They watched as Brianag's eyes slowly regained their green hue, as her teeth became more human, and the blood that soaked her dress and painted her body disappeared. Only a thin ribbon of red remained on her forearm. In the silence, they heard the soft rasp of a long pink tongue removing the smear. Finally aware of her companions, Brianag wondered at their startled glances. Then she understood. "Sorry. Old habits. Where will the civilians be camped?"

✳✳✳

South-west of Dùn Brion, the tall pines of the ancient forests were shrouded in the half-light of a grey mizzle. In a cycle of the moon, a dusting of snow would cover them. As Luag guided the trio down a path well-rutted by wagons, he stopped and faced Brianag. "Will we be permitted to fight, or are we your audience? If so, you should let us know when to clap and cheer."

"Is this pride, sarcasm, or stupidity? None is attractive. Why do you put so little value on your life? Are you eager to die?" Brianag's question was unanswered. "Men do not fear death until the bean-sìth stands at their side. How many warriors do Cè and Fionn command?" asked Brianag.

"At least twenty thousand. Why?"

"Then you will get all the fighting you want and the glorious death you appear to desire." Brianag's talons snapped into view, and her companions recoiled. "Before *this*, I was an adolescent whose sins were to exasperate my ma and to think I knew everything. My only challenge was to avoid boys with fumbling hands who wanted to rut me but didn't know how to, or men who did but should have known better. Sidheag made me watch as she ate my one true admirer."

Brianag choked at the memory. "I was paralysed, helpless to intervene as she devoured him." The talons clicked. "I, too, am a killer. Yet, unlike Sidheag, I wish I were not. I am young, but Death is my companion. My advice is to be brave, not foolish. For the moment, I am your shield. Learn from and make good use of me."

Two events rescued the conversation from a descent into maudlin contemplation. Brianag's sensitive nose twitched. "I smell wood smoke, probably from campfires. We must be getting close." Luag and Malmhìn shrugged. Stale sweat and wet clothes that needed to be washed several sunsets ago were all they smelled.

The proof of Brianag's observation came quickly when a girl of eight or nine summers burst from the wildwood. She bounced off Brianag's legs with an explosive "*Oof!*" and landed in a pool of muddy water.

"Look what you made me do! My ma will kill me for getting my léine dirty, and my da will beat my arse red." Brianag chuckled at the child's righteous outrage.

A man and woman emerged from the forest shouting, "Dolidh!" The man had an unpleasant face, pockmarked from birth. Too much beer had reddened his cheeks and nose and expanded the girth of his belly. Observing Brianag and her companions, he said, "Hand over my daughter." His voice was surly, and a permanent scowl soured his features.

"Who are you?" The ice in Brianag's voice was apparent to all but the man. "How do I know you are the girl's father and not a slaver or a man who preys on children?" Brianag looked closely at the child's mother. Full lips thinned, and her eyes darkened. "By the bruises on your partner's limbs and face, you are certainly a bully, an abuser of the weak."

"This is a family's business. We should not interfere," muttered Luag.

"Will you bear the guilt when one morning the mother and daughter are found dead by *his* hand? You might not want to intrude, but I am an Abomination and have no such qualms." Chastised again, Luag blushed with embarrassment and the knowledge that Brianag was right.

Brianag's hand gripped the man's neck and lifted him effortlessly off the ground. Talons pierced his flesh. He saw his death in her black eyes and whimpered, "Please, no," as Brianag's mouth opened. He felt her fetid breath on his cheek and smelled the meat of those she had recently killed.

A tug on Brianag's dress stopped her from tasting the thug's blood, and she looked down. "He's my da. He's not the best, but he's the only one I have. Please don't kill him."

The father felt his feet touch the dirt and heaved a sigh of relief. Yet his legs had no strength, and he stumbled backwards and fell into the same muddy pool. Brianag grasped his unkempt hair and snapped his head back. "I know and will not forget you. You do not deserve this child, yet she has spoken for you." The click-clack of talons was loud over the forest's silence.

"Harm one hair on Dolidh's head or bruise her or your partner again, and I will come for you. Do you understand?" The vigorous nodding of the man's head had to suffice, as he had lost the ability to speak. "Take us to your camp."

As Brianag followed the family, Malmhìn turned to Luag. "She's frightening and bloodthirsty, but she has a druid's sense of right and wrong. I'm glad she's on our side." Luag nodded in agreement and prayed he would not put his foot in his mouth again.

CHAPTER 10

Dùn Brion & the South-Eastern Forest

"We have two problems," said Cè's shield-man and battle commander. Conn had been Cè's protector since his youth. The hard-headed warrior never minced his counsel to Cè as a young man and had no intention of changing his custom to the would-be king.

Cè's grunt of exasperation was expected. The veteran smiled and continued. "My scouts report over two hundred horse warriors have emerged from the forests at the eastern end of the Sleagh and are riding towards Dùn Brion. They carry the Blood Queen's and the Ravens' banners."

"I did not know the Ravens had mounted warriors."

"Rumours say the Ravens have a new bhanrigh. This is likely her doing."

"Horses will not be of much use in the forests," said Cè, dismissively.

The look from Conn was withering. "Experienced riders have no difficulties fighting in the ancient forests because the trees are widely spaced. Only the dense wildwoods give them problems. However, they will not fight in the woods because there is no need to. Instead, they will travel along the northern slopes and foothills of the Sleagh, which has no tree cover. Once they reach the western tip of the Sleagh, it is a short gallop to the ford across the Abhainn Dubh and then onto Dùn Brion."

Conn tugged on the thin braids of his red whiskers. "Yes, we have warbands plundering the farmsteads along the Sleagh. I expect the riders to sweep these warriors aside." He shook his head in response to Cè's unspoken question. "It is too late to recall them. They are as good as dead. Fortunately, we will only lose about three hundred fighters."

The veteran paused and inhaled deeply. The act had a tone of mournfulness, which made Cè wonder how disappointed his protector was in his judgment. "There is no tree cover for one thousand paces around Dùn Brion. We are forest fighters. This is not our natural battleground but is perfect for riders. My advice is to sound the horns and order a retreat."

"No," replied Cè, "that will give Fionn an additional tail on the whip to lash me."

"You know my position. We have five thousand warriors with clubs and spears against stone walls. Dùn Brion is no more than an elaborate *broch*, but it cannot be taken using the weapons we have. Fionn has sent you here to weaken your army. He knows seizing Cassán's strongholds of Dùn Brion and Dùn Athad is impossible."

"Fionn does not send me anywhere. I am his equal, not his servant," snapped Cè.

"You may change your mind when I tell you the last piece of my spies' reports." Conn's pause for dramatic effect achieved its goal and Cè fell quiet. "A thousand warriors from Seonag's army are jogging through the eastern forests. They will probably gather more warriors before they reach us. A division of Ravens' spears runs to intercept and join them."

"Shite," muttered Cè. "My sister means to finish me. Has the Blood Queen joined her?"

Conn dipped his head. "What did you expect, my king? This war must end, or the Forest People will disappear. Seonag has finally grasped the thistle and her friend, the High Queen of the Eastern Tribes, has chosen sides. I am amazed both waited for so long. We probably have two sunsets before we face the riders and Dùn Brion's garrison. A further ten sunsets and Seonag and her allies will be at our back."

"The Hag's scrawny arse! Even if we win the battle, we will be severely weakened." Cè looked into his guardian's hazel eyes. "I've messed up."

The tall warrior inclined his head. "You are a better tactician than Fionn but lack his single-mindedness. Your initial instincts to avoid Dùn Brion were right and you should have had more confidence in your judgment. Fionn is your brother, but regardless of what happens here, he will dispose of you as he did your other siblings. The better ally was Seonag. She has honour and would have welcomed you and valued your strategic counsel."

Conn knew his next words would anger Cè. "We can save most of the army and negotiate better terms with your sister if we abandon the siege and retreat, immediately."

Cè grimaced at the sour taste in his mouth. "You said there were two problems. What is the second?" The look of dread in Conn's eyes before he regained control of his mien shocked Cè. *What can be that bad?*

"I put little stock in stories of demigods and monsters told by parents to frighten young children into going to their cots." Cè nodded, although his body tensed at what might come next. "The perimeter guards found the remains of a young girl on the edge of the camp at sunrise. Her body had been savagely torn apart and much of it consumed. The druids examined what was left of her. They are certain she was raped before the beast feasted on her."

"The Hag's tits! Increase the camp guards as you deem fit to prevent more of this," said Cè.

"She was the tenth to suffer in this manner." The colour drained from Cè's face. "There are reports of a dog barking after the incidents. The people's imaginations are running wild. They found foot *and* paw prints at each attack. There is talk of the Cú Sídhe."

Cè shook his head. "The Cú Sídhe is a myth. It is some sick, malevolent bastard with a huge, mean hound. Increase the guards around the camp. We need to catch and publicly stake whoever it is." Conn dipped his head. "Now, we must put our heads together and find a way out of our predicament."

Conn sat on a fallen tree near the fire and chewed on a twig while Cè paced the small glade. Finally, Cè faced Conn. "We need an edge. Withdraw our warriors from the siege of Dùn Brion. Send them to the forest south-west of the fort. Cassán's people have fled there." Conn dipped his head. "You will command this action. I need leverage. I want prisoners, not corpses."

***

A war horn reverberated its deep *barrr ewww* from the forests to the north-east of Dùn Brion. Others positioned around the stronghold immediately echoed the message. Cassán watched the Forest People stream from the slopes of the fort's crag. He turned to Neamhain and beamed. "Congratulations. Your tactic worked perfectly." The worried look on Neamhain's face puzzled him. "What am I missing?"

"Dùn Brion's garrison is relieved, but not your people." Neamhain pointed to the south-western forests. "I hope Brianag has prepared her defences well. She will soon have guests."

"The Hag, no!" gasped Cassán as he watched Cè's warriors swarm towards farmers, mothers, children, and old men. "My sister will be safe, won't she? Her powers make her invincible, don't they?"

Neamhain shook her head. "Above all things, Brianag is a warrior. She lives for the fight. In time she will earn the trust of other leaders and become a great battle commander. Of whose army, I do not know, although you and I should pray she is on our side. Her abilities are like the weapons hanging on your belt, and like you, she chooses which to use according to the fight."

The young sídhe held Cassán's gaze. "The Aes Sídhe had two vulnerabilities in the war with humans: they were vastly outnumbered, and man had iron." Neamhain breathed deeply. "Brianag is not immortal. Like me, she can be killed by an iron weapon."

"Shite! What can we do?" asked a white-faced Cassán.

"Pray for her." In her head, Neamhain pleaded, *Please hurry, Sorchae.*

Brianag is in danger.

⁎⁎⁎

Several sunsets earlier, Brianag, Luag and Malmhìn entered the main camp of the Na Mèadaidh refugees. There was no welcome. Instead, Brianag met a wall of revulsion and distrust in the eyes of young and old alike. *It was not me; it was Sidheag,* she wanted to scream, but Sidheag was not here to face their hatred. The bitch and her Brood were gone. Nonetheless, Gaels had long memories, and Brianag was not blameless. Before them, they saw a scapegoat and an opportunity for vengeance.

"Perhaps I should handle this discussion while you remain in the background," said Luag. Brianag was touched by Luag's willingness to intercede on her behalf. The rumbling anger among the crowd surrounding them and mumbles of "Abomination" and "Witch" grew in number and volume.

"Thanks, Luag, but no," said Brianag. She opened her arms and said, "Look at me. I am hardly inconspicuous." Brianag stepped in front of Luag and Malmhìn. "I am Brianag Ni Brion, daughter of Brion Ó Cathasaigh, sister of Cassán Mac Brion, Righ of the Na Mèadaidh, and daughter of Gràinne Ni Fearghal, A 'Bhanrigh Fuil and Àrd-bhanrigh of the Eastern Tribes."

The crowd was unimpressed with Brianag's pedigree. Their mutterings grew louder and more threatening. "My grandmother is the Lady Sídhe, Mongfhionn, and my sister, Neamhain, is her daughter. Neamhain stands with your partners, sons, sisters, and brothers on the walls of Dùn Brion." It took immense strength for an increasingly irritated Brianag to control her body. Instead of talons, flowing green sigils, and obsidian eyes, her body shimmered under the forest canopy.

"That's one way of saying, 'Don't mess with me,'" said Luag.

"I hope it works," replied Malmhìn, gripping her axe's shaft.

Their banter made Brianag smile. The crowd gasped and recoiled at the sight of her needle-pointed teeth. "Please try not to make me laugh, Luag; it could be deadly for Malmhìn and you. I can disappear, you cannot." She turned again to the crowd. "I would like to speak with your civic leader. We need to prepare for what is coming." Brianag spoke confidently, her voice reaching the farthest edge of the crowd.

A grey-haired woman whose bearing refused to acknowledge her age stepped forward. "We know you, Abomination. You and Sidheag slaughtered and fed on tens of thousands. It was your fault that our righ, Brion, died. Why should we trust our children to one who sees us as food?"

Brianag's eyes darkened, amid the clicking of talons. The beautiful shimmering green dress became menacing, and the curling pine-green designs radiated power. "Why, old woman? Would you rather see your granddaughters raped to death and your pregnant daughters' bellies speared? Will you refuse help? Perhaps you prefer to wail helplessly as your sons, daughters, and children are chained, whipped, and driven to the slaving ships?" Brianag stretched out her hand. "Choose, Grandmother. An Abomination's hand or slavery?"

"*I* trust Brianag. She is my friend, and I will accept her help to save my family." Dolidh's small voice rang out. Brianag felt a small hand grasp hers and looked down. She slowed her breath; her talons retracted; and her eyes regained their natural hue.

A tear ran down Brianag's cheek. "Thank you, Dolidh. I'm glad you are my friend."

The crowd parted, and a tall, heavyset man with sun-weathered skin and calloused hands stepped forward. "We will listen to what you have to say. I guarantee nothing more."

"He's a bit cantankerous, but we should take this as a win," said Luag. This time, Brianag kept her lips tightly shut. Seeing Luag in a more favourable light warmed her heart but also made her afraid. *This is too sudden. Perhaps he's just become better at hiding his revulsion of me.*

"Luag's an arsehole at times, but he's honest and loyal. You could do a lot worse," whispered Malmhìn. Brianag blushed at Malmhìn's reading of her body language. Used to concealing her feelings and trusting only a few in the Land of Immensity, how could she be so obvious? *This can only lead to disappointment.*

✳✳✳

Two sunsets later, Brianag surveyed the hastily constructed defences and felt immensely proud of the Na Mèadaidh people. "It is amazing what a thousand children who love digging holes can accomplish." Luag and Malmhìn burst out laughing. Even the dour civic leader could not prevent the broad smile from conquering his face.

Three thousand civilians had taken refuge in the forest. Of that, half were babies and children, five hundred were elderly, and five hundred were in various stages of pregnancy. Brianag's plan gathered everyone into one defensible location. For this, she selected a small, raised clearing about one thousand paces from the treeline and expanded it into a circle with a perimeter of five hundred paces.

They built a berm, from dirt, forest debris, and forward-facing trees. The barrier was the height of a tall man, and five hundred men and women, holding spears, stood behind it. A reserve of half that number, comprising the more mobile elderly and the less visibly pregnant, stood behind them.

Brianag was thankful her father had had the foresight to require every non-slave, whether farmer or artisan, to undergo weapons training. She was also delighted Cassán had continued the tradition. Most of the farmers chose *sleaghan*—spears. Many were also proficient slingers from an early age and always wore three or four slings wound around their waists. Thus, pits were dug and filled with stones.

An army of children, mothers, and the more active elderly covered the area north of the defences in traps. These ranged from holes that would cause the enemy to stumble to those that would snap ankles and calf bones. They planted each with small, sharpened stakes. Brianag sniffed and chuckled. The stench indicated that many had been smeared with shite.

✳✳✳

Brianag muttered, "The Hag!" and, somewhat apprehensively, clambered up and onto the berm's crest. Luag and Malmhìn had persuaded her that leaders spoke to their warriors before a battle to encourage them. Protests that she was not a leader fell on deaf ears.

Brianag coughed, and the people fell silent, increasing her nervousness. "I am very proud of what you have achieved. I do not think well-trained warriors could have done better. So, indulge in a few beers this evening, but no more than a few—drunks make terrible fighters." Laughter rippled through the crowd.

"Fight for your children. Some of you will die. Sell yourself dearly and make your sons and daughters proud. The *seanchaithe*—storytellers—will tell great tales of your bravery, and you will meet them again in Tír Tairngire." The people stood silently. Brianag looked down at Luag and mouthed, "Too sombre?"

He whispered, "Wait."

Dolidh cajoled her da to lift her onto his shoulders. She punched the air and shouted, "Brianag! Brianag!" Soon, the clearing resounded to repeated roars of, "Brianag! Brianag!"

The Abomination created by Sidheag was no more and wept before the people.

***

As a new dawn broke, Luag grasped Brianag's hands. It was a sign of affection at odds with each of their personalities. Luag did not recoil from hands cold to touch, and Brianag accepted the gesture. "Malmhìn and I will fight alongside you."

Brianag shook her head. "No, my style of warfare is best suited to creating terror and is best accomplished alone." She paused, dipped her head to Luag's ear, and whispered, "Find me after the battle. I do not want anyone but a friend to see what I became or may still look like." Impulsively, Brianag kissed Luag on the cheek and hugged Malmhìn. Then she disappeared into the forest.

A short time later, on the plain between Dùn Brion and the forest,

Brianag surveyed the horde rushing towards her. Even with her keen eyesight, they appeared little more than a shimmering blob. She snorted. The fools would exhaust themselves before they reached the forest's edge. She frowned. Her problem was tactics. When and where should she enter the battle… and in what form?

Terror was the key. Like a disease, once started, it would spread through the attackers. She spotted a small hill a thousand paces from her and smiled. *Perfect.*

***

War horns sounded, calling the besiegers to attack those in the forest, and Conn settled into a jog that placed him in the middle of the horde. The veteran had no intention of sacrificing himself by leading from the front. Conn was not a coward; however, he deemed the battle insignificant and not worth his potential sacrifice. Serendipity thrived on such opportunities.

Conn acknowledged the brutal logic of Cè's strategy. Collecting hostages to give him an advantage in negotiations was an excellent tactic. Yet what was he hoping to achieve, and with whom? Had he thought his plan through? Furthermore, Conn had deep reservations about how he and a score of chieftains could stop two thousand angry, frustrated warriors from slaughtering all they encountered in the forest. They howled for revenge for the comrades lost to Dùn Brion's walls.

A chieftain jogged alongside Conn and pointed to Brianag's grassy knoll. Conn squinted, trying to determine the nature of the black shape on the hill, directly in his horde's path. His warriors had little form or organisation as they raced towards the forest. The only thing they had in common were battle cries and curses, which soon become little more than a raw, primaeval growl.

He sensed ripples of fear trickling back from those in the vanguard. The shape on the hill solidified into the most enormous black wolf he had ever seen. Conn watched the wolf's head lift and its mouth open, an entrance to the Otherworld, filled with rows of pointed teeth. Its eyes gleamed obsidian with blazing red tongues of fire.

Yet more terrifying than its physical form was the unnatural howling from its lips. From the forests, numerous packs of wolves emerged to join the refrain and the battle.

✳✳✳

On Dùn Brion's walkway, Neamhain shuddered and muttered, "The Hag!"

A stunned Cassán asked, "Is that Brianag?"

Neamhain nodded. "The battle has begun." She lifted her hands to sing.

Cassán looked at Eimhir, who nodded. "I will not let my sister fight alone, Neamhain. There is one thing I can do." He turned and bellowed, "Assemble the shield-walls. Your families and my sister need our help."

Neamhain put a hand on his forearm. "Thank you."

✳✳✳

In the Royal Crannag, Gràinne dropped to her knees, wept, and prayed to the Goddess for Brianag. Subsequently, she pleaded with Sorchae: *There are too many for her. To survive, she will have to fight without remorse or pity. Seek her out, Sorchae. She will need her family to bring her back from the bloodlust.*

Giosail knelt at her queen's side. She cried for Gràinne's pain and watched the awful Blood Queen rise. Then she shivered at the string of ancient oaths, which promised terrible retribution on anyone who harmed Brianag.

✳✳✳

On the Sleagh, Cè's fourth and final warband fell to the slashing long-handled swords, axes, and maces of Sorchae and Amodocus' riders. Mid-morning, they heard Brianag's howling. Sorchae swore because the horses needed to be fed, watered, and rested. She gritted her teeth as she turned to Amodocus. "We should rest here. Our mounts will be in poor shape for battle if we do not."

The burly Thracian nodded, knowing the pain Sorchae and Gràinne were suffering. He took the reins of Sorchae's mare and watched as she tramped to a grassy hillock nearby. Armour, weapons, and clothing fell to the grass as Sorchae lifted her hands and joined her song with Neamhain's.

Yet something was different this time. Amodocus shook his head and laughed. *Why not?* He watched as curling ribbons sprouted from the dirt and grew like a vine to cover Sorchae's body and face.

⁎⁎⁎

A warband of one hundred fools climbed the hill to battle the wolf. They thought only of how much gold the pelt would fetch and the endless rounds of free beer. They drooled at how tales of their bravery would seduce girls into opening their thighs, even to the ugliest of them.

One look at the wolf's massive head, her obsidian eyes, and the multiple rows of teeth told them they had made a fatal misjudgement. Few had time to fear its long claws before they were on their knees, grasping at slashed bellies or found their guts lying in slippery purple coils on the grass.

Others' final acts were to clutch heads, which clung to their necks by strings of meat. The truly unfortunate smelled the wolf's breath before her jaws closed on their faces, crushing their skulls. One hundred warriors died horrifically in the time it took to inhale and exhale one hundred times. Shock rippled through the horde.

Brianag watched the rebel forces scatter to avoid the mound. Her mouth opened in a nightmarish grin, and she howled. *You cannot elude me.* Keen eyes scoured the horde for its leaders. She spied the first one and bounded towards him, slashing and biting terrified warriors as she got closer. With a leap, she was in front of him. He turned to flee, but in a few steps, his neck was in her jaws. The wolf shook him like a straw doll until she heard the satisfying sound of his spine snapping. Her long tongue lapped at his warm, gushing blood. Brianag growled in disappointment. *There is so much blood and meat, but I have no time to enjoy it. Maybe later.*

One after another, Brianag hunted Conn's chieftains, ending their and their protectors' lives savagely and in ways their worst nightmares never envisaged. Then the wolf paused to search for Cè's battle commander. She was breathing harshly. Her long pink tongue licked the hundreds of weeping slashes that breached her thick pelt. As any wounded animal, she became more dangerous and bit and lashed out at any who came close. *Where is he?* Sensitive ears heard a voice bellowing orders to the horde, and Brianag grinned. *Found you.*

***

"This is impossible," muttered Conn. He roared orders at his army, but its leadership was shattered. In the middle of a charge, there was none to take their place. Hence, the horde kept running towards the forest, if only to stay beyond the wolf's reach. He heard shrieks and saw warriors tossed aside like straw. The unnatural beast was a deliberate and efficient killer, pausing to bite and slash as it came closer.

There was no path to avoid the creature. Therefore, Conn tightened his shield strap on his left arm, hefted his *sleagh*, and strode towards it. He had a veteran's eye for detail. Blood wept from many cuts and the wolf limped from a wound on a hind leg. *If the beast bleeds, it is mortal, and I can kill it.*

In one aspect, Conn was correct; in another, he was dreadfully wrong. He grasped his spear tightly, swept his *sgiath*—shield—around to protect his chest, and advanced slowly towards the wolf.

He's a brave man. The wolf watched Conn get closer and steeled herself. *This is going to hurt.* She ran towards Conn and saw him go down on one knee, stabbing the spear's butt into the soft dirt. *So predictable.* The wolf leapt, and Conn gripped his weapon. A tremendous shriek rent the air as the spearhead plunged through fur and hide to pierce the beast's heart. The shaft snapped as the wolf hit the ground, bowling Conn over.

Around Conn, warriors shouted and cheered his victory and the wolf lying mortally wounded in the dirt. Its great chest rose and fell with each painful breath. With each cycle, the beast's heart beat less frequently, slower, and fluttered. Soon, only muscle memory kept it going, and that did not last long. The wolf exhaled, although it seemed more of a pleased sigh, before it lay still.

***

In Dùn Brion, Neamhain screamed, "*No!*" and lashed the horde with hail and lightning. As Sorchae's riders crossed the Abhainn Dubh River ford, she shouted, "*Brianag!*" In Gràinne's crannag, Giosail watched blood-red tears stream down the queen's face and stain the wooden floor. The runes of the royal crannag glowed silver and red.

***

In his camp in the north-eastern woods, Cè swore as a continuous stream of scouts briefed him on the battle. The reports were full of conflicting information. Hoping to curry favour, the optimists pronounced that Conn's victory was assured. Conversely, the pessimists asserted that the Goddess had turned her back on them and defeat was inevitable.

None gave him cold, hard facts that he could act upon. He noted their faces and would punish them later. The exception was the young woman who stood before him. Her face was grim, and she knew that messengers with bad news rarely had long lives.

Her report was concise, and she refused to be swayed by the gaggle of chieftains gathered around Cè, who declared her account unbelievable or exaggerated. She described an army of almost three thousand who moved through the forest and were two sunsets' jog from Cè's camp. One thousand were Raven spears, and the rest were Seonag's warriors led by Earc.

Cè swore. With his army split, he had only three thousand warriors by his side. The odds were not in his favour. *Why did I not listen to Conn?* The Forest People's tradition was to fight aggressively in the forests. Building defensive positions was abhorrent. *What choice do I have?*

Thus, Cè bellowed two orders, the first to his hornblowers: "Go to the edge of the forest and sound the retreat!" He hoped Conn was within the horn's range. The second was to his chieftains: "Build a berm and dig ditches!"

CHAPTER 11

Loch Eireachd & Loch nan Clàr

Fionn's encampment sat at the northern end of Loch Eireachd in the densely forested northern highlands. It was an idyllic location for those who could appreciate its beauty. Fionn was not one of them. He sat on a rough wooden throne before his pavilion and glowered.

The Goddess did not bless Fionn with a surplus of intelligence, yet he was not stupid. He had begun to question Leannán's perfect solution to his darker needs. Where had she come from? Her accent was not from anywhere in Northern Albu. More to the point, why could he not send her away? Every time he considered it, his body refused to obey his will.

He looked at his trusted chieftains and growled. They paid obeisance to Leannán, not him. However, they did not do this with open displays. Their servitude was much more subtle and thus totally out of character. They appeared to be enchanted, which was a far-fetched conclusion. *Am I paranoid?* He shook his head to clear a fog, which increasingly enfolded his mind. *I will execute a few of them and see what happens.*

A young chieftain, who bowed as he approached, interrupted Fionn's musings. He was a clever young man, a warrior of note, and ten seasons younger than Fionn's current *Àrd Chomhairle*—High Council—members. *Perhaps I should dispose of my Council and populate it with fresher minds and fighters.* He waved the chieftain forward. "You have news?"

The young man dipped his head. "A large force, comprising Ravens and"—the envoy hesitated—"your sister's warriors have passed us in the forests."

"Two armies could march side by side in these forests, and neither would see the other," snapped Fionn. It was an exaggeration. The trees in the ancient woods, which spanned the Highlands from coast to coast, were widely spaced. To thrive, each pine or oak starved its weaker neighbours of nutrients to ensure its survival. It was a model of domination the Forest People had followed for generations. Nevertheless, the forests were vast, providing ample cover for several careful armies.

"Also, a mounted warband of two hundred riders gallops along the Sleagh towards Dùn Brion. They appear to be a mix of the Blood Queen's and the Ravens' warriors." The chieftain hesitated to give an opinion because Fionn's moods were changeable. "Perhaps we should send support to Cè. I'm not confident his army can defeat the forces moving towards him and Dùn Brion's garrison. At the least, your brother will be severely weakened." The young man took a pace backwards and bowed.

"Cè made his cot; let him face the consequences of his decisions. My brother's usefulness has reached its limit," said Fionn.

Fionn's callous response shocked the chieftain, yet he said nothing and merely dipped his head. Fortunately, a commotion at the eastern entrance of the camp diverted everyone's attention. The young chieftain turned in time to watch Fionn's mother, Teàrlag, brush aside attempts to stop her from approaching.

Fionn stood and bowed mockingly. "Have you come to join me for the meadhan-latha meal, Mother?"

For her part, Teàrlag was momentarily stunned into silence by the figure standing at her Fionn's shoulder. The shape of her face, deep-blue eyes, and blond hair bore a striking resemblance to her daughter, Seonag. Only the sardonic curl of Leannán's blood-red lips was at odds with the appearance. *I must be mistaken. What is going on here?* Her senses on alert, Teàrlag took a seat opposite her son.

***

"The Lady Seonag Nic Drostan awaits, my queen. She asks for an audience." Giosail bowed out of habit, and Gràinne shook her head. She had tried to impress on Giosail that such etiquette should be reserved for formal occasions.

"I wonder what Seonag wants. She was here only a short time ago, and it's a long journey from the stronghold of A' Chrìon Làraich."

"She looks anxious, my queen."

"Seonag is a friend, Giosail. She is always welcome"—Gràinne's brow furrowed briefly—"unless we are at war. Please bring her to my private chamber and ask the servants to bring us food and refreshments. She is likely famished." Giosail's knees tensed as if to curtsy, but she overcame the urge. Gràinne smiled, acknowledging the minor victory, and said, "When you have organised the food, please return. I wish you to attend our meeting."

If Seonag thought Giosail's presence odd, she said nothing. Seonag's demeanour witnessed the much weightier issues with which she wrestled. She paced the small chamber, constantly wringing her hands between muttering curses. When she brushed wayward tresses of blonde hair from her face, Gràinne saw anger in her eyes.

"Please, Seonag. Sit down. Eat and take some refreshments. It will help to calm you down."

Instead, Seonag remained standing and held Gràinne's gaze. "Answer me honestly, Gràinne. Am I a weak queen?"

Gràinne shook her head. "No, because you are not a queen." Seonag's mouth fell open, and Giosail's eyes widened. Forestalling any protest, Gràinne continued. "Like your brothers, you are a pretender to the throne of the Forest People. Your father, Drostan, blessed your ascension to the throne, but you failed to seize it with an iron fist. If you had, no one would have challenged you because you would have already disposed of them and their supporters.

"However, *if* you were the Bhanrigh of the Forest People, then, on balance, I would judge you to be weak. A queen cannot please every-one, Seonag. You have a good heart, but that is not enough for a queen. Where is the strength you showed at the Battle of Cùil Daothail or when you fought and defeated eight in Dùn Brion's courtyard?"

Gràinne studied her nails for a moment. "That said, on those oc-casions, you were forced into action. In Dùn Brion you were backed into a corner by Brion's incredibly stupid decision not to support his shield-maiden. You lost your way after Brion's rejection. Cùil Daothail was an escape fostered by the incident. You need to forgive Brion and yourself. Being reactive is a failing strategy for a queen."

The queen paused and laughed, and Seonag's eyes widened at what might be coming next. "You also need to stop rutting eejits like Earc. That said, Earc is more ambitious than some of your previous partners. He wants your throne as well as what's between your thighs."

Seonag slumped on the seat next to Gràinne and smiled wanly. "Well, that was blunt."

"You are intelligent, Seonag. I suspect you asked the question know-ing the answer," said Gràinne. "Perhaps you also thought out of those who advise you, only I would give you an honest answer. Thank you for the compliment, friend. I hope you would do the same for me.

"Are you going to tell me what is really bothering you?" Gràinne shook her head. "No. First, answer me this. Would I have let a tribal war last ten summers?"

Seonag sighed. "No, because you are ruthless. I tried to reach fair agreements with my enemies, and now I fear I have lost my tribe. I have far fewer supporters and warriors than when I started. Many have changed their allegiance to Fionn or rebel warlords."

"As Giosail will testify, I united the Eastern Tribes by blood. She will also agree that I made mistakes, some of which I hope to recti-fy. However, on this sunset, my people are as numerous as the Forest People. Yes, I was merciless and slayed thousands." Gràinne held Seonag's hands. "Still, how many have died in the Forest People's war?

Probably tens of thousands? Whose path, yours or mine, caused the fewer deaths?"

A tear trickled down Seonag's cheek, and her lip trembled. "Maybe I do not have the qualities needed to be queen of the Forest People."

"Nonsense!" Gràinne's rejoinder was fiercer than she intended, but Seonag knew it was heartfelt. "No one will ever doubt your bravery after you fought Sidheag and her Brood at Cùil Daothail. Drostan knew *you* would be the best queen for the Forest People, not your brothers. You need to believe it. Teàrlag stands with you…" The glare at the mention of Seonag's ma's name startled Gràinne.

"Out with it, Seonag. What is the true reason for this visit?"

"I have received reliable reports…" Seonag chuckled. "I still have spies in Fionn's camp. Teàrlag plots against me with Fionn."

"Why is she still alive?"

"She is my mother, Gràinne. Matricide is not looked on favourably by the Forest People or the Goddess."

"I suspect neither is treason. You must deal with this or lose all hope of the throne." Gràinne looked intensely at Seonag. "Do you want to rule the Forest People?"

"My father chose me as he lay dying from his wounds."

"That is a weak answer."

"The Hag, yes! The throne is mine." Gràinne smiled, satisfied at the strength in her friend's voice.

Gràinne looked across the room to Giosail. "What do you say, Giosail? What would be your counsel?"

Giosail gulped and looked at Seonag. "You are generous, my lady, and mean well, but Teàrlag is an infection draining your strength. She must die… immediately. It does not have to be by your hand. Indeed, it should not. That is why kings and queens have shields."

Then she addressed Gràinne. "I have listened to many conversations that perhaps I should not have, but enough to form an opinion. The future of the Eastern Tribes would be ill-served with Fionn as king of the Forest People. He would make an untrustworthy neighbour. Our neutrality was well-intentioned but mistaken. We should have supported Seonag immediately after Drostan's death.

"More blood will be spilt if we do not correct that decision. Your recent decision to send warriors to relieve Dùn Brion must be the beginning. If our children are to have a future, the Eastern Tribes, Seonag, and Cassán must unite against Fionn."

***

As the door closed and a sober Seonag went to fetch her horse, Gràinne faced Giosail. "I did not destroy your tribe, Giosail. Yes, the leaders and warriors died on the battlefield or were executed. However, like you, the women and children were enslaved. The children have grown and are young men and women. With training, they could become warriors."

"What are you saying, my queen?"

"Answer me this, and I will respond to your question. Do you wish to have your tribe reinstated to take its place alongside the other tribes who accept me as Àrd Bhanrigh?"

Giosail gripped the table to maintain her balance. She had sometimes considered Gràinne's question, but only in her dreams. Now, she dreaded what might follow if she answered honestly. Her words might be interpreted as treasonous. She breathed deeply. "I think the children of my tribe have atoned for the sins of our fathers. Yes, we deserve to take our place at the Table of Leaders."

"I have watched you more closely than I suspect you know"— Gràinne chuckled—"although you are sharp-eyed and perhaps, I am mistaken. You have witnessed me as queen and seen Seonag's trials. A queen's path is not an easy one. I had hoped for a longer time to allow you to become accustomed to being royalty again. However, as usual, the Goddess has a timescale of her own."

Gràinne gripped Giosail's shoulders. She looked upon a face whose innocence would disappear and be replaced by many cares. For a moment, she hesitated, but she was the High Queen. "You are the sole heir to your father's throne. Will you accept the burden of that throne and the responsibility for your people? I will not judge you badly if you decline, because it is a dubious honour."

"I accept, my queen," said Giosail. Then she smiled and asked, "May I change the name of the tribe?"

"I would hope so… *and* some of its customs. 'The Smeared' is not a wonderful name, and spreading rancid fat over your bodies is just disgusting." Gràinne thought for a moment. "But not by fiat. Select your chomhairle wisely and seek agreement. There will be times when you must be a tyrant but make them the exception."

"Would it be possible to choose a less harsh location?"

Gràinne laughed. "Negotiating already. Draw up your wish list, and I will call a Council of the Tribes to discuss whatever you propose. I will support you, provided it is not outlandish. Can I announce a new bhanrigh at the next meeting of the clanns?"

"Yes. Thank you, my queen." Giosail paused and frowned. "But how will we find where my people are? It's been nine seasons since the tribe was dispersed."

"I have messengers travelling throughout the north. They bear a notice informing all who wish to rejoin the tribe under your rule to assemble here at the feast of Bealtaine, following the winter. Any who try to prevent them will find a stake pushing against their arse."

"You knew I would accept?"

"Call it foresight. I know a queen when I see one."

***

"Who is the *strìopach*, and why does a whore have a shield, and a dark, handsome one, at that?" Teàrlag referred to the Hound, whose activities at Cè's camp had prompted Leannán to bring him to heel. From the smouldering anger in his eyes, he was unhappy his freedom had been curtailed. He smiled at Teàrlag insulting Leannán and accepted her compliment with a dip of his head.

As for Fionn, he was less concerned about Teàrlag's insult; it was an apt description of Leannán. However, he appeared surprised at the Hound's presence. When had the man entered his stronghold? *More to the point, did I give permission?* He shook his head, and his brow furrowed. *I have too many gaps in my memory. Why?* He stared at Leannán, but she just smiled provocatively.

"She is none of your concern," said Fionn, returning his attention to Teàrlag. He snarled, "You promised to deliver Seonag into my hands at Lugnasad. That was two cycles of the moon ago. Soon, we will celebrate Samhain, and winter will be upon us. Her stronghold at A' Chrìon Làraich is impregnable when the snow falls.

"After ten summers, even my loyal chieftains begin to doubt whether I can bring this war to a close. Their loyalty and reward depend on me being crowned the Forest People's rìgh with no rivals left alive. If you want Drostan's line to keep the throne, deliver on your promise."

Fionn swept a hand in a semicircle. "How long do you think we can keep our arrangement secret? Seonag has spies in my camp." Teàrlag started, and her eyes widened. Fionn laughed. "It seems I have more respect for Seonag than you. My sister is not stupid, Mother, and is wise enough not to tell you everything. My scouts and informers search for her people, but inevitably, we will not uncover everyone."

The panic that surged through Teàrlag momentarily paralysed her. She had grown disenchanted with Seonag's strategy to win the war. Teàrlag firmly believed she had a right to be counsellor to the throne of the Forest People, but she was not getting any younger. Thus, she had turned to Fionn. *Have I made a fool's bargain?* "You should respect your ma. Without my help, Seonag will fight you for another ten summers, and the Forest People will become prey to those around us."

Teàrlag's steel-blue eyes held Fionn's. "Seonag is not your only threat."

Fionn laughed aloud. "If you're talking about Cè, he will be in Mag Mell shortly."

The matriarch shook her head. "The Na Mèadaidh under Cassán

and Eimhir grow stronger and wealthier. The Eastern Tribes are united and thrive under the Blood Queen. Remember, too, Gràinne and Seonag are old friends. Cè's attack on Dùn Brion was foolish. The Blood Queen remained neutral, only because I convinced your sister the war must be settled within the Forest People. The siege of Dùn Brion has changed everything. You need me more than ever, *son*."

She paused as if uncertain whether to share a piece of information but rightly perceived her standing with Fionn was on boggy ground. "And there are the Blood Queen's recent visitors to consider."

"What visitors?" interrupted Leannán.

"Keep the whore in your cot and her mouth shut. She does not belong at meetings such as this," spat Teàrlag.

"Answer her." Fionn spoke slowly, as if fighting the words.

"The Blood Queen's daughter and Sidheag's spawn, Brianag, has returned from the Halls of the Aes Sídhe with a friend, who is the daughter of the sídhe, Mongfhionn. There is also a third friend, Sorchae, who is unexpectedly the new Bhanrigh of the Ravens. I sense there is more to her. All are powerful beings. If they declare publicly for Seonag, our fight for the throne will become much more perilous."

"Go back to Seonag and convince her not to seek help." Fionn bent forward like a buzzard. "Make sure the gates of A' Chrìon Làraich are open when I attack in the spring."

✳✳✳

Apart from the constant drip of blood into pottery amphorae, the cave was quiet. "Indulging your addiction?" mocked the Hound, nodding towards the hanging bodies. "Sidheag was more savage and obvious in her capacity for blood drinking. I wish I had known her."

A withering look is more effective if aimed at someone who respects the originator. The Hound shrugged off Leannán's glance. He feared the enchantress for the chains she wrapped him in, but he had no esteem for her. He would kill her as brutally and slowly as possible when the opportunity arose. In the meantime, he smiled disarmingly.

Leannán knew his intent to be false. "Go to A' Chrìon Làraich and the Blood Queen's stronghold. Your primary mission is to reconnoitre and determine Seonag's and Gràinne's strengths." The Hound looked disappointed and insulted at the menial task until Leannán added, "This time, you may terrorise the population… without restraint."

A smiling Hound turned but halted at Leannán's next order. "Put some clothes on."

"I do not need clothes," replied the Hound.

"Soon, it will be winter in the Highlands, and even the *Cinn Péinteáilte*—Painted Ones—wear pants. Do not make your human presence so obvious that it imperils your mission. There will be those with powers hunting you. You do not want to add me to that list."

"If you are that concerned about trivial matters, then perhaps you should ask your mother, Áine, for help." Leannán flinched at the insult and swore to end the Hound when her quest for revenge was over.

CHAPTER 12

The South-Western Forest

The rebel Forest People greeted Conn's victory with wild cheers and swerved around him as they continued their stampede towards the forest. Meanwhile, in the northern forests, the deep *barrr ewww* of Cè's war horns sounded a persistent call for retreat but were ignored.

Conn's lukewarm support of Cè's forest strategy was supplanted by another pressing priority: the need to remove the wolf's head as a trophy and to skin the beast for its thick, black pelt. Treasure, not retreat, was his goal as he pulled a long knife from his belt. As for his army, they were well past hearing any call to withdraw.

Approaching the corpse, Conn stopped and blinked. Did his eyes trick him? He imagined the wolf moved. *Impossible.* However, it was not that the body moved. The fur seemed to sway like corn in a summer breeze and began to dissolve. The rate was slow at first but increased rapidly. *What sorcery is this?*

The wolf soon resembled a column of thick, black smoke, but it did not disperse or vanish. It hung, a dark mist, five steps from Conn as if waiting for something. Conn rubbed his eyes. The cloud's colour gradually transformed to green, and its core became denser. He watched a shape form at its centre, and gasped, "No!" as Brianag stepped forward.

She took a deep breath as if to savour her rebirth and smiled crookedly at Conn's confusion. "I love my wolf, but the form has limitations on how quickly it can heal. I should thank you for killing *and* saving me."

Brianag laugh sent chills along Conn's spine. "I was not totally dead. Sidheag taught me a little blood can go a long way, and there has been a lot of blood spilt on this grass. From the Aes Sídhe, I learned that death is not all it seems."

"Iron," gasped Conn. "The spearhead was iron. The Aes Sídhe cannot survive steel."

"That is true," admitted Brianag. "Perhaps I am either not a sídhe or am more than a sídhe. That is a topic for philosophers to debate." Brianag's head abruptly turned at the sound of a scream from the south-west.

When she turned back, obsidian eyes held Conn's gaze, and he heard the click of long green talons. "I wish I could spend more time with you, but a friend needs help." Brianag was nose-to-nose with Conn. He gasped when, Brianag eviscerated him. Her talons were so sharp he felt little pain, but she remedied that when her mouth opened, and her jaws crushed his skull. His last memory was the sound of bones cracking and the brief but excruciating agony.

***

Brianag bent her head to the side, trying to shut out the screaming of those who ran past or away from her. From the forest, she heard men and women cry out, their flesh sundered by blades and clubs. She caught the dull snap of bones and the cries of many falling into traps. Yet above that rose Dolidh's scream, *"Brianag!"*

"No!" Brianag was at the berm and searching for her friend in the blink of an eye.

"Over there, Brianag. Over there!" Dolidh stood on the berm, frantically pointing along the defences.

Relief her young friend was safe flooded through Brianag. She would scold her later about exposing herself on the berm. Any respite ended when she saw Luag and Malmhìn bloodied and with their backs against the berm. They fought desperately against enemies frustrated by the obstacle and the defenders' stubborn resistance. The combat could only have one end—their death.

A pink mist of blood and gore tracked Brianag's path as she carved a path to her friends. She stood before them, a beautiful, nightmarish, creature who hissed through a bloody mouth filled with too many teeth. "I told you to hold the fence until others came to relieve you. *Did I not make myself clear?*" Brianag's tone reminded Luag of how his ma chastised him. "Stay *inside* the berm and no more heroics. I do not have many friends and cannot afford to lose any." Luag and Malmhìn had no opportunity to protest. With no effort, Brianag flung them over the berm.

A few well-placed kicks and punches rewarded Luag's and Malmhìn's indignity at crashing into the defenders. Loud protests at their treatment made Brianag laugh, and she turned to face the enemy. Her eyes fell on Dolidh and her horror-filled expression.

The child pointed towards Brianag making her look down at her naked, gore-covered body. When she inhaled, the smell of meat in her teeth filled her nostrils. *I'm sorry I'm a monster, Dolidh. Forgive me.* Her heart broken, she turned her back on Dolidh and waded into the battle. She knew of only one way to assuage her guilt: slaughter.

Still, Brianag mistook Dolidh's intent, for she was pointing beyond, not at, her friend. Her concern was Brianag's safety.

***

They witnessed the transformation of the huge black wolf and watched their leader slaughtered by the green apparition which rose from its corpse. Before a berm built by farmers, snares dug by children broke their ankles and legs. Yet their hopes remained high when they finally stood before the defences. They would rape, enslave, and sell the civilians. None knew of Cè's orders. None would have heeded them.

Two events changed the rebels' ambitions. First, the farmers—husbands, mothers, sons, and daughters—wielded spears like warriors and refused to give ground. Boys and girls unwound slings and lobbed slugs into the air to bruise flesh and break bones. The second was the young girl's cry of, *"Brianag!"* Who was Brianag? When the green horror appeared, they quailed and tried to flee.

Brianag laughed and sang battle cries as she moved through the undisciplined mass. Often, she was nightmarishly visible, and, at other times, concealed. Conflicting emotions of guilt and euphoria filled Brianag. The rising terror of her victims and the blood of the fallen fed her curling designs, increasing her power. She orgasmed repeatedly, overwhelmed by the ecstasy of unconstrained killing.

The weapon that was Brianag paused only when she heard the horns of Sorchae and Amodocus' riders as they entered the forest. Her hearing picked out the battle shouts and heavy tramp of feet of Cassán's shield-walls as they pounded the dirt, marching towards the trees. She savoured the warriors' bellowed promises of revenge for those who threatened their families. On Dùn Brion's walls, Neamhain continued to pummel the enemy with hail.

Brianag looked down at her body and felt nauseous. A thick film of gore obscured her designs. A mask of red veiled every feature of her face apart from her eyes and teeth, which looked garishly white. Her long-braided hair was lank and heavy with blood. It refused to swing or tap her arse when she moved. Streamers of flesh hung from her talons and teeth.

The taste in her mouth was foul, like rotting meat. When she exhaled, the breeze flung the smell of her breath and the stench from her body back at her. She almost puked but did not dare for fear of what she would see. *I smell like death. They cannot see me like this. Sorchae, Neamhain, and Cassán are close. My friends in the camp are safe. I must flee.*

***

Sorchae and her friends could not get near the berm for the bodies. They did not know whether to be delighted at Brianag's devastation or horrified. "Where is she?" asked Cassán, looking at Neamhain.

Tears coursed down Neamhain's cheeks. "I do not know. She has blocked me from finding her... or she is dead."

"Why would she block you?" asked Cassán, refusing to consider the other option.

"Look at the butchery around us, Cassán. She buries it deep within her, but Brianag cares what those who love her think about her. She does not want us to see what she became."

Cassán shook his head. "No. She is my sister and saved my people. We must find her. She may be wounded. Demigods are not immune to iron blades."

"We will track her the human way, without powers, until we find her," said Sorchae.

***

Luag's father and his father before him were hunters and had taught Luag to track and hunt prey. After the battle, Luag told Malmhìn he would find Brianag—alone. Malmhìn was furious at his decision. Consistent in his lack of diplomatic skills, Luag informed Malmhìn she would slow him down. This did not reduce Malmhìn's annoyance. However, she knew Luag had a short time before darkness fell and contented herself with slapping his face, followed by a hug and a prayer for success.

As the sun drifted towards the horizon and the light faded, Luag swore and prayed to the Goddess, promising to be more faithful with his sacrifices. He hoped the trail he followed was the correct one. The battle in the forest had been ferociously bloody, and many paths were available. According to early reports, around a third of the attacking force was dead or wounded. The injured were likely as good as dead.

As he jogged deeper into the forest, it seemed to Luag that Brianag would seek refuge far away from the Na Mèadaidh encampment. Hence, his spirits rose. However, if he was mistaken, the darkness would cover Brianag, and he would have to wait until dawn. That was unacceptable.

He touched the cheek where she kissed him, and his heart pounded. That he cared for someone he had called an "Abomination" a short time ago troubled Luag. Still, as he paced along the path, he could not bear the thought of Brianag being alone. He had witnessed another side of Brianag and knew she deserved better than ignorant condemnation.

"This is silly," he muttered. "I'm not an adolescent boy. We've only met. It was a sister's kiss to a brother." *What if it wasn't?* Life was harsh and few men lived beyond thirty-five summers. If they were warriors, their lives were much shorter.

✳✳✳

The Goddess watched Luag's progress. Truthfully, she had not decided whether Brianag had a future. She had sympathy for Brianag. The young woman had suffered much, none of which was her fault. *Bloody Aes Sídhe!*

Yet could she allow the powerful creature Brianag had become to walk freely among the humans? If she died, would Mag Mell welcome her? There was no place for her in the Land of Immensity. That said, the chaos she would bring to the self-absorbed demigods was a tantalising prospect. The Goddess needed time to think, and that benefited Luag—and Brianag.

✳✳✳

At the far reaches of the forest, Luag stumbled across a small meadow. Squinting in the half-light, he spotted a modest mound at the far end of the clearing. He approached cautiously, sword in hand, stopped a few paces short of the shape, and quelled his stomach.

Brianag lay, curled up like a baby, in a pool of congealing blood. Enrobing her was a wolf with its belly and chest slashed open. Brianag had burrowed into the gash. *Clever, if gory; it's a good way to keep warm.* Luag looked closer at the wolf and saw bite marks. *And to have snacks as well.* Brianag moaned and shivered. Several rows of teeth chattered. The heat from the wolf had almost dissipated. It was autumn, and the night would soon turn bitterly cold.

Luag scavenged for firewood and started a fire close to Brianag. He removed his shirt to cover her and shivered in the chilly, late-autumn night. When his fingers touched her skin it felt waxy, and its coldness shocked him. "The Hag!" he whispered under his breath. He tossed several large branches onto the fire, dropped his *triubhsair*—trousers, lay

101

beside Brianag, and cradled her in his arms.

"You do not look or act like an abomination to me, Brianag. I'm sorry I ever saw you as one." Luag grinned and whispered in her ear, "Please do not eat me when you awake."

CHAPTER 13

Dùn Brion & the South-Western Forest

The battle was over, but Brianag remained missing. Impenetrable darkness enveloped the forest as the sun set. Sorchae had made a promise to Gràinne and only reluctantly ceded to her friends' counsel to return to Dùn Brion to eat and rest. All promised to resume the search at the first light.

Sorchae tossed and turned in her cot. Yet Brianag was not the sole cause of her restlessness. The solitude allowed Sorchae time to think about her recent behaviour and the strange markings on her body. "I'm turning into one of the Cinn Péinteáilte," she grumbled. "But they consented to the sigils." She rubbed and scratched her arms and legs to no effect. "Mine appear to be permanent and resemble Brianag's and Neamhain's," she groused. "Why? I'm not 'special', like them."

Perhaps I should make you 'special', although you are much too modest, Sorchae Ni Íar. Brianag was violated by Sidheag and perhaps her powers are a small reparation. Neamhain is Aes Sídhe and was born with her abilities, although she still does not know their true depths. You have earned yours.

"Shite!" exclaimed Sorchae, and the Goddess laughed.

One day, I will introduce you to Aoife, a delightful young woman who lives in southern Ériu. She, too, has an affection for that word. She also had trouble coming to terms with my gifts.

"Sorry," said Sorchae, although she did not truly mean it. She scanned the chamber for the source of the voice. All she saw were flickering shadows thrown by the wood fire. Yet Sorchae did not doubt that she had company, and the authority in the voice pointed in one direction.

Never apologise for giving pleasure, child, only for being or doing something stupid, rebuked the Goddess. Sorchae growled at being called an infant, and the Goddess laughed. *Consider my age, Sorchae. You will always be a child to me. Get used to it, for I am too old to change. Would you like to see me?* Sorchae's eyes widened at the possibility. *My true appearance is said to be frightening. The shock may send you to Mag Mell, which would be a pity. I would have to find another for the role I envisage for you.*

"That's a clever diversion, Goddess," chided Sorchae. She pinched her arm hard enough to produce tears to confirm she was not dreaming. "What task do you foresee?"

Continue, not foresee, Sorchae. It began when you were a wee'un and battled against great odds to live. Sorchae felt the Goddess pause. *I want you to be my Hand.*

Sorchae shook her head. "I am sorry, Goddess, but I cannot be your Hand. That is Conall Mac Gabhann's role and has been for decades. I will never supplant Clann Ui Flaithimh's *Rí Ruirech.* He is my friend, and I still think of him as my king," said Sorchae.

The Goddess laughed, and Sorchae thought it was a pleasant sound. Still, she suspected any who pissed off the Goddess had brief lives and painful deaths. *Your loyalty confirms my choice. Tell me, Sorchae, how many hands do you have?*

Sorchae automatically looked down. Instantly, she knew she had stepped into the Goddess's trap. "Shite!" she muttered and waited for the inevitable.

Why would you limit me to one? The Goddess's logic was indisputable, yet Sorchae remained convinced a massive prank played out at her expense. *It is not a jest, Sorchae. I leave that to Serendipity. Choose to be my Hand, and you will understand.*

"But Conall does not have a song or these…" Sorchae pointed to the curling designs on her body and instantly felt foolish. *As if she cannot see them.*

I find it maddening everyone assumes I never endowed Conall with special traits. That would be extremely ungrateful, would it not? Perhaps his best gift is to make everyone think he has none. One close to him has strong suspicions, which infuriates her. The Goddess's brittle tone matched her irritation.

Sorchae heaved a sigh. "I accept, Goddess. Now what?"

I will be in touch.

Sorchae looked around and knew the Goddess was gone. "Typical!"

***

Beams of sunlight broke through the glade's canopy and played over Luag's eyes. They sprang open. He breathed easier when he felt Brianag's body pleasantly warm against him. "The Hag. This is embarrassing," he muttered when he realised his hands gripped Brianag's breasts, and his manhood was as hard as a tree trunk snug in the valley between her arse cheeks.

"I wondered when you would wake up. Although parts of you have been very awake for a while." Brianag's sensual huskiness did nothing to help Luag control his hardness or the pounding that began in his chest and revealed itself in his throbbing manhood. "Did you take advantage of me during the night?"

"No!" exclaimed Luag, although the avowal was not said with any great confidence.

Luag's tone told Brianag she had offended him, and she chuckled. "Not even a stolen kiss… on either set of lips? You are full of surprises, Luag. A principled man is a rarity." Brianag made a sound resembling a mournful sigh. "I was fifteen when Sidheag kidnapped me. I was a virgin then and still am. It's a tragic waste of *this* body. Don't you think?"

He grunted uncomfortably, and Brianag sighed impatiently. "Look. Do I have to spell it out? No one has rutted me… *ever.* Place a finger in my pit and you will see I am still very aroused from the battle. And from what is rubbing against my arse, so are you."

"Oh!"

"The Hag, Luag! You're a man of few words!" Silence descended as Brianag reviewed her situation. In a trembling voice, which seemed too fragile to belong to one who had recently slaughtered hundreds, she said, "I apologise. I didn't think. It's entirely different to fulfil your duty to my brother than to care for a monster. I understand." The sob that caught in Brianag's throat was a dagger to Luag's heart.

"That's not it at all, Brianag. I have feelings for you that I don't understand." Luag snorted. "Also, I've never rutted royalty! What's the penalty if I don't perform? What will Cassán say? That's a lot of pressure to lay on a lowborn hunter."

"Now you're being stupid. I never think of your rank and am offended you think so little of me."

"Sorry," whispered Luag.

Brianag inhaled and exhaled slowly. "I am new to living among humans again and have not deciphered the etiquette of relationships. I may be too direct. I'm sorry I've made the situation awkward for you. However, on a purely physical level, my body wants to rut and your manhood rubbing my arse says you do, too."

She deliberately wiggled her bottom against Luag and was rewarded with a moan, bruised breasts, and an even bigger cock. "Let's set emotions to one side. We'll be doing each other a good turn." Brianag giggled. "I'm a wolf, so being rutted from behind is entirely appropriate, and you are positioned perfectly."

The rutting was frantic, and the orgasm, while satisfying, came too quickly for both. They remedied that for the second and third times. Brianag lay on the grass, chuffing as Luag played with her swollen and slippery *brillín*. She resisted grooming him with her tongue—at least for the moment.

"I killed the last man who cared for me, although it was by mutual consent. He was a priest." The statement from Brianag hung in the air as if wondering whether it should return to its source and never be uttered.

"You're telling me this because?" asked Luag.

"I've never had a relationship with a man—or woman. Unlike you, I'm not an honourable person, Luag. I'm evil, and you will be in danger if you get too close to me. The Hag, Luag! I eat people. I might eat you—although not intentionally. Do I need to say more?"

"You're unconventional, a fierce warrior, and cannibalistic. The latter is not unknown among the Celts. I think you're trying to convince yourself you're malevolent. Those who know and love you know that's wrong. Did you ask Sidheag to change you?" Brianag shook her head vigorously.

"Do you kill 'good' people?"

A troubled look settled on Brianag's face. "I don't intend to, but I make mistakes. I *will* slaughter anyone, good or evil, who threatens Dolidh. She is my friend, and I will protect her. I protect my family."

"And me?"

"Malmhin and you are my friends and are under my protection." Brianag smiled at the disappointed look that flitted momentarily over Luag's face. "I have never had a relationship, Luag, that did not end in death. I'd like to try… with you." Brianag choked. "If you can abide an Abomination."

Luag exploded. "Rut the Hag! I wish I had never spoken that word and I swear it will never cross my lips again!" Brianag's eyes widened at his strident tone. "Men and women make mistakes, sometimes terrible mistakes. It doesn't necessarily make them evil, and it doesn't make you evil. It makes you human.

"However, your wolf persona gives me a problem." Brianag's eyes became huge emeralds, and her bottom lip trembled. "I will have to exercise much more to satisfy your unnatural carnal appetites and stamina." The slap rang out across the meadow. Luag rubbed his cheek and said, ruefully, "A romantic kiss to resolve our issues would be good."

"Which lips?"

***

Neamhain pointed the small search party in Brianag's general direction. "Her mind is still closed to me," she said to raised eyebrows which asked, *Why does she not want to be found?*

As the group approached the clearing, the noise was loud and unmistakable, drawing Sorchae and Cassán to it. As Cassán unsheathed his sword and readied himself to step into the clearing, Sorchae put a hand on his arm. "Those sounds are of a different type of combat. I do not think Brianag or Luag will be impressed if we intrude. We should wait a respectable distance from here."

Cassán's face reddened. Then he chuckled. "Do you think she will eat him when she breaks her fast?"

CHAPTER 14

Dùn Brion & Cè's Camp

Bad news rides on the fleetest horses. Reports from messengers filtered through to Cè, informing him of Conn's death and the slaughter of his warriors. The rebel Forest People who besieged Dùn Brion made up half of his army. Many were dead or injured; those remaining had scattered and were hunted by Cassán's garrison and half of Sorchae's riders led by Amodocus.

The foolish tilt at Dùn Brion had achieved nothing, save to humiliate Cè before Fionn and Seonag, and the debacle would likely result in a very public and painful execution. Cè cursed Fionn, yet knew it was his weakness that produced the fiasco. Conn's words of "I told you" reverberated in his mind.

Cè walked the makeshift berm, exchanging confident craic with his warriors. He frantically clutched at a torrent of options in his mind, but they flowed through his fingers like fine, dry sand. Over a hundred riders galloped to link up with the combined army of Seonag's and the Ravens' spears. He expected to break his fast on the next dawn surrounded by his enemies.

What do I have to make Seonag pause before staking me for treason? Cè feverishly searched his memories for morsels of information. *I know Fionn's location.* He dismissed the thought with a shake of his head. Braids of hair slapped his cheeks. *Eejit!* So did Seonag, and she likely had a better count of Fionn's warriors than him. He sighed in despair. News of

Fionn's latest whore and her companion were unlikely to stop the stake from penetrating his arse. Were they?

***

Brianag blushed guiltily as an irate Sorchae and Neamhain railed at their friend for shutting her mind to them. More ominously, she felt her ma's anger float like a thundercloud above her head. *Have I jeopardised my reconciliation?* Brianag knew a reckoning was in her future.

"The Hag, Brianag. We were worried sick about you, but you were rutting *him*." The target of Neamhain's ire switched to Luag, who attempted to merge with the room's rough stone wall. "As for you, what part of 'find Brianag and bring her home safely' did you not understand?"

"When I found her, she was in no condition to be moved," countered Luag.

"So, you rutted an injured, frail young woman. There's a name for that," said Neamhain.

"She is twenty-five summers old, hardly frail, and never defenceless. Brianag needed time to rest and recover," countered Luag. Had he left it there, all would have been well. However, under the scrutiny of Cassán, who seemed to be enjoying the situation far too much, and the women, who were looking for a diversion from their concern for Brianag, Luag wilted.

"The rutting was not my idea," said Luag, looking at Neamhain. The moment the words left his lips, Luag groaned at a blunder only a pubescent boy would make. With those words, he united every female in the room, including Brianag, Eimhir, and Malmhìn. Furrowed brows, thin lips, and unfriendly eyes told him he was about to be savaged. While he had survived the battle of the forest, Luag doubted he would be so lucky in this room. He looked beseechingly at Cassán, but the king was enjoying the entertainment as temporary relief from a bloody war.

"You despoiled my sister, which is a unique situation for me. Should I challenge you to combat as her brother? Or, perhaps, as a king, I should have you whipped for sullying the reputation of a valuable ally," said Cassán. Arms spread, he turned to the women. "Luag did what we could not. He tracked, found, and kept Brianag safe. Should we not just be happy Brianag was found in good health… if perhaps not as pure as she once was?"

Cassán looked at Luag. "My advice to you is simple. In future, state the facts and then keep your mouth firmly shut." A muttered curse was Luag's response. When the women's eyes turned to him, Cassán proved his diplomatic skills had improved by deftly diverting the turbulent waters. "Like everyone, I am delighted to see Brianag." He caught her gaze. "Yet, sister, we thought you died on the battlefield. Only Sorchae refused to accept you had crossed the veil. Resurrection from the dead is a rare feat."

Brianag growled at being put on the spot and then shrugged. "I didn't know it would work. I had a feeling." The explanation was weak, but, unlike Luag, Brianag chose prudence over the truth. Her "feeling" was Sidheag's voice in her head counselling her. That she never doubted Sidheag's instruction shocked Brianag. When a renewed Brianag rose from the wolf's corpse, Sidheag had purred like a feral cat. *She was proud of me.*

A cough drew Brianag from her musing, and she looked at Neamhain. Instead of an apology, she re-committed Luag's sins of loquaciousness and self-justification. "Is it not rumoured that the Womb-Born consider death a deep sleep? Your ma, my grandma, survived her throat being cut while her sisters died." Neamhain nodded, but there was anger in her eyes. For as long as Brianag had known her, Neamhain had studiously avoided any discussion of her mother's experience.

Gaining confidence in her story, Brianag embellished the tale. "I can only imagine since Leannán's mother, Áine, is one of the Womb-Born, she passed certain traits on to her daughter and thence to Sidheag… and me." She shrugged. "Other than that, I took a chance, and it worked. I apologise to everyone for causing pain. I did not mean to."

As adroitly as Cassán, Brianag guided the conversation along another path. She looked at Neamhain and asked, "What is our next move? We know Leannán and the Cú Sídhe are here, and they know about us." The smoking embers of anger in Neamhain's eyes were ominous.

***

The grey-haired veteran alongside Cè had impressive scars on his face and more scar tissue on his arms than his original flesh. Thus, few argued when he was chosen to replace Conn. If anything, the warrior was blunter than Conn. That said, possibly he did not see his life extending beyond the next sunset.

"The men and women in this fortification are among the best of the Forest People. Ask them, and they will fight until none are left." The shield-man held Cè's gaze without flinching or blinking. He pointed to the army gathering one hundred paces from the encampment's berm. "We cannot win against your sister's force. Our defence will not stop horses, and once it is breached, their spear-warriors will flow through the gap. *You* must decide how much value you put on their lives."

"If we cannot defend, should we attack?"

The veteran shook his head. "No… unless you want a quicker death. Again, the horses are their advantage. The moment we charge, so will they. At best, we will be cleaved in two; more likely, our warriors will scatter. At least in this weather, we won't face the Blood Queen's chariots."

"So, it's a glorious death or a humiliating surrender."

"No!" The veteran's words were as painful as a switch across the knuckles. "No, it is death or an honourable negotiation for your warriors' lives."

A few snowflakes landed on Cè's whiskers, and he looked up. "At least it's not raining. Choose our envoy carefully. He has an onerous task."

***

"I was expecting my sister," said Cè. He addressed Earc, who sat astride a tree stump opposite him. Seonag's shield-man did not hide his disapproval of Cè. Before him, he saw an irredeemable traitor who betrayed his sister and their father's dying command. Cè sighed. He had hoped Seonag led those who had trapped him.

"She is in A' Chrìon Làraich." With a flourish, Earc indicated his companions. "You likely know Amodocus, who rules the Na Daoine Tùrsach with the Blood Queen." Cè dipped his head. "The lady is Sorchae Ni Íar, recently acclaimed Queen of the Ravens."

"If only the Forest People could change their ruler as smoothly," said Cè.

"We could have, but you and your brothers decided otherwise," spat Earc.

"That's somewhat hypocritical," retorted Cè. Amodocus' eyebrow lifted in a signal for Cè to continue. "My spies inform me that a handful of warbands in the Highlands have sworn their loyalty to Earc... not Seonag." Cè chuckled. "That sounds like treason to me."

"You asked for this meeting, Cè. What do you propose?" snapped Earc.

Cè looked at his shield-man, smiled wanly, and stood. "Think of me as you wish, but I will not see valiant men and women slaughtered because of my vanity. Therefore, I surrender on one condition. You will absorb my warriors into Seonag's ranks and their families into your camp."

"If we do not accept?"

A glance upwards preceded Cè's words. "It is almost meadhan-latha. If you want a battle, I recommend both armies eat a warm, hearty meal, because it will be the last for many." Cè held Earc's gaze. "Is my sister's army so big she can afford to lose experienced warriors or turn away three thousand skilled recruits? Maybe more, if she prevails on Cassán to cease pursuing and killing those who attacked the southern forest. Do you want to present Seonag with a list of her dead, or her new recruits?

My brother, Fionn, would thank you for the former."

"Your chieftains?"

"They know their fate. All I ask is that you grant them the death of their choice."

Earc looked at Cè's shield-man. "And you?"

"I am a dead man, unless you say otherwise."

"What are *your* personal terms, Cè?" Disgust dripped from Earc's lips.

"You know the Law of the Forest People, Earc. My fate is in my sister's hands—and no one else's."

Earc opened his mouth. Whether to object or protest remained unknown, because Sorchae interrupted him. "I'm good with that…" At Earc's burgeoning objection, she said, "You have no standing here. Amodocus and I are the only royals among us, are we not?"

Amodocus chuckled at Earc's discomfort, and Cè allowed a glimmer of a smile to perch on his lips. "Cè and his chieftains will accompany us to Dùn Brion. The latter will be executed as agreed; Cè and his shield-man will await Seonag's arrival. I will send a rider to her immediately."

CHAPTER 15

The Land of Immensity—Coria

Áine, the Second of the Womb-Born and Queen of the Bright Ones, rarely travelled far from her city of Muria. One of the four Mounds or cities of the Aes Sídhe, Muria stood a glittering example of creative perfection, attracting artists from across the domain of the Tuatha Dé. By acclaim and reputation, Áine was the most talented of them all. However, it was also understood that anyone who might challenge Áine's pre-eminence was unlikely to be granted entry to Muria.

As Áine glided across the marble floor of Coria's Great Hall to join her brothers and sisters, she had a sense of foreboding. The Aes Sídhe had placed Áine on a crystal pedestal as a paragon of creativity and virtue. Not even her links to Leannán and Sidheag had tarnished her image. How could they? In their eyes, Áine had no blemishes. Had she not selflessly punished her daughter, Leannán, by supporting her exile to Oileán Dubh?

However, Áine's veneer of respectability and artistic genius was a deception, sustained by her powers and privileges as one of the Womb-Born. None of her siblings were models of virtue; their dark origins precluded that hypocrisy. Thus, none examined the minor transgressions of their brothers and sisters too closely. For a demigod, "minor" was a relative term.

Áine's true nature was described by her unspoken titles as the Queen of Deceit and the Mother of the Blood Drinkers. She had the blackest heart of any Womb-Born or Sídhe. Beneath her porcelain-perfect body bubbled corruption, a constant fear of exposure, and anger at not being free to indulge her nature. Furthermore, Sidheag was her creation, not Leannán's. Indeed, Áine considered Sidheag the epitome of her many works. Thus, she ground her teeth at being unable to publicly claim her.

Shrewdly, in case her plans went awry—which they had spectacularly—Áine deceived Leannán by planting Sidheag's creation memory in her mind. To this day, the piteous shrieking of Sidheag calling for her true mother to save her from the molten iron grave haunted Áine. *How did Sidheag know I was her creator? Did she tell anyone?* Áine was at once sad and relieved at Sidheag's demise.

Still, with her final breath, Sidheag cursed Áine and, before she fell silent, promised retribution. It was captured in a single word: *Brianag.* Hence, Áine could not believe her good fortune when Mongfhionn dragged Brianag in chains through Coria's gateway. Since that day, Áine had frequently tried to besiege, infiltrate, and control Brianag's mind. She needed to gauge how much the adolescent knew. What knowledge did Sidheag's blood transfer? Was she in danger of exposure? Her efforts appeared successful until she realised the young bitseach was toying with her.

When she tried to withdraw, Brianag would not allow her. Initially crudely constructed, Áine's cage became much more subtle, stronger, and impossible to escape. She was one of the Womb-Born, and hence no mind should be closed to her. That Sidheag had passed this weapon to Brianag made Áine tremble.

Trapped in Brianag's mind, the Queen of Deceit wrung her hands as her mind was examined in minute detail. Eventually, having learned all she needed, and like all adolescents, Brianag tired of her game. She released Áine and slammed the door of her mind and fortress shut. *What had Sidheag created?*

On the surface, Brianag's purpose was obvious: to seek and administer vengeance. Sidheag had been clear on that. Yet Sidheag's motives had never been that simple. *Can I rely on Leannán to destroy Brianag?* Áine's brow furrowed. The answer was an angry, "No."

CHAPTER 16

383 B.C.—Winter—Dùn Brion

Autumn ceded to winter and the highland snowfalls and storms became heavier and more frequent. One more cycle of the moon, and the passes to Gràinne's and Seonag's *dùin* would slam shut. To avoid being stranded in Dùn Brion, Gràinne and Seonag hoped for a speedy resolution of Cè's trial. Regardless of the weather, Cathbad, who accompanied them, was determined to ensure the Law was respected.

Meanwhile, on reaching Dùn Brion's gates, Amodocus and Sorchae exchanged questioning glances when the guards refused Earc entry to the fort. What had he done to anger Cassán? Amodocus, who was better acquainted with Earc, shrugged. "He's an arsehole who uses his relationship with Seonag to bully others. His absence is no loss."

The wait caused by the inclement weather allowed Cassán, Amodocus, and Sorchae to manage the executions of Cè's chieftains in a civilised and efficient manner. All were despatched to Mag Mell in Dùn Brion's courtyard. Several chose to be beheaded and paid the axe- or swordsman handsomely for a keen blade. However, most chose to die at the hands of a friend with a sharp knife and steady hand.

Cassán granted Cè's request to defer his shield-man's fate until he was judged. In the interim, the duo was provided with quarters and treated according to their status. Members of Eimhir's security division shadowed them. If Cè noticed his guardians, he never commented. Still, he was not foolish enough to assume he was not being watched or that

Cassan was not fully informed of every move they made.

✳✳✳

Dùn Brion's Great Hall hosted the hearing. Unlike similar gatherings, it was closed to the garrison and civilians. Despite its cavernous size and cold stone walls, heavy tapestries combined with firepits and fur-lined cloaks to ensure those gathered were comfortably warm. The chamber was too spacious for the meeting, but practicality dictated its choice. Only the Hall's high table was long enough to seat Cè's judges along one side. As northerly winds battered the fort, Cè faced his accusers.

Before the proceedings began, the doors opened. A disarmed Earc, accompanied by two of Cassán's warriors, strode down the centre of the room. Halting before the high table, he bowed deeply to Seonag and less graciously to Cassán. The Na Mèadaidh king glowered at Seonag, then Earc, and finally at his guards. "Were my instructions unclear? *He* is not welcome in Dùn Brion." It was a discouraging start to the proceedings.

Seonag glared at Earc, who was a moment too late in concealing his grin. "I was unaware of your issue with Earc. I apologise. Perhaps you and I should discuss Earc's behaviour after these proceedings, Cassán," said Seonag. "However, he may have information relevant to the trial, and with your indulgence, I ask that he remain."

"Amodocus and Sorchae witnessed my ruling on Earc's unacceptable behaviour. He may remain to give his testimony. After that, my guards will escort him to the dungeons and *I* will decide if he keeps his head," said Cassán. Seonag nodded. The smirk on Earc's face disappeared. "If everyone agrees, Seonag will assume the lead in this hearing."

Before Seonag rose to speak, a second chair scraped the stone floor. Cè stood and bowed. "I appreciate the honour of this assembly, but surely you have better things to do with your time than listen to boring speeches about my many failings and paucity of virtues. Hence, I will make this easier for all of us. I am guilty. I committed treason in opposing my sister and not accepting my father's wishes."

Cè coughed to clear his throat. "I have two requests. First, please extend mercy to my shield-man. It was he who convinced me to sur-render rather than cause the pointless deaths of many warriors on both sides. He deserves your thanks, not a stake in the arse.

"More pragmatically, you will need an experienced commander trusted by my army who will forestall their flight to Fionn. You will not find better. I have released him from his oath to me. Hence, he is free to swear fealty to my sister."

"The second?" asked Seonag. Her voice held tones of despair and frustration that negotiations with her brother had not taken place earlier in the campaign. Fionn had almost certainly killed two of her brothers. *Will a third die by my hand?*

"That I die by my choice of blade and who wields it. I have added over three thousand veteran warriors to your army. It is a fair exchange." Cè smiled, bowed, and sat.

"I smell horse-shite!" exclaimed a red-faced Earc, rising from his seat. "The Law says staking is the punishment for treason."

Earc's outburst surprised most and angered Seonag. However, it was Cathbad who responded. "That is what *man* says, *not* the Law. However, I am open to hearing your arguments. Please cite the relevant sections of the Fénechas in your favour." Earc scowled at the druid. He was not used to being embarrassed or corrected in public, and his temper threat-ened to overwhelm him.

His standing plummeted further when Seonag rose. "You embar-rass me. I believe *I* am the ruler of the Forest People—not you. Lay aside your enmity. If anyone has been affronted, it is me—not you. *Sit down!* Or the king will have you escorted from this chamber."

"I apologise, my queen."

"My brother's proposal has the merit of encompassing an element of healing, which has been long absent in our tribe. Have you anything else to add, Cè?" asked Seonag.

Cè shook his head. "I chose badly sister. The Forest People will have a strong and just leader in you. I wish you victory over Fionn."

"You have no intelligence to share? No mitigating circumstances?"

"I am sure your spies know as much about Fionn's strengths and weaknesses as I do." Cè laughed. "And I'm certain you have no interest in hearing about Fionn's latest whore, who looks remarkably like you"—in an instant Cè's mien became flushed with anger—"or the evil bastard with an equally vile hound that has raped and eaten a dozen young girls in my camp. We still have not found that pair. In that respect, I have a closing request. Find and execute them… slowly and painfully."

"The *tuilithe*—bastards—are closer than we thought, Neamhain," whispered Brianag. The pair were not part of Cè's judgment but stood to the side as observers. Unusually, or perhaps deliberately, Brianag's voice carried to all at the table. Neamhain nodded, Gràinne sighed, and Cè wondered what he could have said to produce such an ominous reaction.

"It appears you have your reprieve, brother," said Seonag. "And quite innocently, too."

***

"It is time you told us who or what we are dealing with and why it is our problem," said Cassán. His expression told Neamhain and Brianag he would countenance no excuses or diversions.

Neamhain looked at Cè. "The evil bastard and hound you speak of are one and the same. His name is the Cú Sídhe."

"The Hag! I mocked Conn for being superstitious when he mentioned the Cú Sídhe," said Cè.

"If I may continue." No sídhe likes to be interrupted, and Neamhain was a signatory to that tradition. "He is a shapeshifter from the dark, violent origins of the Tuatha Dé. Mercifully, we believe he is the last of his kind. Until recently, he and his mistress, the Leannán-Sídhe, were exiled to an island known as Oileán Dubh. The two have no love for each other, but I believe he is bound to her by sorcery."

"Who banished him?" asked Cassán.

"The Womb-Born of the Aes Sídhe." Irritation crept into

Neamhain's tone. Destiny rushed inexorably towards her, making her disposition unusually fragile. "I fail to see how a history lesson on the hierarchy of the Aes Sídhe and their disciplinary methods is useful." She glared at Cassán. "He is here, and so is she."

"You owe us more than that, Neamhain. Unless we understand all aspects of the problem, a solution will be elusive." The fine hairs on Cassán's nape stiffened in anticipation of Neamhain's answer. Eimhir's hand on his thigh briefly diverted Cassán's attention.

"Be careful, Cassán," murmured Eimhir. "The sídhe are sensitive to questions we consider the gathering of basic information." Eimhir's counsel was wise. No sídhe willingly washes the race's dirty clothes in public.

Neamhain's sigh of exasperation ended with a hiss of annoyance. "The Cú Sídhe's mistress is called the Leannán-Sídhe. There are many rumours about why Leannán was banished to Oileán Dubh, but no one knows for certain. Like her mother, Áine of the Womb-Born, she is a powerful enchantress…" Neamhain hesitated. "…and a blood drinker."

"There are more like Sidheag?" growled Cassán.

Like a dog with a bone, he ignored Eimhir's wise and stern, "Tread carefully."

"Sidheag butchered and ate thousands, including my father, Neamhain," rasped Cassán. "Now you reluctantly inform us that more of *your* criminals are loosed on us."

"It is imprudent to antagonise a member of the Aes Sídhe, Cassán Mac Brion, especially one offering help. My patience has limits." Neamhain's eyes were obsidian, and her breathing became faster. She was angry when she needed to be calm and rational.

Cassán stood, placed his hands on the table, and refused to retreat. "Perhaps the Aes Sídhe would have preferred us not to oppose Sidheag. She was your sister sídhe, wasn't she? Are we to prostrate ourselves before Leannán? By your logic, she is superior to us."

"*Hold your tongue, Cassán Mac Brion!* Let someone more rational and experienced lead this discussion." Neamhain's staff pointed at Cassán, and her voice shook the walls of the Great Hall, making most of those present wince. It was the worst thing Neamhain could have uttered and instantly pitted the humans against the gifted.

Sensing imminent disaster, Brianag looked at Gràinne. *Ma, do something. Please.*

Gràinne stood and banged a jug on the oak table. "It is near meadhan-latha. I propose we break for food, refreshment, and reflection. If we cannot resolve this among ourselves, our people are lost." Gràinne's abrupt exit from the Great Hall, followed by Amodocus, Brianag, and Giosail, left wide eyes and open mouths. Seonag, however, had a smile on her lips. *Well done, my friend.*

✶✶✶

"Rut the Hag! Could Neamhain have been more undisciplined? She has set humans against the Aes Sídhe, which did not work well for the Tuatha Dé previously. Does she want lakes of blood?" Gràinne paced the chamber in full fighting mode: red talons clicking, eyes blazing blood red, and curling rivers of crimson in constant motion.

Brianag, Giosail, Sorchae, and Seonag, the latter two having joined the group, stood with mouths open, alarmed by the red miasma radiating from Gràinne. "Modestly, I am more powerful than many of the Aes Sídhe," whispered Brianag to Giosail, "but my ma frightens me. I could use some wise counsel before our troubles multiply."

"Let me talk to her. I have seen such anguish before," said Giosail, detaching herself from the quartet. She walked across the room and gently grasped Gràinne's hands. "My queen, without doubt there will be a time for wrath in our futures, and blood will be spilt. However, at this moment, we need your wisdom to unite us against whatever evil walks our lands."

"She has an old head on young shoulders," said Seonag.

Brianag dipped her head. "She was exiled from her home for as long as I was with the Aes Sídhe. Her wisdom comes from surviving, and that I understand."

∗∗∗

Neamhain fled from the Hall. She had lost control of her temper and feared what might come next. *Why am I so sensitive?* She wrung pale hands as she paced the ramparts of Dùn Brion. The storm raging around her perfectly mirrored the turmoil in her mind. *I am Aes Sídhe. This should not be.*

She understood what had prompted her imperious exit from the Great Hall. Cassán was a pain in the arse. He needed to learn there were consequences for those who questioned a sídhe so brutally and publicly. *Perhaps he is not a good choice for Dùn Brion's king. Maybe Sorchae would be a better ruler.*

You should deal with your issues before attempting to correct those of others. The voice was very familiar, but the harsh tone was not, at least to Neamhain. *And if you think being a sídhe gives you immunity from roiling emotions, then you have learned nothing from me. You must control your outbursts, no matter the provocation or how deserved they may appear.*

"But Ma…" Neamhain cringed at the whine in her voice.

It made Mongfhionn smile before she resumed her rebuke. *Your secret cannot remain hidden any longer, daughter. You endanger your friends. Do you wish to see Brianag and Sorchae die? I do not, nor do I want to watch my daughter grieve for them. Accept what you are. Become what the Goddess meant you to be.*

"But you don't know what that means."

Of course I do, child. I have known since you were born and have carried the burden too long. Neamhain winced under the lash of her ma's tongue. *You are a danger to your friends until you resolve your issue. Go. They have plans to make and do not need a foolish girl distracting them.*

"Shite!"

∗∗∗

About to continue the conversation, Neamhain realised her ma was gone, leaving her alone with the storm. Yet that was not entirely true, and she watched her friends walk towards her. That the snowfall did not af-

124

fect Sorchae made her smile. Brianag had cloaked them both. Neamhain stepped into the protection. "I am sorry for my poor behaviour. Please give my apologies to Cassán and the others."

"Do it yourself!" said Brianag, sharper than intended.

Neamhain shook her head. "I must leave you for a time. There are things I must do… alone."

"No. I will come with you," said Brianag. "You have always stood by my side when I needed support." Neamhain shook her head, and Brianag's lip trembled. "Is this because of what I said about your ma and her sisters? I was wrong. I'm sorry." Emerald tears rolled down Brianag's cheeks. "Please forgive me."

A long, elegant finger plucked a tear from Brianag's cheek. "Silly girl. One tear would be more than enough payment if I needed to forgive you." Neamhain's kiss and hug removed all doubts of a sundered relationship. Turning to Sorchae, Neamhain held her hands. "Look after my sister. When I return, we will talk of secrets—hers, yours, and mine."

Sorchae blushed, and Brianag looked puzzled. Neither had the opportunity to respond. Neamhain had disappeared in a flurry of snow.

"I fear for her, Sorchae. Why would she not let me help? She was there for me in the depths of my despair."

A shake of the head was Sorchae's answer. She grasped Brianag's hands. "Anyone who sees you as a monster does not know you. I sensed Neamhain had a secret, and it is one that she must come to terms with. Our battle is yet to come, and we will need her by our side. She will return."

Brianag traced the curling design on Sorchae's cheek. "When will I know your mystery? I do not recall such designs at our first meeting." Sorchae blushed, but the blast of a horn, calling them back to the Great Hall, rescued her.

"We're needed," said Sorchae.

"This conversation is not over, Sorchae. You will find I am very persistent."

***

"Where is Neamhain?" Cassán's tone had moderated, and his demeanour, while sober, was not antagonistic. This was partially due to Eimhir pointing out that kings who lost the favour of the Aes Sídhe, whether they were in the right or wrong, often had brief lives and painful deaths. Two towering stone strongholds were an inadequate defence against any sídhe.

"She is gone, and before you ask, I do not know where." Brianag's clipped words and harsh stare made it plain to Cassán who she held responsible for Neamhain's precipitous exit. "What I do know is that Neamhain understands more than anyone in this hall about what we face. That insight and her strength are gone, and we are disadvantaged."

"Please tell us what you know, Brianag. You have spent time with the Aes Sídhe and are Neamhain's closest friend. Surely, she told you something about Leannán and the Cú Sídhe," said Sorchae. The dip of Gràinne's head signalled her agreement with Sorchae.

Brianag stood. "The Womb-Born banished Leannán to Oileán Dubh because she claimed to be the mother or creator of Sidheag." A round of muted curses rippled around the table. "I hope her claim is true, although I have my doubts and so does Neamhain.

"Leannán is a formidable enchantress, a sorceress who can change her face to mirror her lover's image of a perfect partner. She is a chameleon and can make you see what she wants. For pleasure, Leannán enthrals mortals by sampling their blood. When she becomes bored with them, she will drain them. No one has ever survived her seduction."

"No!" exclaimed an ashen-faced Cè. "My brother and his senior chieftains appeared distracted on my last visit to their camp." He looked at Seonag, horrified, and said, "The strìopach at his side could have been your twin. What does that mean?"

"I am afraid, and disgusted, the meaning is exactly what you think it is," said Gràinne. "Does Leannán have a Brood like Sidheag?"

Brianag shook her head. "No, unlike Sidheag, she is a powerful enchantress. She does not need a Brood. With enough blood, she can beguile an army and enhance its strength. She is likely building her stocks of blood in a refuge—probably a cave in the foothills near Fionn's camp."

"What about the Cú Sídhe? I assume he's not just a dog to pet," said Cassán.

"In human form, he is a likeable, handsome rogue; in his hound form, he is a rapacious killer, a soul devourer, and a flesh-eater."

"Can iron kill the pair?" asked Cassán.

"Yes…" Brianag shook her head at the sighs of relief before crushing their hopes: "…if you can get near them."

"What do you mean?" asked Cassán warily.

"The Hound is a silent hunter until he has selected his victim. Then he will howl three times. Anyone within hearing range will die, but not instantly. The first bark frightens his prey, the second intensifies fear to terror, and the third frightens them to death, literally. I believe he can modulate his voice and, hence, target specific victims if he wishes. He can devastate a farmstead of thirty or an army of ten thousand in the blink of an eye. It is quite an effective and unique defence, is it not?"

When Brianag spoke again, her eyes were obsidian. She held Cassán's gaze and said, "Stone walls cannot not stop the Hound. The dense forests may limit the range of the sound, but not enough to slow his approach or divert a trinity of deadly barks."

Brianag stared at Cassán and pointed an accusing finger at him. Breaking the silence that descended on the gathering, she said, "I believe Neamhain has or knows where to find the answer to the Cú Sídhe, but *you* drove her away. I hope you will be happy with the bloodshed and wailing of widows, mothers, and children."

"Rut the Hag!" exploded Cassán. He looked accusingly at Brianag. "Why are they here? Is it because of you?"

"The answer is simple, brother. In one thing, the Aes Sídhe and humanity are alike—both seek revenge. Like any human mother, Leannán seeks to avenge the murder of her daughter. She wants to kill me, and anyone she deems responsible for Sidheag's murder. You were at Sidheag's graveside when the molten iron covered her. Leannán has you, among others, in her sights. In her eyes, you are as guilty as me."

"It was justice, not murder," spat Cassán.

Brianag turned to Eimhir. "If she were your daughter, would you not call it murder and seek retribution?" Brianag shifted her attention to Gràinne and Seonag. "We can do nothing here and should retreat to our strongholds in the forests and mountains of the east. In the deep winter, Leannán and the Cú Sídhe may find us inaccessible and more trouble to attack."

She laughed coldly. "The easier prey will be in the Lowlands, in Dùn Brion, Dùn Athad, and the settlements north and south of the Sleagh. If they drink the blood and suck the marrow from the Na Mèadaidh's veins and bones during the winter, it will give us more time to assemble the army of the Eastern Tribes." As a strategy, Brianag's plan was brutally pragmatic.

"We cannot abandon your brother, Brianag," said Gràinne.

"Why not? We can do nothing here but talk." Brianag pointed to Cassán. "He drove one who is closer than a sister to me away. Let him live with the consequences." Brianag turned to Sorchae, who shook her head and mouthed "No" as if she knew what Brianag was about to say.

"Sorchae is Cassán's sister and can rule the remnants of the Na Mèadaidh as well as the Ravens. The bloodline will continue." Brianag turned and stormed from the meeting.

"She's a cold-blooded *bidse*," said Cè to Seonag.

"Yes, but she's not wrong, is she?"

✳✳✳

Eimhir and Cassán sat alone in Dùn Brion's vast Great Hall. Bowed over, Cassán held his head in his hands and muttered, "What have I done? I have alienated my sister and put a knife at the throat of the Na Mèadaidh. Maybe Sorchae would be a better queen than I am a king.

128

Brianag would support her."

"Enough of this maudlin nonsense," snapped Eimhir. "We are victims of the Gaels' temper. Our people wear their hearts on their sleeves and forgive as quickly as they accuse.

"Brianag is wounded because Neamhain departed and did not take her. She's throwing anything she can think of at you to deflect from her pain. I do not believe Sorchae has ambitions to be Queen of the Na Mèadaidh." Eimhir paused, then said, "However, you must, for the sake of your people, build a bridge between you and Brianag. Blood is blood."

"Where would I start?"

"There are two in Dùn Brion who fought alongside Brianag. One she likely loves. They will make excellent ambassadors if they accept. I believe she will not want to see them and the people she saved die."

"More like she'll spirit them away to Loch nan Clàr and Gràinne's crannag," grunted Cassán. "But at least that would save two people." He lifted his head and bellowed, "Send for Luag and Malmhìn."

CHAPTER 17

382 B.C.—Winter—A' Chrìon Làraich

The stronghold of A' Chrìon Làraich held bittersweet memories for Seonag. When they were children, Conall Mac Gabhann's raiders kidnapped Seonag and her brother, Fionn, and used them as leverage to prevent a local skirmish from escalating into a war between Conall and her father.

That was when she first met Cassán's father, Brion. With the support of Drostan, the one-armed warrior became the Rìgh of Dùn Brion and the Na Mèadaidh, and her guardian. She fell in love with Brion, but the relationship was ill-fated. All hope of them rekindling their relationship ended on the ramparts of Dùn Brion when Sidheag killed Brion.

Conall's Master of Defence made the heart of A' Chrìon Làraich, originally a sleepy farming community, into a formidable fortress and bequeathed it to Drostan when Conall's army moved south. Still, the Forest People's strength was in the trees, not strongholds of rock and wood. Hence, Drostan's instinct was to raze it to the ground. His chieftains, including Seonag's mother, Teàrlag, persuaded him not to. For that, Seonag was glad.

Three rivers met to form the broad valley where the Highlands' primary agrarian and trading settlement lay. The slope up to the community was gentle and densely forested with pines. It merged with a level, wooded valley and its wildwood blend of hardwoods and thick undergrowth. Closer to the settlement, the trees had been felled, ostensibly to plant crops. The river on the settlement's far side protected its eastern boundary.

A' Chrìon Làraich dominated the surrounding lands. At its core rose a solid-walled broch. The structure's walls were the width of two men laid head to toe. In peaceful times, the broch served as a substantial home capable of housing several generations. It was deceptively spacious. Steps cut into the inner wall led to a second floor, constructed from cut planks and mainly purposed for sleeping quarters. In the past, the lower stone floor was home to horses and cattle. Now it assumed the loftier role of a Great Hall.

Two circular stone walls, spaced fifty paces apart, surrounded the towering broch. In the winter, they glistened white with frost. Each had a deep perimeter ditch filled with wooden stakes. Scattered around the fortifications, small, shallow pits had also been dug and populated with sharpened sticks.

Numerous wooden halls for the army and shelters for the civilian population were grouped around the walls. Their placement was not random. Areas and channels had been left clear of obstruction. These and the corn fields were the killing grounds. Only the armoury and trades needed for war were located inside the defences.

As Seonag rode through the inner entrance, she yearned for signs of normality: thick grey-blue smoke curling upwards from peat fires and the mouth-watering aroma of the cooking pits. Instead, only the smell of stale sweat and the sounds of war greeted her as blacksmiths' hammers beat iron into swords, spears, and axes.

✶✶✶

The door opened to a small chamber in the broch's ground floor. Fed by wood and peat, the firepit burned fiercely. Friendly fragrances of pine and peat filled the air. They did not reflect the demeanours of those seated at an oak table.

Teàrlag heard the door close behind her and observed that her guards did not exit as usual. Her nose twitched like a rat sensing a trap.

Before her, Seonag sat in a carved wooden chair. She saw her daughter had foregone the use of a fur pad. Therefore, the meeting would not be long enough for anyone's arse to become numb. *Good news or bad?*

If Teàrlag was surprised to see Cè sitting on Seonag's right, she did not show it. However, her heartbeat increased, and her palms felt damp. She took some solace in Earc's disposition. He sat at the end of the table on Seonag's left, and his furrowed brow showed his displeasure at the evident downgrading of his status. Seonag pointed to a seat on the nearside of the firepit.

"Please sit, Mother. It is time to address a weakness in my planning."

"Could you have seated me closer to the fire, Seonag? My arse will have blisters."

"I can have you seated *in* the fire. Would you prefer that?" Seonag's expression gave no sign she was jesting.

Teàrlag looked warily at her daughter. "Are you going to enlighten me, or should I guess the subject of this meeting until I hit the correct answer? Will you reward me, like one of your hounds, with a treat?"

"Sarcasm is not an intelligent defence, Mother. Grovelling might be a better tactic. You misled me when planning this war's tactics. Was that deliberate or due to incompetence?" Seonag's ice-blue eyes gazed steadily. "My brother and I have come to an agreement, and his army has joined with mine. The pity is that we did not reconcile sooner, but *you* told me that was out of the question. Why did you mislead me?"

"You are not my mother to chastise me or query my actions," said Teàrlag.

"*I am your queen,*" snarled Seonag. "Answer me, or do I need to stoke the braziers in the chambers beneath us?"

Seonag's words and the brutal implication of torture shocked Teàrlag. "You have not ascended to the throne of the Forest People and may never sit on it. As Drostan's hand-fast partner, I have as much standing in the tribe as you." Teàrlag looked at Cè and sneered. "Any man will come to an agreement at the point of a sword or with a stake pushed against his arse." Cè bristled at his mother's insult but said nothing.

"That may be so, but Cè had no sword at his throat when he chose to save his and my armies from a battle that would only have benefited Fionn." Seonag looked at Earc, who nodded curtly. "Speaking of Fionn, Earc's spies tell me you have visited him frequently in recent seasons, Mother. Cè has confirmed their reports. Why was I not informed of this?"

"I don't tell you every step I take," snapped Teàrlag. Her heart thudded in her chest. Her tunic dampened with sweat along her spine. The direction and tone of the conversation was ominous.

"That is obvious to me… *now*. Still, regular visits to my enemy's camp, without my knowledge, seems a step too far. I welcome your explanation."

"Traitors will say anything to win favour or stay out of the dungeons," spat Teàrlag. The blazing fire in the chamber raised rosy cheeks on all present, but Teàrlag's became several shades paler, and the vein in her neck throbbed. Seonag played the spider who had begun to wrap its prey in silk. What had changed her? Why was she not like this ten summers ago? *Is all this my fault?*

"I agree. Yet each of Earc's spies witnessed you in intimate discussions with my brother. That seems to support Cè's claim, doesn't it? Who is the traitor?"

"You never had the resolve to end the war. I had to explore other options for victory."

"Not victory for me. Rather, surrender and certain death for me and my people!" barked Seonag. Teàrlag's hand moved downwards to the blade attached to her thigh, and Seonag's eyes narrowed. "If your hand moves a pine needle's width more, I will cut it off, toss it in the fire, and let you bleed out on the floor."

Teàrlag's eyes opened wide in shock. Fionn's warning not to underestimate Seonag echoed in her mind. *How could I have been so wrong?* Teàrlag wracked her brain feverishly for a way out. "I am a queen of the

Forest People. I have rights…" Teàrlag's voice trailed off at the wrath in Seonag's face. Not since her father's death had Seonag shown such emotion.

"A traitor who promised Fionn she would leave A' Chrìon Làraich's gates open has no rights. Familial ties might have mitigated my judgment to banishment." Teàrlag allowed herself thoughts of hope and reconciliation. They were dashed when Seonag said, "However, there is no redemption for one who spat on my father's last wishes."

Seonag glanced at the guards. "Is the stake ready?" They nodded.

Teàrlag gasped, "No!" and Seonag laughed. The sound chilled all in the room.

"You deserve it, and Gràinne, who has been a better friend and counsellor than you, would applaud me. However, I would not be so crude as to have my guards hammer a stake into your arse, Mother." Teàrlag's relief was fleeting. "Take the traitor outside, strip her, and chain her to the stake at the forest's edge." Seonag turned to Cè. "The Goddess will decide which kills her—the wolves or the cold. My gold favours the wolves."

Resigned to her fate, Teàrlag stood, straightened her shoulders, and faced Seonag one final time. She bowed and said, "I was mistaken. You will make a great Bhanrigh of the Forest People."

CHAPTER 18

Loch Eireachd

Leannán was bored. Winter snows isolated Loch Eireachd and the surrounding landscape. The biting, northerly winds and falling temperatures froze the lake and anyone foolish enough to wander too far from Fionn's encampment. Nothing moved in the camp except couples and groups engaged in frenetic rutting. The pleasure gained was brief by necessity, not the usual lack of foreplay. Prayers for constipation bombarded the Goddess. Only the cold held back the stench of frequently pissed *triubhas*.

The enchantress's mood worsened when she realised enthralled men and women made meek, unimaginative lovers. Thus, she loosened Fionn's enchantment just enough to entertain her. Listening to his futile, childish whining and ranting about Cè uniting with Seonag was the price she had to pay for his brutal use of her body. *How could he ever consider himself a king?* Yet she would miss him and the others who serviced her blood and masochistic needs when she returned to the Mounds. *When I return to Oileán Dubh, I will bring some breeding stock. Who would know? The island is alive with my sorcery and not even the Womb-Born can penetrate it.*

In between being abused and rutted by Fionn, Leannán pondered her next moves. Few could match or approach Leannán's powers of enchantment or the fine control she exerted over her victims. Thus, she mostly ignored the unwashed masses of his warriors, apart from the prime specimens whom she allowed to use her body. She saw her gesture as magnanimous, a last moment of pleasure before siphoning their blood into the amphorae.

The sorceress's strategy to totally enthral only Fionn's nobles and chieftains was prudent. It gave her command over the army but committed less of her abilities—and her reserves of blood. The only outward sign of their submission was a faraway stare, which was common to many veterans.

An unexpected benefit of the severe weather was that it kept her stock in perfect condition in the foothill's cave near Loch Eireachd. She had more than enough to power her sorcery and enthral the army, if needed. Once again, Leannán swore at the wintry conditions. She recalled her mother's warning and shivered. She had been among the humans since Lugnasad, almost two seasons ago, and had achieved little. *I have been planning.* Leannán huffed. *Try telling that to my mother.*

Her army was as much use as the hibernating animals in the forests and mountains. It would be Imbolg at the earliest before she could hurl her warriors against the walls of A 'Chrìon Làraich. "There must be something I can do," she muttered as she sipped cool blood. Moments later, she smiled. "I have many thousands of warriors. What does it matter if I lose a few thousand?"

***

It was a cycle of the moon before trudging through deep drifts of snow and fighting against northerly winds became tiresome and then bloody annoying. Alternating between his Hound and human forms made little difference to the Cú Sídhe's progress.

He growled in frustration as he tramped past another farmstead. In any other conditions, the farms were a perfect source of victims for him to violate and feed on. However, buried by the snowfall, his prey slept in the largest of their roundhouses. Extended families of thirty or more, often with animals, slept together as a single amorphous mass. Infrequently, they emerged to piss and shite, but they did this as a group against the home's wall.

The only positive aspect was his immunity to the freezing temperatures. Midway between Loch Eireachd and A' Chrìon Làraich, the Hound's belly rumbled, and he made a decision. He would turn south and make for the Sleagh Mountains and the lands around Dùn Brion. The weather in the Lowlands would be less hostile, the forests would provide shelter, and there would be hundreds of farmholdings and settlements to prey on.

The Cú Sídhe smiled, and rows of pointed incisors gleamed in the moonlight. By making his choice, he had won a victory of sorts over Leannán. Once he was in the southern lands, the bonds that held him would loosen a fraction more. "I will become stronger, and she will not follow me. Her stores of blood are her weakness. She will never leave them."

***

Fionn slumped on the wooden throne at the centre of his pavilion. Glowing braziers radiated heat, keeping the winter storms at bay. The thick, silver-grey wolf's fur draped across his broad shoulders also helped. His fingers beat a rhythm on the seat's arms like knucklebones on a bodhrán. It was his way of focusing his mind while Leannán was in her cave.

During the first few days of Leannán's appearance in his camp, before she tightened her grip on his mind, Fionn had her followed. His instinct for survival meant he trusted no one. He was not stupid. Leannán may have been a whore paid by Cè or Seonag to murder him.

Fionn knew he was a brute, and that people mocked him for his limited intelligence. He chuckled. Most of them were dead, while he thrived. The ridicule was mostly correct, but, by necessity, his weakness made Fionn very focused. Thus, while he gnawed on a freshly cooked *crúibín*—pig's foot—Fionn also chewed on his current predicament. He knew his time of relative freedom was limited. Indeed, by the time the winter storms were over, so would his faux liberty.

A smile formed on Fionn's dry lips. His whining about Cè and his partnership with Seonag was a diversion. *A clever one,* he thought. On the contrary, Fionn was only irritated his brother had not shown this level of initiative when allied with him. A chuckle escaped his lips. He would be surprised if Teàrlag were still alive. If Seonag did not know about her duplicity, Cè would have told her. Another problem solved.

Fionn grumbled at having to stir from his seat, but Leannán did not allow him servants to tend his braziers. Therefore, he had to throw the wood and peat on them himself. *"Bidse!"* he growled. When he retook his throne, his eyebrows knit in concentration. He had to fight the witch, but how? Frustration almost made him kick over a brazier. He refrained. It would be he who had to clear the mess up or sleep in a frosty shelter.

CHAPTER 19

The Na Daoine Cait

The storm's colour palette held a single white hue. It raged like a demented artist constantly, forming and reforming drifts of snow against any object in its path. Neamhain's mother, Mongfhionn, commanded storms, thunder, and lightning. However, only two sídhe were comfortable with the blizzards of deep winter. One was Draighean; the other Neamhain.

Humans often relished the feeling of warm, fine sand from the Great Sea's beaches trickling through their toes. Not so, Neamhain. She loved icy winds and lacy snowflakes. She delighted in the north wind whipping her hair into a blonde halo. When ice rain coated the tips of her braids with tiny crystals, she loved how they sang like chimes in the breeze.

"It must be here," she muttered. Aeons in the past, the Old Ones grew tired of the Aes Sídhe's self-absorption and lack of purpose. They severed their links with the demigods and disappeared. Ironically, many generations later, the fierce battle queen of the Aes Sídhe, known to all as The Mórrígan, had done the same. Were both good or bad portents?

Deep inside, Neamhain knew the Old Ones had powers long since forgotten and could intercede to restrain the Cú Sídhe. They had given oaths to the Goddess to secure their exodus, and Neamhain needed to remind them of one. Yet did she want to? She had a life unshackled by responsibility and friends who loved her. Why put that at risk?

Neamhain whispered "Brianag" into the wind and wished she had said yes to her offer of a travel companion. Still, that would have been selfish. Brianag's talents were needed elsewhere.

Neamhain wondered if the Old Ones had a home and whether it needed to be an actual place. Was it akin to the Aes Sídhe's Mounds? She huffed, embarrassed at her arrogance. Yet something within Neamhain had guided her to this location in the farthest reaches of Northern Albu. Around her was a desolate landscape of rock and snow. To the north, she could hear ocean waves crash against cliffs more ancient than the Aes Sídhe and the Old Ones.

Gràinne's mention of the Na Daoine Cait—the Cait People—had piqued Neamhain's curiosity. The queen had never seen a trace of the tribe and was convinced the Goddess protected them. "Better to leave such a tribe alone," she advised Neamhain. They were peaceable, but who knew how they would react if revealed?

However, Neamhain could not ignore her compulsion or the fact that she was a sídhe with a prophecy to fulfil. As Neamhain scoured the bleak landscape for signs of life, frustration begot impatience. The young sídhe snorted. *What is life or death?* Brianag had turned that on its head.

***

Where is my Brianag? The cursed voice of Sidheag sounded out above the blizzard, startling Neamhain. *Why do you not protect her?*

"She does not belong to you, bitseach!" screamed Neamhain into the storm. "Brianag is my sister, the daughter of A 'Bhanrigh Fuil, and a sister to her siblings. Her friends love her, and she has a home. She has no sins to atone for—they are your burden and the one who created you. You have no rights to her and no arms to embrace her."

Sidheag's shrieking repudiation made Neamhain's ears bleed. Then her mocking voice taunted Neamhain: *Ask Brianag who guides her.*

***

Neamhain shook her head to focus her mind. *I do not need distractions.* When she lifted her head, she saw snow-capped stone walls and steeply pitched, thatched rooftops. The village appeared and disappeared with each gust of the blizzard. There was snow on the thatches and no haze of warm air above the roofs. *Do they not need heat?* She chastised herself. *The Aes Sídhe do not need fires; why should the Old Ones?*

She was sure that the settlement had not been there moments before. Was it a mirage or a sign? Perhaps it was deserted. She smiled and walked towards the gateway. As she came closer, the wall seemed to shrink from her, and the entrance disappeared. "I grow tired of your games, although I should have expected it given your nature," said Neamhain. "Show yourself. You know who I am and cannot refuse me."

Neamhain bit her tongue at her hubris. This was not the way to talk to the Old Ones. "I apologise. I am anxious about my friends and the people of this land. I would be honoured to be granted an audience with the Old Ones."

"You brought evil with you." The voice was male, authoritative, and full of rich textures. It was also unsympathetic.

"Sidheag is dead. Nothing remains but a wraith without substance. She will never return," said Neamhain, feeling the heat rise in her frozen cheeks.

"Why did you assume I referred to *her* and not Brianag?"

"Brianag is my sister and friend. Her mother, family, and friends love her. She is not evil, and I will challenge anyone who says she is." Anger raged in Neamhain's obsidian eyes. "Open your eyes to the true evil walking the land. Reveal the gateway so I may enter, and we can talk."

"You have no authority to command me, child. A reference from A 'Bhanrigh Fuil is hardly comforting, and the black eyes of the Aes Sídhe do not intimidate me."

"You know who I am. You cannot refuse… please." *This is all going so wrong. Why am I speaking in this tone?*

"There is desperation in your voice. How can I know who you are if you have not accepted what the Goddess gifted you? You perpetually kick against your calling, Neamhain, daughter of Mongfhionn. I know this, as do the Goddess, your mother… and you. There is no gateway for one who fears or will not accept what she is. Come back in a millennium when you have overcome your dread."

"*Tuilí!*" growled Neamhain. Still, the Old One's words contained a kernel of truth. She turned, walked to a lone tree she had not seen previously, and sat down with her back to the bole. Icy tears ran down her cheeks. "My friends don't have a millennium to wait."

"Then you had better find yourself quickly."

"Unhelpful bastard!" shouted Neamhain into the wind. "One day our roles will be reversed," she muttered, barely staunching her tears. *Instead of chasing a phantom, I should have stayed with my friends and helped devise a way to defeat the Cú Sídhe.*

* * *

"I have heard tales of the Aes Sídhe but have never seen one. I am told they are tall, beautiful, fierce creatures who are stubborn and have short tempers." The melodic trilling was close to Neamhain's ear. "Are you one, and do you have a temper?"

Taken by surprise, Neamhain's eyes sprung open. She swore at herself for slipping into a much-too-restful state of reflection. She had work to do and a puzzle to unravel. The Aes Sídhe did not need to sleep, but she had a human father. Occasionally, she slept and dreamed. *Was this a dream?*

Neamhain examined, parsed, disassembled, and reassembled the Old One's words. If they made little sense when first heard, they made less sense now. Still, what had she expected? A feast in her honour and those who were aeons older than her grovelling at her feet. She felt her cheeks grow hotter at the truth of that. *Bloody Aes Sídhe arrogance.*

Her thoughts drew her away from the unfamiliar voice until the giggle. It was female, friendly, and, unlike her previous conversation, not combative. Neamhain scoured the immediate landscape. At the same time, she noted the thick blanket of snow covering her legs and lower torso. *That's why I felt warm.* A chuckle came from her right, and Neamhain stared in its direction. Scattered mounds of every size and shape covered in deep snow littered the landscape.

"Did you do this?" asked Neamhain.

"I didn't want you to get cold." The person seemed to pause as if thinking. "Although, I suppose a sídhe does not feel hot or cold, which seems a shame. How can you enjoy one without the other?"

"It would be nice to know who is guarding me."

"I am not guarding you." The voice ceased its trilling yet stopped short of a hiss or spit. It sounded annoyed and insulted.

Neamhain cringed. The tone reminded her of herself. "I apologise. I am not usually this intemperate."

"I know because I can see inside you. Your heart is good, and you are fiercely loyal to your friends. My father is unsure if the latter is wise. He was expecting a traditional arrogant sídhe." Neamhain swore a wet nose touched her earlobe. "You caught him off guard. He is wise and thought someone closer to your age would be a better guide. I volunteered." Again, the voice paused. "I'm glad I did."

"Your father? The one I was rude to? I hope I can apologise face to face." Neamhain sensed her companion nod. She was also relieved she had not been summarily dismissed as she feared.

"You must understand my father is fierce and protective of our tribe—the Old Ones or the Cait People as we are known in the land of the humans. He has kept us safe for millennia, and away from prying eyes, whether human or demigod. Until now, only the Goddess knew of our continued existence. The Blood Queen guessed but was prudent enough not to pry.

"You lay claim to an ancient *geis* which will bring death and set us on a different path. Can you blame him for not being terribly receptive?"

Neamhain shook her head. "No, I cannot. Yet the way of life of the

Cait People will end if evil wins." Neamhain sighed, smiled, and patted the snow beside her. "Please, sit beside me and help me understand your people… and myself. I have much to learn and little time."

Only the sharp eyes of a sídhe could have detected the movement and the slight ripple like warm air over the snow. Neamhain had never witnessed a creature so stealthy. Attempting to track her was pointless. Thus, the sneeze and flurry of snow beside Neamhain caught her by surprise. She laughed, and her new acquaintance giggled.

"May I sit on your lap?" Neamhain dipped her head. "I cannot promise to remain there. Your breasts are much too tempting. They look so comfortable, warm and… soft. Mine are quite small." Neamhain dipped her head and laughed as paws kneaded her chest like bread. Eventually, the head of the most beautiful, long-haired, silver-grey cat she had ever seen rested on her cleavage. By its weight, it was also a substantial feline. Its black-tipped, triangular ears continually twitched, scanning the surroundings.

"I'm not a 'cat'. That is a somewhat generic classification, although we share many feline traits. We are bigger and much closer to the mountain *lince*—lynx—clann."

Neamhain gazed into the lince's green eyes and saw the vertically elongated pupil dilate. She sensed hers do likewise. The low, constant purring made her eyelids heavy, and the reverberations in her chest relaxed her body. "My name is Caoimhe. Take my hand, and I will take you to someone who has waited a long time to meet you."

The idea was ridiculous until Neamhain opened her eyes. She looked into pools of deep green and held the hands of a young woman with long ash-grey hair whose beauty took her breath away. "Welcome to where we rest and play, Neamhain."

***

The lince's fur was beige-white and speckled with small, dark-brown spots. She was the size of a well-fed mountain lynx, although stretched out, which she was as Caoimhe and Neamhain approached, she looked twice as big. She spread her claws before her and licked them with a long, pink tongue slowly, individually, and deliberately.

"Those claws could do some damage," muttered Neamhain. Caoimhe chuckled. Neamhain watched, fascinated, as the lince methodically licked and washed her body. The beast suddenly growled, and Neamhain looked at Caoimhe. "Is there something the matter? Have I done something?"

Caoimhe smiled and shook her head. "Like every type of cat, we are very supple. However, as you will discover, some areas are tricky to reach and clean. If you do not mind, I will help her." Without waiting for permission, Caoimhe became the silver-grey lince and padded gracefully over to the other. The bigger lynx turned and lay on her back, revealing its snow-white belly and chest fur.

Neamhain watched, fascinated by the thorough and tender washing Caoimhe administered. Then, she reddened as she realised which areas needed specific attention. The larger animal's purrs became louder, and Neamhain's breathing and pulse rate increased symbiotically. She found the scene intensely erotic and embarrassing. Yet it was impossible to look away. When Caoimhe returned to her human shape and stood beside her, her face was flushed.

"Does it hurt when you change to your lince persona?" Neamhain asked, hoping to steer the conversation towards safer ground.

"No. However, your perspective is mistaken. Your friend, Brianag, changes to a wolf, doesn't she?" Neamhain dipped her head, wondering where the conversation was heading. "Brianag, even after her awful abuse by Sidheag, remains human, does she not?"

Neamhain nodded although there was a hint of uncertainty in her mien. Caoimhe paused, frowned, and said, "Brianag has powers none of us understand, but for all her trials, her core humanity has not changed, which speaks well of her."

Neamhain's eyes widened when she realised what Caoimhe said. "You're a lince. That is your natural state. This human form is not who you are, is it?"

Caoimhe smiled and held Neamhain's hand. "No, it isn't," she winked. But it does allow for some unique and pleasurable experiences." Caoimhe inhaled deeply and exhaled slowly. "You are very observant, Neamhain. However, you need to take one more step."

"No."

"Is it that difficult to comprehend? You are neither sídhe nor human. Rather, you are a lince and belong to the Cait People—a race that is aeons older than either. You are also unique and none of us know how that happened. Only the Goddess knows. Also, by the Goddess's edict you are our queen, and we have never had a queen." Caoimhe pointed to the other cat, who sat looking intensely at them with pale, topaz-blue eyes. Its pupils were constricted as if it was unhappy with something or someone.

"I don't think she likes me," said Neamhain. The statement made her sad.

"She is you, Neamhain. Think about how you would feel if someone you were born to be with kept you waiting for so long. She feels unwanted by the one she was born to love and be a part of."

Tears formed in Neamhain's eyes. "I'm so sorry."

"Tell her, not me." Caoimhe's eyes twinkled. "Make nice with her. Afterwards, I will teach you the hygienic necessity and pleasure of mutual washing."

✳✳✳

As Neamhain walked resolutely towards the lynx, it, with equal resolve, did not move and stared at a point far in the distance. *At least she's not making me crawl on my belly. That's something, I suppose.* Yet the closer Neamhain got to her lince, the more the knots in her stomach tightened, and her legs grew weak.

"No, I must not fail." She set her jaw and continued, one step after another.

Several paces from the lince, the animal had neither moved nor acknowledged Neamhain's presence. *The Hag. She's more pig-headed than me. This will make a great fusion. What do I say to her? Will she even allow me to get close? Will she spurn me?* The last thought made the knots in her stomach tighten more. She gasped, and her lip trembled. *Does it mean that much to me?*

Taking a deep breath, Neamhain sat down beside her lynx. *At least she didn't run away.* Neamhain looked into the pale-blue eyes and saw pain, loneliness… and fear. "Are you afraid of rejection?" whispered Neamhain through a veil of tears. "I will never do that, I promise. I feared what I would become, but I didn't know you. Can you understand that?"

Neamhain's answer was a pale-pink tongue licking away her tears. She reached out a nervous hand to smooth the lynx's back. The fur felt softer than any she had known. She heard a soft purr, smiled, and stroked more. The purring became insistent and louder. Neamhain felt the lince relax as they fell together onto the grass. "Thank you," whispered Neamhain, and she hugged her lince.

"I'm glad you came. I was very lonely," trilled the lynx in a voice that was the mirror image of Neamhain's. Blue eyes held Neamhain's, the pupils dilated impossibly large, and the two merged.

A short distance away, Caoimhe smiled. Where there had been two, there was one. She would let them adjust to each other until night-time. Then they would run together. Neamhain had a lot to catch up on.

∗∗∗

Neamhain had no idea how long she had been in the land of the Old Ones, and she rarely knew who was present—lynx or sídhe. *Does it matter?* With Caoimhe's guidance, the transformation became seamless. The pair played and loved together. She gave a long sigh, or was it a purr?

"Is it time to be responsible?" asked Caoimhe.

Neamhain stretched, licked down her leg to her toes, and dipped her head. Pale-blue eyes met pools of green. "I am afraid of what may have happened in my absence. I love you, Caoimhe, but I do not want to lose the family and friends I left behind."

"I understand. I sensed your dilemma, and my father awaits us in the settlement."

***

Neamhain smiled. The village was no longer a mirage, and the gates swung open as they approached. A tall, straight-backed, elderly man with golden hair awaited them. Neamhain suspected that, like the Aes Sídhe, he adopted his age to suit how others perceived him. She smiled at the cry of "Da!" and watched Caoimhe hug and kiss him.

Yet there was a wistfulness in Neamhain's delight. Seeing the elderly man reminded her she had not seen her father, Fearghal, in a while. She loved and missed him. *Will he like my lynx?* It was a silly question. Fearghal would accept any form she took without hesitation.

The Elder's voice was pleasant, but Neamhain detected a note of pain. *Why?* He pointed to a large roundhouse at the settlement's centre. "There are food and refreshments ready in the building. We do not need a Great Hall, and indeed, there is no need for the Cait People to meet to discuss topics of importance physically."

The man chuckled. "Our large gatherings are for parties and céili! However, I think that would be one step too far for you on this occasion. The Council of the Cait People await you in the roundhouse."

As they passed the dwellings, Neamhain's now extra-sensitive nose twitched at a smell that rose above the coldness. She sneezed several times and felt her lynx unamused at the scent. Caoimhe's cheeks reddened.

The Elder stopped and faced Neamhain. "I apologise, my queen." It was the first time he had recognised her position or right to the title, and she heaved a sigh of relief. He shrugged. "We are felines. Until the Goddess aided our departure from the kingdom of the Tuatha Dé, we had an army of servants to take care of our daily needs. The Goddess decided we needed to learn humility and forbade us from having servants."

The Elder's tone suggested he did not agree with the Goddess. With a flourish of his hand, the Elder indicated the village. "As you can smell, we are appallingly bad at hygiene. In our defence, our time is spent mostly in the land of the Old Ones, where such bodily functions and wastes are magically absent."

"So, I smell millennia of shite, piss, food scraps, and hairballs? Thank the Goddess for natural decay." The Elder nodded. "That will change," said Neamhain.

"How? We are naturally hedonistic."

"You are naturally lazy," retorted Neamhain, and father and daughter blushed. "However, I may have a mutually agreeable solution to your hygiene challenge, but first, we have a war to fight and win." The Elder dipped his head and indicated the roundhouse's entrance.

*** *

"The *Rígan* of the Na Daoine Cait has arrived, and the prophecy is fulfilled," announced the Elder. "Greet your queen." One side appeared to be as embarrassed as the other. The Old Ones had never had a queen, and neither had the Aes Sídhe. Hence, Neamhain had never considered she might be elevated to royalty—except in her dreams. What was the protocol?

"Shite," muttered Neamhain. Caoimhe tittered. A cough from Neamhain drew everyone's attention to her. "This is a novel situation for everyone. I am not one for formalities, but perhaps we should begin by affirming you agree with my role and swearing loyalty to me as your rígan. That is the practice of the humans." She was relieved as, one by one, all the council members bowed and made their oaths.

"Good." Neamhain pointed to the circle of eleven chairs. "Let us sit and discuss why I am here. There are always wars among men." A round of agreement and some less complimentary observations on humanity followed. "However, one that is not of their making is among them. Leannán-Sídhe and her pet, the Cú Sídhe, aim to destroy them.

"Humans, including my family and friends, have no defence against the Cú Sídhe. I am informed that the Cait People know how to defeat the Hound."

"That is not strictly correct," said the Elder. Neamhain's heart skipped several beats, and she fought to keep her face neutral.

"Please explain."

"First, let me introduce other key parties to this discussion." The Elder dipped his head to Caoimhe, who immediately left the round-house, leaving a bewildered Neamhain. When Caoimhe returned, nine females accompanied her. Each young woman stood behind a council member.

"These are our daughters. Caoimhe, whom you have grown to know well, will be your protector, in human terms your shield-maiden. She will die to defend you." Neamhain's hand went to her mouth to stem a cry of "No!" The Elder continued. "There is only one way to stop the Cú Sídhe's triple bark and the subsequent deaths of many—a lince's yowl."

Neamhain's shoulders relaxed. The relief was premature. "Each of the Cait People's daughters has one chance to stand before the Cú Sídhe and prevent his bark. The cost is their death—a final death. We cannot use deception or sleight of hand to return them to the land of the Old Ones. We can only pray that the Goddess has a place for them." A sombre silence descended on the room.

Neamhain stood and shook her head. "The Hag, no! There must be another way. I will not permit the sacrifice of innocents. It is barbaric. The practice of tyrants."

"There is no other way. If our daughters die, another ten will replace them. This will continue until the Cú Sídhe is destroyed. We hope you and your friends succeed sooner rather than later."

"I wish I had never come to this place," said a stricken Neamhain, gazing at Caoimhe.

"Then you would never have been complete, and only the Goddess knows the implication for you, the Cait People, and the humans. You are a bhanrigh, and queens must make hard decisions. Ask your friend, the

Blood Queen. Her reign has not been easy."

Neamhain glared at the Elder until he shrunk from its ferocity. "I will accept Caoimhe as my shield-maiden, and she and the others as my *caomhnóirí*—personal guard." The council members heaved an audible sigh of relief. It ceased at one word. "*However*… they will be trained to fight alongside me in battle against the Cú Sídhe and other enemies. They will not stand and be slaughtered without a fight."

CHAPTER 20

A' Chrìon Làraich

Leannán prided herself on the subtlety of her sorcery. From her perspective, taking over victims' minds was not violent. Most humans were weak. Thus, only the strong suffered any discomfort or pain, and they were rewarded by the fulfilment of their most depraved fantasies. Most times, Leannán's need for blood was modest. There was no need for blood and gore unless she wanted to indulge herself and drink deeply.

Yet every rule has exceptions, most of which are justified by circumstance. Fresh blood was preferable when she had a project and needed to boost her powers. The stores in the amphorae were her reserves. Thus, Leannán felt no guilt as she drained the blood from another of the fresh bodies hanging from the cave's roof. All were fully sentient, but unable to resist Leannán's rapacious appetite. She released their vocal cords near their deaths because the final moans and pleadings of their sacrifice triggered intense orgasms that overwhelmed her.

Sometimes, she deliberately bit into an artery. Instead of a steady flow, the lifeblood would gush and splash her, making her skin tingle. Leannán revelled in the perfect temperature of the liquid. The indulgence was a waste of fuel, but she had an abundance of donors. *I deserve a little treat.*

Sated, and still naked, Leannán walked to the cave's exit, looked to the foothills beneath her, and gave herself a pat on the back for her patience and ingenuity. Further down the slope, an army of three thousand warriors barely recognisable as men and women assembled. For several cycles of the moon, she had overfed her selection until they were morbidly obese. Then, she moulded them to her will.

Sorcery was both art and science and Leannán knew some rules cannot be broken. A potter's genius requires clay to demonstrate his expertise. So, it was with human flesh. Leannán could not create it, but once it was available, she could transform it.

In Leannán's hands, the three thousand became gross caricatures of their former selves. Fat was converted into hard muscle, and bones lengthened and thickened. Their minds collapsed under the strain of the alterations, and they lost the ability to communicate. Leannán created an army of giants, massive brutes who followed only her commands.

It was time to attack A' Chrìon Làraich and teach the humans a lesson.

* * *

The snow fell thick and fast. Therefore, Sorchae and Amodocus agreed that he should take the riders and return to Gràinne's crannag before they were trapped in A' Chrìon Làraich. The veteran horse warriors were a precious and finite asset, and the toll required by the gods of the Highland mountains would be too high to risk.

Sorchae remained with the foot-warriors. Ardghal insisted on staying with her as her shield and exchanged places with Niall. Still, a sojourn in A' Chrìon Làraich was not an intolerable price to pay for pleasant quarters and regular meals throughout the winter. The stronghold had an abundance of solid barracks inside and outside its walls, many of which were currently empty. Much of Seonag's army, taken by surprise by the heavier-than-usual snowfall, remained in the forests. They would hunker down beside blazing fires and trickle back over the next few cycles of the moon.

Seonag's and Cè's warriors numbered about five thousand; Sorchae had one thousand Raven spearmen; and A' Chrìon Làraich's permanent garrison was five hundred. Half of the latter manned the ballistae on the ramparts. Hundreds of braziers, always lit, formed rings of fire. Behind the stone-and-dirt walls, huge, smoke-blackened cauldrons filled with oil and water sat near piles of wood ready to be set alight.

The small group sat around a table in the stronghold's broch and shared food, beer, and craic. Sorchae's skin tingled all over, and she constantly shifted in her seat. Mostly, she refrained from scratching herself to pieces, but it was a challenge. *What is going on?* Sorchae was unaware that her curling symbols were in constant motion—but Seonag, who sat beside her, was.

She put a hand over Sorchae's. "What is the matter? Are you unwell?"

Sorchae shook her head. "I fear an attack. Are there lookout towers beyond the treeline? An army could hide in the forest and be on us before the alarm is raised."

Earc laughed loudly, which pleased neither Sorchae nor Seonag. "Erecting guard towers in the forest would be a foolish waste of warriors. They would see fewer than a hundred paces in front of them. There are archers on the treeline who will signal if an attack is near." He laughed again. "Don't worry, you're safe. The snow is knee deep already, and by the next sunset, it will be thigh deep. Who can attack quickly in such conditions?"

Seonag's former shield's patronising tone was mocking at best and insulting at worst. It angered Seonag, but not wishing to air an internal dispute, she settled for glaring at Earc. *What did I ever see in him? How did I consider him a partner to share my throne and cot?*

I agree, Seonag. He is not suitable for you, but who am I to judge? I, too, have challenges in finding a partner. Sorchae's newfound ability startled Seonag. To Earc, she snapped, "I can think of two that winter will not stop: a sídhe and a Cú Sídhe." Earc glowered at Sorchae's riposte but had no answer. She turned to Seonag. "My senses tell me something approaches. With your leave, I will send Ardghal with twenty Ravens to scout north of the stronghold. Fionn's stronghold is not too distant, even in these conditions."

Seonag dipped her head. "Take twenty of my warriors, too. They know the forest paths." At Earc's grunt of disapproval, she snapped, "It is better to be prudent beforehand than to build funeral pyres afterwards." After a moment's angry silence, Seonag glared at Earc. "Cè will immediately assume the duties of my battle commander and shield. You will confine your duties to ensuring *my* warriors remain in full readiness."

Red-faced at his public demotion and humiliation, Earc rose to object, but Seonag dismissed him with a curt, "Remove your belongings from the broch. Henceforth, you will quarter with the army."

***

Fionn sensed a change in the strength of Leannán's enthrallment. He no longer felt locked out of his mind and began to consider the random snippets of information permeating it were fragments of Leannán's thoughts. Yes, his brain felt like travelling through marshland, but his ability to think had increased. He had first observed the improvement a moon cycle ago when Leannán began to create her army.

He chuckled. *The bidse is overreaching.* It made sense. She was far from her home among the Aes Sídhe; the blood stores in her cave would not last forever, and there must be an ongoing allocation of power to control the enchanted leaders.

It puzzled Fionn why Leannán wanted to attack Seonag. The journey south to A' Chrìon Làraich was relatively short. In the summer, a warrior could jog the distance in five sunsets. It was folly in the winter over treacherous mountainous terrain with passes blocked by snow. *Stupid bidse!* Why could she not wait until spring? Who was she trying to impress? More to the point, who did she fear?

Fatigue descended on Fionn. He staggered to his cot and tumbled into it. Unused to prolonged mental exercise, his physical fitness was determined by the winter snows that restricted movement and how often Leannán wanted to be rutted. "Stupid bastard," he muttered, castigating himself. "How did I ever think I was in charge?"

Yet as sleep overtook him, Fionn smiled. Every pace Leannán took away from him weakened her enthrallment. She had no stores of blood save the brutes she pushed towards A' Chrìon Làraich. Fionn also knew that Leannán had not enchanted the entire army. To do so would quickly drain her strength. If he could free just one hundred veterans, he would break the bidse.

⁂

Apart from random clumps of snow falling from tree branches and small animals scurrying to find food scraps, the forest was quiet. The larger predators, wolves and bears, prefer to hibernate unless their food gathering has been poor. Thus, the crashing noises coming from Ardghal's northern flank signalled danger. His band followed the sounds and smell of woodsmoke and shuffled over the snow towards them.

"The Hag's arse!" muttered the wiry veteran who lay beside him in the snow.

"What are they?" grunted Ardghal. The question was rhetorical, but his companion was unlikely to make that distinction.

Seonag's choice of leader for her warriors had caused Ardghal to raise an eyebrow. Beira was small, barely reaching his chest. She was not unattractive, but her forwardness made him uneasy. The less-than-subtle hints of rutting later increased with each step taken. Ardghal knew he was no catch, although he was novel to her. Still, he was used to leading in most things, including liaisons. It seemed, however, that his apparent bashfulness only increased Beira's fervour. He groaned aloud.

As if sensing his thoughts, she said, "I'm just being friendly. It can be a long and lonely winter here, isolated from friend and foe." After a moment, she said, "I don't bite," but then she winked mischievously. "Unless you like that." By the time Ardghal's brain had delivered a suitable, humorous rejoinder to his lips, she had moved the discussion to safer ground.

"I make it about three thousand of the brutes. They keep shuffling around, but it's a reasonable estimate. What are they? They may have originally been human, but by the Hag, what did the witch do to them?"

Any opinion Ardghal might have formed dissipated at a scream from the camp. One from Beira's band, wishing to impress, had drifted too close to Leannán's encampment. They watched as several brutes dragged the scout by her braided hair and threw her down in front of the enchantress.

Ardghal and Beira watched the scene unfold by the flickering light of the fire. There was nothing they could do to rescue the warrior without exposing the warband. An apparently bored Leannán snapped at one giant and waved a hand towards the prisoner. Four brutes picked her up by her limbs. With a communal grunt, they tore her arms and legs from her torso and threw them onto the fire. The limbless trunk followed. The woman's screams seemed to take an eternity before they were silent.

"They're strong bastards," said Beira, grinding her back teeth until her jaw ached. "I wish I could mark them for later, but how do we tell any of them apart?" She paused. "At least they didn't rape her. That's a mercy."

"They're strong and fast—faster than any of us. Once Leannán gives the orders, they will be at A' Chrìon Làraich in two sunsets, maybe three, if the Goddess favours us. We should return immediately." Ardghal paused. "I hope you know an open and straight path back to the stronghold."

"This is the Highlands, and it is winter. You can have neither," she replied, adding with a wide grin, "but you're welcome to rut me as an incentive—if you get us back safely."

CHAPTER 21

Dùn Brion & Loch nan Clàr

"It's the wind," said Cassán. He had repeated the mantra every evening since Brianag stormed from the dùn. On each occasion, the statement was true. Yet, on this evening as he and Eimhir stood on a walkway lightly dusted with powdery snow, the fine hairs on the back of his neck stood stiff. On this night, he was suddenly unsure. Why? What had changed?

"Call for her. She's your sister. Name me siblings who do not fight. Apologise for upsetting Neamhain. Even if it's not true, someone must open the door to reconciliation. Ask for her help. Brianag's temper is fierce but short-lived." Cassán shook his head, dashing Eimhir's hopes. *Bloody, stubborn family. They would rather their bones were broken and crushed than say, "I'm sorry."*

"My words were honestly spoken but ill-chosen for a king. My sister will not listen to me, and I cannot blame her. Our hopes lie with Luag and Malmhìn."

I may have misjudged him… again. Eimhir pointed to the forests and the clouds of snowflakes drifting and swirling over the landscape. "Be realistic, Cassán. Think of the terrain they must cross and the winter storms in the Highlands. It's a hazardous journey. They might die before reaching Loch nan Clàr." Frustration slipped into Eimhir's tone. "What will we do then? How can we face the Cú Sídhe on our own?"

"We will fight with everything we have, and the Goddess will determine if we live or die."

"The Goddess provided a weapon in Brianag," snapped Eimhir. "She has no time for those who disregard her gifts and is not one to forgive petty foibles." Eimhir spun around and walked a few steps before descending to the courtyard. Her last words, "Call Brianag," hung in the air.

✷✷✷

Cassán understood Eimhir's position. He also knew humans could not forever rely on gods, demigods, and other unnatural creatures to fight their battles. At some time, men and women had to make a stand. Was that time now? It was a question that would be debated over future campfires by old men, philosophers, and the seanchaithe. Cassán sighed, shook his head, and walked along the parapet to where his garrison commander stood.

"How many horses do we have?"

"Including the queen's and yours, twenty." Cassán cursed under his breath. Building a sizeable force of horses and riders had been on his "actions needed" list for several summers. It was yet another task he had neglected to follow through on. Just that summer, Pytheas had offered to transport prime horses from Curraghatoor in Southern Ériu. Cassán had said he would think about it and did nothing. *Stupid tuilí.*

"Dùn Athad should have a similar number. Send a rider to the fort. Direct its commander to dispatch all his mounted warriors to Dùn Brion, immediately. At dawn, send our cavalry out to patrol: ten along the Sleagh and the rest to the farmlands south of the mountain."

The commander dipped his head. "What shall I ask them to look for?"

"Dead, horribly mutilated bodies. I doubt the Hound will take the trouble to bury his prey." The veteran dipped his head and trudged through ankle-deep snow along the walkway to the steps.

Cassán looked into the night sky and whispered, "Brianag." Unknown to Eimhir, it was not the first time.

***

Luag and Malmhìn journeyed a half-cycle of the moon in harsh conditions before their exhausted horses collapsed and became food. They, too, would have died well before reaching the queen's crannag, if a group of Gràinne's scouts had not chanced across their path. Hence, they were saved from a frozen fate.

Unfortunately, their rescue did not fully dispel the duo's troubles. The Na Daoine Tùrsach warriors were suspicious of all strangers. Thus, it was debatable whether freezing to death or being killed as spies would be their path to Mag Mell. Yet, the *mná-sídhe* had not cried; thus, there was hope.

"The Hag's arse, Luag. Call out to her or just think of how precarious our situation is. She will come and you know it."

Luag shook his head. "You call her."

"Bloody stubborn man!" shouted Malmhìn. "I'm not the one who rutted her. She knows our thoughts, but she wants to hear from you." A round of laughter rose from their captors seated around the campfire enjoying the entertainment. In frustration, Malmhìn lashed out. Whether deliberate or not, Malmhìn's kick was exceptionally well placed. Luag cried out. Bent over double, he rubbed his crotch. Raucous laughter from their guards rose into the still, crisp air.

"Why did you do that?" Luag's question never received an answer, unless the vision of Brianag tossing their custodians into the air like straw dolls counted.

Black eyes glared at the guards. Instantly, they stopped complaining about their bruises and cuts. The sight of the green apparition and the awful clicking sound of her talons turned their blood to ice. The needle-pointed teeth gave every indication Brianag might be hungry. "You dare to mistreat *my* friends," she spat. To Brianag, ignorance was an insufficient defence.

She turned to Luag. "If you wanted to join me, why didn't you just call out or say something before I departed Dùn Brion?"

"That's what I said," muttered Malmhìn.

This elicited a brief smile from Brianag and a sigh of relief from Malmhìn. *She still cares for us.* Then Malmhìn shivered violently, and her teeth chattered uncontrollably. Brianag saw that her friends' dire state was not due to their capture but to being left without heat or warm clothing. Hence, they were half-frozen. She glowered at the scouts again, and they shrunk further back from her.

"The Hag, Luag. If you want to die, that's your choice, but why include Malmhìn in your madness? We will talk about this later."

In the blink of an eye, the trio were in Gràinne's crannag, and Giosail was shouting orders to the servants for roaring fires, thick woollen *brait*, and food. Brianag paced the floor railing at a miserable Luag.

Finally reaching the limits of his patience, Luag stood, called on his remaining strength, and roared, "I did not come to join you! I came to talk some sense into you." Then he collapsed on the wooden floor.

✳✳✳

The Hound breathed deeply, savouring the fresh Lowlands air. The landscape was blanketed in unblemished snow; ice rain converted trees and bushes into glittering crystalline sculptures. On the Sleagh, the snowfall barely reached his calves. He smelled the peat- and pine-scented wood smoke from hundreds of farmsteads and small communities and heard the shouts and laughter of their occupants. The potential bounty exhilarated him.

"This will be *my* hunting ground," he growled. Leannán wanted him to rape and slaughter without restraint. He was her diversion while she pursued her revenge for Sidheag's death. *No, I will not do that.* Inevitable discovery and the curtailing of his food and pleasure lay along that path. The humans would retreat to their strongholds, and he would become the hunted. *Where is the joy if I kill my prey by the thousand?*

The Cú Sídhe smiled crookedly. "I need to test and refine my powers. Who would blame me for indulging my vices while honing them? Better that than barking three times and massacring everybody north and south of the Sleagh." He changed into his hound form. There was no point in being human. The Hound sniffed the air, and drool dripped from his lips as he padded towards the nearest farmstead.

The screams of terror when he entered the roundhouse instantly raised his pulse rate and removed any fragments of compassion. Babies, mothers, daughters, sons, and grandparents shrieked with the uniformity of certain death. His lips drew back in a merciless grin, exposing huge incisors, and his claws extended. The slaughter was over too soon. *Humans are so frail, but they taste delicious.*

A sob from the shadows made him pause from gorging on his victims' flesh and wallowing in the blood and gore. He smiled and transformed back into his human form. She was pretty and well-developed for her age. He had deliberately saved this one. *I have other hungers to satisfy.*

Frozen with horror, the girl had watched what he did to her family. As he walked towards her, she screamed herself hoarse. When he grasped her long blonde hair, only croaks came from her lips. That was a pity. He loved their pitiful cries. *Next time, I will choose one a few summers older with a stronger voice.*

***

Luag awoke to find himself in strange quarters and an unfamiliar cot, but in a position well-known to him—albeit reversed. He felt Brianag's breath on the back of his neck. One arm curled around his shoulders, pulling his body tight to hers, while the other casually stroked his manhood. He tried to resist, but inevitably he was soon as hard as an oak staff.

"I am recovering from a harsh journey and near death. This is not helping."

"Are you sure?"

The cot shook as the wolf furs were displaced. A long tongue with the texture of fine grit licked from his balls to tip of his manhood. He gritted his teeth and swore to resist but failed. His shaft became thicker and harder. The independent traitor throbbed more and demanded satisfaction. Brianag's hand exposed the smooth, bulbous tip; her lips kissed, and her mouth enveloped the shaft. The battle was lost.

He watched her head bob up and down as she sucked his manhood, synchronising it with the slow stroking of his shaft. The movements became faster and faster until he groaned, climaxed, and gushed into her mouth. He heard her gulp down his milk and the smack of lips and could not resist a smile.

Weariness demanded rest and his eyes closed. They opened when Brianag straddled his chest. The pressure should have hurt, yet she felt surprisingly light. Two full breasts and a cloud of red hair descended. Her mouth went to work again. *Is there a better way to cross the veil?*

The slap was gentle but sent a clear message. "Forget any thoughts of crossing the veil today or in the future. I intend to keep the bean-sìth well away from you." Brianag frowned. "I concede you're too weak to rut me, but it seems a lifetime since I have had this in my mouth."

Brianag's lips glistened provocatively, and a small tear-shaped pearl escaped. Its freedom was brief as the pink tip of her tongue captured and devoured it. "Are you hiding any more?" Luag felt his manhood squeezed. "Got it." Her triumph made him chuckle. Then an unguarded thought made his brow furrow.

Irritated, she growled. "Why couldn't you enjoy our moment together? You had to think of those you left behind. What is wrong with you? Perhaps you are better suited to a life as a druid. I do not know if I can live with your gallantry." A firm hand pulled Brianag down on top of Luag, and she nestled against his chest.

"I'm starving," said Luag.

Brianag demonstrated the benefit of having the gifted partner. As they stepped from their cot, a fist banged the chamber door and a bevy of servants entered the room followed by Giosail. Without a glance at the naked occupants, they efficiently stoked the fire and added wood and peat, put fresh meadowsweet and straw in the cot, and laid a small table with food and refreshments.

Before exiting, Giosail sniffed the air. Her nostrils quivered in distaste, and she announced, "You stink and cannot meet anyone before bathing… both of you. Your baths will be ready when you have broken your fast."

"Too many people in this crannag abuse their power," grumbled Brianag.

***

"Three farmsteads were attacked, if you can call the butchery he left in each an attack." Dùn Brion's garrison commander's sour demeanour reflected someone wanting to throw up but refusing to permit it.

"At each scene, one victim was obviously raped. The bastard posed each of them to show their violated lower torso." The warrior choked on his words and his throat burned. "I saw their soulless eyes. He wanted us to see how they suffered before he tore their throats out and snacked on the rest of their bodies." The tall warrior had daughters the same age as those violated. His hand constantly rubbed the pommel of his sword as if wanting to draw the weapon and administer justice—or revenge. Did the motive matter?

"Where did the attacks take place? Is there a pattern?" asked Cassán.

The commander shook his head. "Two were in the foothills north and south of the Sleagh's foothills and one was where the Abhainn Dubh meets the Linne Foirthe. Given the timing, no human could have travelled the distances." The warrior paused. "When there are more attacks, we will have better information and may detect a pattern."

The man, realising what he had said, slumped down on his seat. "The tuilí is taunting us and wants to draw us out." Were more slaughters inevitable? Were they powerless in the face of evil?

Cassán turned to Eimhir. Her knuckles were white as she gripped the table, and her face matched their pallor. Her eyes asked one question. In answer, he placed a hand over hers and said softly, "I have asked many times for Brianag's help. Whether she will come, I do not know."

Tears flowed down Eimhir's cheeks. *How many times will I misjudge*

Cassán before he tires of me? The calloused hand that held hers and the love in his eyes gave her his answer.

✳✳✳

Pride, a hot temper, and misplaced blame had got the better of Brianag—and she knew it. Luag's arrival exposed her weakness to all who mattered. For a cycle of the moon, her ma, Amodocus, and even Heilasa had said nothing, but their eyes shouted their thoughts.

All sympathised with her over Neamhain and would stand with her, no matter what path she took. Nevertheless, their unspoken words condemned her. Luag's arrival made things worse. She licked the last drops of grease from a fat chicken leg, briefly wondered where her ma got the fowl, and pointed the bone at Luag.

"Well, are you going to berate me for being selfish and uncaring? For deserting my friends... and brother?" In her head, Brianag heard the echoes of Cassán's whispered pleas and shook her head as if to erase it from her mind. "I'm also hot-headed and irresponsible. Have I omitted anything?"

"You hurt because you are loyal to your friends, whom you have defended and given your life. You feel guilt and shame for what you are, although everyone who loves you knows that's nonsensical. If I go to Gràinne or Amodocus or your brother and sisters, will they recoil when asked if they love you or will they look at me as if I'm mad to ask stupid questions? You have a temper and overflow with fiery passion, but you are a Gael. For better or for worse, that is part of us."

"You have not asked me to go back," said Brianag. "That is why you are here, is it not? Cassán sent you."

"I am here because I love you." The confession stunned Brianag and Luag. "Cassán did not need to send me. I would have come, anyway... as would Malmhìn," said Luag. "You know that you must go back. I do not need to ask or tell you this, and neither do I need the ability to read your mind to see this."

"Cassán insulted Neamhain," sniffed Brianag. "Who are you to demand I ignore that? I have lost my closest friend."

"You are a woman, not an adolescent, Brianag. Stop the drama. You have not lost Neamhain." Luag's stern tone startled her. "She chose to search out something very important to her. That she left you behind is a measure of the enormity of that choice. Do you think she wanted to do that?" Brianag shook her head.

"It is for Neamhain to seek reconciliation or retribution. She is a sídhe. When did they ever have any problem in asserting themselves? What will you do if Neamhain reconciles with Cassán, but you have put your relationship beyond healing? She trusts your judgment, Brianag. That's why she did not take you with her."

"You're much too wise, Luag," said Brianag. "Which is surprising given the arsehole you were when we first met. I am not sure…"

"Yes, you are, and you knew Cassán would respond. Your brother is a king who has a tribe to keep safe. Is he not allowed to be angry that his people are in danger—the same ones you rescued in the forest south of Dùn Brion? Is he not to be forgiven for words spoken? Can't you understand the fear that grips him? His people are being raped and slaughtered by the Cú Sídhe."

Luag took a deep breath. "Cassán and the Na Mèadaidh have no choice. They will fight the Cú Sídhe until the last of the tribe bleeds out on the Sleagh's gorse and heather." He inhaled. "That includes Dolidh, her family, and all those you saved in the forest. Will you let her stand defenceless against the Hound? She counts you as her friend. Is she mistaken?" Luag's words left a bitter taste in his mouth.

"I will remove Dolidh and her family from the Sleagh. They will be safe," snapped Brianag.

Luag shook his head. "You know Dolidh. She is a child, yet she will not leave her people. If needed, she will die with them. How will you sleep when you hear her screams night after night?"

"Bastard!" shrieked Brianag. The wooden walls of the crannag shook as if an avalanche of snow fell on it. However, Luag refused to retreat from the terrible creature who stood a breath away.

In another room, Gràinne gripped Malmhìn's arm to prevent her from going to Luag's aid. "They must resolve this between themselves. We cannot help or intercede."

Luag's faith in Brianag's sense of justice was unshakable, but neither he nor anyone in the crannag ever found out how the conversation would have proceeded. Brianag's fierce confrontational demeanour changed in an instant to terror.

She whispered, "Dolidh," and was gone.

CHAPTER 22

A' Chrìon Làraich

Ardghal and Beira ran, jogged, walked, and stumbled along rutted forest and mountain paths. Hidden by a thick blanket of snow, the trails were doubly treacherous. Mercifully, the pair avoided twisted or broken ankles, although several of their band were not as fortunate and were left behind in the trees. Beira prayed they would find hiding places beyond the reach of Leannán's army.

Back in A' Chrìon Làraich and covered with thick woollen brait, the pair sat exhausted and shivering beside a roaring firepit. Both eyed the food and beer servants laid on a small table beside them and wondered if they had the energy to raise the food to their lips. They also pondered whether they should eat or talk first.

"How long until they attack?" Seonag's question correctly assumed the pair's physical state was because of an imminent threat. Thus, they chose to sip cups of hot beer flavoured with meadowsweet. They would eat later.

"We have one sunset to prepare A' Chrìon Làraich's defences and devise a strategy," said Ardghal. His companion nodded in agreement. "Leannán's horde numbers three thousand…"

Before Ardghal could expand on the statement, Earc banged the table with his jug and laughed aloud. "Just three thousand. There are over six thousand warriors in A' Chrìon Làraich. We have sturdy walls, a hundred ballistae, and several hundred hounds. An attacking force would need overwhelming odds to breach our defences…"

This time, an angry Ardghal interrupted Earc's flow. "A wise man would keep his mouth shut and listen to the full report before embarrassing himself… and his queen."

Earc rose unsteadily, his face flushed from too many cups of beer. "I will not be insulted. I am the commander of the Forest People in A' Chrìon Làraich, which is also my clann's home, and demand respect. Face me man to man in the courtyard."

"Warriors do not demand respect, they earn it," retorted Ardghal. "I will be happy to fight you, but only when you are sober. I would not wish to be accused of taking advantage of a drunk as well as a fool." Beira bit on her fist to stop tittering.

"Where on earth did you find this eejit, Seonag?" asked Cè. His voice was little more than a murmur, but loud enough for Earc to hear. "Surely you have better taste than him?" After a moment's reflection, Cè put his hand on his sister's arm. "I am sorry you are that lonely. I have no doubt the Goddess has a partner for you, Seonag. Be patient."

It was difficult to determine whose face was the redder or who was the most embarrassed—Earc or Seonag. Seonag looked at Sorchae, who sat unperturbed by Earc's challenge to Ardghal. "If you have no objections to a contest to the death, then neither do I," said Seonag.

Sorchae looked at Ardghal, smiled, and dipped her head. "The challenge poses no difficulties for me. However, like Ardghal, I suggest the contest should wait until after the attack. We should let Ardghal finish the report he started to deliver before being rudely interrupted."

"Agreed." Seonag turned to face a scowling Earc. "As for you, since you are incapable of learning or behaving properly when in the company of my guests, you are of no use to me. Whatever commissions you retain are revoked, and you are stripped of all ranks and privileges. Retire to the barracks. Perhaps time spent in the front row of my warriors will adjust your demeanour."

Earc rose to leave the table, but before he had gone more than ten steps, Seonag had reflected on his earlier words. Anger suffused her face, and she stood. "Never presume to speak for your clann and do not put your threat to the test. They are *my* people. Like my mother, you will be disappointed. Unlike her, you do not have a familial bond to save you from a stake in your arse." As the broch's door slammed shut behind Earc, Seonag smiled, relieved at having rid herself of a problem. She looked at Ardghal. "I apologise. Please continue."

"We face giants, although that description usually encompasses an element of humanity. Many are two spears in height, and some were taller. Their girth is as big as a barrel of beer, their legs are like tree trunks, and their arms are the width of an oak tree's bottom branches.

"They are monstrous, musclebound creatures who are devoid of mercy. We watched four of them tear our comrade's limbs off and toss her torso onto a fire while she still lived. I still hear her screams, and the smell of brimstone as her hair burned fills my nostrils."

"Shite!" exclaimed Sorchae, reflecting the horror expressed by the others.

"They are solid and agile—faster than anyone could expect from their height and mass. All bear clubs and spears, but their massive fists are likely as dangerous as blacksmiths' hammers. They have no free will. All are Leannán's creations and under her thrall."

Ardghal reached for a cup of beer and dipped his head to Beira, who stood and bowed. "Based on our observations, each of Leannán's monsters is worth three of our warriors, perhaps even five." She looked at Seonag and Sorchae. "Earc could not have been more wrong when he said we had strong defences and nothing to worry about. We are outnumbered and need a battle strategy… fast."

Cè broke the sombre silence that descended. "We need a plan to whittle their numbers before they reach our walls. Here's what I suggest."

* * *

Beira climbed one of the few oaks in a forest dominated by pines. She sat on a sturdy branch; muscled thighs gripped the rough bark. Below her, smoke curled upwards from the small fire at the tree's base. The edges of lips, which had not lost their youthful softness, opened and a broad smile spread across her face. She recalled Ardghal's explosive, "*No!*" when she volunteered for the mission.

An integral component of Cè's battle plan needed the positioning of a handful of lookouts a hundred paces beyond the treeline. They were to fire flaming arrows into the sky immediately after Leannán's army was spotted. Beira smiled wistfully. It was a mission with a high probability of death. A long sigh, witnessed by a cloud of white crystals, followed. After a score of arseholes, she had finally found a man she liked enough to want him to stick around. Now she hoped her brashness had not frightened him off.

"What am I thinking?" She wanted to shout it into the forest but only murmured so as not to reveal her position. "I'm on a suicide mission and I'm thinking of a potential hand-fast partner." She looked upwards and shook her head. "The Hag, but this is poor timing, Goddess."

Beira's train of thought ended abruptly when she heard the crack of a branch breaking. She slithered down the tree, grabbed her bow, and moved cautiously towards the noise. She had to make sure it was not a bear taking a break from hibernation. Beira had walked only five paces when a lumbering, grunting brute emerged from the trees.

"Shite!" she murmured, ducking behind a broad trunk. She hoped the creature was a lone scout as she took a handful of tinder from a pouch. *All my dreams might go up in flames if I light this.* With a sigh, she struck the flintstones and watched the glowing spark carry her fate.

✶✶✶

Leannán tasted an emotion she rarely experienced in the Mounds or on Oileán Dubh: excitement with a hint of fear. Hubris, an affliction often attributed to the Aes Sídhe, overpowered her mind and she strode ahead of her monstrous army. That said, "strode", while a fair description of Leannán's intent, did not take into consideration that her bare feet scarcely touched and rarely broke through the icy crust of the snow.

Sensitive nostrils quivered as her army approached the stronghold. She was close enough to smell the first hints of woodsmoke and peat carried on a northerly breeze. There was another fragrance carried on the wind, but she could not place it. Neither could her sensitive hearing identify the strange squealing sounds from A' Chrìon Làraich. Thus, Leannán ignored both as being of little consequence, just as she had ignored the benefit of sending scouts to reconnoitre the stronghold. That said, since her hulking warriors could barely speak beyond primal grunts, how would they have imparted what they saw?

She heard the slap and crack of wood against wood and the whoosh of displaced air but did not understand their meaning… until the screeching began. While her army was unable to speak coherently, they remembered how to scream.

∗∗∗

Once she sent her arrow into the air, Beira dropped the bow stave and quiver and ran. "I wish I were taller and had longer legs," she muttered as her lungs filled to bursting with frigid air. She was almost at the treeline when she heard the first "*whoosh*".

She roared, "Run!" to her comrades, but apart from praying to the Goddess for mercy, that was all she could do for them. Everyone was on their own now. Behind her, the forest exploded into an inferno of sweet-smelling pines as volleys of hundreds of flaming ballistae bolts slammed into the trees.

Beira threw herself onto the snow beyond the forest line and rolled down the gentle slope before starting the long trudge across the fields to the outer wall of A' Chrìon Làraich. Almost at the wall, she took a moment to steady her breathing and turned about. The sight shocked Beira. For five hundred paces along and one hundred back from the treeline, the forest was an inferno.

Cè claimed that, whether man or monster, all feared fire. The nightmarish screaming and smells from the forest stunned Beira's senses. Still, the trees were life to the Forest People, and all Beira could think was that it would take generations to plant and grow new pines. Beira shed tears for the trees, not for Leannán's brutes.

Her sorrow was abruptly curtailed when she was lifted from the snow and held in a hug that almost cracked her spine. "Never do that to me again," said Ardghal. He released her and took a step back. "Are you hurt? Do we need a healer?" All Beira could do was shake her head, grin stupidly, and hope they had time to rut before the main battle commenced.

"The others?" asked Beira. Ardghal shook his head. "The Hag!"

***

Leannán discovered even a sídhe has limits on how long she can scream before her voice becomes a meaningless series of croaks. Flames she could survive, but only a sídhe's reflexes saved Leannán from the arm's-length iron heads of the ballistae bolts. She almost jumped out of her skin when the first bolt slammed into a nearby pine. The flaming missile split the tree trunk and the sap turned it into a torch.

All around, she heard the shrieking of her army burning in the fires created by A' Chrìon Làraich's bolt-throwers. Leannán watched them run aimlessly in a patch of forest that became their funeral pyre. She had no control over them. Her sorcery proved no match for primal survival instincts.

Leannán shrugged. She would go back to the forest encampment and drink the blood of the handful of brutes she had left behind. Her well of power had diminished alarmingly, and her blood stores were far away. Feeding would solve the immediate challenge of calling her giants back to the camp. Once gathered, she would throw them at A' Chrìon Làraich and punish the stronghold's insolence.

***

In Loch Eireachd, Fionn sensed that things were not going as planned for Leannán and that her sorcery's strength had weakened. His mind was clearer. He also understood Leannán's feeding on his blood had forged a link between them. Still, that had its dangers. If he could sense Leannán's general disposition, could she peer into his thoughts?

He shivered at the possibility. How much of his plans did she know or suspect? So far, she had not acted, which gave Fionn hope. However, his plan to recruit a warband of one hundred warriors from those not enthralled had hit stumbling blocks of derision, fear of Leannán, and suspicions he was Leannán's spy. Any respect for his former position as their king and commander had largely dissipated.

Yet Fionn was dogged in his execution of his strategy. From an army of over twenty thousand, he gathered a band of brutal, ill-disciplined warriors. Copious jugs of beer and promises of gold, cattle, and *striopaichean*—whores—persuaded them to join him. Fionn was cunning enough to know that once the warband had committed one act of defiance, there was no turning back. There would be no forgiveness from Leannán.

On this crisp winter morning, Fionn and his warband, who were still hungover from several sunsets of binge drinking, trudged up the foothill towards Leannán's cave. The air filled with curses, retching, and for some, feelings of remorse. The latter group recommitted to the plan when confronted with knives and fists.

At the cave entrance, the smell of rotting flesh greeted Fionn's band. It was ominous, because the season and frigid weather usually masked foul odours. As Fionn led them deeper into the cave, he gave a satisfied smile at the curses and retching at the sight of bodies strung up like deer to age. Some were recognised as comrades; others were family.

Outrage inevitably led to violence. Thus, Fionn had little to do but watch as the warband swarmed into the cave and smashed Leannán's amphorae of blood. The act consolidated and reinforced the band's unity. The containers' destruction transformed the refuge's floor into a slurry of blood.

Fionn's suggestion to cut down and burn the victims found no sympathy or compassion. "They're dead. We can do nothing for them." Comradeship only went so far.

CHAPTER 23

A thick wolf's fur swathed Cè's upper body; heavy, plaid woollen pants protected his legs; and sheepskin-lined boots his feet. Yet he shivered as he paced A' Chrìon Làraich's inner wall. Perhaps he considered his likely death, or perhaps it was simply a cold, windy, cloudless night. Stars speckled the sky, and the moon was full. Sporadic showers of red and orange meteor tails added to the beauty of the firmament. The scene was the perfect setting for a winter celebration. But the fireballs were flaming bolts from the array of ballistae protecting the outer and inner perimeters.

A' Chrìon Làraich's armourers' and blacksmiths' muscles cried out for relief as the craftsmen pounded iron into arm's-length spikes and cut and shaped wooden shafts. In the frigid night, sweat flowed from pores opened by roaring forges and intense, unceasing effort. There would be no relief on this night. Indeed, they would not rest until the battle was over, and who knew when that would be?

"Where will they attack from?" asked Seonag.

Cè's shrug gave her no solace. "Pine woods surround us on three sides. To the east, the river protects us. Thankfully, it is not frozen enough to walk across. This time, Leannán's intent was to attack our northern flank. She will probably switch to the southern and western approaches. However, the snow in the forest is not as deep as on the cleared land surrounding the stronghold. They could skirt us and attack from any or all sides."

A chuckle made the duo turn to Sorchae. For one who had lived most of her life in balmy, Southern Gaul, she looked the readiest of the three for battle in the frigid conditions. A heavy fur swathed her torso, covering a boiled leather cuirass. Underneath that, hip-length chainmail rested on a soft woollen tunic.

Heavy woollen triubhas covered her legs. She wore leather, fleece-lined boots with thongs tied to above the calves. An assortment of knives was slipped into each boot, with only the pommels visible. A broad, carved-leather weapons' belt rested on Sorchae's hips. At this time, two ribbed, short swords and several daggers populated its scabbards. Her spears and long-handled rider's sword and axe rested against the wall.

"If I was one of Leannán's brutes, I would be afraid of you," said Cè. All three laughed. Nearby defenders picked up the mirth, and it rippled along the wall.

Sorchae pointed to the ring of fire at the forest's edge to the north, south, and west. "Do you intend to burn all the trees down? If so, you might have to rename your tribe." She referred to the random flaming bolts that continued to be shot from the ballistae.

"If need be, I will burn every pine, oak, and alder." Cè's response was brief and brutal. "We will know the direction of Leannán's attack from the screams of her monsters." Seonag flinched at the nightmarish vision.

***

Nepotism and gold had bought the young man a place as a *ceannard ceud*—leader of one hundred—in A' Chrìon Làraich's permanent garrison. It was a rank usually preserved for veterans. In the case of A' Chrìon Làraich, it was also a prized appointment.

Most of Seonag's warriors roamed the forests in warbands. They were well-outnumbered by Fionn's army and faced death every sunset. In A' Chrìon Làraich, the young man had high expectations of minimal action and a cot in a warm barracks. He also intended to take full advantage of the stronghold's social calendar to ingratiate himself with influential contacts. His career would proceed upwards with the least risky trajectory.

To his credit, he felt a degree of shame at his lack of experience and knew the futility of justifying his position. Excluded from the comradeship of his peers and the hundred he commanded, his face reddened at the loud taunts flung at him as they warmed their hands over perpetually burning braziers.

Worse, the hard eyes of the dozen veterans in his band, any of whom deserved his position, and the slow grinding of their blades on whetstones were a constant reminder of how tenuous his position was. Undoubtedly, they would kill him if he put them in peril. In the heat of battle, he would not be missed.

Until Seonag, Sorchae, and Cè's arrival, the young man was confident of his future. What could happen in this sleepy post at the centre of an agrarian, trading community? The nightly volleys of flaming bolts into the forest, the explosion of pine trees, and the constant smell of pine, smoke, and burning flesh disabused him of his comfort.

His triubhas were cold and wet from pissing himself each time he heard unearthly screams from the forest. People talked of giants and nothing in their eyes said they were jesting. As he stood on the outer wall, the young man wished he had protested his father's lofty ambitions for him. He should have volunteered as a simple spearman, along with his other less politically ambitious friends.

On this night, as he watched the full moon reach its zenith, his only prayer was for a quick death. He had been diligent in his sacrifices to the Goddess… at least over the last seven sunsets. Surely that should permit him entry to Mag Mell.

✳✳✳

Leannán was impatient for a victory. Few doubted she was a powerful sorceress. Nevertheless, she was unproven when it came to commanding an army in a war—even a mindless one she could direct to do anything. She had no battle commanders to develop a strategy and execute it. *Why didn't I bring Fionn and some of his chieftains?* The threat of dismemberment by her loyal brutes would have kept them compliant.

Thinking of Fionn made Leannán frown. The distance between them weakened her hold over him—and the Hound. However, the continual drain on her powers to command her army had a much greater effect. She had already consumed the blood of five of her brutes. Her disquiet regarding Fionn rose with each dream she experienced. Yet Leannán refused to concede their message might be accurate. *I'm an enchantress, not an Oracle, but I must finish this quickly and return to my blood stores.*

A crack sounded and made her flinch. A tree burst into flames and another of her brutes shrieked. "Tuilithe," she muttered. Leannán stood and determined to bring the battle to an end. She called a handful of her hulks to her side. She watched as they shambled over to her fire. In their eyes, there seemed to be a reluctance to obey her.

Did they know she would drain their blood and leave their carcasses to rot on the forest floor? *Impossible! Their minds are empty of all thoughts but mine.* She sent a message to them, and they whimpered and moved closer. *I should crack the whip more often.*

More trees burst into flames. "Act, Leannán," she chastised herself. Then she shouted, "*Ionsaí*—attack!" Half of the brutes proceeded towards the southern and half towards the western flank.

* * *

The flaw in Cè's plan became clear almost immediately. Leannán's ogres burst from the treeline to attack the southern and western walls. In response, the ballistae teams sent fiery volleys into the mass. When an ethereal song rang out from the pines, they stopped. Slack-jawed and vacant-eyed, they stood by their machines. Caught unawares, none could resist Leannán's song of enchantment.

"Rut the Hag!" said Seonag. "How did we forget Leannán's powers?" She pointed to the hordes moving rapidly towards the defences.

"They'll be upon us without a shot fired. Can she enthral us too?" In desperation, Seonag turned to Sorchae. "You're the only gifted one in A' Chrìon Làraich. Can you do anything to help?"

Sorchae hesitated. "I don't know what my powers are. This is new to me. The Goddess did not provide instructions, and my only possible mentor is in Gaul." She shook her head in resignation. "Rut the Hag's bony arse! I should be naked, but the battle will be over before I get out of my battle armour. I will need help."

The alacrity with which Ardghal and Cè stepped forward made Sorchae withdraw a dagger from her belt. "Anyone who gropes me should consider the painful retribution I will dispense after the battle… if we're still alive." She paused and looked at a grinning Seonag and Beira. "That goes for you two, as well."

There was a moment in the freezing cold when Sorchae's fingers and toes turned blue, and her nipples stiffened. *Please, Goddess. I need help.* In the darkness, Sorchae's curling sigils were black. When struck by the moonlight, they became rivers of silver, in constant, turbulent motion. As she raised her hands, warmth flowed through her body.

"She's beautiful," said Seonag. Everyone on the defences echoed the sentiment.

***

"The bitseach!" shouted Leannán when she recognised the voice of the one she had been unable to identify. Fear rippled along her spine when she stepped beyond the treeline of burnt pines and espied the glowing silver figure on A' Chrìon Làraich's ramparts. The demigoddess stamped her feet. Humans were irresponsible and should not have powers.

Leannán redoubled her efforts to counter Sorchae's song and keep the ballistae teams enthralled, but, like Sorchae, she had never tested her abilities to their limit. In the Land of Immensity and on her island, it was a game. There were none who opposed her or knew their lives depended on winning.

Now, Leannán understood she was unprepared to battle the

humans. Even without the witch on the ramparts, their numbers were overwhelming. There were other armies in the forests and in the north. Unaccustomed to making rapid decisions, Leannán's dilemma momentarily paralysed her. A' Chrìon Làraich's ballistae teams were released.

The squeal of skeins tightened, the crack of bolts released, and the shouts of incomprehensible pain from her army jerked Leannán from her indecision and replaced it with anger. Leannán's wrath at her mother, Áine, burned bright. *The narcissistic bitseach wants me to fail. She sent me unwarned and unprepared. Why? What is Sidheag to her? She is my daughter, not hers.*

Unwilling to admit defeat, Leannán gathered her remaining army and flung it at A' Chrìon Làraich's walls. Yet not before a terrible thought entered her mind: *Am I Sidheag's mother?*

CHAPTER 24

The Sleagh & Dùn Brion

It was a humble farm labourer's home, but it was dry and with minor maintenance resisted the elements. Eventually, the father hoped to own a farmholding. Until then, he and his two older sons took any work that was available. An old, worn pelt covered the entranceway, but it was a poor defence against the winter winds, rain, and snow, and flapped constantly in storms. Thus, the family huddled together around the roundhouse's firepit.

A sharp-eyed Dolidh thought it odd that a section of the hide appeared to move with intent. Squinting in the half-light of the fire and rushlights, she stared at the doorway. Her eyes widened when the tip of a large wet snout poked its way through, followed by a massive, brutish head.

She opened her mouth to scream a warning, but in the beat of a drum the Hound was inside the home. There were no weapons in the roundhouse, save chairs and a few farming implements. Dolidh's family recognised the danger and knew who was in their midst. The beast had attacked a score of farmsteads and small settlements, slaughtered the people, and raped the young women.

The Hound's lips retracted in a terrifying grin to reveal a mouth with too many incisors. When he breathed, the small roundhouse filled with the stink of rotting flesh from his recent victims. He snorted at the folly of their futile attempts to defend themselves and wondered if he should bark.

His control of his talent had improved substantially since his first kill. The Hound shook his head. There were only ten humans in the home, and half of them were young. *It's disappointing, but I suppose they'll do as a snack.* He opened his mouth and growled.

Everyone shrieked, except Dolidh She shouted one word, "Brianag!"

***

The shimmering green figure who appeared between the Hound and his victims elicited a deep rumbling growl from the beast and a loud cheer from Dolidh. It was a small home. The doorway was too narrow to offer the option of a fast escape, and besides, the Hound was between it and Dolidh's family. Significant losses were inevitable and Brianag would not risk her friend. *We'll just have to wait the bastard out.*

Predator and killer locked eyes, sizing each other up. The "getting to know you" phase ended when Brianag lashed out and slashed long cuts across the Cú Sídhe's muzzle. Her attack elicited the response she wanted… apart from the cheering of Dolidh, her parents, and siblings. Surprised, outraged, and distracted, the Hound retreated several steps. In a few breaths, Brianag created her illusion and concealed Dolidh's family.

Dolidh jumped up and down with relief and excitement, and soon her family joined in the celebrations. Brianag hissed, "Quiet!" and bared her needle teeth. Even Dolidh fell silent. "You are far from being safe. The Cú Sídhe is not stupid, and I cannot fight him without losing some of you.

"Your home gives me little room to manoeuvre, but if you remain silent, he cannot see the 'real' you and cannot hurt you." Dolidh's newborn sister, ignoring Brianag's order, began to gurgle. A stern, black-eyed look from Brianag and the mother swiftly popped a long nipple into the child's mouth.

"If the Hound barks three times without pausing, you will die… and likely so will I," said Brianag.

The father stepped forward. Ignoring Brianag's hostile look, he said, "Use me as a distraction to get my family to safety." Murmurs of "No!" rippled through the family. Dolidh looked hard at Brianag, and her eyes said, *Don't.*

If I can change then why not him? Brianag thought about smiling but ruled that out. An open maw filled with her teeth and the screaming would restart. She dipped her head and allowed her eyes to return to their natural green. "Thank you. I will keep your brave offer in mind, but I think it must be all or none of us."

***

The Hound, smarting from the parallel cuts to his face, prowled the roundhouse's inner wall. Occasionally, his paws lashed at the family, but soon he realised they were an illusion. "*Cailleach*—witch!" he growled. Still, he was cautious… and impressed. He had never witnessed Leannán maintaining a mirage while simultaneously hiding a group of people. Hence, he chose prudence. *Do I want to tangle with a formidable sorceress? What are the limits to her powers? Is she immune to my bark?* The Hound continued to prowl, sniff, and scratch at the deception.

Dolidh tugged at Brianag's sleeve. When she looked down, the child smiled and whispered, "Thanks, Brianag. You didn't have to come for me."

"Of course I did, Dolidh. As I told Luag, I have too few friends to lose any. You are my first friend and are under my protection… as are your family."

"Can you make us disappear and reappear somewhere else, like you do for yourself?"

"Honestly, I don't know. I can transport myself mostly anywhere, and I have done it with two others, but I've never tried with ten. I don't know what would happen to you if I lost strength or where you would end up." Brianag twisted her fingers in frustration. Playing with her gifts was fun to annoy the Aes Sídhe, but not when lives were at stake.

"Let us talk, witch." This time, the human form of the Cú Sídhe spoke. His voice was deep and persuasive and Brianag admitted he would have been rather handsome before her talons spoilt his perfection. She wondered if her cuts would ever heal. "I see you have an affection for this family. Agree to stay out of my way, and I give you my word you may take them wherever you want, safely. It is a fair offer. I am not usually so generous."

Another tug on her sleeve distracted Brianag. Dolidh held Brianag's gaze and shook her head. "He's lying. You can't trust him, Brianag. He'll just kill us another time when you're not around."

"I know, Dolidh." Brianag inhaled and exhaled several times to calm herself down. She smiled at her friend. "Signal your family to make themselves as small and tightly packed as they can... quietly. I am going to try something."

"My offer will not stand forever, witch. What is your answer?"

"I am not a cailleach. I am Brianag, the creation of Sidheag. I am sure you have heard of her. Leannán, your mistress, claims to be her mother. You are not stupid, Hound. Do you want to tangle with one whom the Aes Sídhe fear?"

"You're bluffing," said the Hound, as Brianag's shimmering figure with obsidian eyes, green talons, and curling sigils stood before him. When she opened her mouth, he saw a maw filled with needle teeth. Instinct told him his life had become much more complicated. His preference for tasting his prey's fear before eating and raping them might be limited. There was no satisfaction from killing from a distance. Still, it was tantalising to be both prey and hunter. This was a true test of his skills.

"I have a counteroffer, Cú Sídhe. Leave this land and my friends. Do this and I will not hunt you until the festival of Bealtaine has passed."

"You know my talent; you cannot harm me," retorted the Hound.

"Can you perform your gift with your throat ripped out? How will you speak? I am faster than you and I can hurt you." Brianag chuckled, and the Hound shivered. "Your muzzle still bleeds. The wound will weep and fester until you die."

"Bitseach! My race is older than the Tuatha Dé and has vanquished beings and tribes greater than you."

"And yet you are alone. Where are the others? Where are your armies?" taunted Brianag. "You are outnumbered in this land."

"Humans?" scoffed the Hound.

"Not just humans, although they number in their tens of thousands and defeated the Tuatha Dé because of it. My ma is A 'Bhanrigh Fuil, and she is much older than you." The Hound paced to and fro. Brianag sensed his agitation and looked inward to steady her pulse. Wagering with her friends' lives left a sour taste in her mouth.

"Well, Hound. Do we have an agreement?"

There was no answer and Brianag did not expect any. However, the Hound was distracted by having to think rather than rely on instinct. She hoped she had enough time and strength to take advantage of this. The illusion dissipated; the Hound changed to his beast when he saw the family. Yet he only spotted them for a few moments before they were gone. Outwitted, he howled in frustration… but only once.

∗∗∗

Cassán knew an unhappy population who perceived the nobility as weak and unable to protect them was fertile ground for malcontents to foment rebellion. Hence, the discussion between Cassán, Eimhir, and their chieftains in Dùn Brion's Great Hall focused on the rising civilian death toll. Swords were drawn and spears hefted when Dolidh and her family appeared amid the meeting.

A small voice from the centre of the group spoke. "I am Dolidh, a friend of Brianag Nic Brion, and this is my family. We wish you no harm"—Dolidh giggled—"You have all the weapons." The atmosphere in the chamber warmed a little. "Also, I think Brianag would not be pleased if you harmed us. Moments ago, she rescued us from the Cú Sídhe." Dolidh smirked mischievously. "I think you are well aware of her tendency to get angry."

Cassán laughed, smiled at Eimhir, and bellowed, "Set a table with food and drinks for our guests. They are the first to survive the attentions of the Cú Sídhe and are exhausted after their experience. Also, find them warm chambers where they can rest. They will be my guests in Dùn Brion until they wish to leave." He looked at Dolidh. "Perhaps you would join Eimhir and me at the high table and tell me how you know my sister."

Dolidh giggled, stepped forward, and curtsied. "She and I are old friends." She pointed to a spot behind the king. "However, she stands behind you and can tell you herself."

Once more, swords and spears appeared as Brianag stepped between Cassán's and Eimhir's thrones. Cassán sighed. "Put your weapons away. Given how many she slaughtered to save *your* families in the forest, I suspect my sister would not break a sweat to send you to Mag Mell. She is my guest, and according to our laws and traditions, she is under my protection. Treat her with respect or face me."

"Thank you, brother… and sister," said Brianag, and then braced herself to receive an enthusiastic hug from Dolidh.

"Perhaps she's mellowing," whispered Cassán to Eimhir. Brianag's wolfish bark disputed that.

Eimhir touched Cassán's arm and whispered in his ear. He nodded and addressed Dolidh. "Perhaps you would accompany me, my queen, your friend Brianag, and a few others to another chamber, where we can eat, drink, and talk. I think your presence would be extremely helpful in keeping the adults harmonious."

Cassán stood and announced, "This meeting is adjourned for the rest of you. Enjoy Dùn Brion's hospitality. We will break fast together on the next sunrise."

＊＊＊

The gathering, in one of the dùn's more intimate rooms, ensured none of those present could avoid eye contact or miss the body language of the others. Of those present, only Dolidh, who sat next to Brianag, and

186

Cassán's shield-man appeared at ease, possibly in expectation of the the-atre soon to commence.

The oak table was rectangular, which instantly divided the small group into two sides. Dolidh, inquisitive and observant as always, asked, "Are round tables banned in forts? They would seem friendlier to me."

Cassán smiled at Dolidh. The emotion was honest, not patronis-ing, unlike how adults often address young children. "I think it would be a wise decision to appoint you to my *Àrd Comhairle*—High Council, Dolidh. However, I will delay that until you are older and have enjoyed your youth. In the meantime, I will take your advice and have the dùn's carpenters fashion a circular table."

A whispered, "Stop procrastinating. Apologise!" from Eimhir made Cassán flinch.

He looked at Brianag, took a deep breath, and released it slowly be-fore speaking. "The last time we met, my words to you and Neamhain were intemperate and boorish." Brianag flinched at Neamhain's name. Her eyes glittered and her talons clicked. "For that I apologise. My only excuse is that I worry about my people, but that doesn't justify being ignorant and rude."

Another inhalation followed, and it was clear that Cassán struggled with what he was about to say. "I, Dùn Brion, and the Na Mèadaidh need your help to fight the Cú Sídhe. He has slaughtered hundreds and raped many young women. My warriors can track him and mea-sure the death he brings, but we have nothing to stop him or slow him down. Furthermore, his appetite grows, and he targets ever larger communities."

He looked at Dolidh, smiled, and coughed. "I am very glad to see that you have rescued one family from the Hound's clutches. Brianag, if need be, I will abdicate the throne of the Na Mèadaidh. You are from Brion's bloodline and, with your talents, are better placed to protect the people than me."

Gasps of "No" escaped from Eimhir and Cassán's shield-man.

Both knew of Cassán's apology; neither thought he would abdicate.

"Queen Brianag has a certain ring to it, don't you think, Dolidh? The Aes Sídhe would be furious, and what would my ma and grandma think of their errant daughter and granddaughter's rise to the nobility?"

A tug on her sleeve caused Brianag to lower her ear to Dolidh. The girl whispered, "Be nice." Brianag smiled and her eyes regained their natural hue.

"They would ask if I had taken leave of my senses to even to contemplate such a status… unless it was to tease you, brother. And they would be right. I don't know what I am, but I am certain I am not a queen. I am much too selfish and quick-tempered for that honour." She looked at Dolidh. "This child is my conscience, and I have much to learn from her."

Brianag looked at Cassán and Eimhir. "I apologise for my behaviour. Indeed, I have no intention, and never had any, of claiming the throne of the Na Mèadaidh. Neither does Sorchae. Indeed, you will do me a service by not mentioning it to her. She would be infuriated at me for suggesting it.

"I was furious at Neamhain for leaving me behind and it was easy to direct my ire at you. However, it was misdirected, and I was being self-centred. Neamhain had to unravel a mystery, and this time, I could not go with her." Brianag choked, and an emerald tear fell into her cup. "I pray she is well." A small hand slipped into Brianag's.

It seemed an eternity of silent contemplation passed before Dolidh said, "I'm starving. I missed out on the food with my family when we came to this room." She looked at Cassán expectantly, and he roared with laughter.

"I apologise, Dolidh. Would you prefer to eat with your family or stay with us?"

"Brianag is my family, and since she is your sister, that makes you and Eimhir family, too. I'd like to eat here, please."

Cassán bent towards his shield-man. "Can you organise food for us and have the servants stoke the fire? Then come back. We have much to discuss."

***

"I hate to broach the subject…" Cassán hesitated as Brianag tensed. "I remember you saying that Neamhain knew of a way to stop the Cú Sídhe. Was that part of her quest?"

Brianag dipped her head and attempted to control her roiling emotions. On the cusp of desperation, she felt Dolidh slip a hand into hers. "It is all right to cry when you miss someone you love, Brianag. I do it when I miss you."

"Aww shite!" said Eimhir and ran to embrace Brianag and Dolidh. Soon, the oak table was saturated with tears; the men looked embarrassed and wondered what the correct response should be. They decided to keep their mouths firmly shut.

Brianag sniffed, wiped tears from her eyes, and said, "I left some friends behind in Loch nan Clàr. I will return shortly." It took her less time to arrive back than to make the declaration. Accompanying her were a nonplussed Luag and Malmhìn.

"The Hag's hairy arse, Brianag. My belly cannot handle this form of travel. And you can't expect to drag us with you whenever and wherever you want. I… we need boundaries."

"Look around, eejit," hissed Malmhìn.

A quick survey of who was in the room elicited a moan of "No!" from Luag, followed by a deep bow and apology to Cassán and Eimhir. The glare to Brianag said, "We'll talk about this later." At this, the room dissolved into rolling peals of laughter. Sadly, the meeting marked the last time laughter was heard freely among the Na Mèadaidh.

***

Cassán coughed to bring some order to the gathering and to approach the topic he had previously started. "We need to form a strategy to combat the Hound. It is unlikely we can kill the monster, but from Dolidh's description of what transpired in her home, Brianag hurt him and made him bleed. That gives me hope he is vulnerable." Cassán looked at Brianag. "Do you think Neamhain will return, and if so, when? What can we do in the meantime?"

Those present flinched at the cracking sound when Brianag gripped the table's edge. Emerald talons dug into the oak and splinters fell to the floor. This time Luag enfolded her hand in his. "You have a bigger heart than you imagined, Brianag, but the consequence of that is that you hurt much more when the ones you love suffer or are in danger," whispered Luag.

She looked at Luag and squeezed his hand. "I am more volatile and vulnerable with a heart. Whether that is better for me, or the ones I care for, is unproven." As she stood, Brianag's eyes regained their natural green colour, and her talons retracted. The tension in the chamber diminished when she smiled at Cassán and said, "If you permit, I will stand. It is a habit from my time with the Aes Sídhe, which stubbornly resists change." Cassán inclined his head.

"Truthfully, without Neamhain, I do not know how we can stop or even slow down the Hound." The statement caused a ripple of consternation while she paused to sip spring water. "However, Neamhain's leaving had little to do with you. Yes, she went in search of a weapon to fight the Cú Sídhe, but she has talked about visions and an ancient prophecy of which she is part. Neamhain is on a journey as much as I am."

"Have you any idea when she will return or, indeed, if she will return?" asked Cassán.

"I am convinced she will come back to us, but I do not know when." Brianag took a deep breath before speaking again. "As Dolidh described, I was able to hurt the Hound, but I took him by surprise. That will not happen again. We cannot underestimate him. He is a clever beast and a superb hunter. Also, so far, I cannot infiltrate his mind. That is not surprising since his race pre-dates the Tuatha Dé, but it means I cannot foresee his next attack."

"Is there anything we can do?" There was an undertone of

desperation in Cassán's voice.

"The season makes hunting easier for the Hound. In the winter, the people huddle together to keep warm. Reduce his prey. He can devastate thousands but prefers to savour the terror he creates. Genocide deprives him of that pleasure. Send riders out to keep a watch on the Hound and tell the people as far as possible to stay in small, scattered groups.

"The Cú Sídhe is addicted to flesh and violating young men and women. He has a ravenous appetite for both, which will only increase. In the Mounds of the Aes Sídhe, he was forbidden to hunt for aeons. Here, he has a feast laid before him every sunrise."

"I had comrades who fought Sidheag and her Brood at the Battle of Cùil Daothail," said Cassán's shield-man. "Gossip has it that the Sídhe, Mongfhionn, designed a sigil that protected against the Brood's song. Each warrior painted it on his or her forehead. Can you devise something similar?"

"Mongfhionn is my grandma," said Brianag. Eyes lit up around the table until she shook her head. "Only a sídhe can do that, which means Neamhain or my grandma. I will ask Mongfhionn. However, I suspect that a sigil to protect against Sidheag's Brood is a simpler task than against one of the ancient races."

"We will do what we can, but I am resigned to losing a lot of people until Neamhain returns," said Cassán.

"I will patrol alongside your riders—in my wolf form." Brianag chuckled. "Please tell your warriors I am not to be hunted. My previous death was a useful tactic but bloody painful." Cassán smiled and dipped his head. "The Cú Sídhe did not know what to make of me or my pedigree. That could be an advantage and may make him more cautious."

"I will be going where Brianag goes," said Luag. Brianag's protest got no further than a thought when he added, "There will be no objections."

"I'm going, too," said Malmhìn. This time both Brianag and Luag opened their mouths, but Malmhìn's stare stemmed their words.

"You should also take a cohort of Eimhir's warriors," said Cassán, to Eimhir's surprise and agreement.

"You mean her spies and assassins." Brianag chuckled. "Do you not trust me, brother?" Brianag's attempted pout fooled no one.

"They're the stealthiest among our warriors," growled Cassán.

Brianag, Luag, and Malmhìn discussed the offer for a few moments before Brianag turned to Cassán. "We agree to your generous offer. Luag says that they will make excellent decoys." Silence fell as the others pondered how serious Brianag was.

CHAPTER 25

A' Chrìon Làraich

Sorchae looked along A' Chrìon Làraich's walls and sighed. "If I had a wish, it would be for a thousand-man shield-wall. I don't care how huge the tuilithe are. Let them try to get past that."

"It is not in the Forest People's culture, Sorchae. The forest is our strength. We fight in the trees with clubs and spears. Even your Ravens don't use a shield-wall. They prefer speed, spears, and skirmish lines. In this region, only Cassán trains his warriors in that formation, and it is because of his father's heritage," responded Cè.

Sorchae pointed to the horde about to crest the first line of ditches and berms. "How's that working out?" She turned and gestured towards a treeline of charred, smoking forest. "I see no trees to give cover or advantage." Finally, she pointed to A' Chrìon Làraich's walls and broch. "If trees are your strength, why didn't you return this land to the forest? Instead, you kept a stronghold built of stone. I think your father, Drostan, knew it was time to change or die."

"Have you any suggestions?" Seonag's tone was dry. Sorchae's youth and assured demeanour irritated the more mature woman. That she enjoyed Sorchae's body troubled Seonag. The Queen of the Ravens had not donned her armour and looked like a sensuous, twinkling star. *Get a grip on yourself, Seonag.* A cough from Cè drew a reluctant "Sorry," from his sister. Sorchae's song had saved the fort from disaster and slaughter. Seonag looked at Cè and Sorchae. "We need a solution fast."

"We cannot fight these giants one on one. That's a reckless and short path to Mag Mell," said Cè.

"Do we have to?" asked Sorchae. "We outnumber the bastards three to one." She looked at Seonag. "May I?" Seonag dipped her head. Arms uplifted; another song flowed from Sorchae's lips. This time, it carried a simple command to the defenders: "Fight in threes." Around the walls, men and women shuffled into small, well-armed groups.

Seonag smiled and touched Sorchae's arm. It was a first step to friendship between a lonely queen and a Hand of the Goddess new to her role. "Thank you. I apologise for forcing you to use your gifts so soon after you received them. Not acknowledging their value was thoughtless of me."

Sorchae shrugged. "I don't want anyone who doesn't get angry in the heat of battle at my side. The Goddess used you to give me a deserved kick in the arse."

The de facto queen of the Forest People watched as Sorchae sorted her weapons, laying them within an arm's reach against the wall. Perturbed, she asked, "Shouldn't you put your armour on? You look very… exposed." It was a crisp night, and Seonag's words carried along the wall. Instantly, there were groans of, "Please, no," from the warriors—both male and female.

Sorchae laughed and shook her head. "The enemy is already at the outer ditches. I don't think I have enough time to don my armour." She flexed and stretched well-defined muscles. Silver rivers awoke from their slumber and cascaded around her body. She grinned and, with a wink at Seonag, directed attention to her designs. "I am well-enough armoured."

I chose you and made you special, Sorchae Ní Íar, not immortal. Do not be a stupid bitseach.

"Yes, Goddess," muttered a chastised Hand.

***

From beginning to end, the stench of battle is unmistakable and unavoidable—and rightly so. Usually, loosened bowels and bladders begin the olfactory assault. However, Leannán's brutes had no comprehension of why they should fear the berms and ditches and did not understand what lay beyond the earthworks. Leannán's insistent voice in their heads commanded them to go forward and kill.

Cè watched the attackers surmount the forward berms of the perimeter ditches. "Bastards!" he growled as he saw the giants rip out the earthworks' sharpened stakes. Some gripped them to use as better clubs; others pulled them from the earth and hurled them at the walls. The tactic was unexpected. Cries along the defences demonstrated its success.

"Do they not feel pain?" asked Seonag as she watched a wave of the enemy tumble into the ditch. At a minimum, injuries from the sharpened stakes would have caused a "normal" army's attack to stall. The ogres shrugged off hurt and most were little more than inconvenienced by the pales. "*Ignite the ditch!*" bellowed Seonag. Pitch- and oil-soaked straw covered the bottom of the trench. She watched hundreds of smoking arrows arc into the air and wished she had many more archers. Soon, the channel filled with choking smoke and fire.

Screams and the awful smell of burning flesh rose to clog the defenders' ears and noses. "Why don't they stop, Ardghal?" asked Sorchae. She grimaced as ravenous fires devoured flesh, turning it into ash and cinders. The sounds of choking and coughing rose as the monsters tried to clear their lungs. It was the first sign of humanity from the monsters. Still, they did not stop. Any who fell became stepping stones and bridges.

"They have no fear or respect for their bodies," said Ardghal. "They are below animals, for they have no pack, partners, or friends." He grasped Sorchae's shoulders and spun her to fasten his eyes on hers. "I am your shield-man, my queen, appointed by Mòrag to protect you." He looked at Beira, and she nodded. "You will allow Beira and me to do our jobs. You are a queen, and it is our duty to die for you, if needed. Agreed?"

The muted "Yes," from Sorchae held tears in its tone. Further along the rampart, Cè turned to Seonag. "You heard the conversation?"

Seonag inclined her head. "I have not been a good brother to you, Seonag, and for that I am sorry. However, I will be the best shield-man that ever stood with you." He looked around. "Where's Earc? He should be at your side, too."

"The bastard is nowhere to be seen."

"Coward," spat Cè. He inspected the warriors nearby and spotted a woman whose limbs were striped with scars. He smiled at the veteran, and she scowled back. "She'll do. If she survives the battle, you can officially promote her. Seonag nodded and turned away so Cè would not see her tears. *Why does facing death illuminate character? Could I have rescued Fionn rather than sought his end?*

Then the screaming erupted, rising to a level best suited to the Otherworld.

✳✳✳

Sorchae ducked as another massive rock—or was it frozen dirt?—crashed onto the ramparts. Leannán's army did not need long-range missile throwers. In their arms, they had the strength to throw boulders. The Hand flinched at the sound of massive clubs hammering against A' Chrìon Làraich's oak gates. "They won't last much longer."

Seonag looked along the walkway and concurred. Apart from the gates and their stone supporting piers, several sections of the walls were little more than rubble. The defences were solidly built, but their designer never anticipated such an enemy.

A' Chrìon Làraich's defenders continued to empty hundreds of cauldrons filled with boiling oil, pitch, water, and glowing cinders from the braziers. But the ogres kept on attacking. Few of Seonag's and Sorchae's warriors fell. Still, that piece of fortune was because they had yet to stand toe to toe with the monsters. Seonag turned and looked at Sorchae. Her demeanour was one of helplessness and anger.

"They will break through the outer defences soon. Before they reach our last ramparts, they will face the deep pits, final perimeter ditch, fire, and our war hounds." Seonag waved at the destruction.

"So far, we have killed or badly injured five hundred. The same number died in the flames in the forest. That leaves about two thousand. I cannot envisage how our final defensive line will stop these beasts. They will massacre my people and warriors. My broch can hold a few hundred at the most and there's no guarantee it will stand."

Seonag looked desperately at Ardghal, Beira, Cè, and Sorchae. "What can we do? What are we missing? They must have a weakness. I am open to suggestions."

"We should abandon the walls. Fighting on the battlements will not save the people. Use the dogs as a distraction and fight alongside them," said Cè.

"I hope their handlers are good and constantly remind them who is the enemy," chuffed a sceptical Ardghal.

"What do you think, Sorchae?" asked Seonag.

"Cè's plan is good but it will not change the outcome. Leannán's ogres will kill our warriors and breach the defences. The surviving remnant will slaughter the civilians. If we arm the people, then some may survive. They may even endure until more of your warriors arrive."

"I was told you were an optimist," growled Cè.

Sorchae chuckled. She had grown to like Cè. Then she said, "The source of the brutes' power is Leannán."

"Are you suggesting we attack and kill Leannán?" asked Seonag, smiling for the first time. "That would be better than certain death in A' Chrìon Làraich, although the civilians would be left defenceless."

The Hand shook her head. "Not 'we' just me. Killing the bitseach would be the best outcome. However, I will settle for pushing her far enough away from her army until she loses control and her enchantment cracks." Sorchae pointed towards a lone figure at the smouldering treeline. "Leannán controls her army from the edge of the forest. It must be an immense strain and drain on her powers, especially if she has also enthralled a portion of Fionn's army. If I can threaten and push her back even a few hundred paces, I might break or weaken her hold on the giants and tilt the balance of the battle in our favour."

"It would be folly to attempt this alone, Sorchae." In the background Ardghal and Beira signalled their agreement with Seonag. "You must take a warband with you. How many warriors will you need?" asked Seonag. Her tone brooked no disagreement.

"Two hundred Ravens. I don't expect Leannán has another army, but she'd be stupid not to have bodyguards. My strategy is to get me close enough to Leannán, not to fight her or her guards—at least not with normal weapons." Sorchae's brow furrowed. "This is new to me, but if I can break her enthrallment with my song, then A' Chrìon Làraich might have a chance."

"I'm going with you," said Ardghal.

Sorchae shook her head. "Seonag will need all the veteran warriors she can get."

Ardghal bowed. "My queen, it was not a suggestion or request. I am going with you."

"So am I," said Beira. "There's no way I am letting Ardghal out of my sight again."

CHAPTER 26

At the riverside defences, the fighting was less frenzied. Leannán's giants appeared reticent to test the icy surface. Perhaps, they feared drowning as much as burning. The few who stepped onto the thin, frozen crust crashed through into the frigid waters.

It was not a deep river, but its undercurrents could knock the burliest off their feet. Thus, the waterway proved stronger than Leannán's ogres and a better defence than A' Chrìon Làraich's walls. Many were dragged downstream, never to resurface. Only sporadic hulks emerged on the river's nearside bank and were largely ignored by the defenders.

***

The child, a girl by her long flaxen hair and berry-stained léine, could not have been older than six. She looked about the same age as the young man's sister. *Where the Hag are her mother and father?* He cursed them both. Barefoot and gripping a straw doll, she ran screaming between the army's barracks. *Keep quiet, child. Please keep quiet and they might ignore you.* His hopes were dashed when a lumbering brute spotted the girl. The ogre roared, and the child shrieked, "Ma! Where are you?"

Many of the Forest People looked disdainfully upon armour, but the young man was wise enough to know he needed every advantage he could get. Thus, he had gratefully accepted the boiled leather cuirass, with iron scales sandwiched between its layers, his mother bought him.

However, deeming it insufficient, he used savings to purchase a sleeveless, thigh-length coat of mail.

When he gripped his spear, slipped his arm through his shield's straps, and grasped its wooden handle his intentions were obvious. "Don't do it, lad," said the flinty-eyed veteran beside him. For the first time, he saw more than an indulged brat who did not deserve his rank and would get men killed. "She'll be dead before you reach her, and you'll be dead moments later."

"You're probably right, but I won't let her die thinking no one cared." He smiled and roared, "Open the small gate!" In his favour, he had practically lived in his armour since the day he bought it, and his muscles had grown to meet the challenge of its extra weight. Thus, when he ran, he was not out of breath, and that pleased him.

The two gnarly veterans who had stood on either side of the young man looked at each other and sighed. "He's an eejit and a piss-poor warrior, but the Hag's bony arse, we can't let him show us up. He'll end up as a *ceannard a' mìle*—leader of a thousand—if he rescues the child." As they passed the gate guard, the elder of the two said, "Close the gate after us and reinforce it. I doubt we'll be back."

***

The girl saw the young man run towards her. She smiled at her rescuer with child-like trust. He screamed and shouted at the giant who stood before her with his club raised. When he got within a spear's length of the creature, the warrior yelled, "Get away from her!" and stabbed at a thigh wider than an oak tree's trunk.

The ogre appeared caught between two minds. Who was its priority? The tiny human who was crying, or the warrior who stabbed him. It looked at the child with eyes devoid of compassion, and the huge club descended. She did not have the chance to scream one last time. Mercifully, in an instant, the little girl's head was little more than pulp. By the time her body fell and bled out on the snow, the bean-sìth had already guided her to *Tìr nan Òg*—the Land of Youth.

"No!" roared the young man and attacked the brute.

If he had run away, the girl, free of pain and happy in Tìr nan Òg, would still have claimed him as her hero. She had no wish to see him harmed. Reaching out a hand, she shouted, "No!" as loud as she could. *He cannot hear you or feel your touch, child. Come with me and explore your new home.* The Goddess took the girl's hand and guided her towards the sounds of children playing. Yet before she entered the garden, the child turned around. One last tear rolled down her cheek.

The young warrior looked at the perfectly formed snowflake on his hand, looked upwards, and said, "Thanks." Then, gripping his spear firmly, he renewed his attack on the ogre. The brute had strength and speed on its side. The young man's only advantages were courage and nimbleness. He struck and ran, struck and ran. He had watched mounted warriors use the tactic. Yet his efforts garnered scant reward. The beast's skin was tougher than an animal's hide. He was a gnat attacking a cow.

"Push the bastard towards the man-trap," roared the veteran as he and his comrade joined the young man. He pointed to a deep, rectangular hole ten paces beyond them. The snare was planted with fire-hardened stakes. "It's our only hope of disabling it." The three separated and attacked from different angles.

The ogre roared, although it seemed more annoyed than concerned and certainly not afraid. Its strength remained undiminished as three spears jabbed and slashed its flesh. Still, blood streamed from a hundred cuts, and the strategy appeared to work as it retreated and came closer to the pit's edge.

Was it luck, or did Serendipity take a hand? Shouting curses at the ogre, the young man thrust forward one more time with the spear's leaf-shaped iron blade. The brute roared, this time in genuine pain and surprise. With one hand, it grabbed its crotch. The spear had pierced the hulk's most vulnerable spot, leaving its balls in the snow before him. Instinctively, the ogre swung the club in its free hand towards its assailant.

The young man's comrades heard the sickening thud of the club striking flesh and the dull sound of ribs breaking. In the corner of their eyes, they watched him land on the hard, frozen earth. They could not help him. The brute was weakened, perhaps badly wounded, and the advantage was theirs. More stabs with bloody spear tips pushed the brute backwards with increasing speed until, with a bellow of surprise, it tumbled into the pit.

As they looked into the snare, there was only satisfaction in the veterans' eyes as the giant struggled to free himself from the stakes piercing his body. The warriors looked at each other and nodded. They raised their spears and thrust downwards. The ogre roared as the spearheads pierced its eyes. Several twists of the blades destroyed the monster's brain. As they turned away from the pit, the hulk's body refused to accept its death and twitched… but not for long.

The young man had crawled to a nearby boulder and sat with his back to it. Soon the snow covering the rock was stained crimson. Blood dribbled from his mouth, and he breathed harshly. In pain, he asked, "Is it dead?" The veteran nodded, and the young warrior smiled and said, "Good. Thanks."

"Don't worry, Sir, we've seen worse injuries in battle. The druid healers will have you back on your feet in no time," said the senior veteran.

The young man smiled at the respect but shook his head. "There is no return for me. The damage is too great. Move me and I will be dead before we reach the healers' roundhouse." He coughed raggedly, and more blood splattered his chest. "Grant me one request, please." The veteran looked warily at the young man but knew in his heart what his leader would ask—a sharp blade.

As they carried their comrade back to the stronghold, one remarked, "He was a brave warrior."

"It's a pity he had to die for us to recognise that," said the other, blaming the tear that rolled from his eye on a speck of ash.

* * *

The warrior was young enough for the Goddess to allow him to choose between Tir na nÓg and Mag Mell—the Hall of Warriors. He picked the former, hoping he would see her again. As he walked towards a gate that shimmered like a tree after an ice rainstorm, his steps faltered. *Will she remember me? Will she want my company?*

He felt a small hand grip his and looked down. "I've been waiting for you. Come with me and I will show you our home." He smiled and happily walked to where she guided him.

CHAPTER 27

Fifty paces from A' Chrìon Làraich's outer wall, Beira, wrapped in a thick wolf's fur that made her look twice her girth, stopped and looked at Sorchae. Then she eyed Ardghal, shook her head, and muttered, somewhat enviously, "She hasn't even got a single goosebump." Sorchae and the shield-man chuckled.

"This is new to me, too," said Sorchae. "I was never this immodest, even on the hottest days of Southern Gaul. My Cinn Péinteáilte friends, and even my aunt Mòrag, would be shocked. Delighted, but shocked."

As the full moon rose above the horizon, Sorchae bathed in its soft yellow rays and soon her curling designs resembled seams of pale gold. She stretched out her arms and moaned. To those accompanying her, it appeared she was about to orgasm. Her proud, prominent nipples supported their observations.

A cough from Ardghal drew Sorchae reluctantly from her momentary pleasure. "Apologies, I haven't fully uncovered the mysteries of the Goddess's bounty. So far, the evidence points to her having a mischievous, perverse sense of humour… and a dirty mind." Sorchae reconnoitred the landscape before them. "Beira, you know the land. Is there a way to approach the treeline unseen?"

Beira shook her head. "Not fully, although drifts of snow have accentuated the small hills and ridges of what were previously ploughed fields. That's in our favour. We can use that and get to within five hundred paces. However, won't Leannán be able to discern your presence?"

"Probably, but I'm hoping she's focused on controlling her ogres and it lasts until we are in place." Sorchae turned to Ardghal. "Organise our warriors into five groups of forty. One cohort will remain with me, the others will drive Leannán and whoever is with her northwards." She smiled at Beira. "Please take the lead and get us as close to Leannán as possible."

* * *

Seonag and Cè watched the warband disappear into the white landscape. Like a meteor, Sorchae's glimmering sigils marked their progress. "Thank you, Goddess," she muttered. At Cè's raised eyebrow, she said, "Leannán's attack on our western and southern flanks left a gap on the northern side. I must believe that is part of the Goddess's plan."

Loud *barrr ewwws* of the war horns positioned on the outer wall signalled that the giants had breached the battlements. "Order the horns to signal the retreat. Under your command, half of our warriors will man the inner wall along with the civilians of all ages and sexes who can wield a spear or use a sling.

"Supported by the hounds, the remainder will fight between the walls. I will lead those fighters." Something in Cè's eyes disturbed Seonag. "Is that understood?" she asked.

Cè's answer was an unexpected brotherly kiss on the forehead. It was swiftly followed by a fist to his sister's chin. Seonag's head snapped backwards, and she slumped to the snowy walkway. Cè called five burly warriors to his side. "You have fought loyally at my side. These may be my last orders. Give me your oath they will be carried out." The group dipped their heads.

"Convey the queen to the wall and see that she is well. When she awakes, under no circumstances is she to join the battle down here. The future of the Forest People rests in my sister's hands. She must survive this war."

* * *

"Your Ravens are stealthy. I'm impressed," said Beira.

Sorchae dipped her head, accepting the compliment. They had advanced to the treeline undetected and closer than she had hoped for. The Ravens' wings—two groups, each comprising eighty warriors—spread out on either side of her band.

They each divided into two and slithered their way through the snow towards Leannán's position. Each carried a bow, a quiver of arrows, several javelins, and a spear. She wondered, come sunrise, who would feast in Mag Mell and who would break their fast in A' Chrìon Làraich. Sorchae shook her head. *I can't think of that now.*

"Can she see us?" muttered Sorchae. Brianag's abilities allowed her to extend her vision and senses over long distances, but her friend had unique talents. *Can I?* A few tests produced little more than a nosebleed and a headache. That said, her night vision had improved considerably. She spotted Leannán's position. On a still winter's night, the sound of fighting in A' Chrìon Làraich overlaid Leannán's insistent chanting.

"The Hag's arse!" she muttered. "I'd better start before the bitseach enthrals the warriors with me." Sorchae stood, raised her hands, and opened her mouth.

Ardghal bellowed, "Protect the Queen. I'll kill any man or woman who shirks their duty."

"That was motivational," said Beira.

✶✶✶

Leannán shrieked as her ears picked up the opening strains of Sorchae's song. *Who is the bitseach?* She was simultaneously affronted and anxious that anyone would challenge her sorcery.

Battle shouts to her left drew her attention to a band of warriors rising from the snow. Twenty-five volleys of arrows followed in the wake of their taunts and insults. When the arrows' iron barbs thudded into the earth and trees around her, Leannán screamed again. *How dare they attack me?* A score of brutes were commanded to attack the Ravens' warband. Moments later, she detected a subtle adjustment in Sorchae's song.

This time, a group of Ravens on her far left stood with lit arrows. The diversion of their comrades had covered their small fires and the smell of woodsmoke. Showers of arrows struck the trees surrounding Leannán. Those still green with pine needles and cones, and wet with sap, burst into flames.

Attacked on two flanks with fire and slings armed with iron slugs, by Sorchae's remaining Ravens, Leannán became incandescent with rage. Her response was instinctive, and she acted like any being, whether demigod or human, with no battle experience. She panicked. It lasted for only a few breaths but created an opening for Sorchae to force her song through the veils of Leannán's mind.

Veils protect human and demigod minds from invasion, misuse, and destruction. The greater number an attacker can spoil, the weaker the target becomes. Destroy all the curtains and the body dies. Human babies receive three veils from the Goddess to protect their minds and spirits. At puberty and the onset of adolescence, a fragile and turbulent time for young men and women, they are gifted three more. Finally, at eighteen summers, the Goddess gifts humans three more for a total of nine.

In a decision she came to bitterly regret but could not rescind, the Goddess gifted the Tuatha Dé twelve veils and the Womb-Born kings and queens fifteen. Thus, she raised them above all creatures, except a handful of ancient races and, of course, herself. Still, she was wise enough to make only nine of the veils self-healing. After ten, any damage was permanent.

Where are you, bitseach? Inside Leannán's mind was as black as pitch and as foul as a decomposing body. The Ravens' queen's nose crinkled. *Have you never washed?* Sorchae's song transformed into a sword of light in her hand, and she began to slash the first veil.

Leannán was new to massed battles, but she was not a novice in sorcery. She rose to challenge Sorchae, mocking and taunting her and wrapping her in black tendrils of enchantment. *You will soon serve me, bitseach.*

Simultaneously, she directed another score of ogres to confront the new threat on her right.

***

Concerned about Sorchae's health, Ardghal and Beira looked at each other and wondered what to do. They could not see her slash Leannán's third veil, the black tendrils that embraced her, or the evil black liquor that splashed Sorchae's body.

In the human domain, blood dripped from Sorchae's chewed lips, her gums bled, and her teeth ground together. Her nose bled freely, and bloody tears leached from eyes reddened by broken blood vessels. Her body recoiled as if under attack and bruises intermingled with her flowing designs. Yet Sorchae remained defiant and on her feet. She willed the moon to recharge the rapidly diminishing stores of her power.

"The Hag, Ardghal," said Beira. "This is too much for her. She'll kill herself trying to save us."

"We have one option remaining," said Ardghal, and he spoke to the horn blower. The war horn reverberated its call for each of the five warbands to attack Leannán. He grumbled, "Horns are useless for detail. Let's hope our warriors have enough common sense to concentrate on Leannán and avoid the brutes where possible."

Beira nodded. "But what do we do about Sorchae? Her sigils are flickering, not flowing. Surely her strength can't keep up for much longer."

"We'll walk her between us and, if needed, we'll carry her. We can only pray the closer our warriors get to Leannán, the more fearful of the iron in our weapons she becomes. Surely, there's a limit to Leannán's ability to simultaneously control so many and fight Sorchae. Our distraction must divert her from Sorchae."

***

Seonag awoke on A' Chrìon Làraich's walkway to a thumping headache, a foul temper, a freezing arse, and her scarred shield-woman confronting five others. *What was Cè thinking?* She ruefully rubbed her chin and tried to stand. Strong hands on her shoulder made that impossible.

"Cè has taken charge of the warriors below us. He commanded us to ensure you remain on this wall." The band's leader coughed. "If needed, we will chain you to ensure his orders are executed." The tall, barrel-chested veteran's larynx had been crushed by an axe shaft in a battle in his youth. Hence, his voice resembled quern stones grinding grit. Neither his words nor his eyes gave any hint that he and his comrades would deviate from their instructions.

"I can have you executed, very painfully and slowly, for this," said Seonag. The warriors shrugged. *The Hag! They expect death.* What caused the fighters to remain loyal to Cè? *Don't you dare die on me, brother. I need you at my side.* "I will not. Instead, you will join *my* shield-woman. May I please rise? I promise not to contradict my brother's orders or make you break your oath"

A calloused hand, overlaid with scars, gripped Seonag's and pulled her to her feet. Simultaneously, a commotion and loud voices approached. Seonag's newly appointed guards hefted spears and encircled the queen.

"Seonag is a pretender and has no authority. Who can follow a queen weak enough to allow her brother to disobey her commands and punch her to the ground? The Forest People deserve a strong leader, not a mewling princess." Earc's voice rose above the clamour.

"The Hag's tits! We're in the middle of a battle for survival and this arsehole chooses now to challenge me," snarled Seonag.

Earc paused to savour the raucous support from his band of supporters. Most were drunk malcontents, who had been promised gold. Yet he was not blind to the people and army drifting away from the two groups. "Fight me, Seonag Nic Drostan. Or show the tribe you are a coward who has no right to claim the Forest People's throne."

"Orders?" grunted the veteran beside Seonag. "There's only a score of them. We can take care of this." His voice and grunts of "Yes!" gave no indication that the band could not.

Seonag smiled and shook her head. "You will know when to strike." She looked at her shield-woman. "I need a spear." Instantly, a sleagh was slapped into her hand. The queen dipped her head and refused to wince at the sharp pain.

The warrior's lips spread in a toothy grin and said, "Kill him." That it glinted with several gold teeth startled Seonag. Few in the Forest People cared much about their teeth or smile. The small group opened, allowing Seonag to stride forward.

The antagonists were about twenty paces apart. At ten, Seonag hefted the spear into a throwing stance. Relishing the surprised look on Earc's face, she hurled the weapon. It struck him in the chest, erupting from his back in a melange of blood and bone. Nevertheless, it was not an instantly mortal blow. Earc stumbled backwards and slipped on the icy stone, grunting at the jarring pain.

Seonag reached out and felt a second spear slapped into her hand as her protectors stormed past to crush Earc's supporters. She brushed aside Earc's feeble attempts to push her away, knelt on his chest, and grasped her spear in both hands. Her intent was clear. "It seems the treasonous are not clever. A wise leader and experienced warrior would have protected himself with a shield."

"You have no honour, bitseach!" gasped Earc. The first spear in his chest trembled with each forced breath.

"I have no use for honour. I am fighting for my people's survival."

To Earc, the spearhead took an interminable time to descend. He felt the tip tickle his nose for a fraction of a moment before it destroyed the cartilage and plunged through bone into his brain. His body spasmed several times before life finally fled from it and the bean-sìth took his soul to the Otherworld.

Seonag looked around the bloody rampart and heard Earc's band's last pleadings for mercy and dying gasps. "Throw them over the wall. There is no room on my defences for traitors." She raised her spear, turned to face the warriors and people in the courtyard, and shouted,

"The Forest People will be victorious! Fight for your children… fight for your families!"

The roar of defiance from the walls of A' Chrìon Làraich was deafening and became thunderous when one voice rose above all and shouted, "Fight for Seonag, Bhanrìgh of the Forest People!" She would have cried had she not spied a group of ogres converge on Cè.

"No!" she bellowed.

***

Sorchae walked a line between dreams and reality and knew the lack of focus on either was dangerous. She felt Leannán's tendrils suck power from her designs and prayed to the Goddess it would remain a cloudless night. She was dead if just one cloud obscured the moon. Chin set and grinding down on teeth that ached and bled, she drew strength from Ardghal and Beira and forced her legs to walk on.

Leannán's anguish and fear of failure gave Sorchae hope. Slashing the veils—she counted five damaged—split the sorceress's focus and diminished the effectiveness of her enchantments. Sorchae heard Ardghal urge the Ravens forward and sensed Leannán move her brutes to confront them. Battle cries and taunts rang out. Sorchae shed bloody tears for those who fell.

***

Wide-eyed, Leannán thrashed around, looking for relief from the drain on her powers. She had not drunk blood since the beginning of the Battle of A' Chrìon Làraich and had no opportunity to top up her reserves. Inexorably, she felt herself weaken. A slow drip at first, the loss soon became a bubbling spring.

I cannot bind the bitseach, control the battle, and protect myself. Leannán faced her weaknesses and had no answer to the force moving closer… save one. With an eardrum-shattering shriek, Leannán abandoned the brutes who attacked A' Chrìon Làraich. Gathering up her remaining ogres, she fled the battle.

***

With a whimper, Sorchae collapsed into Ardghal's arms. Her breathing slowed and her heartbeat dropped to little more than a flutter. The flowing designs became dormant. All she wanted was to sleep… forever.

As my Hand, your role is to inspire others to greatness and deeds of valour. How often do I need to remind you? You cannot do that if you are in Mag Mell, Sorchae Ni Íar.

The voice was tetchy, but Sorchae sensed tones of anxiety and pride. She smiled, said, "Yes, Goddess," and fell into a deep slumber. Perhaps she would not wake up. "No. I did not say goodbye to my friends," she whispered.

***

Bodies of dogs, men, and ogres littered the freezing slush of blood and snow in A' Chrìon Làraich. Waterfalls of boiling oil, water, and pitch poured from smoke-blackened cauldrons, sloughing skin from broken bodies. There were no more braziers. All had been emptied into the final ditches, setting the pitch-soaked straw alight. Man and brute tumbled screaming into the trenches and man-traps and died. The humans' plight was curtailed quickly because they were more fragile.

Seonag closed her ears to the screaming of mothers and children and stabbed another giant whose huge hands grabbed the stone wall to pull itself over it. Her protectors had learned to stab the brutes' eyes as soon as their heads appeared above the battlements. That the walkway was a frozen river of blood, gore, and corpses testified to how many times they had failed. *There are so many heroes. How will I remember them?*

Once again, Seonag looked over the wall, searching for her brother. Once again, she was disappointed. In frustration, she screamed, "Sorchae!" Was the Bhanrigh of the Ravens dead? Had she failed in her mission? Was A' Chrìon Làraich doomed? Despair swept over Seonag, numbing her mind. Her body froze.

A rough hand grabbed her shoulders and shook her. Her leading shield-man, in a gruff voice, said, "Fight or die!" Yet the omens said death was to be their fate. She looked behind her and saw fathers and brothers fingering knives. They knew the time approached when they would have to send mothers, daughters, sisters, and wee'uns across the veil. They would not allow them to face Leannán's monsters.

In a voice hoarse from shouting, she rasped, "We will fight." She raised her spear, even though her mind told her she was too tired and should rest. A bit lip flowed blood—this time hers—into her mouth. She bellowed, "Fight!" and the call was taken up around the stronghold.

And then, it stopped. The cacophony of battle ceased and those left alive—a pitiful remnant of the garrison, farmers, artisans, and their families—looked at each other unbelieving and expecting death. Seonag looked across the bloody courtyard and ramparts of A' Chrìon Làraich. Ogres stood motionless, waiting for orders, which never came.

"Kill every last one of the bastards!" she bellowed. "Burn them until only ash remains to dress the fields."

✳✳✳

The tall figure threw back the hood of her crimson cloak, releasing a cascade of waist-length flame-red hair. Natural green eyes and full, deep-pink lips were the perfect complement to the tresses and her smoke-white skin. However, they did not suit Áine, Queen of the Womb-Born's mood. Thus, her eyes glittered obsidian and the lips were thin and shone black. The sound of her teeth grinding over each other silenced the few birds and animals left in this part of the forest.

Initially she was surprised and pleased at Leannán's assault on the stronghold of A' Chrìon Làraich. It was a good strategy, and the moulding of men into mindless brutes was a nice touch. Original, too. Perhaps she should have stepped in and supported her daughter when the one tainted by the Goddess revealed herself. She may have tilted the odds in Leannán's favour. The Hand of the Goddess was new to the role. Hence, she had no understanding of the power she could wield.

Instead, Áine did nothing… except watch the debacle unfold. Her daughter fled, pursued by the humans, and her spell over the brutes attacking Seonag's stronghold broke. They became huge mindless toddlers who stood waiting to be slaughtered. Áine huffed. *My daughter thinks too much of the present and cannot see the long game.* Leannán should have at least given them the mind and instinct of animals. That way, they would have fled, continuing to be a nuisance and to kill. For a sorceress, it was an unforgivable waste.

"It is right she faces the consequences of her actions… alone," muttered Áine. "Victory should have been hers. Now, she will own the defeat and learn from it." Áine smiled. "And I will not be tainted by failure… just like it was with Sidheag."

The spike of pain in her head forced Áine to her knees. She clutched at her breasts, her pulse raced, and her chest heaved. Then it was gone as quickly as it came. Áine's lips thinned into a sneer. "You are weak, Sidheag. You do not have the physical or mental strength to bring me down or destroy me."

That may be true, Mother, but Brianag does. She will come for you.

CHAPTER 28

382 B.C.—Spring—Dùn Brion

Due to Dolidh's status as Brianag's friend, she and her family were frequently invited to share evening meals with Cassán and Eimhir. This delighted Dolidh but embarrassed her parents who held that the low-born should not mix with the nobility. The king and queen perceived their conversations as a means of gaining insights into what the civilian population of Na Mèadaidh considered important issues. Brianag, Luag, and Malmhìn, recently returned after a fruitless half-cycle of the moon chasing the Hound, joined the meal on this occasion.

After a few cups of wine, Dolidh's father volunteered, to the surprise of his hand-fast partner and children, that he had been apprenticed to a local blacksmith in his youth. Blacksmithing was a much sought-after trade. However, he had been easily led and did not complete his training.

Cassán signalled to a servant and whispered a message in her ear. A short time later, a huge man with a ruddy face and massive arm muscles entered the chamber. He wore a leather apron over a naked torso marked with burn scars. His imposing physical traits belied his inward discomfort. The dùn's senior blacksmith bowed deeply. "You sent for me, my king." The man's body language screamed his obvious ill ease in Cassán's presence. His anxiety increased when Cassán indicated a seat.

"Please be seated. I have a request."

"Anything, my king."

Cassán chuckled. "Don't be so eager to please when you have no idea what I may ask. Kings are notoriously capricious." Beads of sweat collected on the blacksmith's brow and began to dribble down his face. The king pointed to Dolidh's father.

"This man has informed us that in his youth he was apprenticed to a blacksmith but never completed his training. It is a valuable trade, and I wish you to assess whether he can complete his apprenticeship under your direction." Stunned, the table fell silent. "I want an honest opinion. If he is not suitable, there will be other opportunities to find productive work for him. Am I understood?"

The man nodded, relieved to be on firmer ground. He pointed to Dolidh's father and said, "Stand." As Dolidh's da rose, the black-smith also signalled to Dolidh's older brothers to rise. Father and sons squirmed under the scrutiny. The blacksmith turned to face Cassán. "We need more blacksmiths in the dùn and to service the settlements. I'll take all three." He grinned. "At least one should survive my training."

The blacksmith turned to the trio, who stood open-mouthed. "Be at the forge at sunrise." Then he chuckled and pointed to the jugs of beer and wine. "Go easy on that for the remainder of the evening and get to bed early. A hot furnace is a place of torture when you're parched and have a thumping headache."

✳✳✳

In the babble of excited conversations, no one saw Dolidh slip from the room. When she returned, she staggered into the chamber, struggling to carry a large, reddish-brown cat in her arms. Still, the cat appeared to welcome the attention and purred loudly—much more loudly than a feral cat.

Shocked, Dolidh's ma rose from her seat and bowed to Cassán. "I apologise, my king. She's a child." To Dolidh, she spoke sternly, "You can't bring a cat in here without the king's permission or when meals are served. It may have fleas or carry disease."

Dolidh took umbrage at her ma's words, hugged the animal tighter, and pouted. "She is a lince, not a cat, because she has spots, and black tips on her ears. She is perfectly healthy and free of sicknesses. Also, she likes me." The lynx purred extra loudly as if to support her new friend.

"How do you know she's a lince, Dolidh?" asked Eimhir.

Dolidh smiled. "Originally, I, too, thought she was a big, friendly cat, but she corrected me. Her friends are nice, too." While, her family attempted, unsuccessfully, to convince a stubborn Dolidh she was dreaming, Brianag examined the cat closely. Hope rose in her breast, but when the cat opened its eyes, they were deep pools of green.

Cassán looked at Brianag with mounting curiosity at her demeanour. "Something is troubling you, sister."

"I think we should investigate Dolidh's new friends before the sun sets."

* * *

No one had comprehended why Cassán's father insisted on preserving the tree when the fort was under construction. Indeed, it seemed as if the dùn was built around the oak. Was he prescient or did he yearn for a glimpse of natural beauty among the stone and iron?

Located at the centre of Dùn Brion's courtyard, the tree's familiarity and longevity also bestowed invisibility. Only the younger children, who loved to climb and swing from its branches, gave it any attention and love. Most thought the oak was a nuisance and should be cut down for firewood. Dùn Brion's grove of druids defended the tree's presence, mainly due to the mistletoe that coexisted with the oak.

The sun drifted towards the horizon as Brianag walked closer. Acorns crunched under her feet, and she saw the oak had a distinctly green sheen. She nudged Luag. "Have you ever seen the tree bloom or throw off acorns?"

"Never. I thought it was dead," replied Luag, suddenly becoming wary. Sensing danger, his hand gripped his sword, and he whirled around.

Brianag tittered. "Do you intend to challenge a tree? Or maybe the *lincean*. You may be outmatched."

The sun set, and the brightest moon seen for generations in the Lowlands rose high in the sky, bathing the stronghold with silvery light. In the moonlight, eleven pairs of luminous eyes sought and caught Brianag's attention.

Their heads swivelled constantly, yet not smoothly, taking in and analysing every element of their surroundings. Every facial aspect—nose, triangular ears, whiskers, and eyes—moved. Their tails were much shorter than those of feral cats, but like with all felines, the appendages spoke a language the lincean understood and responded to. Their movements were languid, but muscles rippled beneath the fur, waiting to be called upon.

A large lynx, with beige-white winter fur and dark brown spots, lay perfectly balanced on a thick lower branch. Neamhain slowly and deliberately licked her paws and pondered why a minor activity gave her such deep pleasure. She purred, loudly. An adjacent cat leaned over and licked her throat and behind her ears. This time the purring took on a distinctly erotic tone, making Brianag feel uncomfortable. It was as if she intruded on a private moment.

Brianag's sharp eyes counted nine more cats, with coats from red to brown and grey. All enjoyed Neamhain's hedonism. The collective sound of purring multiplied and echoed off the courtyard's stone walls. Neamhain looked around with eyes that glowed luminous blue in the moonlight. Ten pairs of green met her gaze. All respected her position, but one pair adored her.

Neamhain rose and arched her back. Front legs reached for the farthest twig sprouting from the branch. Her white belly lowered to the wood while her arse rose. Long, hooked claws pierced the bark and pulled backwards. Ten curling oak ribbons drifted downwards to join the acorns and catkins. The bobbed tail signalled a warning to her watch.

Be wary. Humans are intimidated by the unfamiliar. If approached, retreat, do not confront. The exception is the children. They will want to love you.

Neamhain jumped down from the branch, although that was a

pathetic description of her movements. Rather, she flowed seamlessly from the branch to the courtyard dirt. Alongside, but at her shoulder, was a beautiful silver-grey lynx. Both seemed to become much larger as they approached Brianag and Luag.

"Be careful, Brianag. Even one as insensitive to the spirit world as me can feel the ancient power radiating from these creatures," said Luag.

Brianag nodded but took a step towards the beige-cream cat. She knelt on the frozen dirt so that their eyes would meet and peered into pools of blue. The lynx's vertically elongated pupils dilated in remembrance, and she drew Brianag in.

No! gasped Brianag. *This is your secret.*

Why not? If you can be a wolf, why can't I be a lynx?

The voice in Brianag's head was Neamhain's. The lynx smiled and Brianag felt a compulsion to reach out to stroke and scratch her fur. The other cat moved closer, and a low rumbling growl replaced its purring. *A protector or much more?*

"Neamhain!" cried Brianag, throwing her arms around the lynx's shoulders. Tears cascaded, soaking the cat's fur.

Cassán looked at Eimhir and shook his head. "I thought I was beyond being surprised, but I am speechless." He stepped forward and coughed to get Brianag's and Neamhain's attention. "Perhaps we should continue this reunion inside." He looked at Eimhir. "I hope they can understand me. I doubt we have lynx translators in Dùn Brion."

We understand humans perfectly well, Cassán, said Neamhain. The choice of words caused Cassán to bristle but caught himself before saying more. He pointed to the entrance to the Great Hall. *Thank you. You will soon learn that my choice of words was not an insult.*

✶✶✶

The meeting was held in the smaller chamber where Dolidh and her family had eaten earlier with Cassán and Eimhir. Dolidh had given her parents the slip and sat quietly in the shadows.

"Do they always have confrontational furniture?" asked Caoimhe, looking at the rectangular tables. Neamhain dipped her head. Brianag and Cassán chuckled.

"Dolidh made the same comment recently and I agree. However, in a time of war, it is hard to justify furniture-making over arrows and spears." Cassán coughed and his cheeks flushed. "I mean no insult, but I feel quite awkward conversing with a lynx. My mind does not think as fast as yours. That said, if you wish that we continue as is, I am sure I will learn quickly."

Purring, like sighs, followed a moment of silence. "Oh wow!" exclaimed Dolidh, giving her position away. She watched the lynxes transform into two beautiful young women, neither of whom she had seen before. "Are you goddesses?"

Neamhain laughed. "Not quite, Dolidh. That title is reserved for the Goddess, and she is quite jealous of it."

"Is my lynx like you, too?"

"We do not belong to anyone, Dolidh," said Neamhain a bit more sharply than was necessary.

Upset at Dolidh's embarrassment, Brianag shook her head and chastised her friend. *She is an innocent child, Neamhain, who defended her family from the Cú Sídhe. Her bravery cannot be contested, but more than that, she is my friend. What does she know of gods, demigods, the Aes Sídhe, Ancient and Old Ones… and Abominations?*

Neamhain's hand went to her mouth, chastised. She went to Dolidh and dropped to her knees. "I am so sorry, Dolidh. That was a hateful thing for me to say and I have no excuses. Please forgive me." Neamhain's lip trembled as she wiped Dolidh's tears away with a pale hand. Each of Dolidh's was matched by one of Neamhain's. "May I hug you?" Dolidh nodded.

As the scene progressed, Caoimhe came to Neamhain's side, knelt, and whispered in her ear. Neamhain smiled and dipped her head. A short time later, the chamber door opened, and a tall, red-haired female entered. She looked around the room, smiled when she spotted Dolidh, and gracefully sat beside her.

"I am Íde, Dolidh. We have not been officially introduced." Dolidh's eyes widened as she gazed into Íde's eyes and grasped who she was. "This is a meeting for adults. Wouldn't you rather come with me? We can talk about my people and your family, and I can introduce you to my sisters."

Íde took Dolidh's hand and led her to the doorway. Before exiting she bent down and whispered, "We really love being stroked and cuddled." The beam that Dolidh flashed before exiting the chamber warmed everyone's hearts.

* * *

"I think introductions are needed, and then we can discuss strategies to destroy the Cú Sídhe," said Neamhain. She held Caoimhe's hand. "This is Caoimhe. She is my guide and friend. Caoimhe is the daughter of the Leader of the High Council of Na Daoine Cait—the Cait People. In human terms she has the rank of a princess."

Neamhain saw that her choice of words rankled Cassán. "Please humour me. I will explain. You know me as Neamhain Ni Fearghal of the Aes Sídhe, but that no longer applies. I fulfil an ancient prophecy and am Neamhain, Queen of the Na Daoine Cait." Neamhain nodded to Caoimhe, who instantly became a lynx.

"Unlike my dear friend, Brianag, who is human and can change to a wolf, we are lincean." She pointed to Caoimhe. "This is our natural state, but we can change to a human form. *I* am a cait." Neamhain chuckled. "If we want to be petty, our precise species is lincean."

"Shite!" muttered Luag. The room became silent, digesting the new information. Brianag's stillness had little to do with Neamhain's announcement, but rather her description of Brianag being human. In the depths of her mind, she heard Sidheag's cackling.

"In my experience, a retreat to the mundane can prepare a path to a discussion of more serious matters," said Cassán. "First, should we introduce ourselves—at least to Caoimhe?"

"Everything I know, Caoimhe knows. However, I am sure she would appreciate a personal introduction," said Neamhain, and then she laughed. "We are a very ancient and open race. Only the Goddess's mind is shut to us." She glanced at Brianag and chuckled. "And sometimes, yours.

"Likely the members of our tribe also share our knowledge. It takes quite a bit of getting used to but does promote a high level of honesty among us and our friends."

"That could get embarrassing, quickly," said Luag, looking at Brianag.

"We do have rules and boundaries, Luag." Neamhain smiled and Luag braced himself for the "but." "However, we *are* cats."

"What sleeping accommodation can we make ready for you?" asked Eimhir, picking up Cassán's conversation. "Do you require a special diet? I am sure the kitchen servants can prepare whatever you require."

"Thanks, Eimhir," said Neamhain. "The oak tree in the courtyard is perfect for us. Indeed, Caoimhe and I wondered if it had been planted by Cassán's father in anticipation of our arrival. Imbolg and spring approach, and rain is likely in the Lowlands. Hence, it is curious how the stables were built close to the tree."

Neamhain paused and looked at Caoimhe, who instantly appeared as embarrassed as any cat could. "Aside from that, the Na Daoine Cait are not *trained* for indoor living." Neamhain rubbed her chin. "As for food…"

Caoimhe whispered in Neamhain's ear, and she nodded and laughed. Brianag looked at the pair and was momentarily jealous. *Will I lose my friend?*

"We are carnivorous," continued Neamhain, "so meat is good, although we prefer it bloody. Caoimhe has reminded me of the pink-fleshed fish in your rivers to which we are quite partial." She looked at Brianag. *In answer to your question, Brianag: Never.*

Cassán leaned over and whispered to Brianag, "It is too late to discuss battle tactics, and I believe this more informal conversation is valuable. Perhaps you could you ask your ma to join us at sunrise? I am aware that, like you, she has no need for 'normal' modes of transportation."

＊

It was sunrise and Gràinne's senses tingled as she, Giosail, and Brianag passed the oak tree. The sensation was like how she felt when standing at the borders of the Land of the Cait. However, this time, the intensity of the lincean's scrutiny would have crushed a lesser being. Gràinne smiled at the obvious testing of her abilities, although she was disappointed at the lack of subtlety. She decided to take the bull by the horns.

"I am Gràinne Ni Fearghal, High Queen of the Eastern Tribes, and A 'Bhanrigh Fuil. We both claim ancient origins"—that elicited a rolling growl from the lyncean, but a bark from Neamhain cut off the dissent—"but I respect your lineage as being from a time before mine." Gràinne glanced from face to face, ascertaining and evaluating old identities in new forms. "If we are to fight alongside each other in battle, then we should respect our individual journeys to where we stand on this sunrise."

She scrutinised the oak tree and the luminous eyes that peeked from behind the leaves. Spotting a pair of blue eyes, she smiled. "The shape of your eyes has changed, Neamhain Ni Fearghal, but I hope the one whose mother I share has not." Gràinne pointed to Giosail. "Brianag, Sorchae, and you took an oath to train Giosail. Circumstances may have changed but I have not released you from your vow."

Gràinne stretched out her arms towards Neamhain. "You are a beautiful creature, but I prefer to embrace the Neamhain I know. Come, sister, I have missed you." Heaving a huge sigh of relief when Neamhain took her human form before her, Gràinne threw her arms around her. "Welcome back. I am delighted you found your destiny." Then she whispered, "Your mother and father also await your return."

＊

The room crackled with constrained power as Gràinne rose. "I had a brief conversation with Seonag before arriving here. She will address you at another time but has given me leave to summarise recent events. A half-cycle of the moon ago, Leannán created an army of monstrous creatures and attacked A' Chrìon Làraich.

"Out of six thousand defenders and a similar number of civilians, only one third survived, including Seonag…"

"No!" gasped Brianag. "What of Sorchae?"

"If it were not for Sorchae, A' Chrìon Làraich would lie in ruins. She is drained of strength but recovering."

"Thank the Goddess," said Cassán to a round of agreement.

"Agreed. However, Seonag's brother Cè lies in his cot. His injuries may be mortal, and that may be a blessing. The pitiless savagery of his fight against Leannán's ogres drove him berserk. His mind may never recover."

"We know Sorchae's a great warrior, but how could she prevail against Leannán?" asked Neamhain.

"As I recall, Brianag and you thought Sorchae had a secret to resolve," said Gràinne. "I think you will be surprised when you meet Sorchae, or as she is now known, the Hand of the Goddess. Unlike us, she was not gifted or forced to don her powers but earned them."

"I feel quite inadequate among all these powerful ladies," quipped Luag. Laughter rippled around the chamber.

"I could always bite you and turn you into a wolf," said Brianag, flashing needle-pointed teeth. Luag was torn between being horrified and fascinated by the possibilities. "I was only joking, eejit. I am not sure what I am, but I am certain I'm not the *Dearg Due*."

Gràinne turned to Neamhain. "Cassán and Eimhir await what you have to say." She touched Neamhain's arm. "Be honest but remember the power you hold and the needs of your tribe."

Neamhain sipped a cup of ice-cold spring water and gripped Caoimhe's hand for support. "The Cú Sídhe are a race as old as the Cait

Sìth. Both tribes were violent and merciless hunters of flesh and souls."

"The Hag!" gasped Cassán.

"We are not proud of our history," said Neamhain. Her face coloured at the confession. "In our favour, we realised our path was wrong and unsustainable." Neamhain looked at Caoimhe and she dipped her head. Exposing dirty laundry is never pleasant. "We consulted the Goddess, and she gave us a choice: go to war and annihilate the Cú Sídhe or be destroyed. We agreed to a geis to be ruled by a queen if we failed.

"I am the Queen of the Cait Sìth and the fulfilment of the geis and associated prophecy. I am also a testament to our failure. One Cú Sídhe escaped the war, likely hidden by one or more of the Aes Sídhe. It is he who roams Northern Albu to rape and to consume flesh and souls. He is bound to Leannán. I am here to see the Hound killed and his soul, if he has one, destroyed."

"The Gaels have a talent for assigning blame and seeking retribution," said Cassán. "I apologise to Neamhain for what I may have said in the past. However, I fail to see how any of this can be attributed to Neamhain or the Cait People. How can they be blamed for missing one violent tuilí millennia in the past?" said Cassán.

"The Goddess is a tough negotiator, Cassán, and more fastidious than the Aes Sídhe in ensuring all terms are complied with," said Gràinne.

Cassán dipped his head. "We must focus on how we can work together to kill the last one before he massacres more of my Na Mèadaidh and the Forest People." He looked at Neamhain. "Also, Neamhain and the Cait Sìth deserve to be released from their geis."

"There is a solution," said Neamhain.

"I sense I am not going to like what you will say next," said Cassán.

"You have hidden talents, Cassán." Neamhain considered carefully before speaking again. "We have a special yowl which will consume the Cú Sídhe's bark. It will stop him from barking three times and should give us enough time to strike him down and destroy him."

"That's good," said Cassán. More warily, he asked, "What is the catch?"

"Each time one of us presents herself before the Cú Sídhe to stop his barking, she will die when the yowl ends." Neamhain choked on her words. "Including Caoimhe, ten sisters travelled here with me. Each is a princess of the Cait Sìth. All are prepared to die. If need be, they will be replenished until the Cú Sídhe is destroyed."

Aghast at what he had heard, Cassán stood and scratched his shaven head. "No. I appreciate the offer, but I cannot allow the sacrifice of innocent young women or lincean. It is barbaric, and I am not a tyrant. No. Just no."

"My sisters and I thank you, Cassán. Yet what is the alternative? With Brianag, the Blood Queen, and Sorchae, you may harass and even injure the Cú Sídhe. However, none of you can bind him or serve him up for execution. In the past, we failed to complete our mission. This is the Cait People's price for redemption. Will you cheat the Cait Sìth of our future?"

Cassán slumped back in his chair. "There has to be a way to destroy the Hound without this cost."

"I agree and said the same before the Cait Sìth's Council of Elders. There is none. That said, we should consider a battle plan to minimise the loss of my sisters," said Neamhain.

✳✳✳

Dùn Brion's stone walls had witnessed many unnatural incidents. However, the sight of eleven lincean ascending the steps to the walkway may have been the strangest. As the lincean passed Cassán, they dipped their heads in respect. It was the first phase in a strategy to put the Hound off balance.

The troubled king had not slept; his eyes were red, and dark circles gathered under them. Neamhain's rough tongue licked his hand as she passed. *There is no guilt for you to bear.* Cassán heard the words, but it did not relieve his pain.

The lincean stopped, sat, and purred. Then they looked towards Neamhain. She stared at the red-orange sun rising above the horizon. *My people deserve to be free of the geis laid on them, Goddess. Please help us to hunt and kill the last of the Cú Sídhe.* Neamhain lifted her head and a long yowl flowed from her lips. Instantly, she was joined by ten others.

Brianag grimaced and turned to Luag. "Not one word."

Gràinne shrugged. "They are not the best at harmonising or keeping a melody going, are they? Given they are cats, should we have expected anything different? We should help. If you make the tempo, I will sustain the metre. I doubt Neamhain will be upset. At the worst, it will give the Cú Sídhe something to mull over."

Two dresses fluttered to the stone walkway as Brianag and the Blood Queen raised their hands and began to sing. In A' Chrìon Làraich, Sorchae rose unsteadily from her cot and demanded to be carried to the walls.

✱✱✱

South of the Sleagh, the Hound paused as he approached the settlement. It was located on the eastern bank of the Abhainn Dubh, where the river met the bay of the Linne Foirthe. Due to its favourable position and deep water, it was a major trading centre. Hence, it was one of the more populous centres of the Na Mèadaidh.

At first, the Hound grinned, if a dog could, at the discordant yowling of the cats. The effort made the skin of his muzzle tighten around the ten slashes and he cursed Brianag. When Serendipity commanded a north-easterly wind take the song and carry it to his ears, one more time, the Hound shivered, and long-buried memories of ancient battles and enemies flooded his senses.

He instantly became alert, fearful, and angry. The Old Ones and lincean bitches had made an agreement with the Goddess and brought genocide down on the Cú Sídhe. Still, that was not the main source of the Hound's anger. The yowling broke a curse, a memory spell cast by Áine.

The Hound saw Áine of the Womb-Born removing him from the battle. She took his memory and made him Leannán's pet. He saw that, like him, Leannán was a pawn in Áine's game. The Cú Sídhe's vision of freedom from Leannán's enchantment was an illusion. He had been deceived. Wrath welled up from inside the Hound and he howled. He barked three times and thousands in the trading community died in terror. Afterwards, he cursed his lack of control, the waste of human flesh, and the absence of young women to rape.

He howled again but this time held back his bark. Anxiety gnawed at his mind. The bitseach and spawn of Sidheag had marked him. He did not know if she could kill him, but the memory of the war with the Cait Sìth told him the cats could. A trickle of fear ran along his spine. It was fun hunting and violating the humans, but on this sunrise the game had changed. He was in real peril. *I must find Leannán.*

***

As the performance ended, eleven lincean stood and stretched. All looked to Neamhain. The queen purred, dipped her head, and growled. It was time to hunt. As the watch of lynxes crossed the courtyard moving towards the gateway, Dolidh ran from the stables. She threw her arms around Íde and tearfully begged her friend to be safe.

If the Goddess wills that I should live, Dolidh, then you and I will live happily together for a long time.

"I am going with them," said Brianag. "A wolf may be useful."

Gràinne dipped her head. "I must return to A' Chrìon Làraich and determine what Seonag and Sorchae need. Leannán remains a threat, and she commands Fionn's army. That could be over twenty thousand warriors."

"I have selected a warband of forty riders. They will accompany you and Neamhain." Cassán handed Brianag a hunting horn. "Sound this if you need help and they will be at your side."

"Thanks, brother," replied Brianag.

"We're going with you, too."

Brianag grinned at Luag and Malmhìn and her heart warmed. "I wouldn't have it any other way."

CHAPTER 29

Loch Eireachd

A deep abyss lies between level-headed planning and deception, and drunken discussions. Bravery bought by beer and promised gold is never a strong foundation. Fionn's belated revelation that Leannán was a sorceress and his boast he had overcome her enchantment failed to produce his hoped-for boost in confidence. Instead, his band of one hundred warriors looked anxiously from one to another.

"How can we be sure we're not falling into *her* trap? We're within sight of Leannán's cave and now you choose to tell us she's a sídhe and an enchantress," said one whose courage rose above the low standard set by his comrades.

"Something went badly wrong for Leannán at A' Chrìon Làraich. I sense it. Her grasp on us is less than the witches' covens in the mountains, and who cares about them? Leannán never enters her cave with her brutes. They always remain in the camp while she feeds and restores her powers. Half of us will hide in the cave and the remainder in the trees nearby. We will trap and kill the bidse."

Warming up to his topic, Fionn stood and glared at his band, daring them to challenge him. This was the Fionn of old and they shrunk back. They were caught in a snare between Fionn and Leannán. Still, Fionn had always treated those who stood with him well. "Better the demon you know," they muttered before grasping spears and moving into place.

***

Fifty of Leannán's brutes survived the Battle of A' Chrìon Làraich. It was a number much easier to control than three thousand. Hence, as she entered the subdued camp on the shores of Loch Eireachd, Leannán exhaled in relief.

The debacle of A' Chrìon Làraich taught Leannán she needed thinking leaders, as well as mindless battering rams. Many chieftains remained enthralled, and after restoring her strength, she would loosen their bonds. She needed real commanders and a more subtle approach to tethering them to her. As to the rank and file, it was past time for her to reveal her true self. She was a powerful enchantress and a demigod. How could they choose Fionn over her?

Curt orders to her monsters ensured none followed her to the cave in the foothills. It was a mistake. As her refuge came into view, Leannán inhaled deeply and exhaled slowly, relishing the calmness. She barely resisted drooling at the thought of the amphorae of blood awaiting her. Inside her refuge, she would drink, replenish her sorcery, and take revenge. She had unfinished business in A' Chrìon Làraich.

As she neared the cave, her instincts screamed, "It's a trap!" Millions of tiny hairs on her neck and limbs bore witness, as did the breeze that carried the scent of decay to her nostrils. Still, Leannán's need for blood overwhelmed caution, and her disdain for humans blinded her to the possibility of a rebellion. Even without blood, she was a sídhe. Without hesitation she crossed the cave's entrance.

The scream was visceral, growing in intensity as it echoed, over and over, off the dank cavern's walls. Fionn's men gasped as eardrums, noses, and eyes bled freely. Leannán's feet sank to her ankles in the slop of blood and mud. Pierced by hundreds of shards of smashed amphorae, her feet became a mass of torn flesh. The shock of the loss stunned Leannán—but only momentarily.

Drawing from her reserves, Leannán's gleaming obsidian eyes scoured the cave, seeking those who dared challenge her. Fionn's band closed in with spears held at waist level. Iron blades taunted Leannán, yet the points trembled. False courage is ephemeral. Fionn had told them she would be helpless, and the fools believed him.

In the darkness of the cavern, she plundered their memories and showed them the faces of their daughters, hand-fast partners, and lovers. She displayed them naked and violated by their fathers, their fathers' comrades, and others they trusted. Innocent faces stared, shocked and accusatory, as long, leaf-shaped spearheads punched through their soft bellies.

Duped by Fionn, his followers discovered that the awful price for disrespecting any sídhe, even one at her lowest ebb, was a terrible reckoning. Fionn knew this. A hundred paces from the cave, he stood with his remaining fifty warriors. He listened as those inside Leannán's sanctuary turned on each other. Crazed fathers killed to defend and save those they loved, and no quarter was given.

A few from Fionn's band moved closer to the cave. "Take one more step and I will gut you," he growled. "Our comrades are fighting for us. They will drain Leannán's remaining strength." He paused, looked around him, and wished he had one hundred more—even a thousand. Doubts crept into his head. Was the bidse still manipulating him?

As the melee in the cave subsided, he shouted, "Ionnsaigh!" and the fifty charged forward. "Kill her before she drinks blood."

✳✳✳

A rockfall sealed the cave as soon as the last of Fionn's men crossed its entrance. It may have been the work of Serendipity or simple coincidence. However, trusting either explanation necessitated believing the second voice echoing off the cavern's walls was in their heads. The will and strength to move their bodies dissipated, provoking panic and loosened bowels. The ability to either fight or flee deserted them.

"You dare to confront and threaten one of the Aes Sídhe. In itself, that is worthy of prolonged, excruciating pain. Yet, you compounded your offence by challenging one of the Womb-Born's daughters.

Therefore, much more deliberation is needed." Áine's teeth flashed in the darkness. "But I will find a way to make you beg to enter the Otherworld."

"*Mother!* I have this under control. Please leave." The tones of fury and frustration woven into Leannán's voice momentarily stunned Áine. When had her daughter ever stood up for herself?

"*Under control!* If I had not timed my entrance perfectly, the humans would have spitted you on an iron blade. Instead of holding this discussion, you would be a shade awaiting judgment by the Queen of Death, The Mórrígan." Leannán scowled and opened her lips to protest. Áine's open palm signalled she had not finished.

Ignoring Leannán, Áine returned to inspect the rebels. "Your enchantments are sophisticated and surprisingly strong, and it was amusing to watch you play with the humans. *That was not your mission!*" Leannán winced as Áine's voice thundered around the cave. "You were sent to find and destroy Brianag and all who participated in Sidheag's execution. Yet they are still alive. Worse, the Old Ones have revealed themselves and aid them. As I speak, the Cait Sìth hunt your pet."

"No!" gasped Leannán, and then she growled, "I have a plan."

"We do not have time for *your* plan. You have remained too long among the humans. Even with blood, your powers wane. This was supposed to be a quick search-and-destroy mission. You have broken the Accord negotiated by the Tuatha Dé with the humans. The Womb-Born fear wider human involvement in our affairs and will vote to remove the sanction that allows you to hunt here."

"No! It is my quest," shouted Leannán.

"No, it is mine because you have failed," retorted Áine.

Two pairs of black eyes held each other's unblinking gaze. "Is your plan to embarrass me before the Womb-Born and force me to openly declare Sidheag was my daughter?" Áine's revelation stunned Leannán. "Such a stain on my reputation would be impossible to recover from and I would be banished. That I will never allow."

"*Bitseach!* You may have created Sidheag, but she was always *my* daughter. Unlike you, I mourned her death. To you she was a failed project and only fit for destruction." Leannán straightened her back and mocked Áine.

Where has this Leannán been hiding?

"With blood, I can enthral an army of ten thousand. Can you? You are a voracious blood drinker, Mother, but face the facts. Your sorcery, like your art, is mediocre at best. Even if you slaughter and drink the blood of hundreds, you can never approach my powers of enchantment. You will never command the humans' army."

Áine's cackle was chilling. "All this time spent rutting humans, you never learned how to rule them. Instead, you performed magic tricks." With a wave of her hand, the rockfall disappeared and the sun's rays beamed into the cave. "Follow me, and I will show you how to ensure cooperation without making them senseless fools."

* * *

It took Áine until sunset to assemble her pageant. A bound Fionn knelt before his comrades. Beside him, on the still-frozen ground, lay a fire-hardened stake. An arm's-length hole to receive its unsharpened end stared at Fionn. Before him were his fifty warriors, and alongside them were fifty stakes and fifty holes.

They looked at him over their shoulders with eyes filled with wrath and blame, and their lips cursed him. Unrepentant, Fionn snarled at them. "I forced no one to join me. Your motives were greed and power, not addressing injustices. You made your choice. Now die like warriors."

Áine stood on a great boulder. Her voice boomed across the loch and deep into the forest. "My daughter sought to control you with seduction and sorcery. I have no time for such foolishness. You will obey me because you fear me." Murmurs of rebellion rippled through the ranks of the Forest People's army. They stopped when Áine cackled, "How curious you think you have a choice."

The clank of chains, loud sobs, and pleas for mercy followed as the families of the rebels were marched forward. All generations and even distant cousins were represented. Only babies sucking at their mothers' breasts were unbound. Those who resisted were beaten with clubs or prodded with spears. None were allowed the relief of death. Áine had forbidden that.

Each extended family was chained to the thick bole of an ancient pine. They shrieked helplessly as tinder and straw were stacked against them and soaked in pitch and oil. The rebel warriors who knelt facing them fought against their restraints, but their efforts were useless.

"This is how I reward treachery. Remember it. Disobey me and you and your families will receive the same or worse justice. I hold your lives in my hands. Serve me faithfully or die like these."

Áine snapped a finger and the fifty rebels were lowered onto sharpened pales. All screamed as the stakes penetrated their arses and slowly pushed their way up through their abdomens, finally erupting from their chests. The dull crack of thighs broken by blacksmiths' hammers elicited curses and shrieks and quenched all hope of escape.

Fionn was the last to be staked. Defiant, he cursed Áine and Leannán when he was bent over a tree stump. As he felt the stake press against his arse, he needed all his mental and physical strength for a final act of defiance. The pale was hammered into his arse, and he was dropped with a shuddering thud into the receiving hole. Still, Fionn refused to cry out or scream, and for that the Forest People always remembered him.

He was grateful not to see his warriors' eyes. Yet that was scant solace when shouts of "Fire!" rang out and the screaming of men, women, and children filled the forests and his ears. The smell of brimstone as hundreds of heads of hair blazed, and the stench of burning flesh, clogged his nostrils.

⁕⁕⁕

Áine turned to Leannán. "Don't you love how pretty pines are when set alight?"

"This was foolish, Mother," said Leannán. "Have you forgotten our history? The humans defeated the Tuatha Dé because there are multitudes of them. They are fertile and we are barren. It was inevitable they defeated us. You have lit a torch to guide them to us. What will you tell your brothers and sisters when they are rampaging through the Land of Immensity?"

"Never, we are too powerful. Our gateways are hidden from men."

"That is hubris. They know the portals' locations. They have Brianag, A 'Bhanrigh Fuil, a Hand of the Goddess, and the Queen of the Cait Sìth to show them. Are *you* so sure the Womb-Born can defeat these and the humans?" Leannán laughed. "I leave you to your campfire and burning forest. Goodbye, Mother."

Rage bubbled up from the pit of Áine's belly which could not be contained, and she lashed out. Long black talons slashed across the back of Leannán's neck, and her head fell to the forest floor. For a moment, Áine was horrified at what she had done. Yet had she not warned Leannán of the price of failure? How could she be guilty? Nevertheless, Áine was perplexed. *Why was it so easy?* Why did Leannán not sense and anticipate her actions? She was a sídhe.

The laughter from deep in the forest was her answer. "You disappoint me, Mother. The Queen of Deceit is easily fooled, and, as with your artistic reputation, your talents are unexceptional." Áine ground her teeth and scoured the wildwoods, to no avail. "A final piece of advice, Mother. Count your warriors in the morning. The number will be less than you expect."

Áine spat in the direction of Leannán's voice as she disappeared into the deep forest with her remaining brutes. Her brow furrowed at her daughter's parting words. "I have no need of anybody's advice. Neither do I need the Womb-Born nor the Accord with men. I have my human army."

Áine smiled at the thoughts of conquest that infested and spread through her mind. She reached out and grabbed the nearest warrior.

Her mouth opened and needle teeth bit into the woman's neck. It did not take long to drain the body of lifeblood… nor the many others she drank from that night. As the families burned, Áine lost any sense of discipline and gorged herself on a luxury she had not tasted for millennia—fresh blood.

***

Taking advantage of Áine's euphoria, a group of chieftains gathered and hatched a plan. Many of their people were already moving south through the forest towards A' Chrìon Làraich. Now it was the warriors' turn. Unfortunately, the advent of spring brought rain and muddy ground. With the young and the elderly, it would take at least a half-cycle of the moon to reach Seonag's stronghold.

In all, five thousand warriors and double that number of civilians moved like ghosts through the ancient forest. The woods were their home, and even the youngest children sensed that through bare feet and receptive minds. Caught between Áine and Seonag, they prayed to the Goddess for journeying mercies.

They knew that, with Fionn's death, Seonag had no rival for the throne of the Forest People. Hence, the people, but more so their leaders, were understandably anxious at the reception they could expect in A' Chrìon Làraich.

CHAPTER 30

A' Chrìon Làraich

The sounds of mourning were unceasing as seemed the clearing of the bodies from A' Chrìon Làraich. Those of the fallen garrison and the stronghold's civilians were burned on pyres alongside each other. All were given the ceremony and reverence due to those who defended A' Chrìon Làraich and paid with their lives. Their surviving family members wept as the flames consumed their loved ones' mortal forms.

The same dignity was not afforded to Leannán's brutes. Yes, they were burned, but in anonymous, mass graves, beyond the community's walls. A sizeable minority were left in the ditches and man-traps where they fell and died, pinned by stakes; none thought it worthwhile or relished the task of extracting them. Thus, pitch was poured over them and set alight. The fat of their bodies spat a final curse but accelerated the burning. When the corpses were sufficiently degraded, the holes and trenches were filled in with rocks and dirt.

⁕⁕⁕

Gràinne choked as she crossed the crumbling walls of the first line of defence. A thick miasma of smoke particles undulated above A' Chrìon Làraich, coating skin and lungs, and clogging noses. The usual fresh spring smell of the pine forests was overwhelmed by brimstone and burnt flesh. She wondered why the winds, which normally rolled down from the mountain peaks, had ceased. Was it punishment from the Goddess, and if so, why? Surely, A' Chrìon Làraich was the victim of evil.

Gràinne shook her head as she passed the first defensive wall. She could have taken her choice of hundreds of gaps in the wall. It was not destroyed, but it was a porous barrier. As she approached A' Chrìon Làraich's inner wall, it was much worse. The profusion of dried blood splashes provided the only relief from the grey rubble.

At the centre of A' Chrìon Làraich, Seonag's broch stood tall and largely undamaged. Gràinne strode towards it, past rows of temporary shelters. Ragged coughs and sneezes raised the spectre of disease and infection. Only the cries of babies raised hopes the Forest People might have a future. Sullen, smoke-smudged women with spears at their feet grieved as they cooked over makeshift firepits. Others watched and sharpened weapons.

Everyone had been touched by Leannán and her monsters. Still, none believed their troubles were over. The Forest People, with some justification, believed the Goddess had tired of the endless squabbling between Drostan's children and the many thousands who died because of their vanity. To chastise them, she had visited unimagined horrors on the tribe. Would their leaders learn the lesson before it was too late? Probably not.

* * *

Seonag stood by Cè's cot in a section of the Great Hall. Her brother had barely survived the short journey from the battleground to the broch. The druid healers judged it unwise to move him again. "The Hag's arse," muttered Gràinne as she took in the extent of Cè's bruises and lacerations. No part of his body or mind was untouched.

He constantly moved, mumbled, and occasionally shouted. His words were unintelligible. Gràinne marked the ropes that restrained him to his cot. That he was a guest, not a prisoner, was shown by the sheepskin lapped around and under the restraints.

"He is much improved," said Seonag. At Gràinne's raised eyebrow, she added, "Honestly, he is. I thought the bean-sìth would take Cè, but now I have hope." A dip of Ardghal's head confirmed Seonag's words. "Without Sorchae, A' Chrìon Làraich would be destroyed, and its people massacred."

"A' Chrìon Làraich *is* destroyed, and its people slaughtered, Seonag," said Gràinne, laying her hand gently on her friend's arm. "Best to raze the ruins to the ground. Who will want to live among the shades of the dead? You need a new stronghold."

"Let's go to Sorchae's chamber. We can eat and talk," said Seonag.

* * *

"You must move your people to Dùn Brion and safety. Send messengers to gather your warbands from the forest. They will be needed to protect the civilians. The people can shelter in the forests beyond Dùn Brion or travel to Dùn Athad and the safety of the marshes surrounding it. The warriors must join Cassán and his allies. The Highlands and Lowlands can only defeat this evil if we are united."

Gràinne glanced across the chamber at Sorchae, who lay in her cot. The Blood Queen grimaced at the haunted look on the young woman's face and the livid bruises and puckered scars all over her body. Even minor adjustments of position made Sorchae gasp in pain.

I wish you had remained in Gaul with Conall, and Mòrag had not laid this on your shoulders.

Thank you, but I am where I was meant to be.

"The Eastern Tribes cannot stand aside for this battle, and the Ravens and Na Daoine Tùrsach must set an example." Gràinne smiled at Sorchae. "With your permission, I will send a rider to Niall in Càrn Liath and raise an army."

Sorchae's injuries from her battle with Leannán were such that it was agony to move her head. Thus, she was grateful for the Goddess' gift and gave her consent silently.

"When I return to my crannag, I will speak with Amodocus and Giosail. They will send riders to the other tribes and encourage them to

240

join with us." Gràinne's eyes narrowed. "I will remind the reluctant that they gave the Blood Queen their oath and she has a long memory…"

Further conversation was interrupted by a loud banging on the door. Seonag's four remaining shields grasped spears and moved towards the entrance. Furious words were exchanged, before Seonag's protector returned to the table. "A messenger from Fionn wishes an audience." At a dip of Seonag's head, the envoy was searched and allowed to enter.

✱

The envoy was five paces from the table when he dropped to his knee, bowed, and said, "My queen."

"The most senior chieftain in Fionn's army is a strange choice for a messenger," rasped Seonag. "Is your recognition of my status a recent conversion? Is it permanent or will it change with the breeze?"

Sidestepping acrimony, the envoy answered, "I observed Cè as I crossed the broch. I trust the healers will enjoy success in restoring your brother to full health. I also saw the damage done by Leannán's ogres. I am truly sorry for the deaths of so many of your warriors and people…"

"The sentiments are welcome, if tardy, but I have limited time. My allies and I need to develop a plan to confront Leannán." Seonag stared at the man. "Deliver your message and ignore protocol. I have no time for flowery or weasel words."

The chieftain bowed and smiled. This was a changed Seonag. *A more dangerous one, too.* "Fionn is dead. You are the uncontested Bhanrìgh of the Forest People." Seonag's hand covered her mouth. "He, along with fifty of his guard, were staked after a failed attempt to kill Leannán. As you are aware, staking is a slow death. They were made to watch as the conspirators' families, from babies to grandparents, were burned alive."

"That bitseach, Leannán," growled Gràinne.

A shake of his head was the chieftain's answer. "It was a sídhe called Áine, not Leannán. Áine tried to kill her, too, but underestimated Leannán's sorcery. She fled north, along with her remaining brutes."

"Who is Áine?" asked Seonag.

"I am unversed in the hierarchy of the Aes Sídhe. She claimed she was Leannán's mother and is known as Áine of the Womb-Born. Apparently, she is a blood drinker and is Sidheag's true mother."

"The Hag!" muttered Ardghal. "I sense we are even deeper in the shite."

"Are you alone?" asked Seonag.

The chieftain shook his head. "Five thousand warriors and their families follow me. We fled while Áine burned the families and became drunk on blood. Our hope was to find refuge in A' Chrìon Làraich, but it is in ruins."

The elderly chieftain smiled wanly. "Our fate is in your hands, my queen. The nobles and chieftains will swear an oath to serve you." He chuckled. "My advice is to accept our pledge. This war is fated to become bloodier, and you need warriors. Worst case, put my five thousand in the front ranks to be slaughtered."

"They are not your five thousand any longer. They are mine, and I do not waste brave warriors." Seonag's eyes narrowed. "Only the arseholes who lead them. Return to your people and have them march to Dùn Brion. Thankfully, we are a good distance south of Loch Eireachd and Áine's army, so we have a respectable start on them. We will meet you at the Na Mèadaidh's stronghold."

Seonag glanced at a stricken Gràinne. "What is it, Gràinne?"

"Leannán has fled to the north and will want to demonstrate she is better than her ma. My stronghold is defended only by a skeleton winter garrison. She will rightly see my family as an easy target for revenge. I must leave." No one had an opportunity to agree, object, or offer help before the Blood Queen disappeared.

Sorchae winced as she rose slowly from her cot. She nodded to Ardghal and Beira, and then Seonag. "I will leave now, too and will see you in Dùn Brion."

CHAPTER 31

Loch nan Clàr

Gràinne's royal crannag and its adjoining building were in the mountains far to the north of the conflicts at Dùn Brion, A' Chrìon Làraich, and Loch Eireachd. Guarded by the lake's frozen waters and towering snow-covered peaks, a garrison of five hundred commanded by Amodocus protected the royal family. In normal times, it was enough.

Constantly frustrated at having to travel at the same speed as her score of brutes, Leannán once again stretched out her vision towards the crannag. This time she smiled. A 'Bhanrigh Fuil was not at home and the garrison's meagre size was no match for her monsters. She cajoled her army to move faster.

A blast of a lookout's hunting horn was Amodocus' first inkling of Leannán's imminent arrival. He stood on the bridge between the shore and the Great Hall's crannag and watched the attackers' approach. Even at a distance, they appeared huge. The burly warrior swore at Leannán's timing. In a cycle of the moon, the ice would have lost its strength. Leannán's brutes would fall through, and the loch's deep black waters would accept the enemy's sacrifice. With the land bridge destroyed, the crannags would have scorned any attempt to overwhelm them.

Amodocus looked upwards and was disappointed. Even this far north, darkness was a long way off. There was nowhere to hide. He spotted Giosail and called to her. "Take my best fifty fighters and the children to the royal crannag and barricade yourselves in. Defend the young until victory or death."

Giosail looked at him. "You had no need to remind me or the warriors of our duty to your children."

Amodocus dipped his head, acknowledging the reproach. "I'm sorry. I meant no insult. The ones who attack are unnatural and I fear for my son and daughters. I will fight better, knowing they are with you."

Giosail's heart broke at the fragility in Amodocus' voice. She put a hand on his forearm. "You are the bravest and greatest of warriors, Amodocus, and this without the powers so many around you were gifted. Be the bear we all look up to. The Goddess will protect you."

Amodocus smiled and extracted an "Ooof!" from Giosail as he hugged her. Then he roared, "To the bridge! Defend the Royal Crannag."

***

In the gloom of dusk, Gràinne walked barefoot through the ashes and smoking timbers of the first crannag. With each step, her heart beat faster, and she braced herself against discovering the mutilated bodies of her loved ones. With each step, her blood boiled, and the Blood Queen was set free.

Now was not the time to mourn those whose final act of defiance was to set fire to the crannag. They died in the inferno, along with the monsters they trapped. All would be honoured later. A blood-red tear ran down the queen's cheek and her face became implacable. *Where is Leannán?* She padded towards the Royal Crannag.

Flung off its hinges, the crannag's solid door fell onto the floor, throwing dust and splinters into the air as Gràinne entered. She coughed and sneezed to clear the cloying smells of smoke and burnt flesh. Scanning the chamber with anxious eyes, a sigh of relief escaped her lips when she spotted Amodocus and her children. She ignored Leannán— for the moment

Amodocus lay slumped against the far wall, a bloody mace grasped in his hand. Behind him, a red stain crept slowly outwards, like mould. His ragged breathing echoed off the building's timbers, giving Gràinne hope. Before him lay a berm of bodies formed by his veteran guard and the enemies they slaughtered. To a man and woman, they kept their vow to protect the king and his family with their lives. The heat of Gràinne's anger climbed to new heights.

Cradled in his arms, Thrax and Mùirne, hoping to impart childish strength to their da, ignored the blood seeping from Amodocus' many cuts. The eldest, Heilasa, only ten summers old, stood defiant and legs apace before him. She gripped a bloody knife in her trembling hand. Beside her stood a gore-covered Giosail. One arm hung limp by her side. Her jaw was firmly set; a spear was wedged under her armpit.

"Are you well, my love?" The brief dip of her partner's head partially relieved Gràinne's anxiety. "Can you walk, Amodocus?" His look said he would, no matter the pain. To Giosail, Gràinne said, "Please help Amodocus and my children to my rooms. If any servants remain, have them tend to his and your wounds. All will be well, and I will join you shortly."

Leannán's cackle disputed Gràinne's words.

"She killed our friends, Ma. Show no mercy." Heilasa pointed to Leannán as she helped Amodocus to his feet. The sídhe stood near the chamber's central firepit. Blue smoke from the smouldering peat bestowed a spectral aura on the enchantress.

Amodocus groaned in pain as he stood. It drew a chuckle from the enchantress. Gràinne turned to face a smirking Leannán. A hand raised, palm towards Leannán, froze the sorceress's expression and elicited a gasp of surprise.

✳✳✳

"You dare to come into *my* lands and threaten *my* partner, *my* children, and *my* friend, and kill *my* people with your puny magic, bitseach. And now, you taunt me," snarled Gràinne. "Your narcissism, and ignorance of who stands before you, betray you. You should fear me and flee."

The affront to Leannán's sorcery was a sharp slap in the face and threatened to disrupt her composure. Doubts surfaced in the sídhe's mind. The strange runes carved into every piece of the crannag's timbers had not prevented her brutes' slaughter but had slowed them down. Worse, they accelerated the drain on her abilities. She had not foreseen the Blood Queen's traps or drunk sufficiently to restore her strength since the Battle of A' Chrìon Làraich.

Leannán should have recognised the danger of the sigils and their ancient origin. She should have retreated. She had sufficient power to flee and knew she could feed later and fight another day on another battlefield. However, she was a sídhe and arrogance would not let her withdraw… again. "I am the daughter of Áine of the Womb-Born. Stand aside, witch, and I will spare those who remain alive in this hovel."

"You are evil and lack the basic intelligence that would tell you to flee, bitseach. This fight is between you and me, and you are outclassed."

Gràinne's words startled Leannán. No one had ever called her evil, and she never considered herself in that category. *Am I not a famed artist?* In the eyes of the Aes Sídhe, such a talent washed away many transgressions. *I act according to my nature. How can that be evil? It is who I am, and I will not change.*

The cackle that rattled in Gràinne's throat should have been sufficient warning. Leannán watched Gràinne's red chiton drift slowly, hypnotically to the floor's wooden slats. It was a mistake. She should have been watching Gràinne. This time, it was the sorceress who was enthralled. By the time Leannán dragged her eyes from the crimson gown, it resembled a pool of blood about Gràinne's feet… and it was too late. Fate had withdrawn her options.

Like a buzzard selecting its prey, ruby eyes sparkled and gripped Leannán's gaze. Rivers of crimson flowed over Gràinne's body, drawing power from the air. Every drop of spilt blood migrated to the Blood Queen. Leannán felt her already depleted blood power leach from her body. Long red talons clicked ominously as Gràinne walked towards the sorceress. The leisurely and graceful glide of her steps added to the horror.

"Shall we see if a sídhe is a match for A 'Bhanrigh Fuil?" Gràinne smiled malevolently. "Sidheag wasn't."

Leannán's screech shook the charred beams of the crannag. In an instant, she appeared where Gràinne stood, yet the Blood Queen was not there. Leannán knew this from the searing pain and wetness of her back. Blood flowed from multiple slashes. Shock filled the enchantress's eyes. In all her millennia of life, until entering the human kingdom, Leannán had never suffered so much as a cut from a blade of grass. Her battles were from a distance and fought by dupes. Now she stood nose to nose with an apparition from whose talons dangled strips of her flesh. Leannán fought to control herself and reassert her dominance.

A derisory laugh greeted her ears. "Arrogance has killed you. You should have taken the time to learn about your enemy. I am the *Blood Queen*. Any power you have is from the blood of your victims and that rightfully belongs to me." Gràinne signalled her crannag. "You made my family and warriors bleed. I own the blood you have taken or spilt, and I will have every drop of it back."

Gràinne's hands were a blur; Leannán moved like a snail. The pain in Leannán's chest was excruciating. Blood-soaked ribbons of her gown fell to the floor, and she stood naked. Long, parallel tears criss-crossed her breasts and belly. Leannán's mind became foggy and sluggish as life-blood flowed from her. Her pulse raced and sweat beaded on her brow. *Had A 'Bhanrigh Fuil deliberately avoided major arteries to prolong her agony? How?* Bravely, perhaps, Leannán staggered forward intending to attack Gràinne, but she had no claws. Her weapons were the hands of others, and in this room she was alone. *What foolishness made me attack the Blood Queen's stronghold?*

"Is it sad to discover your mother valued you so little that she did not prepare you for me?" Gràinne's chilling laugh froze the blood streaming from Leannán's wounds. "Fortunately for you, I cannot take my leisure and prolong your suffering. I must finish this. My daughter and I have a reckoning with Áine." Another blur of movement drew shrieks from

Leannán as Gràinne's talons cut her face to the bone. The visage that had taken on countless guises became a blur of memories until it rested on the one she was born with.

"You cannot end me, witch. I am of the Aes Sídhe."

"Ending you would be a mercy, and I am in no mood to be compassionate."

Time slowed for Leannán. She watched Gràinne reach out a hand. Her body shuddered as she felt her chest open and her ribs crack. When the hand withdrew, it held her heart. She watched spellbound as the Blood Queen bit into it and ripped off a piece. "I haven't eaten since breaking my fast. This will have to do." Heart blood slithered down Gràinne's throat, and she gulped down the chunk of muscle. For the first time, she relished and enjoyed the taste.

There is no bean-sídhe to guide demigods to another plane. Caught between life and death, Leannán teetered like a straw doll balanced by a child. She yearned to cry, "Ma!" but what use would that be? Instead, she looked at the only one who was close to her and said, "Please."

Gràinne reached back over her shoulder, grasped the blackthorn grip of her longsword, and pulled it free its loop. As if recently drawn from the blacksmith's forge, the blade glowed orange and red from the firepit's flames. It hissed as it cleaved Leannán's neck, cutting off one last scream before the head rolled over the floor and tumbled into the flames.

✳✳✳

In the encampment in the forests north of the Sleagh, Áine looked up from the roaring fire, her face troubled. It was as if an emotion she had never experienced was trying to break through. With it came thoughts of loss and a need to cry.

Still, Áine had never been a caring or nurturing mother for Leannán or Sidheag. She shed no tears. Her only emotion was exasperation for a plan whose execution failed. Once again, she swore to avenge Sidheag, albeit for selfish motives. Leannán's memory, however, was forgotten before the fire was cold ash.

CHAPTER 32

Dùn Brion & the Lowlands

It's strange to hunt in a pack. Brianag stood on a grassy mound recently uncovered by the retreating ice and snow. Her tongue lolled over razor-sharp canines, eventually emerging on the right side of her mouth. Although the spring air held a nip of winter, she panted loudly, to cool herself. Around her, lynxes stretched, licked various body parts of themselves and each other, and purred. Their noses and ears constantly twitched, sampling the landscape. *They have perfected the art of appearing totally relaxed while remaining on high alert.*

Alongside Brianag stood an anxious and annoyed Caoimhe. Black, elongated pupils, little more than slits in a green background, looked at the wolf. They accused Brianag of encouraging Neamhain to scout ahead without the pack. *I am her shield. I should be with her, protecting her.* Her lips drew back, exposing long, razor-sharp fangs, and she growled.

I understand your concern for Neamhain, but how can you protect her when you do not know how to fight? Caoimhe's expression became one of protest and despair. The wolf shook her head. *You should know three things, Caoimhe. First, I am not a rival for Neamhain's affections and never will be. We are friends since childhood and are sisters, not lovers. I am glad she found someone to share her cot with, as I have.*

Caoimhe growled, although the level of hostility in her tone diminished. *The second?*

Neamhain is adjusting to being a queen. Like her ma and my grandma, she is arrogant, wilful, and single-minded. However, she is also fiercely protective of those she loves and for whom she feels responsible. She stood by this Abomination. The wolf's pink tongue moistened its lips. *If I had to guess, she is scouting ahead so that she can be alone to think. She is more than a Cait Sídhe, or a Sídhe, or a human. That is a heavy load to carry.*

Caoimhe growled, and the wolf shook her head in disapproval. *What cause have you to be displeased? On Neamhain's shoulders sits a great burden, and it is one that would crush a weaker person or being. While we talk, she is desperately searching for a way to prevent the sacrifice of any of her subjects... including the one she loves. Your Council of Elders see the death of your companions as an acceptable price to pay to kill the Cú Sídhe and be released from their geis to the Goddess.* The wolf's large eyes held the cat's gaze. *That is something Neamhain will never accept. Any of their deaths will devastate her, and she does not deserve that. Know this, she will sacrifice herself rather than allow that to happen.*

Helpless, Caoimhe whimpered for her love. Then she stood, looked in the wolf's face, rubbed noses, and licked her snout. *Like many others, including my people, I judged you without knowing you. I apologise and hope we can be friends.* Brianag dipped her head. *How can we help Neamhain? Both of us will die before she is offered up to the Cú Sídhe.* Caoimhe paused and tilted her head. *You said three things. What is the third?*

I will destroy anyone who hurts Neamhain. Brianag's tone was pitiless and her eyes gleamed.

Caoimhe shivered. *Even me?*

You would never hurt Neamhain, so your question is absurd... isn't it? The wolf howled and the cats yowled.

Further ahead, Neamhain paused and smiled. *Thank you, Brianag.*

✳✳✳

Luag dipped his head and smiled at Caoimhe. Then he ruffled Brianag's lush winter fur. "We need to talk," he whispered into a black velvet ear. "*Now!*" The urgency in Luag's voice troubled Brianag, but she kept her demeanour under control.

Is there something wrong, Brianag?

Brianag chuckled. *No, Caoimhe. I think he is feeling lonely among us and not hearing normal conversation.*

I am sorry he feels that way. It was not our intention to make him feel unwelcome. I will tell my sisters to assume their human form in his presence.

Thanks, he will appreciate that. He and I will go for a walk, and I will reassure him everything is well.

A few hundred paces down a hunter's path, Luag turned to Brianag. "Please change. I would rather not converse with a wolf."

"Are we just talking, or do you envisage other more vigorous activities?" Luag stood open-mouthed at Brianag's naked body, and his manhood stirred. "I miss that, too."

"The Hag, Brianag. Don't make this more difficult than it is. Please put a léine on. I can't concentrate when you're naked... and please cloak us." Luag's closing words troubled Brianag. In an instant, they were cloaked, and she stood in a green chiton that hugged her curves like a second skin. Luag rolled his eyes.

"Out with it, Luag. What's bothering you?"

"When was the last time you hunted man or beast?"

Brianag's brow furrowed. She sensed the conversation taking her along a perilous path. But for whom? "A cycle of the moon, perhaps less. What is your point?"

"How long has it been since the Cait Sìth have hunted?"

"They're lincean and natural predators, like my wolf."

Luag's face said everything and Brianag felt her belly flip. "Look at how they act, Brianag. They've never hunted, have they? At least not in many millennia. After the war with the Cú Sídhe, they've never needed to stalk and kill their prey. Since then, they've lived in an alternate world and have had no enemies."

"But they are the Cait Sìth... the Old Ones..." Brianag's voice trailed off and the sick feeling in her stomach grew worse.

"If you or I had not hunted in millennia, how good would we be?" Luag grasped Brianag's hands. "Look, I am not saying they are useless—far from it. They are powerful lincean… demigods. However, I am saying we need an honest discussion with Neamhain and Caoimhe and a plan that plays to all our strengths."

Luag sighed. "The alternative is the Council of Elders' strategy, which, from my perspective, relies on throwing innocents at the Hound until one of them gets get a lucky yowl in. That is unacceptable to Cassán, Malmhìn, and me. I hope it is offensive to you and Neamhain."

"Shite!" exclaimed Brianag. "Can we at least rut a few times before we go back to the camp and face Neamhain and the watch?"

✳✳✳

The Hound sat on a large oak branch brought down by a combination of winter snows and lightning. Before him a fire crackled happily. He cursed the fire for its frivolity while he faced the misery of being hunted. The Cú Sídhe had not been prey since the wars with the Cait Sìth. His face smarted from Brianag's perpetually bleeding cuts. They reminded him of his vulnerability, and he swore again. Beside him, a plump hare struggled in the snare. It was the Hound's only consolation. Still, it also increased his anger. *Why am I reduced to feeding on animals?*

Yet what was the source of his profanity? Humans often invoked the Hag in various forms when angered, sometimes when happy or when they rutted. Sometimes they substituted the Goddess, but that was rare. She had a low tolerance for those who abused her name. Who could he use as the focus of his oaths? Who was worthy of the honour? To the Hound's frustration nothing came to mind.

A white-hot spike was driven through his skull and into his mind, interrupting his speculation. The Hound gasped and barely saved himself from tumbling into the fire, along with his food. Composure lost, he howled and instantly regretted it. The Cait Sìth were close. He sensed their twitching noses and feared their eyesight—they could spot a mouse at a thousand paces. As for the wolf, her hearing had no limits.

The pain in his head spiked again. He resisted howling, but only at the price of bleeding gums and lips. This time, he saw Leannán's heart in A 'Bhanrigh Fuil's hand. He watched the Blood Queen rip a bloody chunk off and swallow it. In his vision he saw Leannán's head severed by iron and followed it as it tumbled into the fire. Soon her lush black tresses were consumed by the flames. Then there was no more pain, only a sense of emptiness. For the first time in aeons, the Hound was alone.

Where can I go? To Áine? The Hound shook his head. The Cú Sídhe had protected the Aes Sídhe and the Tuatha Dé before them, but when they needed support, the Womb-Born had turned their backs on the race and watched as the tribe was slaughtered. *Backstabbing bastards.*

The Hound ripped a leg off the mountain hare, staining its white fur red. He smiled cruelly as it shrieked, and slowly he tore each of its limbs from its trembling torso, before finally ripping its head off.

✳✳✳

"My sisters are displeased at your assertion and criticism. Neither will the Council of Elders accept them," spat Caoimhe. "We are hunters, predators since the dawn of time. In this, we have no rivals." She paused for emphasis. "The Elders may withdraw our help."

"And face the wrath of the Goddess, the Blood Queen, and me, Caoimhe? The Cait Sìth will be cursed and become pariahs. I think not," said Brianag.

"Is Luag's deduction incorrect, Caoimhe?" asked Neamhain. Her calm tone and sídhe-like mask of impartiality hid her emotional turmoil. "When did the Cait Sìth last fight or hunt? Was it during the war between the tribe and the Cú Sídhe? If so, that was aeons in the past. Did the Elders pass on their knowledge of battle to the young?"

Neamhain signalled the other lyncean with a flourish of her hand and received a round of unfriendly mewling. "Are there veteran warriors who mentored you and your friends? If yes, why are they not with us? Or, as Luag suspects, is your sole role to be sacrificed to the Hound?" Neamhain gazed into Caoimhe's eyes.

"What is wrong about serving the Cait Sìth with our lives? None of us are children who were misled. We always knew our duty and accepted

253

the inevitability of sacrifice when the prophecy was fulfilled. The surviv-al of the tribe matters, not us." Caoimhe's lip trembled, and she barely held back her tears. Her fear was not death but losing Neamhain. In Neamhain's eyes, she saw only pain. Her eyes widened when she tried to "talk" to Neamhain but found her mind closed. How? None of the Cait Sìth possessed the ability to be totally alone. The idea frightened Caoimhe.

My friend, Brianag, found it an advantage to shut her mind to the prying of the Aes Sídhe. She taught me how she did it, so we could share and be confident of privacy. I never thought I would need it between us. The sorrow in Neamhain's voice broke Caoimhe's heart, but she had no way to tell Neamhain how she felt.

"Death in battle is heartbreaking, but the courage shown can be cel-ebrated and remembered," said Brianag. "Throwing away a life that is unable or unwilling to defend itself is unacceptable to those with hon-our. It is the weapon of the despot, of tyrants who put children in the vanguard to draw arrows and uncover traps."

Brianag turned to Neamhain. "Luag, Malmhìn, I, and the riders who accompany us will not fight alongside those who are no more than babies. We will find another way to destroy the Cú Sídhe. My advice is to send them back to their settlement and life in their alternate land. We bear them no malice and wish them well."

"Please, no!" gasped Caoimhe. "We would be disgraced." The mewling from the other cats echoed her anguish.

"Better that than an undeserved and futile death," growled Brianag.

"Who am I, Caoimhe?" Neamhain's calm tone and question startled Caoimhe.

"You are the Queen of the Cait Sìth," said Caoimhe.

"You swore an oath to obey me."

Caoimhe hesitated. "Yes, my queen."

"I will hold you, and your sisters, to your pledge. From this time forward, there will be no talk of meaningless sacrifices. If any of you disobey me, *I* will kill you. I told the Elders you would form my cao-mhnóirí—my personal guard. I do not think they understood me.

"Among the humans, this honour is given only to the bravest of the brave. You will fight at my side in battle until you deserve the title or die. Am I clear?" Caoimhe bowed but was ashamed to meet Neamhain's eyes as she straightened. "We will develop a plan to kill the Hound. Following that, you will fight at my side with the humans, to defeat Áine, her horde, and any other enemies who may arise," said Neamhain.

"That was not our understanding," said Caoimhe.

Brianag laughed. "For one so ancient, you have an awfully naïve understanding of how the Goddess works."

Neamhain dipped her head. "I agree." She turned to Luag and Brianag. "You have a half-cycle of the moon to resurrect the hunting and battle skills of the Cait Sìth. Hopefully their ancient brains have not atrophied, and they are fast learners."

A round of spitting and growling greeted Neamhain's disparaging comment. She smiled. *At least they have some pride left.*

***

A short time later, Brianag drew Neamhain aside and hugged her. It was agonising to see how badly her friend suffered. "Caoimhe hurts as much as you do, Neamhain, but from a different perspective. Please do not use the concealment I taught you as a means to run away from challenges."

"Thanks," sniffed Neamhain. She looked across the camp to where a silver-grey lynx sat alone, isolated from the watch.

"Go to her," said Brianag. "You'll regret it if you don't." She smiled as her friend changed into her beige-white lynx and padded across to Caoimhe. Brianag breathed deeply. "Maybe I have a career as a matchmaker," she muttered.

"What?" asked Luag.

Brianag jumped and rounded angrily on Luag. "Don't do that. I could have sliced you open."

Luag's answer was a rib-cracking hug and a whispered, "Let's rut." Yet Brianag was reticent, and he followed her gaze until it fell on Malmhìn. He laughed. "I will never forgive myself for being so wrong about you. Don't worry about Malmhìn. Her lustful needs and appetites would make the famed Queen Medb of the Connachta, whose thighs were always open and friendly, blush. One man will never satisfy Malmhìn." He chuckled. "She doesn't broadcast her predilections but, believe me, all of the fifty riders who are with us are in for a treat."

CHAPTER 33

The Highlands

Áine's partialities belonged to an age the Womb-Born wished to put behind them. Thus, the Mother of the Blood Drinkers could not be true to her origins in the Land of Immensity. For millennia Áine lived a lie as the Queen of the Bright Ones and an artistic genius. Indeed, she played the role perfectly. In the domain of the humans, Áine had the freedom to release her brutal nature and indulge her dark roots. The experience was intoxicating and addictive.

My avenger is coming for you, Mother.

Startled, Áine looked around for the voice's source, unwilling to accept Sidheag was in her head. Still, the words jerked her from her musings. She was furious at the scene revealed as her army stepped out of the treeline and onto the meadowland of A' Chrìon Làraich. Not even a stray goat chewed on spring grass.

There was no sign of Seonag's army or her people. The sole evidence a huge settlement had existed in the valley were piles of rubble, which could have been explained by mountain avalanches. In a few summers, trees, grasses, and wildflowers would conquer the vale and reign again. Seonag's broch, the defensive walls, and the civilian and warrior quarters were ash or broken rock. The perimeter ditches were no more. Only the Goddess could have done a better job at erasing A' Chrìon Làraich.

Later, Áine sat on an ornate, cushioned, and bejewelled throne she had conjured. *Why shouldn't I have some luxuries?* The seat was placed on a mound to give her a commanding view of the vale and what had been A' Chrìon Làraich. An army of over twenty thousand thwarted from raping and pillaging stood, disgruntled, stood at her back.

As Áine scoured the valley, her anger simmered. *I am humiliated.* Worse, it was the second time within a short period. The first was the escape of five thousand warriors with their families. Magnanimously, she assumed part of the blame for that incident. Addicted to blood, but un-used to the unlimited, fresh supply, she had over-indulged. Like humans who drank too much beer and wine, euphoria captured Áine. Her senses became dulled and reeled. However, she learned her lesson. She was one of the Womb-Born. A demigod and should not debase herself to the levels of humans... at least in public.

As she surveyed the valley, Áine reflected on what she deemed a defeat. Seonag had outwitted her and spirited her people away. *No, she outsmarted my commanders, not me.* Black eyes sought her battle commander. He shrank from her gaze, hoping to make himself invisible. He failed, and unable to resist Áine's compulsion he stepped forward.

"You failed me. Where is my victory over Seonag? Why is her head not spiked on a spearhead? Where are my blood sacrifices? Why are the ranks of my army not swollen with her warriors?" The man flinched at every word from Áine's black lips and each lash of her tongue. He knew he was a dead man and prayed the Goddess would preserve his family. Acknowledging he had no words to change Áine's intent, he bowed and accepted his fate.

The cackle that rattled in Áine's throat sent shivers along the commander's spine. As if he were an outcast, his former comrades shuffled backwards to separate themselves from him. Cowardice made them re-fuse to meet the challenge in his eyes. The clicking of long, black talons came closer, and he felt his chin lifted. His body refused to respond to his will, and frozen, he waited. There was no mercy in her eyes, but what else could he expect? "It seems that humans are stubborn and slow to learn. Fortunately, there are many of you."

"Please, no," he begged. His voice was the one function Áine had left the brawny warrior, along with, of course, the ability to feel pain. She heightened that sense.

"Arrest his family. It seems I was too merciful the last time. Let the army violate the females and young boys before throwing them onto the flames of their funeral pyre with the rest of his family." None challenged Áine's orders or would fail to carry them out. By the same token, none would cross the green meadows to Mag Mell. The Goddess had commanded the Otherworld to be their fate.

"Bidse!" The insult was strangled and the sweat on the man's brow demonstrated the effort needed for his defiance. It was his last word, unless the gurgles of him drowning in his blood counted. That did not last long when Áine's talons cleaved his head from his shoulders.

As his headless body tumbled to the earth, the fountain gushing from his arteries soaked Áine in gore. She relished the sensation of the warm liquid on her body and opened her mouth to catch the blood. She would have fallen on the still-warm corpse and drunk deeply, but that would have been unseemly. Licking her lips, Áine turned and pointed to a young chieftain. "You are my battle commander. Make sure you do not disappoint me."

"Yes, my queen," he said, bowing as he dropped to one knee. In his mind, he feverishly planned to remove his family from the encampment. The chilling laugh in his head disabused him of any chance of success. All he could do was say "Sorry" to his hand-fast partner and children and pray their deaths would be quick and painless.

***

Áine and a small warband journeyed to Loch nan Clàr and a confrontation with the Blood Queen. She knew her army would remain largely intact in the valley of A' Chrìon Làraich due to their base human nature. Added to this was her promise to publicly sacrifice one hundred of her chieftains' families if anyone, high- or low-born, deserted her.

One hundred warriors accompanied Áine on her journey. The number was the limit of how many she could transfer from one location to another without arriving at her destination weakened and at risk of being overpowered. Áine would not repeat Leannán's error. She ignored the retching into the snow by her guard after their sudden transportation. *Humans are pathetically frail.*

The scent of woodsmoke tickled her nostrils and became stronger as they approached Loch nan Clàr. Her band struggled through deep snow. In the far Highlands, it would be a cycle of the moon before spring established a firm grip on the season and ousted winter. She thanked herself for not bringing them close to the crannag. Gràinne's warriors would have easily overpowered them.

"No!" she gasped and then shrieked. Warriors' ears bled, and on the high mountain peaks, the ear-shattering yell shattered the virgin ice and snow. Snow, rock, and ice tumbled down the slopes. Áine stood at the edge of the frozen lake and stared at... nothing. All that remained of Gràinne's crannags were their fire-scorched pilings.

Like Seonag, A 'Bhanrigh Fuil had outfoxed her. Áine knew going further north would reveal nothing. The Eastern Tribes and their armies had fled, but where to? She paced to and fro, until one of the warriors shouted and pointed to the pilings. Áine screamed again, and more snow and rock tumbled down the mountains.

A spear was secured to one of the pilings. Spiked on its blade was a scorched, hairless skull. Leannán's lidless, empty black eyes stared accusingly at Áine. Blackened lips, twisted into a sneer by the flames, taunted her mother.

I am disappointed. Are you sure you're my mother? At least Leannán fought A 'Bhanrigh Fuil, face to face. This will be much too easy for Brianag.

Another screech drew a chilling laugh from Sidheag. In a fit of rage, Áine slaughtered her hundred warriors. Temporarily satiated, she fell onto the blood-soaked snow and rested until her composure was restored. She needed to think.

CHAPTER 34

The Lowlands

Though they were affectionately referred to as cats and kittens by the children of Dùn Brion, when Neamhain and her lynxes hunted, each one's physique became bigger than a wolfhound's. Large, wide paws allowed them to travel rapidly over snowy terrain. Each had four toes with long, wickedly curved, retractable claws. Yet these were not their main weapons. Rather, it was the razor-sharp teeth and long fangs that gripped and tore out their prey's throat.

Powerful legs propelled the lincean to run faster and further. They could jump the height of four spears, and leap across ravines and rivers over twenty paces wide. They were ambush predators who hunted in packs. No prey, whether human or animal, would survive an attack by a watch of lynxes.

Luag inspected his students lolling about, grooming each other's fur, stretching their bodies, and arching their spines. It was a beauty pageant for lynxes. He sighed at the hopelessness of the task Brianag and Neamhain had assigned him. Luag had a few basic challenges but the foremost was how to communicate with the cats.

If he had no means of speaking to them, how, after aeons of hedonism, could he encourage the narcissistic cats to work together? Also, encouraging the lincean to rediscover their natural hunting instincts came with the peril of Luag becoming a victim of his success and their next prey. Thus, Luag spent the first quarter cycle of the moon in endless rage and with flailing arms. He signalled, shouted, and cursed… and failed abysmally to organise his students into a cohesive hunting pack.

One evening, he and Malmhìn shared a rabbit spitted over the campfire. Sensing his frustration, Malmhìn whispered in his ear, "Observe them carefully, Luag. They are ancient and while their instincts have been dulled by neglect, they learn quickly. Ask yourself, who is being hunted and which of *your* skills do they need?"

Luag slapped his forehead and roared with laughter. His eyes opened, Luag realised what he observed as an annoying avoidance of his training was a seamlessly coordinated and executed plan of deception. They had absorbed his initial lessons rapidly and, bored, used him for play. He smiled, rose, and walked to the trees where the lincean slept. A few paces away, he bowed deeply. "I apologise, ladies. I underestimated you and made stupid assumptions. Perhaps we can start over, by you telling me what knowledge I can impart to you."

A large red lynx leapt down from the tree, shifted into her human form, and walked up to Luag. She smiled. "My name is Íde. I, too, apologise for my sisters. Working with us while we are in our lynx persona must have been awful for you. Yet, you never gave up." Íde paused to consider Luag's request. "Among other things, I think if you can guide us in being as patient and stubborn as you, then that will be extremely helpful." She turned to face the trees. "Ladies, we have teased Luag and yet he never gave up on us. Transform and ask him all the questions with which you have been plaguing me."

"This process would be a lot easier if I could also talk to you in your natural state," said Luag.

Íde laughed and was joined by the other lynxes. Luag looked at his feet in embarrassment at having obviously said something stupid. *My apologies, Luag, we had no intention of making you uncomfortable. The fault is shared equally. You should have mentioned this before, and we should have suggested a resolution. It is quite simple, as you can now see… or hear.*

"Shite!"

***

Brianag looked across the campfire and smiled. It was good to have Neamhain at her side again. Nevertheless, in an instant her expression changed to a frown.

"Spit it out, Brianag. What is worrying you… besides the secret you stubbornly refuse to share? If you cannot be open with me, then who else?" Neamhain's mien became one of disappointment. "Perhaps you have shared it with Luag. That I can understand, although we have been friends since childhood, and I am sorry you do not trust me."

"It's Sidheag," said Brianag.

"She's dead," responded Neamhain.

"Is she? Many of the Aes Sídhe believe she lives."

"No, Brianag, a small number *wish* she were alive. It is a fantasy; she is dead. My mother witnessed her encased in molten iron, and no sídhe can survive that."

"She was more than a sídhe… as am I. Death is a flexible concept for the Aes Sídhe. Perhaps she found a way to return."

"No, she did not. Iron is the ultimate destroyer of the sídhe, and with it comes the final death."

Brianag's lips trembled. "If she is dead, then why is she speaking to me?"

"What?"

"I hear her in my head. She spoke to me when I was in the Mounds but contacts me more often in this realm. It was she who guided me through my 'death' at the hand of Conn and my subsequent rebirth. She addresses me as her daughter."

"She is not your ma. She never was and never will be. Have you spoken to Gràinne about this?" Brianag shook her head. "Then you should. She has more experience with ancient spirit voices than anyone, including the Aes Sídhe."

Brianag shook her head again. "No. After Leannán's attack on

Loch nan Clàr and Amodocus' almost fatal injuries, I don't want to add to her worries."

"You underestimate your ma's powers of observation and her abilities. You will worry her much more by not telling her. Promise me you will."

"I promise… after the Cú Sídhe and Áine are defeated—and dead."

Neamhain sighed but knew this was the best she could get from Brianag, at this time. "What else worries you?"

Brianag pointed to the lynxes gathered around Luag and Malmhìn. "They hunt and kill animal prey well, but if they are truly to be your caomhnóirí, they must kill humans. When they do, will they get a taste for human flesh and blood? I still do and bear that guilt." Neamhain's demeanour changed to one of shock. "Don't worry, I'm selective. I only kill and eat bad people and those who hurt my friends. I feel nauseous and ashamed afterwards. So, it's not as if I enjoy it." Brianag smiled hopefully at her friend.

"I'm not sure that is totally comforting, Brianag. As for my lincean, I pray their inner voice will guide them."

"I suppose that's the best any of us can hope for." Brianag stood and shouted, "It is time to hunt." Then she changed to her wolf and howled.

Luag turned to the lynxes. *I am proud to hunt along with you.* The round of discordant caterwauling he took as agreement.

As Malmhìn swung up and onto her mount, the leader of the riders' warband looked nervously at her. "Are you sure they know we're on their side?" She laughed and rode off, leaving the warrior without an answer.

***

The Hound stood, flexed his muscles, and heard the crack and pop of his joints. *I have been in the land of the humans too long, and its awful climate infects me with annoying ailments.* He looked up at the full moon and was tempted to howl at the orb. He swore. "I'm a dog, not a wolf." There was disdain and dismissal in his voice until the slashes on his nose reminded him of his vulnerability. He grunted. "All I need is time for three barks."

The howl and yowling in the distance halted his reveries, and he instantly transformed into a dog the size of a bull. Distance was deceptive on chilly spring nights and those he faced were unnatural. He had to be certain of their demise. *I will look into their feline eyes as they die and celebrate my race's victory.*

The Hound sniffed the air. He would not underestimate his enemy. They had roughly equal hearing, but his sense of smell was far superior. Lynxes had a distinctive smell, if only he could dredge it up from his memory. The danger was their speed, which he could never match, and their stealth, which leant to them hunting in packs.

He growled in frustration. His ego and hubris would not allow him to kill this enemy from a distance. Yet how could he close on them until they exchanged stares without putting himself in mortal danger? *Why did Leannán have to die? We were a good team, and I could have made good use of her sorcery. Too late for useless reminiscing.* Then the Hound grinned. There was one sure way of finding the Cait Sìth.

CHAPTER 35

Self-reflection was a talent Áine never claimed. However, she reluctantly, if belatedly, conceded that Leannán had been a powerful enchantress who could enthral an army. Her daughter's weaknesses were the execution of a battle plan and her short-sightedness.

Áine's gift in sorcery was much less impressive. Indeed, there were many among the Tuatha Dé and Aes Sídhe more accomplished. Her human army had grown to twenty-five thousand warriors but realistically she could enthral and control no more than a tithe of them. *I was wrong to dismiss Leannán's value.* The admission stunned Áine and she immediately refuted the confession of inadequacy.

Like her siblings, Áine could enthral several thousand minds simultaneously. By the same token, it followed that if she could control their minds, she could also turn their brains to pulp. Hence, if she found herself about to be overwhelmed, mass slaughter was an excellent way to retreat. *Why did Leannán not do this? Did my intervention put her on a path to death?* If Áine could have felt guilt, this was the moment, but it passed.

From a craggy outcrop, Áine watched her army battle the change of seasons from winter to spring and march agonisingly slowly towards Dùn Brion. Instead of snow and ice, they faced swollen rivers, constant rains, and lakes of mud. Her noble senses were offended by the army's stink of piss, stale sweat, and rotting clothes and feet.

Furthermore, Áine experienced the law of diminishing returns.

Public scenes of cruelty, mass torture, personal violations, and executions eventually reaped a decreasing impact. Worse, they slowed the progress towards Dùn Brion and her retribution. Moreover, Áine was left with the worst of Fionn's warriors, who were well-acquainted with his brutality and sadistic tendencies. Therefore, punishments were ineffective.

Enthralled chieftains and warriors kept the army moving while sanctioning the raiding, rape, and plunder of people and settlements who had the misfortune to lie in their path.

* * *

As he broke his fast with Eimhir, Cassán wondered how Brianag and Neamhain fared in the hunt for the Hound. Beyond that, he worried at the lack of news from the wider war. *Where is Áine?* Thus, the garrison of Dùn Brion remained on high alert. The people of the Na Mèadaidh who resided on the Sleagh and the land north and south of the mountain range had fled. Most crossed the Abhainn Dubh, settling in the forests on its west bank.

In a time of great turmoil, one thing delighted Cassán and gave him hope for the future—the swell of Eimhir's belly. "Thanks, Brianag," he whispered. The smile on his face disappeared when a guard charged into the chamber, interrupting his time with Eimhir. "What is it?" he snapped, glowering at the man.

Regretting his impetuosity, the messenger gulped. He inhaled and exhaled to control his racing heartbeat. "Apologies, my king. Five hundred riders and twenty chariots crossed the Abhainn Dubh ford at dawn. They'll be at our gates soon. The ballistae teams are readying the machines. The cauldrons of oil, water, and pitch are prepared and simmer on the braziers."

The envoy was pleased with his report… until Cassán spoke. "What eejit gave those orders? It had better not have been my battle commander. I'll flay the skin off the backs of anyone involved." The guard stood shocked. His mouth hung open and his heart pounded in his chest.

"The only ruler in the north who has that many chariots is A 'Bhanrigh Fuil. The riders are probably hers and the Queen of the Ravens. I do not want a war with the Eastern Tribes."

Cassán looked at Eimhir. "I may need a woman's touch to prevent a disaster. Out of my way," he said as he pushed the red-faced messenger aside. Then he stopped abruptly, turned, and faced the envoy. "You delivered the message you were given, and no fault lies with you. I suggest you get some food and put your armour on. War will soon be at our gates."

* * *

Cassán looked over Gràinne's shoulder. "Amodocus, Sorchae, Seonag?"

"While I was in A' Chrìon Làraich, Leannán and her brutes attacked my crannags. Amodocus lies near death in his cot in the Ravens' settlement of Càrn Liath. Leannán is dead by my hand."

"No!" gasped Eimhir, holding her belly. "Your children?"

"They, along with Giosail who was also badly injured, are safe in Càrn Liath." Red eyes glared at Cassán, and he recoiled. "But I must be *here* rather than with my hand-fast partner and children." Blood-red talons extended, and crimson sigils flowed as the Blood Queen stood before them. The air crackled ominously, threatening to tip over into an abyss of terror and blood.

At a loss, Cassán looked to Eimhir. Sensing the source of the turmoil roaring through Gràinne, Eimhir ran to her. She hugged Gràinne, barely refraining from flinching. It was as if she embraced a fire. "I am so sorry for Amodocus and will sacrifice to the Goddess for healing mercies for him and Giosail. We have skilled druids and healers in Dùn Brion. Fast horses will take them to Càrn Liath." Eimhir sighed with relief when she felt the heat subside. *I hope my baby is unharmed.*

Fingers lifted her chin. The talons had retracted, and Eimhir looked into golden eyes. "Thank you, Eimhir." Gràinne smiled. "Your baby is healthy. I would no more harm your child than mine." She looked at Cassán and dipped her head. "I apologise for my temper. Times have been quite trying recently."

Cassán nodded and pointed to a small table. "There is no need for apologies between family, and I like to think you are part of Eimhir's and my family, and we yours. Shall we eat? I assume you have not broken your fast yet. Then we can talk."

Gràinne inclined her head and then put a hand to her mouth. "Shite! My riders and chariot teams. They have ridden hard from Loch nan Clàr. I would appreciate food and refreshments for them and their horses, more than for myself."

"That has already been taken care of, as well as cots and a warm fire in the barracks for those who wish to rest."

"Thank you," said Gràinne and sat down.

***

Cassán was impatient to hear the news from Gràinne although he dreaded what she might say. He coughed to clear his throat and speak. Eimhir's hand on his thigh and a whispered, "Let her eat and gather her thoughts," stopped him.

Gràinne lifted her face from eating and smiled. "Thanks, Eimhir. However, time is precious, and we have much to organise." She inhaled to settle her mind. "A' Chrìon Làraich is little more than rubble and likely will be reclaimed by the forest. The bean-sìth has stepped back from Cè but hovers awaiting the Goddess's instructions. Seonag and the survivors of her army and people march towards Dùn Brion."

The Blood Queen tugged her braids. "Ironically, it seems that Dùn Brion will, once again, host the final battle and its walls will be soaked in blood." She paused. "Seonag is the closest of the allies, and I estimate she will be here in a half-cycle of the moon."

"How many?" asked Cassán.

"We need to prepare for eight thousand warriors and double that number of civilians."

"The Hag's tits! Is that all remains of the Forest People?" asked Cassán. "They numbered in tens of thousands."

"By my scouts' last report, Áine commands twenty-five thousand. The Goddess has turned her face from the Forest People. Drostan's once-great tribe is shattered. Many of Seonag's warbands fight rebel warbands in the trees and cannot be counted on to join us. I expect many civilians fled and are hiding in the far forests, but they are at the mercy of Áine and her army. I would not like to be in their position."

"Sorchae?"

"Your sister is very stubborn. Instead of resting to recover from her wounds, her compromise was to travel on a litter with Seonag's army. Ardghal is with her." The sighs of relief from Cassán and Eimhir prompted a smile on lips but little joy. "She is much changed, Cassán. Indeed, you will hardly recognise her, and she has a new title: the Hand of the Goddess. The young woman has proven to be full of surprises."

"I'm not sure anything about my family surprises me anymore," retorted Cassán. "The Eastern Tribes?"

"Niall oversees the gathering of the armies of the tribes, which will mostly be the Ravens, my Na Daoine Tùrsach, and a smattering of smaller clanns. It is spring but melting snows have made the terrain in the Highlands treacherous. They will not make good progress until they reach Cùil Daothail. From there the winds will help dry out the land." Gràinne paused to sip a cup of cold milk, relishing its creamy taste and texture. "I do not expect them before a full cycle of the moon. If we're lucky, there will be about ten thousand from the Eastern Tribes."

"That's more promising," said Cassán.

"How many from Dùn Athad and Dùn Brion?" asked Gràinne.

"No more than five thousand." Cassán saw a frown creep across Gràinne's face and smiled. "You surely are aware the Na Mèadaidh never had a large army. Instead, we have our shield-walls, and my warriors boast each of them is worth ten of any other tribe."

"We shall soon put that to the test, Cassán," said Gràinne. "Are they at hand?"

"They are already assembled, either in Dùn Brion or in the barracks located nearby."

Both looked at each other knowing they had avoided one topic: Áine. "The bitseach will be at Dùn Brion's walls in a half-cycle of the moon. The ravaging and rape of the land and its people slows her down," said Gràinne. "My latest reports are that she has twenty-five thousand warriors, although that is a much too honourable description for the savages who follow her."

"We have little time to plan," said Cassán. Gràinne nodded in agreement. Cassán looked at Eimhir and she inclined her head. "We should appoint a battle commander. Decisions will need to be taken as the war flows." A raised eyebrow greeted Cassán's proposal. He laughed and shook his head. "Not me. There is only one who has experience and success… the Àrd-bhanrigh of the Eastern Tribes." Relieved at Gràinne's agreement, Cassán asked, "What news of Brianag and Neamhain? I have heard nothing since they departed to hunt the Hound."

"Nothing," growled Gràinne. "My daughter can be infuriatingly secretive when she has cause. Still, it's a good strategy."

CHAPTER 36

The Hound was cunning and powerful and had used his time in the human domain wisely. Thus, like a whetstone on a good blade, he honed the edge on his gift until he had absolute control over it. In hundreds of lowland farmsteads and settlements, thousands of lives brutally ended, and souls reaped attested to his dedication.

Now, alone, hunted, and weary of looking over his shoulders, he changed tack and decided to offer himself up. The hound reasoned that presenting a more amenable target would draw the cats out of hiding. In doing so, they would be exposed to his singular weapon. It was an excellent, if high-risk, plan but needed persistence in its execution. The Cú Sídhe's well of patience was shallow and after a half-cycle of the moon, he became bored with waiting.

In the half-light of dusk, a scent teased the Hound's senses. He loped cautiously towards the fragrance. With each synchronous movement of his legs, he sniffed the air, testing it. The smells he tracked were woodsmoke and horse shite. *It must be the warriors who ride with the lincean.* He smiled and snuffled again. This time there was a faint but unique smell of lynx. *Yes!*

He took another pace towards the smell and stopped. *It's too easy. Where's the wolf?* Wolves have a musky, ancient forest fragrance, and it was absent. *Why don't I smell her?* The hackles along his spine raised. It was an involuntary action, but a warning he would never ignore. The Hound dropped to his belly and waited. His ears were erect and vigilant, while his nose sampled the air thousands of times.

The Hound growled, although, given the need for caution, it was more like a low rumble. The hunt excited him, but he wearied of it. He wanted it over, to return to having the freedom to prey on and violate the humans. He drooled as he thought about previous victims' delicious flesh and their screams and piteous pleading for mercy. This was an idyllic land, perfect for the Cú Sídhe and he was resolved to keep it.

When he considered the forest safe, the Hound rose, walked several hundred paces away from the camp, and circled it several times. With the Hound's sense of smell, the encampment could have been lit up by bonfires and only several paces away. He mapped the positions of the warriors and horses and calibrated the loudness of his bark to slaughter them. He shrugged velvet shoulders. *It's a trap.*

＊＊＊

In the encampment, Luag turned to Brianag. "He's here."

She nodded. "Yes, but he senses a trap. As much as I hate to compliment him, the Cú Sídhe is not rash. Also, hunting in the Lowlands has sharpened long-unused instincts." Brianag turned to Neamhain. "He is learning and only improves with time. We cannot allow that and must attack him on the next sunset." Luag and Neamhain nodded.

"Good. I'll hold the illusion for a while longer to be sure he has gone."

＊＊＊

"The Goddess has prepared the battlefield for us," commented Brianag. She pointed to the wide valley stretching before them. In the russets and pinks of dusk, the undulating fog that curled and threaded its way through the trees bestowed an ethereal atmosphere. The dense pine forests of Northern Albu swept from coast to coast and from the Lowlands to the Highlands. It was a forest that followed the natural, mountainous contours of the land. The hunters were on the hilly ground, which marked the transition to the Highlands.

273

"To whose advantage is it?" asked Neamhain.

"Whoever wins."

Neamhain shivered at Brianag's rows of needle teeth and what substituted for a grin. Did Sidheag know what she was creating? Was it by accident or design? If the latter, at whose feet did the blame lie—Fate, the Goddess, or Serendipity? *Brianag is perfectly beautiful, yet perfectly terrible… and one of a kind.*

"Yet I hope I am not alone anymore," said Brianag. Neamhain started and blushed, knowing her thoughts were exposed. Cats' emotions were much more visible than those of the sídhe. "I have Luag to share my cot; Dolidh is my conscience; and you are my steadfast friend. Also, after ten summers imprisoned in the Mounds of the Aes Sídhe, I am reunited with my ma, and my brother and sisters. I have a family."

Brianag paused and pursed full lips. "I have spent many summers asking, 'What type of monster am I?' Now, I ask, 'Does it matter?'" Black eyes held Neamhain's luminous blue gaze. "*Does it?*" Neamhain regarded it as the most important question she had ever been asked.

"No. No, it doesn't, Brianag. Your friends are true. You and they chose well."

✳✳✳

The Hound stripped the meat from the deer's bones and, having cracked its thighbone, he sucked and licked the succulent marrow. The fog that floated around and above his hollow dampened noise and smells. He had chosen his stand well—a large mound with a shallow depression at its summit. As a bonus, a copse of pines and bushes shielded the hill. That said, those hunting him had unnatural abilities, which mitigated his advantage.

His ears pricked up at the crack of a small branch and he sniffed, sampling the foggy air. He could not place the noise, but it confirmed his suspicions. His hunters were as tired of the game as he was and getting careless. The final battle was close. The Hound breathed deeply and slowly. He needed to be cold and methodical. Passion would remove his massive head from his broad, muscled shoulders.

"I'm ready," he growled. "Come and get me."

***

"He has chosen well," said Brianag. The hint of admiration in her voice drew a stern look from Neamhain and hissing and spitting from the quintet of lynxes accompanying them. Brianag laughed and bared her teeth in response. "If you underestimate the Cú Sídhe, I will stand at your pyre and grieve for you.

"It is time to be cloaked. You will make no noise as we move towards the Hound. If you do, *I* will kill you. Understood?" Brianag paused. "When it is time to attack, I will drop the concealment. Do not throw your life away foolishly. I pray when we break our fast at dawn, you will be seated alongside me." Brianag lifted her hands, and the group became a shimmering mirage in the forest.

South-west of the Cú Sídhe's hill, a second group of five lincean carefully picked their way over thick forest debris, avoiding even the smallest of twigs. They used their broad paws to sense any movement. Íde and Caoimhe took the lead together.

If anything should happen to me, promise you will take care of my daughter, Caoimhe. Please take her to Dolidh.

Don't be silly, Íde. We'll celebrate our victory as the sun rises.

North of the mound, Malmhìn brought her mount to a stop and said to the leader of the riders, "It's our time. Keep to the plan." The leader barked a quick order, and the riders removed the rags and strips of sheepskin muffling the horses' tack and hooves. Each hefted a javelin but had three more, plus the same number of heavy darts, in sheaths strapped to the horses' flanks.

Malmhìn inhaled and exhaled. They were to be the first into battle. "Ionnsaigh!" she shouted.

***

The Cú Sídhe was relieved to hear the shouts and blaring horns from the riders. He responded with a bellow, challenging them to face him. Then he mocked them. "Where are the cats? The cowards let the humans die for them?" His last words melded into a growl as he transformed into his dog persona.

"The Hag's arse! Look at the size of that beast. I've seen smaller bulls on my da's farm," said the leader.

Malmhìn snorted. "What did you expect—a family pet?"

The mound proved no challenge to the powerful horses, and soon they crested the hill. A hail of spears and darts swept the summit, surprising the Hound and making him flinch. Yet his hide was thick and tough, and the missiles barely pierced his skin. Most sank a fingernail's depth into the Hound, trembled, and fell to the ground.

The leader was a skilled horseman. He was also young and untested in anything more than skirmishes with cattle thieves. In the heat of the first assault, he ignored his orders to retreat after launching the initial missile bombardment. Hubris swelled his chest. He saw a glorious victory and ordered his warriors to attack again.

"No!" shouted Malmhìn and galloped to close with and stop the eejit. By the time she reached him, his head tilted to the side. Vicious claws had removed his throat and opened his chest to the bone. His horse's flesh was shredded by the Hound's talons. The young man spent his last few moments in agony and regret, waiting for the bean-sìth. Half of his command were dead or mortally wounded from the Cú Sídhe's crushing jaws and claws. The Hound had barely taken a scratch.

Without Malmhìn, the slaughter should have been greater. The Hound steadily worked his way through the screaming horses and warriors, intending none would escape. Malmhìn roared, "Retreat!" over and over until her voice was little more than a dull croak. She sighed in relief as a third of the riders managed to withdraw and turned to join them.

A gore-soaked snout and long canine incisors with strings of flesh and dripping blood was Malmhìn's final vision. The smell of his maw as he opened it made her nauseous. She stared defiantly into the beast's eyes and reached for the dagger in her boot. Before she could touch the pommel, the beast ripped open her throat and flung her body aside.

I'm sorry, Luag. It was Malmhìn's final thought before the bean-sìth took her to Mag Mell.

* * *

A shocked Caoimhe tore her eyes from the massacre on the hill and looked at Íde. *What were they thinking? They were to be a diversion while we attacked from the south-west. Do we stay with the plan? There is no surprise or feint.*

They were brave men and women. Let us hope we can match their courage, but not their recklessness. Íde looked to the south-east. *We are the distraction for Neamhain and Brianag. It is time for the Cait Sìth to stand and fight for our people.* Elongated pupils shrank to a black slit in luminous green eyes. Ears, noses, and whiskers twitched, measuring the landscape.

Five huge cats approached the mound, carefully side-stepping the bodies of horses and men tossed aside by the Hound. Blood splattered their paws and coats. They felt the Hound's delight and his challenge to the Cait Sìth. *We are coming for you,* was the lincean's communal reply.

* * *

No one informed him, yet Luag knew Malmhìn was dead. Brianag and the lincean knew, and in the intimacy of Brianag's mirage, there was no avoiding their eyes or ignoring the tears Brianag fought but failed to hold back. He smiled sadly at the hand on his arm. "She fought well and saved many. Her courage will be spread abroad and celebrated by the largest pyre," said Brianag.

He dipped his head. "I know, but it doesn't help. She was my friend and, like you, I have too few of those to lose." He brushed a tear from his eye and said gruffly, "Let's kill this bastard before other good warriors, whether lince or human, die."

In the space of a breath, Brianag dispelled the cloak, and transformed into her wolf form. She, Neamhain, and her lincean bounded for the mound.

* * *

He smelled the Abomination and the cats coming in from two sides and paced back and forth on the mound. Exhilarated from the battle with the riders, his confidence was high. Yet in his mind, the voices of his tribe burdened him. Many called for revenge; more shouted, *"Traitor!"*

Long-buried memories surfaced. He watched as he was led, not in chains but by the hand, from the final battle by a Womb-Born sídhe. The bitseach, Áine, had made him a pariah for eternity. He laughed derisively at the irony. The only one who could preserve the memory of and avenge the Cú Sídhe was despised by his race. *I'll show the bastards who's a coward.* He bounded towards Caoimhe's group.

The lincean scattered, knocked over by the momentum of the Hound. Yet the apex predators regained their composure quickly and surrounded the Hound, spitting and hissing. Long claws extended and vicious fangs threatened. He could not match their speed. Propelled by their hind legs, with one leap they would be on him. The Cú Sídhe wanted to howl, but that would have been a mistake. He needed a predator's discipline to win this war. He smelled the other watch of lynxes and Brianag come closer and knew he could not fight both groups.

He had one weapon that would destroy them, and so he waited silently until they were all in his killing circle. Terror momentarily stalled the lincean's attack. Then the Hound barked… once… twice… In the blink of an eye, Caoimhe was before him, sitting and staring. He saw her smile and her mouth open. *What does it mean?* Suddenly, Caoimhe spun away, knocked aside by Íde.

It is not your time, sister. Íde turned to the Hound. *But it is yours.* As the rumble of the Hound's third bark formed in his throat, Íde opened her mouth and sang. It was the most beautiful sound anyone had heard, especially from a cat, and consumed the beast's final bark. His voice gone, the Cú Sídhe stood vulnerable. Íde fell lifeless to the grass.

No! screamed Caoimhe. Fangs unveiled; she leapt for the Hound's throat. The Cú Sídhe's voice was gone but his strength remained undiminished, and he swatted her aside. Multiple claws lashed out and incisors tried to find purchase as Caoimhe's group attacked *en masse*. All that happened was a profusion of cuts, bloody tears, and broken bones. The Hound was untouched. Worse, he croaked.

"You didn't tell me that our 'weapon' was time-limited," growled Brianag. "We've already lost half the lincean because of injuries and deaths."

I did not know. It has been a long time since anyone used it, said Neamhain.

"The cats, Luag, and I will attack from all sides. You must damage his throat. He cannot be allowed to heal and bark again."

***

The Hound would have howled if he had a voice. Instead, he emitted a broken whine. The lynxes had caused him minor damage, apart from the one who robbed him of his gift. However, Brianag's raking talons opened long wounds along his flank. He remembered the effect of them on his muzzle and knew they would never heal. He snapped at her, but she was too fast for him. Luag's sword breached his hide. The iron burned him and brought tears to his eyes. *Bastard!*

Neamhain stood back from the affray, in front of the Hound. She watched intently as her lincean and Brianag attacked.

We do not have much time, Neamhain. His voice strengthens.

The Queen of the Cait Sìth hissed, *Tell me something useful,* and resumed her observation of the Hound. Her eyes followed as his head swiftly shifted from left to right, snapping at his assailants. *Move the attacks. Make him stretch to bite you.*

She crouched. Powerful hind legs tensed, ready to spring. The leap was fifteen paces long and timed perfectly. As the Hound overstretched his neck to bite Brianag, Neamhain's claws fastened onto and sank into his chest. She felt his body tremble and smiled. Before his head could turn round to snap at her, the Queen of the Cait Sìth opened her mouth and sank long fangs into his throat.

Blood gushed into Neamhain's mouth. She felt like she was drowning as it filled her mouth, making her gag. *No. I was destined for this.* She bit harder with jaws that had the strength of a blacksmith's vice, and felt the Hound's flesh weaken. Her head rotated back and forward, making her dizzy. She bit down one final time and tore the Cú Sídhe's throat out. *You'll never bark again, bastard.*

Nonetheless, the Hound's strength had not gone. He trembled at the blood gushing from his throat and lashed out in a frenzy of fear and anger. Whimpers from the lincean who attacked all along his body told of his success.

In the melee, Luag scrambled onto the Hound's broad back. Legs clamped to the Cú Sídhe's flanks, he raised his sword, shouted, "For Malmhìn!" and plunged the weapon into the massive head. The Cú Sídhe shuddered and collapsed.

Above the sighs of relief and muted cheers of victory, Brianag bellowed, "Build fires, dismember the bastard's corpse, burn it, and scatter his bones and ashes wide. He cannot be allowed to rise from the embers."

* * *

At the gates of the Otherworld, the Cú Sídhe stopped and blinked several times. The entrance was closed to him. "No," he gasped. The Otherworld was his right.

You have no rights, Devourer of Souls.

"Mother?" The Hound watched the Goddess manifest herself and shrunk back in terror.

I bear that title in disgrace, beast. I did many foolish things and made many mistakes in my early years. Giving life to the first of your kind was one. Now you will join them. In the Otherworld, there is light, and that you do not deserve.

The Cú Sídhe would have shouted, "No!" but the Goddess had expelled him into the black void from which she had formed him. He had no voice but for a while he experienced the terror he had inflicted on others.

CHAPTER 37

Dùn Brion

All who stood around Íde's pyre knew two truths: grief is lonely and personal. What words are fitting when there is no body and no certainty as to the destination? Cassán, as Righ of Dùn Brion, had an unenviable task. "I knew Íde briefly. She sacrificed herself for her friends, those she loved, the Cait Sìth, and the people of Na Mèadaidh. That is all I need to know. My deepest regret is not having the chance to know her better. I mourn her passing."

Cassán looked up into the clear night sky and pointed. "I see a new bright star and have named it Íde. So perhaps we do know where she is, and that she watches over us eternally. Goodbye, Íde."

"Well spoken, brother," said Brianag, wiping away emerald tears.

"We have had our disagreements, Cassán, Righ of Na Mèadaidh. However, from this moment, you may call upon the Cait Sìth and know that we will come." Neamhain dipped her head to Cassán and embraced him. That each of the lincean placed their paws on his shoulder and licked his nose with rough tongues was discomfiting and the single source of laughter on a sober occasion.

***

Everyone in Dùn Brion knew Íde's death had desolated Dolidh. No well-intentioned words, such as courage, bravery, and sacrifice, brought the child consolation. Thus, for several days after the reports of Íde's passing and the killing of the Cú Sídhe, the young girl retreated to the solitude of her sanctuary—the stables. There Dolidh sobbed until the Goddess touched her and sleep carried her to where she could hold Íde again. When the sun set, there was always one who would lift her into their arms and carry her to her family's quarters.

As the meadhan-latha sun rose high on a fresh spring morning, Dolidh sat on the hay in the stables. The horses were subdued, respecting the young girl's need to mourn, although Dolidh did not understand the word. She rubbed tears from already reddened eyes. Heartbroken, she asked the Goddess once again to take her to Íde.

You are not the first child to ask me to take their life and will not be the last, Dolidh. If only adults could retain such feelings of love and self-sacrifice.

"Goddess?" breathed Dolidh. Her innocent heart knew instantly who spoke to her. "I'm lonely. Íde was my friend and I loved her, but I will never see her again… not even in Tír Tairngire, for she is not a Gael."

The Goddess was surprised and impressed at Dolidh's knowledge of where the bean-sìth guides people's spirits. Yet, sadly, Dolidh's observation was true. Íde would never walk the meadows of Tír Tairngire. *She died so that you, your family, and your people would live, Dolidh. Does that not count for anything?*

Does she not deserve to be remembered and her life celebrated by one who loved her unconditionally? Only you can do that. Adults are fickle at keeping memories and promises. Íde knows only you—and perhaps one other—will always treasure her memory. Will you allow her to be forgotten?

"The burden you lay on me is unfair, Goddess," said Dolidh. "I'm only a child."

The Goddess laughed at the child's honesty. Yet it was not a cruel or false laugh, and that Dolidh appreciated. *Yes, it is. I must go, Dolidh. Sadly, there are many children who grieve lost friends. However, I will watch over you, and you will never be alone.*

Dolidh frowned and pouted. "She could have given me something more than words." The laughter from the depths of the stable startled her, and she muttered, "Sorry, Goddess." The sound of the stable doors' hinges squealing diverted Dolidh's attention from her grieving, and she watched two figures approach. One she recognized as Caoimhe. She looked equally sad and Dolidh felt guilty, although she did not understand that word either.

Beside Caoimhe walked a child who looked about the same age as her. Dolidh was sure she did not know the girl, yet something about her face and long red hair was familiar. They sat beside Dolidh, with the girl on Caoimhe's lap. It looked as if the girl had been crying as long as Dolidh. *Why are they here?* For a moment, Dolidh was angry her sanctuary had been invaded. Then she remembered the Goddess's words, reddened, and muttered, "Sorry."

"This is Éile, Dolidh," said Caoimhe. A tear rolled down the older cat's cheek. *Why?* "Éile is Íde's daughter." Dolidh's eyes widened, and her mouth fell open. "Before she crossed the veil, Íde made me promise to bring Éile to you. Like you, she is very lonely. Íde hoped you and she would become friends, and you would cherish each other, like sisters."

Two pairs of small hands reached for each other. Soon embraces and tears followed. Yet among the tears of sadness were the beginnings of joy. Caoimhe turned before exiting the stable and smiled. Éile had become the lynx kit and purred contentedly in the arms of one she knew she could trust.

Before they fell asleep on the hay, Dolidh whispered, "Thanks, Goddess," and so did Éile.

✳✳✳

At sunset, Caoimhe returned to remind the girls that it was time for bed, but they were gone. "Shite! How will I explain this to Cassán and Eimhir, and to Dolidh's parents?" Anxiety increased with each breath. In her mind, she heard cries of "Kidnap!", the beat of war drums, and the Cait Sìth forced into war with the humans. "No, please no. Why did you do this, Éile?"

"Éile is blameless. They have gone to the place where I met my lynx," said Neamhain, smiling at Caoimhe's startled reaction as she appeared at her side. "Éile wanted to show Dolidh her home. I guided them to ensure their safe arrival."

Startled, Caoimhe turned around and snapped, "I know *that*. Why did you not stop them? This is beyond foolish, Neamhain. We are in the middle of a war. It is the first time in history humans have fought alongside the Cait Sìth. We do not need a confrontation between the humans and our tribe. They will see Dolidh's disappearance as an abduction, not a visit to a friend's roundhouse."

Neamhain's eyes blinked fast as she reflected on her well-meant but suddenly imprudent support of Éile. "You and I will speak with Cassán, Eimhir, and Dolidh's parents, *now*. If they wish, we will take them to where Dolidh is…" Caoimhe's eyes widened in shock. Before Neamhain, no such thing would ever have been contemplated, let alone permitted. "They will see that Dolidh is happy and safe, is there of her own free will, and can leave at any time."

"What about Brianag?" Confused at the question, Neamhain looked helplessly at Caoimhe. "Brianag sees Dolidh as her special friend. A friend who took her hand when no one else did and made her feel normal. She has sworn to kill anyone who hurts Dolidh. She slaughtered hundreds in the forest because she thought Dolidh was in danger. It was Dolidh who drew Brianag out of exile to save her family from the Cú Sídhe."

Caoimhe glared at Neamhain. "How will you explain Brianag's demands to visit Dolidh to the Elders? You know what they think of her, and you know she will not be stopped."

"Shite! I have made a real mess."

Caoimhe squeezed Neamhain's hand and nodded. "Yes, you have, but your intentions were pure. We will navigate a path through this." She chuckled. "Besides, you're the queen, so the Council of Elders can object all they want but the power is with you." Caoimhe paused. "Will

Dolidh return?"

Neamhain smiled. "Yes, she will… at a time of the Goddess's choosing." She kissed Caoimhe. "Let's go and explain my foolishness to Brianag, Cassán, and Eimhir."

CHAPTER 38

Cassán's spirit and hopes were raised when news came that Sorchae and Seonag had crossed the Abhainn Dubh and would enter Dùn Brion on the next sunrise. It was counterbalanced by messengers from the Highlands army who told him that the combined force of Ravens, Na Daoine Tùrsach, and other Eastern Tribes were still a cycle of the moon away.

A battle-weary Seonag entered Dùn Brion's courtyard and was instantly taken aback by the large cats reclining in the oak tree's branches. A short time later, in the Great Hall, she was stunned to see two of the creatures relaxing, if uncomfortably, on benches at the table. The seats barely contained the lincean and creaked under their weight. Sorchae nudged Seonag and whispered, "This is quite exotic, isn't it?" Apart from pleasantries to Cassán, Eimhir, Gràinne, and Brianag, Seonag kept her mouth firmly shut.

Cassán coughed and inclined his head towards the lincean. "Now would be an appropriate time to introduce yourselves to our new arrivals."

"What is going on, Sorchae? Is everyone under a spell? Are *we* enchanted?" Sorchae's reply was a ripple of chuckles, leading Seonag to snap, "You are as infuriating as Brianag." Still, her eyes widened, her jaw dropped, and she emitted an unqueenly squeak when the cats transformed into Neamhain and Caoimhe. She turned her ire on Gràinne, sitting opposite. "A little forewarning would have been appreciated… *friend.*"

An unrepentant Blood Queen's eyes narrowed, and she held Seonag's gaze without blinking. "Until now, the Forest People have suffered the most. Everyone acknowledges the devastation of your people, army, and lands. It pains all of us." Gràinne's red-gold eyes glittered, causing Seonag to dread where she would take the conversation.

"Nevertheless, the fault for the Forest People's destruction lies not with Áine or Leannán. They merely took advantage of a dispute between siblings. *Am I correct?*" Seonag blushed. "A united Forest People would have overwhelmed both sídhe." Gràinne took a deep breath. "In the next cycle of the moon, Cassán's, Neamhain's, Sorchae's, and *my* people will die to preserve *your* throne. Perhaps then you will be satisfied with the division of the dead."

Gràinne took a breath and sipped on a cup of wine. Her eyes reverted to more gold than red, and she asked, "Is Cè recovering?" A mortified Seonag raised her head from staring at her fingers and nodded. Smiling at Neamhain and Caoimhe, Gràinne said, "Our guests sacrificed close friends to kill the Cú Sídhe, as I am sure you will learn later. Therefore, forgive us some mischievousness at your expense. It lightens our sober thoughts."

Thoroughly embarrassed, Seonag stood, turned to Neamhain and Caoimhe, and bowed. "I apologise for my insensitivity and absence of a sense of humour. My life has been tightly focused on death and survival recently. I have witnessed little joy." She looked at Neamhain and smiled. "You, I know…"

Brianag paused chewing on a particularly bloody slice of deer, wiped her chin, and laughed loudly. "I very much doubt you do. She is my closest friend and surprised me."

Sorchae's belly laugh was followed by a painful ouch as she was not fully recovered. Still, it joined Brianag's and echoed around the cavernous Great Hall. "I agree, Brianag. I knew Neamhain had a secret, but this surpassed anything I imagined."

For a moment Seonag again teetered on the cusp of anger but she managed a chuckle. Those present recognised the victory. She looked at Neamhain, stood, and bowed to Neamhain and Caoimhe. "Perhaps a new beginning is needed. I am Seonag Nic Drostan, Bhanrigh of the Forest People." It was the first time Seonag acknowledged her royal title, and it felt uncomfortable on her lips. A frown fluttered on Gràinne's brow.

Neamhain rose and bowed. "We are not strangers because, within me, I keep the 'old' me. Yet, I am also Bhanrigh of the Na Daoine Cait." She giggled, although it came out as a purr. "The honour came with surprising revelations and changes. Discovering you are a cat is quite… disturbing." She looked fondly at Caoimhe. "But only for a little while."

At a nod from Neamhain, Caoimhe stood and bowed. "My name is Caoimhe, and I am a Princess of the Na Daoine Cait. I am my queen's shield-maiden"—Caoimhe laughed—"and frequently her ambassador. Neamhain's training as a sídhe lacked any lessons in diplomacy." She rolled her eyes. "But is that a surprise to anyone?" Laughter rippled around the table.

"And the rest, Caoimhe," said an impish Brianag. Both lynxes blushed.

"Neamhain is my partner as well as my queen." Caoimhe paused and let out a long, sensual purr. "It is a relationship that gives rise to stimulating discussions on domination in our cot." Those gathered laughed freely and loudly, which they had not done in many sunsets. Cups and jugs were banged on the oak table and their contents stained the table. It made a brief and welcome change from tears.

✳✳✳

As the sun rose, painting the sky with a blush of red, Dùn Brion's War Council broke their fast. Ghostly ribbons of white mist floated over the forests. Neither omen was promising. Before the meal concluded, iron-grey clouds deluged the stronghold and surrounding landscape.

"Bloody unpredictable spring weather," groused Cassán. He received grunts of agreement in between the slurping of thin oatmeal and crunching of fresh berries.

Eimhir smiled as she saw Cassán tug his earlobe. "Your mind is on other matters. What are you thinking?"

"The marshes," he replied.

Blank expressions greeted Cassán's brief explanation. In his youth, Cassán would have taken the reaction as an insult. Instead, he laughed and elaborated. "The north-western portion of the land bordering the Clota estuary and river is bogland. It dries and freezes during the winter. However, with spring and the recent rains, once again, it has become treacherous. The Clota will likely overflow its banks, too."

He motioned to Luag. "According to Luag, only a handful of hunter families know the paths through the marshland." The puzzled expressions remained. Cassán sighed. "Our battle strategy is obvious and simple, which is a good thing. We drive the bastards into the bogs or the waters of the Clota. Our blades will slaughter them, and the dark depths of the marshes and Clota will be their graveyards."

"What about the civilians?" asked Brianag, sucking noisily at a piece of berry skin wedged in her back teeth.

Manners, daughter.

Sorry, Ma.

"They will be escorted to the forests and mountains to the south-west of Dùn Brion. There is ample room and cover. The trees and the river will provide an abundant supply of meat and fish."

"They will need protection. Something always goes awry in any battle plan. Remember the last time," said Brianag to mumbles of agreement.

Cassán scratched his head. "If Seonag agrees, I propose positioning a thousand of my shield-wall warriors and a similar number of her forest fighters with them, and all our war hounds. At the worst, the force is large enough to stall a stronger attack on the civilians until help arrives."

Cassán was relieved to see Seonag dip her head and hear the members around the table voice their approval.

"Speaking of numbers, how many are in Áine's horde?" asked Gràinne.

"Our latest reports estimate about twenty-five thousand. They may have picked up more warriors, whether by force or voluntarily, on the journey," said Eimhir. "They have entered the mouth of the Sleagh Valley. Hence, my scouts will be able to provide regular and more accurate updates, soon."

"Allowing for the warriors needed to protect the civilians and the absence of the Eastern Tribes' troops, we are outnumbered three to one." Glum expressions settled on the group's faces until Gràinne said, "I have faced worse and won."

She added, "We have a unique advantage in our horses and chariots, even if the ground is not perfect. There are, of course, those of us with special gifts, although we may be occupied neutralising Áine." She took a sip of milk, relishing its cold creaminess. "We also have the strongholds of Dùn Brion and Dùn Athad to retreat to, if needed."

Gràinne looked at Neamhain, who could not forestall shivering at the unsettling gaze. "Áine is Womb-Born and, like the Aes Sídhe, can influence the weather." Neamhain breathed in sharply, guessing where Gràinne was going. "Did you lose your ability to use the climate during your transformation?"

"The honest answer is that I do not know." She laughed. "My singing voice has changed. Those who heard my sisters and me on the walkway will agree the new sound is not an improvement." Cassán nodded in agreement.

Gràinne's next target was Sorchae, who also found it challenging not to wilt under the Blood Queen's intense stare. "Seonag told me about your songs at the Battle of A' Chrìon Làraich. Can you influence the weather?"

Sorchae shrugged. "Like Neamhain, I do not know. I am learning on the job." She knew, as with Neamhain, that her answer was weak, and she awaited Gràinne's riposte. It came quickly and sharply.

"There is an army marching towards us and we are substantially outnumbered. I suggest Neamhain and you come together and sort out what you can and cannot do… *now.*" Although it was presented as a proposal, the recipients understood they had been scolded like a mother reprimanding her children.

There was only one response. Neamhain and Sorchae stood, bowed, and said, "Yes, my lady." Along with Caoimhe, they exited the chamber.

Ardghal nudged Luag. "This battle will be one of surprises." A sombre Luag dipped his head. With Malmhìn's death, he felt as if he would be fighting without his right arm.

⋆

In the broad valley north of the Sleagh, Áine's vanguard walked barefoot over wet, yet firm, ground. Twenty rows back, the army tramped through thick, glutinous mud. At one hundred rows, they were up to their calves in a dark, foul-smelling slush.

Brògan and skin were sucked from poorly maintained feet. Most of Áine's warriors came from humble forest families. Thus, if they wore footwear at all, it was handmade, using low-quality hides. Under constantly wet and muddy conditions, the protection disintegrated.

Áine had the power to improve her army's situation by using strong winds or reducing the rain to a light drizzle. However, the demigod was mean-minded, blaming the slow journey to Dùn Brion on the warriors' need to satiate a long list of depravities. When she finally emerged from the Sleagh Valley into the plain, she smiled. In this, she was alone. Before them, Áine's warriors saw a large, treeless plain, stretching into the distance with no end in sight. The landscape was an aberration, even for the less mountainous Lowlands.

Generations of Na Mèadaidh farmers had felled the timber. Initially, they used the wood to build shelters, but soon, they planted corn and other crops in the newly created plain. It was not long before they cut down more trees to create more fields. As the warriors gazed ahead, the only breaks in the lush grassland were deserted farmsteads and drystone walls. To a forest fighter, whose refuge and shield were the dense trees, the scene was nightmarish.

Vengeance drove Áine. The shimmering, purple silhouette of Dùn Brion, a sunset's march to the south, became the focus of her hate. To anyone who would listen, she swore to reduce the stronghold to rubble and slaughter those she blamed for Sidheag's death along with their off-spring and families. She would savour their excruciatingly painful demises and return triumphantly to the Mounds.

In her visions, Áine saw the Womb-Born and the Aes Sídhe hold her up as an example of how they should deal with humans. *"Tá ár lá tagtha—our day has come,"* she breathed into the air. Áine's self-indulgent reveries ended abruptly when her recently promoted battle commander appeared at her side. Given the number who had occupied the position recently, it was deemed a death sentence, not an honour. He gestured towards the west. In the distance was a flickering, multicoloured line.

The Womb-Born queen pushed her vision closer, enough to discern the individual faces of the warriors. When Áine attempted to breach the veils protecting their minds, she was brutally rebuffed. Brianag's maw opened wide to reveal rows of needle-point teeth. Her mocking voice reminded Áine of how helpless she had been in the Mounds of the Aes Sídhe.

"I am prepared and stronger, bitseach!" shouted Áine.

And yet I am in your head but mine is closed to you.

Those around Áine shuddered. They wondered what creature could inspire such raw emotion in the sídhe.

Brianag is coming for you, Ma, and I will have revenge on the one who aban-doned me. Sidheag's voice echoed through the halls and chambers of Áine's mind, ripping asunder veils of protection constructed over aeons. Áine's eardrum-shattering shrieking resounded over the plain.

"How many are there?" rasped the burly battle commander, ripping Áine from her trance.

She was thankful for the mercy but would never show it. "About ten thousand; they are arrayed quite prettily."

"You will be more respectful when you watch their shield-wall grind our flesh and bone."

"Are you afraid? I can replace you."

The man snorted. "Go ahead. Whether leading or following, my fate will be no different than that of our warriors."

"Advice?"

"Their strategy appears obvious. Force us closer to Dùn Brion's walls and crush us between the assembled army divisions and the stronghold's heavy bolt-throwers," said the battle commander.

"Is that what they will do?"

"They have mobility, organisation, and experienced leaders, so probably not." The warrior held Áine's gaze without flinching. He did not wait long before her talons sliced through his neck, leaving it hanging by a small strip of skin. It was as good and quick a death as he could have expected and likely a better one than his comrades would receive. Still, he wished that his last memory was not the sound of the bitseach drinking his gushing blood.

***

Cassán swore as his shield-man checked his sleeveless, hip-length chainmail tunic and tightened the straps of his boiled leather cuirass over the mail. The body armour was also inlaid with small, iron scales. "I am supposed to be able to fight, which assumes I can breathe," grumbled Cassán. His battle commander was unrepentant.

Both stood in the front rank of the shield-wall. The wall comprised four rows, each with one thousand warriors. They stood an arm's length from each other. Each held a javelin in one hand and an oblong, chin to mid-calf *sgiath*—shield—in the other. Three more spears were stabbed into the soft earth. Once the javelins were thrown, the formation would tighten up.

Ten paces back from the wall stood a reserve of one thousand fighters. These were the least experienced members of the shield-wall. If they were needed, the battle was likely lost.

Every warrior had three darts strapped to the inside of their shield. All had short, ribbed, steel swords hung in sheepskin-lined scabbards on their belts. Some had longswords, and others carried axes, suspended from leather loops on their backs. It was impossible to count the number of knives secreted in or on their bodies.

All wore plain, smooth iron-and-bronze helmets with an acorn at the apex. Ribbons of varying colours fluttered from the bronze nub. They were the one piece of individualism permitted in the shield-wall. Most were gifted by partners, lovers, or children.

Apart from the autumnal skirmish in the south-western forest against Conn, Dùn Brion's shield-wall had not been tested in a major battle for ten summers. Cassán looked anxiously around him, trying to read his warriors' body language. Their eyes and faces gave nothing away, and he hoped that was a good sign.

"They will perform well and, if needed, die well. That is all you can ask of them," said the shield-man.

"Thanks," said Cassán. He shrugged his shoulders and grinned. "Are you sure this cuirass is tight enough?"

✳✳✳

Behind Cassán's shield-wall were the riders and chariots. The latter's long scythes were a source of anxiety among the foot and horse warriors. "I wish we had several thousand of your Ravens' spears with us," said Gràinne, looking over her shoulder at Sorchae.

The queen's charioteer, a veteran of many battles, played with the reins to keep the team of four shaggy-haired horses' steady. Gràinne's arse cheeks rippled gently as the chariot's *cret* rocked. *Am I getting fat?* The team's tack sang like wind chimes and plucked the thought away. It was a sound that always soothed the Blood Queen before battle. She laughed at the earthy comments and suggested rutting positions from those behind her. Men and women about to die deserved a little tolerance.

"So do I, and no, you're not getting fat. Of more immediate concern to me is that you keep your chariots' knives far away from my horses," said Sorchae, answering Gràinne's question and wish.

"I've never hurt a friendly horse—yet—but I might start with your bastards," retorted Gràinne.

The riders arrayed behind Sorchae roared their support and she laughed. Like Gràinne, the Hand of the Goddess and agreed leader of the mounted warriors was naked astride her tall, chestnut mare. Her curling sigils lay dormant, waiting for the emergence of a timorous sun or early moon from the blanket of clouds. Neither looked promising.

On either side of Sorchae were Ardghal and Beira. The latter constantly complained it was unnatural for a forest warrior to be mounted and asked who would soothe her aching arse. Sorchae fought to stem a grin at the deluge of volunteers from the riders. She eventually gave up and joined in the laughter.

****

On Cassán's right flank, Seonag was conflicted and uniquely dressed. Many years as Cassán's father's shield and battle commander in Dùn Brion had acclimatised her to wearing armour and chainmail. Her choice of weapons—swords, maces, axes, and javelins—reflected that period, also.

Seonag knew her Forest People would fight courageously and selflessly and give no quarter. The latter was the problem. Most had had family or friends slaughtered by Leannán's brutes and were determined to serve retribution on those they blamed. Could they fight coldly and pragmatically? She huffed. *When did my people ever fight without passion?*

The Forest People's queen divided her army into two, with each forming the wings of Cassán's battle formation. It was a tried and tested shape better known as *Sgiath an Fhithich*—the Ravens' Wings. Like the Ravens, the Forest People mostly fought naked or wearing plaid trousers.

The differences were in the choice of weapon and terrain. Seonag sighed. Sometimes, she was envious of the freedom to fight unfettered like Sorchae or Gràinne.

No one is stopping you but yourself, Seonag. Gràinne's intrusion was echoed by Sorchae.

Next time, and after several strong brews, perhaps, laughed Seonag.

While the Ravens fought with spears to force attackers onto the shield-wall, the Forest People preferred clubs. These ranged from basic tree branches enhanced with iron rings and spikes to impressively ornate, flanged maces with hardwood shafts, and repurposed blacksmiths' hammers. *We are tree fighters. How will we adapt to an unnatural open field denuded of natural cover?*

She looked at the quintet of shield-warriors, three male and two female, who were her protectors. After the Battle of A' Chrion Làraich, neither she nor they could decide who should be her shield, so all were officially appointed to the position. They had quickly become her family.

The oldest female looked at her and gave her a toothy smile. "You'll be fine, and we'll be fine. What's the worst that can happen—dying and entering the feasting halls of Mag Mell? Look at your army. Most of the warriors come from poor families. Mag Mell, and relief from the drudgery of life, are the dreams of many."

The veteran tugged on long copper-red braids and laughed. "After the battle, you will be proud of your army. You will cry and mourn alongside their families at the funeral pyres. You will drink yourself into oblivion, rut strangers, and awake with a raging headache and a sour belly." The veteran winked. "You will, of course, not forget to bathe in a freezing cold river. Celebrating Samhain with a wee'un would be embarrassing."

"Thanks," said Seonag. Then she sighed. "It has been a long time since I have been rutted." At the raised eyebrows of her shields, she added, "That is not an invitation… and you are not to follow me at the victory celebrations."

The wily veterans bowed deeply and winked to each other. Of course, they would follow the queen. That was their job.

***

I have brought her to you, daughter. Slaughter the bitseach and set us free. Sidheag's voice was full of anticipation.

I am not your daughter, Sidheag. I never was and never will be. Áine will die by my hand because that is what I want. Without her, you would not exist, and neither would Leannán. Without your interference, I would be normal. Brianag ground her teeth until her jaws ached.

I deserve respect, Brianag. Who saved a stubborn adolescent from freezing to death in the Highlands and provided nutrition? And it is time you stopped lying to yourself about being normal. I did not plant the seed which germinated in you.

Liar!

We can debate causes and meanings, Brianag, but the fact is that ever since you tasted that first drop of my blood, you and I have been joined, albeit unwillingly. We are at opposite ends of the same chain. The laugh that rattled around Sidheag's throat was chilling. *Whatever you may think of me, I am and will always be a part of you. I care for you more than my mother ever cared for me. However, this I know. Kill Áine and the chain between her and me will sunder, as will the cord that binds you and me. I will seek another world to bend to my will.*

The tone of sadness that infused Sidheag's last words shocked Brianag. For the first time, she considered Sidheag might have feelings. Also, what freedom would she have? She would still be a powerful creature, feared by all but those who knew and loved her. And now she had another riddle to solve. Who planted the seed in her, and who would she ask?

"How can I trust you or your words, bitseach?" shouted a frustrated Brianag. There was no answer. Eleven pairs of lynx eyes opened, and eleven heads tilted to the side. "Shite! My apologies. I have creator issues." Brianag took the communal purr as sympathy.

CHAPTER 39

The Lowlands

Áine's vision swept across Cassán's chosen battlefield. She sensed the impatience of her enemy, whether human or gifted, to engage and their determination to destroy her. She empathised with and understood their cold, disciplined, and unforgiving fury. It contrasted starkly with the picture presented when she looked over her shoulder.

In her army, she observed the faces of the subdued, the terrified, and the rapacious. A moment of intense disappointment flooded her mind. *Why do I not engender loyalty?* She spat on the dirt. *I require sacrifice, not devotion.* She scoured the layout of the battleground, looking for weaknesses—every plan has one—and she found Cassán's. Áine turned to her latest battle commander. He flinched. *Spineless arsehole.*

She pointed to the forests in the south-west. "The mothers, daughters, and children of those who want to kill you are in the trees. You are forest fighters. Surely, your ineptitude does not include being defeated by the weakest members of the tribe." Black held hazel eyes. A sharp talon lifted the man's bearded chin, and he trembled. "Rape, pillage, and kill. Indulge your worst lusts. Fail me, and you will die slowly as I crush your skull and drink your blood."

***

"The Hag's bony arse! How could I have been so wrong? I should have anticipated this." An anguished Cassán pointed to Áine's horde who, like a flock of birds in a green sky, wheeled around and jogged in a south-westerly direction. He turned to Gràinne, Seonag, and Sorchae. "The bitseach's target is our people in the forest." He scratched his shaven head so hard it bled.

"No plan is executed perfectly, Cassán. Our mistake was to parade our strength. We should have used the forest cover better. Áine's response is exactly what I would have done," said Gràinne. "What are your orders?"

Cassán rubbed his chin. "Even at a fast jog, our foot warriors cannot intercept Áine before her army reaches the forest. Let us pray the ones we left to protect the people hold firm. That said, Áine's rabble cannot reach the camp before night falls; they will have to make camp tonight and attack at sunrise." He looked at Gràinne and Sorchae. "Harass them with our chariots and horses, but not foolishly. Use Dùn Brion to resupply."

Gràinne dipped her head. "Brianag and Neamhain?"

A crooked smile settled on Cassán's lips. "They know what to do when darkness falls."

***

Led by a shimmering red Blood Queen, twenty chariots wove in and out of the loosely organised body of Áine's army. Once their stock of javelins and darts were exhausted, the warriors hefted their favourite weapons: longswords, axes, and maces. Soon, covered in gore, the gaily coloured baskets and banners became a uniform crimson.

Affixing long scythes to the vehicles' axles transformed a useful transporter of leaders across the battlefield into a fearsome creator of terror. It took courage and a cold temperament to defend against and then to attack a chariot. Áine's horde claimed neither. They ran and were harvested like ripe corn. Limbs were scattered wide across the meadows. Legless men and women sobbed and begged for a sharp knife to the heart. They discovered charity had fled Áine's army.

Instead, their comrades spat on and mocked them as they ran past.

Those who had not bled out on the grass found relief of a kind when the sun dropped below the horizon and the first predators emerged from the trees.

***

Sorchae stood on the thick, black, gold-fringed *diallait* covering her horse's back. Instantly her sigils caught a shaft of sunlight and exploded into rivers of gold and red. She pointed with a javelin to the front of the enemy's formation, howled like a bean-sìth, sat down, and led the formation forward at a gallop.

Cassán had tasked Sorchae to disrupt Áine's momentum, thus giving those in the forest more time to prepare their defences. Fortunately, her warriors sat astride an excellent weapon. Fiercer than the riders were the five hundred horses with bony hooves and huge, grass-stained teeth. Each weighed the equivalent of eight warriors.

The queen of the Raven's decision to attack the enemy's column far from the rampaging chariots was prudent, saving man and beast from the spinning knives. Áine's horde had long replaced battle training and tactics with rape and pillaging. Feeble leadership, no discernible strategy, and a poor choice of weapons proved disastrous against the horses who slammed into the vanguard. Volleys of javelins and darts were hurled, leaving thousands grasping at the trembling wooden shafts and iron that sprouted from their bodies.

When the missiles were exhausted, the riders unsheathed long-handled swords, maces, and axes. The horses joined in with furious kicking and biting. Only Cassán's instruction to fight wisely made Sorchae blow the horn to withdraw. "Return to Dùn Brion, re-arm, and eat," boomed her voice across the field. Áine's army gave a communal sigh of relief and prayed for a restful night. The Goddess spurned their prayers.

***

The veteran *ceannard mìle*—leader of a thousand—in command of Cassán's forest defences looked down and smiled. The young woman at his side claimed she was fifteen summers. She held a spear in soft, trembling hands. Likely, several sunrises past, her duties were milking the family's cows. On the morning, the veteran called for volunteers to man the hastily erected defences, she was among the first to step forward.

Her jaw was set defiantly, and her face looked northwards, to Áine's encampment of thousands of campfires. Experience told him she would not be persuaded to change her mind, and she would be dead by sunset. He reached out, took her spear, stabbed the butt into the soft dirt, and said, "Let the sleagh do the work. A wise warrior does not waste her strength. Seasoned fighters conserve energy." The veteran breathed deeply. "You will stand with me until I tell you to retreat behind the defences. There you will rest your weapon on the stockade until you need to stab the enemy."

The young girl's eyes misted over. She knew if she withdrew, he would not. He would stand and die. She looked up at him and thought his blue eyes set in a weather-worn face were beautiful. "Thanks," she said. Then she smiled and risked squeezing his rough, calloused hand. Both knew the opportunity might never come again.

***

Áine's camp's mood was fractious but grateful the chariots and horses had retired. Still, apart from Áine, who had no need for sleep, the makeshift encampment had a fitful rest. Fear was the army's constant companion. Night was the perfect environment for the huge black wolf and chain of eleven lynxes who noiselessly approached the camp. To the heightened senses of the hunters, it was as if the camp was in full daylight.

Another, much larger, four-legged army waited beyond the treeline. Hundreds of wolf packs padded forward and took up positions. Steam from a thousand panting mouths rose into the chilly spring night. They awaited orders from Brianag and would attack only when she allowed it. No matter what, before dawn, their bellies would be bloated with two-legs' flesh. They did not wait long until Brianag howled, followed by Neamhain and her lincean.

In Áine's camp, those who survived the night had terrible nightmares of bones crunched by iron jaws, of throats torn out by teeth that never lost their edge, and of the cries of those dragged into the forest to feed pups with equally sharp incisors. The visions lasted for the remainder of their lives. Still, for many that was not a long time.

***

In the forest encampment, the veteran shivered at the shrieking and screaming from Áine's camp. Yet his imagination was insufficient to describe the litany of horrors inflicted on his enemy. He had heard rumours of a great wolf and watch of lincean but put it down to foolish gossip. The camp's hounds howled incessantly, angry at not being allowed to join the night battle, and he swore at their handlers: "Keep those bloody hounds quiet!"

A small figure stirred beside him, and he smiled. She had been fretful and unable to sleep because of the Otherworldly noises filling the night air. He made her lie beside him and covered her in a heavy woollen *brat*. She had fallen asleep against his chest as he smoothed her long blonde tresses. He growled at the vulgar suggestions to rut her from those younger than him, which was most of his command. There was nothing to stop him. No one would object. It was one of the benefits of his position. He had the strength and authority to overwhelm any protest she might make, and she would have no redress. None would support her.

He smiled. *Would I have said anything different, even just five summers ago?* He shrugged. *Probably not.* He knew the younger version of him would have rutted her. The veteran smiled again and muttered, "I'm getting old."

***

An overcast dawn of persistent mizzle, mist, and the smell of death greeted Áine. In common with the humans, what annoyed her the most was the curtain of rain. Still, whether cold or warm, wet or dry, the climate did not bother any sídhe because they could meld it to suit their personal preference. Áine extended her vision over her army, cursed her naivety, and reviewed the many mistakes she had accrued. Thin, dusty pink lips curled into an ugly sneer. *Hindsight is a useless tool.*

Áine's grumbling marked a deeper anxiety, which the abundance of fresh blood and bodies, many incapacitated by injuries, could not remove. *How will I gather those who killed Sidheag together?* The battle did not matter to her. Whether one or twenty thousand died, she would not shed a single tear. It was a deception, perhaps her finest. She wanted her prey to look into each other's eyes like they did when they judged Sidheag. Like ghouls, they had watched molten iron poured over her living, writhing, and screaming body. They had celebrated Sidheag's awful death; now Áine would balance the scales and serve justice.

A hint of magenta crept above the dawn horizon. Its purity was quickly adulterated by pink, orange, and yellow hues. It was a magnificent display, but few in Áine's horde appreciated it. Some broke their fast with bread, cheese, oatmeal, berries, and spring water. Most drank the remaining beer to give them courage.

The wiser among the army used whetstones to grind a sharp edge on blades dulled and notched in the previous sunset's battle. Too late, Áine understood that these were the men and women she should have relied on. Yet could running, terrified and screaming, from the incisors, claws, hoofs, and blades of their foes be counted as a battle? Winning the imminent mêlée might redeem the tale, if not the warriors.

Áine stood, pointed to the forest, and spoke. Her voice was chillingly calm and heard by the farthest warrior. "You will attack, despoil, and slaughter everyone. Fail me and I will drink your blood and make you and your kin suffer such that you will beg for the Otherworld. Succeed and I will lead you to conquer other tribes and nations."

✳✳✳

In the forest, the horde faced a man-high berm of dirt, rocks, and trees. In front of the earthworks stood a thousand-man shield-wall, supported by a thousand farmers and their sons and daughters. Spears sat as comfortably in work-hardened hands as hoes or pitchforks. Indeed, many preferred the latter's familiarity. A man is easier to impale and toss aside than a bale of hay. High in the trees, a thousand of Seonag's Forest People waited.

With the berm in sight but still unable to make out individual faces, Áine's horde neglected to survey the field before them and charged through ground sewn with iron thistles and arm-deep holes planted with sharp, shite-smeared stakes. In their frenzy to get to the people, few noticed the fluttering ribbons, marking safe paths for the defenders.

The horde had a single strategy: to overwhelm by numbers. In their zeal, they also forgot about war dogs, until a thousand grey and brown shapes with a thousand snapping jaws bounded through and over the berm. A desperate and bloody struggle between defenders and attackers built a second berm of bodies one hundred paces from the defences. The slippery, gore-soaked wall of the dead and dying became a challenging barrier.

Fear rippled through the aggressors' ranks as Cassán's war horns blared out at their rear. Gripped by the need to survive, they knew they must overcome the defences and take hostages before the enemy cut off any path to retreat. They fought with desperation and died by the hundreds.

***

Cassán's and Seonag's warriors engaged the rearguard. Sorchae's riders rode in a wide arc to bypass the horde and blunt the assault on the berm. Brianag, Neamhain, and the lincean continued to terrorise Áine's army. Brianag relinquished her wolf-persona, preferring to slaughter as an iridescent, green nightmare.

The unhappiest of the combatants were Gràinne and her chariots, who were banished to the edges of the battle. Still, she conceded the rationale behind the tactics. Chariots were ineffective in close-quarter fighting in a forest. Still, it did not prevent the group's disgruntlement. Only when her driver, a wise veteran, tapped her shoulder and said, "Go," did the Blood Queen and her warriors step down from their chariots and enter the battle alongside her daughter. Wails of terror and anguish ascended as A 'Bhanrigh Fuil and her daughter, Brianag, meted out justice, cleaving a bloody gorge through Áine's army.

Thousands died on the edge of the forest as Cassán's shield-wall ground its way closer to the civilian defences. Nevertheless, caught in the jaws of an implacable foe, the horde's resistance became more determined. They knew they had no defence for their actions and would be shown no mercy. Therefore, they attacked the civilian defences with increased ferocity. They needed its sanctuary.

The veteran observed his shield-wall and the reserve were reduced by half. Of those remaining, all bore wounds and verged on the edge of exhaustion. He bellowed, "Hold!" to the warriors. Then he turned to the volunteers and shouted, "Get behind the berm. Protect your families." The girl shook her head but the look in his eyes said, *do not disobey me*. Her shoulders slumped; she grasped her spear and sobbed as she trudged through the narrow opening in the berm.

***

Cassán called Seonag to him. "The berm will not hold much longer, and we cannot break through this horde in time. I am open to suggestions."

"They are desperate. We have them trapped and they will fight like cornered rats." She paused and rubbed a smear of blood from her cheek. "Give the vermin an escape route."

The king's eyebrow lifted and Seonag laughed. "I did not say to let them escape. Withdraw warriors from the western flank. Make it look like a new tactic. Signal Sorchae to stop any of the horde running south." Seonag's eyes glistened. "You wanted to drive them into the Clota estuary and marshes. It was a good strategy, and we can still execute it."

War horns blared out across the battlefield. The veteran chieftains of Áine's horde watched as divisions of their enemy assembled and reassembled. Spotting the weakness on the western flank, they grinned and signalled the retreat. Fifteen thousand warriors flowed westward. Too late, they realised the deception as Cassán, Seonag, and Sorchae guided them to the river and the marshland beyond it. Their cries rose into the sky as the real slaughter began.

✳✳✳

The forest battle over, the young girl searched a battlefield of horrors that no one of her youth should have witnessed. From meadhan-latha to dusk she walked and stumbled through the broken and the dead. On occasion she thrust her spear into a wounded enemy; sometimes she sent a mortally wounded comrade to Mag Mell.

Her stomach, long empty from puking, felt bruised. She scavenged a strip of almost-clean tunic to cover her mouth and nose to resist the cloying tastes and smells of the slaughter. The adolescent considered tossing her léine aside. Soaked in gore, it clung to her slender body, a constant reminder of the slaughter. However, modesty prevailed, and she kept the garment. The dress was not much but at least it kept her one layer removed from being bathed in blood. That said, to anyone she passed, she appeared a sylph covered in gore, from head to toe.

She rested momentarily on a fallen tree and immediately drew the attention of a group of warriors. The fever of battle sublimated into a need to gratify their desires, and the whores had not yet flooded the battlefield. The girl understood the rationale of their crude threats. However, the stance of her feet, steel in her eyes, and the unwavering spear held in bloodstained hands stated her intentions. She would not submit and would wound, maybe kill, a few of them. They dipped their heads in respect and walked away in search of less dangerous prey.

She looked up through the forest canopy and whispered, "Please, Goddess. I need help." The great eagle in the sky opened its bill and a sound like a child's laughter flowed from it. The girl saw and heard the bird and was annoyed. *Am I mocked?* She saw the huge bird circle several times before flying in a north-easterly direction. "Thanks, Goddess. I'm sorry for my impatience," she murmured and jogged in the direction of the bird's path.

The sight of his body slumped against a tree made her heart miss several beats and the blood drained from her face. A bloody spear lay across a broad chest, which no longer lifted with each breath. He was caked in blood. Deep wounds on his torso continued to weep. *Was that a good sign?* The veteran's legs and arms were not much better. His left arm hung awkwardly, and a ring of livid bruises around his ankle pointed to a break. In his right hand he gripped a sword; however, she doubted he could raise it—if he was still alive.

The girl chastised herself for her lack of faith. The Goddess had guided her to this place for a reason. She ran towards the veteran but paused when she heard a spring bubbling nearby. The young woman removed the cloth from around her mouth, dipped it in the spring, and ran to her veteran.

"You will not die," she whispered in his ear as she moistened his lips and dribbled water into his mouth. The young woman—she had earned the title—began to clean the gore from his face. She flinched at a new, long scar from cheek to chin but resolved to continue her work. She would sew his scars later. Many times, she returned to the brook, and each time she said, "You will not die. I will not allow it." She never abandoned hope, even though her reserves of faith and physical strength were greatly depleted.

The bean-sìth stood at the man's side and stretched out its hand to take the veteran's spirit. It stopped when it looked into the girl's fierce eyes and glanced upwards. The Goddess smiled. *Leave this one. There are many others to guide to Mag Mell or the Otherworld.*

The veteran coughed, faintly and painfully. His chest moved and he gasped as broken ribs pricked his lungs. The girl's tears cascaded onto his face and drummed against his eyelids. "I might drown," he croaked. She resisted the temptation to slap him. That would wait until he was healthy and they could reminisce about this moment.

"Thank you," he murmured and signalled her to come closer to his mouth. "I wish you were my daughter."

The young girl smiled. "I can be. I'm an orphan."

✷✷✷

Ten thousand avoided the marshes and evaded the shield-wall, clubs, chariots, and riders. They heaved sighs of relief when, spent, they flowed into the western mouth of the Sleagh Valley. Wails of despair and curses filled the air when they discovered their path to the Highlands and safety blocked by the Eastern Tribes' army.

Late to the battle, the spears of the Eastern Tribes aimed to match their allies' death toll. The Blood Queen had given them their orders: "Spare no one and show no mercy." All hope of retreat or disappearing into the great forests ended for the remnants of Áine's horde when their heads were spiked on leaf-shaped blades and displayed as a warning for all to witness.

✷✷✷

A scouring of the battlefield revealed one thing: Áine was nowhere to be seen. "Did we think she would stand and fight with her army? It was always a means to an end," said Brianag.

"I agree. However, the 'end' has always been our deaths to avenge Sidheag," said Cassán. "We are gathered here. Where is she?"

Eimhir's scream from the battlements of Dùn Brion gave him the answer.

CHAPTER 40

Dùn Brion

Huddled in a corner of Dùn Brion's ramparts, a blood-enrobed Eimhir sobbed and prayed. She rocked to and fro, constantly caressing her belly and assuring the baby she would protect her. Eimhir was not severely injured. A painfully twisted ankle limited her movement, and she had suffered multiple lacerations and bruises when Áine dragged her up the walkway's steps and along its length.

The grey, stone battlements of Dùn Brion were awash in blood and gore and a haze of shimmering air floated above the still-warm bodies of the garrison. Mercifully, due to the ongoing forest and Sleagh Valley battles, only a skeleton cohort of two hundred warriors guarded the fort and the queen. Still, that would be of no comfort to their families and lovers. None of the garrison survived. The gore was from the brave warriors who had attempted to save her. Their deaths were bloody, ago-nising, and delivered with contempt.

Amid her comrades bleeding and awaiting the bean-sìth on the cold stone, Eimhir watched the youngest and last of them, a girl of no more than sixteen, struggle to stand and face Áine. Eimhir prayed for the young woman, but knew the warrior faced impossible odds. More tears cascaded onto the parapet as she saw Áine grasp the girl by the throat, effortlessly lift her off the walkway, and eviscerate her. Coils of steaming guts slithered onto the stone, to join scores of others. The flesh on the girl's chest was shredded, exposing gleaming white ribs.

Yet the young warrior refused to cry out or scream, infuriating Áine. Helpless, Eimhir watched the sídhe's maw open and long bloodstained incisors descend. In desperation, she shouted, "What is your name?" Through the blood spouting from the young woman's mouth, Eimhir barely made out the word "Ròs" before her throat was gone. The vision of her sacrifice would never leave Eimhir.

Áine's grazing and slurping sounds as she fed on the girl's blood and flesh revolted Eimhir, and she threw up. As she caressed her belly, she whispered, "Ròs. Your name is Ròs." Eimhir prayed once more. This time, she pleaded with the Goddess that Cassán would not come to Dùn Brion. In her heart, she knew it was a forlorn hope.

Therefore, Eimhir prayed again. This time for lightning to strike the fort and fire to destroy it and every trace of life within its walls. The evil had to be vanquished, and for that she would gladly sacrifice herself and the unborn Ròs. The Goddess was sorely tempted by Eimhir's request. However, she knew fire would not guarantee Áine's death, and so she forgave Eimhir's curses.

***

Cassán swore as he was unceremoniously dumped on Dùn Brion's stone walkway. Brianag did not want to bring her brother, yet if anyone deserved to be included, it was Cassán. That he was deposited in the farthest corner of the walls from Eimhir prompted a stream of frustrated oaths. He rose with every intent of making his way to Eimhir, but two lynxes blocked his path.

"They have instructions to prevent you getting any closer. If needed, they will break your legs," said Brianag. Her expression said she was not bluffing.

"Bitseach!"

Brianag smiled. "If I let you fight Áine, you will die, brother. That is unacceptable. Eimhir is good for you, and your baby needs what I never enjoyed—a father. This is not a fight for humans. Seonag and you have commanded with courage and have gained a great victory for Northern

310

Albu." She nodded in the direction of Áine. "Leave this final battle to the darker side of our family." Cassán would have objected and risked the loss of his legs but for one small word. For the first time in their relationship, Brianag said, "Please."

And so, Cassán dipped his head. "Keep Eimhir safe and… and kill the bitseach." He paused and added, through tightly pursed lips, "Slowly and as painfully as possible. I want to hear her scream and beg for mercy."

***

"Why here, Ma? It's a poor position to defend," said Brianag. When Gràinne, Brianag, Cassán, and the lincean appeared on Dùn Brion's walls, Áine retreated to the corner where Eimhir sat rocking back and forth.

"She holds us in contempt because she assumes we will sacrifice everything to preserve the human."

Brianag looked warily at her ma, but Gràinne was gone and in her place was A 'Bhanrigh Fuil. The Blood Queen was ready for battle with red eyes and long red talons. Swirling crimson sigils in perpetual motion were enhanced by an opaque, pulsating, aura. It sent blood-red fingers towards Áine who visibly recoiled from the tendrils.

"She *is* right, isn't she, Ma? We will do everything to keep Eimhir safe, won't we?" The Blood Queen's long silence made Brianag shiver. "Ma?" Brianag remembered Sidheag's words about the seed, which had slept within her, and wondered if she was right. She questioned who was the most powerful: Áine, Gràinne, or herself?

Gràinne's aura retreated, leaving her skin a vibrant, pastel pink. She smiled. "*You* are the most powerful, but Áine and I are the most experienced. Often, in battle, knowledge and practice tips the balance." Gràinne inhaled deeply and exhaled several times. "Of course we will rescue Eimhir; she is your sister through Cassán, and you are the baby's aunt. The challenge is how."

A scream from Eimhir broke the conversation and removed an

opportunity for a tactical diversion. Áine bent over and grabbed Eimhir by her long braids. The queen's scalp stretched to breaking and she cried out for relief. Dragging Eimhir through the bloody slop, Áine walked a few paces towards Brianag.

"Leave her alone, bitseach. She has nothing to do with our conflict. Release her," demanded Brianag.

"An Abomination, who is a child in comparison to me, has no authority to make demands of a Womb-Born," snapped Áine. She peered over Brianag's shoulder to Gràinne and chuckled. "It must have been difficult for her to grow up with two mothers."

"She has one mother, bitseach. *Me*," growled Gràinne and braced herself.

"I can feel her nascent power straining at the shackles with which her human part seeks to bind her. With Sidheag, she had the freedom to cast that off and set her true self free. She might have been a worthy opponent of one of the Womb-Born. Unlike you, she is naïve and holds to the delusion she can be normal. Both of you are tainted by your feelings for humans…" She looked down at Eimhir. "…like this one."

"You cannot win, Áine. Your vengeance can never be accomplished. Only Brianag, Cassán, and I face you. One is missing from those who oversaw Sidheag's execution: the sídhe, Mongfhionn." Gràinne laughed and the sound echoed around the walls of Dùn Brion, taunting Áine. "Did you think she would come to rescue her daughter and granddaughter? She has no need, for she knows we are stronger than you."

Eimhir screamed as Áine lifted her effortlessly as if she were a feather. Áine was tall, even for a sídhe. Thus, Eimhir dangled like a straw puppet a forearm's length off the walkway. She felt the bones pop, her neck stretched, and she felt her belly push against her blood-soaked léine. A sharp talon dragged leisurely across Eimhir's pale throat. Flakes of dry skin were carried away on a breeze, layers of skin parted as the nail dug deeper, and Eimhir felt blood trickle from the tear. The pain was no more than a cut from a blade of grass. Eimhir sensed it was not a mortal wound and sighed at the respite.

"You are perceptive for a human," mocked Áine. "My next demonstration will not be to your liking." A talon sliced through the ties securing Eimhir's gown, and it sloughed off, coming to rest in the gore. Eimhir flinched as she felt the sharp nail trace designs on her belly. She pissed herself, and the warm fluid flowed down her thighs to join the bloody walkway.

On Dùn Brion's ramparts, Cassán bellowed, "No!" as he watched the talon travel down Eimhir's belly. This time the path was vertical, the cut was deep, and blood flowed freely. Eimhir grasped at her stomach and attempted to push the edges of the slash together.

"Kneel before me or I will pluck the baby from the human's womb. I will drink both mother and child's blood, and feast on their flesh."

***

"Why?" asked Brianag, and Áine stopped. "Why does one of the vaunted Womb-Born need a baby as her shield?" She glanced at Gràinne and laughed. "The answer is obvious. She is terrified of facing us, Ma." Brianag bent in an exaggerated bow. "She should be, because are more powerful than this pitiful sídhe. The Goddess demands judgment, and we are her servants."

Brianag looked to Neamhain. *Be ready.* An imperceptible inclination of Neamhain's head was the answer. *The bitseach is mine to kill, Ma, but I need you at my side.* Gràinne smiled at Brianag's unspoken words, and once again a red aura emerged to envelope her body. Crimson tentacles embraced Brianag, menacing, yet warm as if blood pumped through them.

"No, Abomination, because her agonies and death will hurt you and everyone who caused Sidheag pain. I will delight in your pitiful cries for mercy before I kill you," snarled Áine.

"Liar!" shouted Brianag, causing Áine to wince. "You cared for neither Sidheag nor Leannán. Your heart was stone and your ears deaf when they called on you for help. *You* let them die alone and unloved. Your vanity has no bounds, and you will go to any lengths to mask your corruption."

Áine shook Eimhir like a rat, eliciting a shriek from her victim.

Move speedily, Brianag. Eimhir is in dire peril. The cut triggers the baby's delivery, and we cannot cover all the possibilities. Brianag nodded at Neamhain's counsel.

"Let us examine your erroneous assertion. You badly misjudge me, Áine of the Womb-Born. Sidheag made me an Abomination, a monster. The humans and Aes Sídhe alike fear me but have no love for me. In return, I owe them neither love nor loyalty." Áine glanced warily around her. Controlling humans was effortless, but those arrayed before her had abilities, and she had not fought on equal terms in millennia. Insidious doubts and fears multiplied in her mind. *Are they mine or the bitseach's?*

Brianag continued to prey on Áine's mind, taunting her and moving closer. "It is you who needs this woman and her baby because you are not strong enough to destroy me. I respect Leannán more than you. She had the courage to fight A 'Bhanrigh Fuil, face to face. She will be remembered fondly in the lore of the Aes Sídhe… not you. Your reward will be everlasting laughter and ridicule because you are a coward who used a baby as your shield."

She breathed deeply. In the slop of Áine's slaughter, Brianag stood a shimmering green beauty with obsidian eyes, green talons, and curling green rivers. She opened her arms wide. "Prove me wrong." Then she opened her mouth in a nightmarish smile. "I tire of your procrastination. Kill the baby. Kill the mother. You are the greater evil. Do it, or are you scared to fight me, face to face?"

"No!" roared Cassán.

***

To an impartial observer, the events immediately following Brianag's challenge were executed in a heartbeat. To those involved, it was chaos, and an agonisingly long period. Enraged by Brianag's insults, Áine's lips curled and she tossed a screaming Eimhir over the parapet with a flick of her wrist.

Red tendrils from Gràinne's aura stretched out and wrapped around Eimhir's belly, stemming the flow of blood and slowing her fall. Wisely, the Goddess mistrusted Serendipity's promise to deliver Eimhir to safety. Hence, she intervened, directing Eimhir's descent into the courtyard and not Dùn Brion's rocky crag.

As Eimhir fell shrieking onto the oak in the yard, the tree's spring foliage broke her fall, and she was immediately caught and surrounded by a huge ball of lynxes still wearing their winter fur. Thus, she gently descended until transferred into the arms of a relieved, if very shaken, Cassán.

∗∗∗

Thwarted, Áine lifted several bodies from which to drain blood. She screeched at the foul taste. Nauseated, she threw up most of what she had recently drunk, which was a first for any sídhe. Demigods were not supposed to suffer the inflictions of humanity. She spotted the thin, red mist undulating over the gore and glared at Gràinne.

"I am A 'Bhanrigh Fuil—The Blood Queen. All blood serves me, and, as with Leannán, I have removed your rights to its power." Gràinne chuckled, but it was not a joyful sound. "Yet, you are one of the Womb-Born, Áine, and I have no authority to remove a sídhe's abilities." Gràinne's lips drew back into a spiteful grin. "Surely a Womb-Born can fight my daughter without blood or a baby as her shield. In your words, she is a child."

Áine strode towards Brianag but promptly tripped over Eimhir's dress and fell on her face. As she struggled to rise from the slop, Brianag was bent over double laughing. At one time, the blood drinker relished bathing in gore. Now she felt disgust as she wallowed in the guts of her victims.

"First justice to Eimhir," said Brianag.

"I will flay the flesh from your body, bitseach," said Áine, regaining her balance, if not her dignity.

"How will you do that? I am inside your head," mocked Brianag.

"Eimhir's diversion was very clever for a human." She shivered as she slashed the protective veils in Áine's mind and walked through the maze of dark pathways. "Your mind is loathsome, but I have not forgotten its secrets."

The screech of fury and fear from Áine burst eardrums across the surrounding landscape. She stepped forward to kill Brianag, but uncertainty gripped her. *Which Brianag should I fight? The one who tears through the veils in my mind or the green nightmare who dances before me?*

"Both, bitseach. We are one and the same." Brianag leapt forward and slashed, reducing Áine's chiton to ribbons and watching them flutter to the walkway. From breast to belly, rows of diagonal cuts parted Áine's porcelain and hitherto unblemished skin. Only her face remained untouched.

Áine grinned as Brianag watched the wounds mend. "Killing a Womb-Born is not that easy. You are young, so your conceit is understandable. However, it will be your downfall." Áine's hands were a blur of movement, and her nails slashed unceasingly. Brianag's taunting laughter and the realisation she made no impact on her enemy curtailed Áine's fury. Her mouth fell open as Brianag's mirage dissipated.

"Did *you* think killing *me* would be so easy? I am insulted."

Áine whirled around to face Brianag, but was it the real one or another illusion? Still, how had an illusion caused the physical wounds? Áine's mind was in turmoil. She needed an enemy to confront, but where was hers? The answer arrived when she was brought to her knees with spiking pains in her head. Brianag had torn down the final veil. Áine felt her mind crushed.

"No!" she shrieked as Brianag destroyed the centre of her existence. Yet the image that petrified Áine was not a determined Brianag slashing her essence. Behind Brianag stood Sidheag.

I warned you, Mother.

In the physical world, Áine collapsed to her knees. Her body streamed blood from multiple injuries, and she could do nothing to stem the flow. The Blood Queen had removed her blood's ability to clot. One thought consoled her. *I am Womb-Born. I cannot die.*

"Only the Goddess cannot die, fool, and she would not be stupid enough to put the claim into words," said Brianag.

Áine looked into Brianag's obsidian eyes and a maw full of savagely pointed teeth. She winced at the pain from a thousand bleeding wounds. From her head to her feet, she was a mass of bleeding flesh. She looked down and laughed. "How appropriate. The price of your victory is to kill me in the manner of Sidheag… and me."

A hand with long, wicked talons lifted, ready to strike. In her mind, Brianag saw a ripped face and torn throat. Áine's eyes glinted in expectation and in the belief a Womb-Born would find a way back. Her mouth opened. "Do it!" she snarled.

"No!" shouted Gràinne. "You are the monster; my daughter never was."

Brianag's arm reached out with an open hand. She exclaimed, "Ma!" Gràinne knew what her daughter wanted. The longsword glinted in the meadhan-latha sun as it turned cartwheels. It slapped against Brianag's palm, and she closed her fingers around its hilt.

In a smooth movement, the blade arched towards Áine's swan-like neck. She gasped, "No!" at the red-hot touch of iron and smelled her flesh burn. Still, Áine's eyes told of an absolute belief in her rebirth. She smiled as the sword carved through her neck effortlessly and her head fell into a pool of gore.

"You got off too easily, bitseach," said Brianag.

"Dismember her. Burn the pieces to ashes, crush the bones, and mix the remains with ingots of molten iron," commanded Gràinne. In a plane between reality and the void, she heard Áine scream and smiled. "Maybe not, Brianag. Maybe not."

CHAPTER 41

382 B.C—Summer—Loch nan Clàr

It was the full moon, and Giosail watched Gràinne slip from another victory feast and cross the bridge to her newly built crannag. She prayed to the Goddess for mercy as she had on every full moon since she was eight. Hidden in the shadows, Giosail wept for one she thought of as her mother. She watched Gràinne open the door to her private chamber and go inside.

Gràinne saw the platter and the cloth covering the foul heart. She sighed sorrowfully and then chastised herself. *I should be thankful. I have Brianag back and my family is healthy and at my side. Many of my people were not so fortunate. Thank you, Goddess.* With a long sigh, she lifted the corner of the tray cloth and took the heart in her hand. It felt warm, and she shivered in the summer breeze. Steeling herself, she bit into the muscle. Then she threw up, again and again until nothing remained in her belly. The sour taste of vomit and bile suffused her mouth, and its foul odour filled the room.

The laughter in the chamber told Gràinne she was not alone. Conflicting emotions of anger and anxiety roiled, but she held her tongue.

Did you think so little of me that you believed I would not reward you? Shame on you, Gràinne Ni Fearghal.

"What have you done to me, Goddess? Am I no longer A 'Bhanrigh Fuil?"

Even my powers are not such that I can remove a blessing bestowed by the ancients.

"Not so much a blessing… a curse maybe," huffed Gràinne.

Don't be ungrateful, child. Without the Blood Queen, Brianag would be lost. Now she has a chance to be part of a family and has friends who love her.

"Sorry."

Keep the title if you wish. It has an impressive cachet attached to it and many fear what it represents. I made some adjustments to remove the nastier elements of the gift, such as its cannibalistic elements.

"Have I lost my powers?" Before the Goddess could answer, Gràinne quickly added, "Not that I care. They are more of a burden than a blessing."

That is yet to be determined. What I have done is unorthodox and will probably have unforeseen consequences… for both of us. You may have lost some powers of A 'Bhanrigh Fuil, but more likely they have changed or been enhanced. Only time will tell. The Goddess suddenly burst into laughter, which made Gràinne wary. *However, I recommend a long conversation with your ma. I have made you a sídhe.*

"Shite!"

CHAPTER 42

The Land of the Cait Sìth

Anxiety overwhelmed Giosail as she looked across the landscape. Behind her, a thousand families, aged from babies to grandparents, waited. From the rumblings of her subjects, they too had misgivings. She had led her people to a wasteland, not a paradise. Giosail mused that perhaps the original barren terrain of her tribal home was not as bad as she thought.

Gasps from the crowd diverted Giosail's thoughts, and she peered north towards the coast. An iridescent mist formed a thousand paces ahead of her. She blinked several times and frowned. She had no doubt that the phenomenon was not present a few moments ago. Perhaps it was a weather event created between the land and crashing seas. In her mind, she stamped her feet. *Where is Neamhain? She promised to meet me.*

Still, the more she strained her eyes, the more she became convinced two shapes were forming in the mist. *Hopefully they are friendly.* Nerves knotted Giosail's belly. *Shite! Why did I want to be queen?* What Giosail had not considered was the figures coming towards her solidifying into lincean. The cats were huge and walked confidently towards Giosail with a grace no human could emulate. Muscles rippled under their lighter summer fur. Giosail watched as one lince deliberately fell behind until its head was level with the other's shoulder.

Amodocus and she had heard legends of cats fighting against the Cú Sídhe and Áine's army in the Lowlands while recovering from their injuries after the battle with Leannán. However, she thought that was just a tribal nickname, like Sorchae's Ravens. *They could not be real lincean. Could they?*

***

"The Hag's tits!" said Neamhain.

"What's the matter?" said Caoimhe.

"Giosail has never seen me as a lynx. She was battling in the Highlands when we were fighting in the Lowlands. What must she think watching two huge lincean approach her?"

"I hope there's no hunters among her people. That could be embarrassing." Caoimhe giggled.

"I don't think you're taking this seriously, Caoimhe. We do not want to start another war. Remember the diplomatic and family issues we had to resolve with the Dolidh and Éile incident?"

"What's the worst that can happen, my love? Recently, the humans of Northern Albu have encountered Áine, the Cú Sídhe, Leannán, Sidheag, Brianag and her wolf, and multiple sídhe. Surely a couple of cats will not alarm them.

"Moreover, if any problems arise, we can vanish immediately and return later to have a private conversation with Giosail and her council." Neamhain looked as unconvinced as only a cat can. "Show Giosail what she thinks is the real you and look queenly. We can explain later."

***

Later, Giosail confessed she nearly pissed her new plaid triubhas when the lincean turned into Neamhain and Caoimhe. Only Neamhain's eyes convinced her she was not going mad. The three stood in silence for what seemed an eternity before a diplomatic Caoimhe said, "We should hug and show the people we know each other and are friends. Dolidh and Éile are visiting the settlement for a few sunsets, so we can call on them as backup if needed."

Neamhain nodded and said, "Before we do that, I should formally introduce you. Giosail, this is Caoimhe. She is a bana-phrionnsa of

Na Daoine Cait—the Cait People—my partner, and our best diplomat. Caoimhe, this is Giosail, bhanrigh of a tribe that needs a name. Perhaps we can help with that."

More curious than fearful, the crowd edged closer while the trio talked. When all three hugged and kissed, they burst into relieved applause and excited chatter. When the embracing ceased, Giosail looked awkwardly at Neamhain. "What is it, Giosail?"

Giosail's arm swept in a semicircle before her. "We are honoured to share this domain with the Cait People, but the landscape is more desolate than our traditional lands." She frowned slightly. "However, I made an agreement and will stand by it."

Neamhain chuckled, looked at Caoimhe, and nodded. "Please ask your people to close their eyes… and no peeping, not even the children." It was a strange request but transpired to be just one of many on that sunset. When Neamhain shouted, "Open your eyes!" gasps of awe greeted her as the adults beheld a land of meadows, forests, rivers, and springs. Then came the squeals of joy from hundreds of children as they spotted hundreds of extremely curious kits. Childish voices pleaded to be allowed to pet the young lynxes.

Giosail looked uncertainly at Neamhain. "My tribe have waited a long time for your people, Giosail. It is appropriate for our young to engage first," said Neamhain. She laughed at the fierce threats of smacked arses and switches from parents should the children harm the cats. "I think the children will soon learn how sharp kits' claws are and where the boundaries lie.

"My council waits in our Great Hall to greet your leaders, Giosail." Neamhain paused and laughed nervously. "But keep your noses closed! You will soon find out how much my tribe needs your people. While we talk, your people are free to roam. It is your land as well as ours."

* * *

A half-cycle of the moon after Giosail's arrival, Neamhain and Caoimhe called a meeting of the Na Daoine Cait's Council. Caoimhe's father, and the council's leader, outwardly looked calm but anxiety made his pulse race. The demeanours of Neamhain and his daughter pointed to an imminent storm.

As a queen who had recently triumphed over Áine, Leannán, and the Cú Sídhe, Neamhain might have been expected to be in an amicable and forgiving mood. However, when she pushed the throne backwards and searched the faces of all seated before her with narrowed elongated pupils, it was not a promising omen. *What have we done?*

The Leader's answer came quickly. "You deceived me, your queen," growled Neamhain, and instantly every cat in the room became alert. "Worse, you sent your daughters, not to fight the Cú Sídhe, but to surrender and be sacrificed to that beast." A ripple of objections and arguments percolated through those present. A threatening growl and incisors revealed by drawn-back lips stopped it.

"In the human world, this is the act of the depraved and dictators who put no value on life. I expected much more from the Cait Sìth, but it seems you are not as enlightened as humanity." This time, the growling came from the council members. "*Bi 'nad thost*—be silent!" bellowed Neamhain.

"I have spoken with the Goddess…" The chamber instantly fell silent. "*We* will take no rebuke or excuses from a leadership who betrayed their founding principles and their young. The Cait People *never* sent their daughters into battle to be sacrificed. It seems there is a history you conveniently forgot. It was the Elders who had that honour."

Neamhain breathed deeply. "*Your* duplicitous behaviour is unforgivable." Gasps met a statement that left no room for discussion, and the Council of Elders dreaded Neamhain's next words. "The Elders of the Na Daoine Cait are banished to the Land of the Old Ones for a thousand years. There, you will have no contact with any of the Na Daoine Cait." Neamhain paused to let her judgment sink in. "You may be accompanied by those family members who are foolish enough to travel with you."

"You cannot do this," snapped the council leader.

"I can because I am your queen," said Neamhain. "If you have objections, I suggest you take them up with the Goddess or her Hand. However, I would not count on a warm reception. The Hand is a childhood friend of mine and the Goddess is angry at you for twisting her generosity. Both are of the opinion that exile is much too lenient."

The leader looked beseechingly at Caoimhe. "Daughter, can you not intercede on our behalf? Please persuade Neamhain to reduce our punishment."

"She is my queen. Strangers valued me and my friends lives more than our fathers. Go. As the queen's shield-maiden, it is my duty to enforce the sentence. You have one sunset to say goodbye."

CHAPTER 43

The Land of Immensity—City of Coria

Nine thrones of polished, black granite, marbled with emerald-green veins, dominated the chamber. They looked impressive, if impractical and certainly uncomfortable. Each had a large, fringed cushion to alleviate sore arses, but the smooth, slippery stone defeated the intent. Only seven were occupied. The Leader of the Womb-Born glanced to his left and right. Four brothers and two sisters returned his gaze. All anxiously awaited news from Áine.

They needed a measure of how the Aes Sídhe would fare in a second war with men and had used their sister's desire for vengeance to test the resolve of humans. The siblings knew Áine was unstable but hoped the Womb-Born would see the bigger picture of freeing the Aes Sídhe from the confines of the Land of Immensity. Pre-occupied with their infertility and the unsustainability of their race, they thought to conquer the humans and use the females to breed a new generation of Aes Sídhe.

The other dilemma for the Womb-Born, which became evident shortly after Áine commenced her campaign, was that their vision had deserted them. They could neither see into the realm of man nor use the portals. Thus, the pathways and doorways to the Kingdom of Men were closed… but by whom? A score of scouts had returned blind and dumb.

Self-preservation, always the foremost priority for the Aes Sídhe, begat division and the blame game. "It is the Goddess's work. She has moved against us." Only Daghdha was brave or foolish enough to openly state what his siblings were thinking. "Who else could imprison us in our domain? Men are not powerful enough… yet."

"But why?" asked Oghma.

The Leader looked incredulously at his brother. "Is that a serious question? Áine, Leannán, the Cú Sídhe, and let us not forget Sidheag and her Brood. We let the beast and the blood drinkers loose. We broke our covenants with the Goddess and men."

An uneasy silence pervaded the chamber as the Womb-Born wrestled with conflicting emotions. It was broken by a raucous laugh, emanating from everywhere and nowhere. The demigods reached for their legendary swords and spears.

"What use are your weapons if you cannot see me or if iron cannot kill me?"

The voice was young, harsh, and resonated with a desire to inflict pain. An apology followed a cough. "Sorry, Grandma… us." The veil dropped, revealing Brianag, Mongfhionn, Draighean, Medb, Gràinne, Neamhain, and Sorchae, standing before the nine thrones.

Daghdha recovered first from his and his siblings' shock at the disruption. His lips curled in contempt. "I see a gaggle of disaffected sídhe tainted by men, a Cait Sìth, a Blood Queen, and her spawn—or is she Sidheag's issue?" He looked at Sorchae and momentarily curbed his screed, but Daghdha was committed and not the sharpest blade among the Womb-Born. Thus, he blundered on. "And a human with a fancy title." He stood and bowed. "We tremble before you."

The other Womb-Born hid their mouths with their hands and giggled like children, although nervously. Daghdha's bombast had barely finished before Brianag was in his face. Green talons encircled his neck and bit into his flesh. He gasped as pain seized his body for the first time in aeons. "The 'human' is both my friend and the Hand of the Goddess. *She* does not welcome her servants being mocked. Hold your tongue, fat one, or I will rip it out—permanently. Shite! Perhaps I will anyway."

Daghdha's siblings were stunned and shouted, "No!" as Brianag's mouth opened into a dark maw with multiple rows of needle teeth.

"Brianag, we have an agreement with the Goddess, and unlike those before us, we will keep it," said Sorchae. A reluctant Brianag loosed Daghdha, although not before the talon on her little finger sliced through his neck, narrowly, but deliberately, missing his artery.

"See how quickly you can heal that, arsehole. The Cú Sídhe's never mended," hissed Brianag, before retreating to her ma's side. Daghdha scrambled to stem the blood. He was unaided by his siblings, who considered Daghdha an obese boor and were inclined to sympathise with Brianag.

The Leader changed tack to regain ground and assert the Womb-Born's authority. "Your tricks and petty defiance will cease immediately," he ordered. "Return to wherever you consider your home, and we will ignore your behaviour. You cannot and will not be allowed to defy the Nine." The smile on Mongfhionn's face as she stepped forward should have been a warning to the Leader, but history and self-importance blinded him.

"There is no 'Nine'," stated Mongfhionn. The ice in her voice chilled the chamber. She produced a hessian sack from the folds of her cloak, held it up, and tossed it towards the thrones. The bloody head of Áine emerged and rolled towards the leader. "Áine is destroyed." Mongfhionn watched a glimmer of a smile alight on the Leader's lips and shook her head.

"There will be no reincarnation. We removed her brain, burned it to ash, and scattered it over molten iron. Her body was dismembered and burned, her bones crushed, and her ashes put in iron ingots, which were scattered and buried across the domain of men. The Goddess delivered her to the Void." Gasps of "No!" and "Bitseach!" echoed off the room's crystal walls. "Leannán and the Cú Sídhe are also destroyed... *permanently.*"

"We have The Mórrígan, and no one can stand against her," snapped the Leader.

"On that we agree. None can stand against The Mórrígan. You would do well to remember that. But where is she?" Mongfhionn barely controlled the snarl in her voice. "You do not know and have not known for generations." The leader's hands gripped his throne until the granite arms began to crack and crumble. An ominous inevitability gripped him when he examined the smiling faces before him.

"You do not know where she is, do you?" Mongfhionn laughed, and it was a harsh sound. "The Goddess and we do." The leader and his siblings shook with anger at having been outplayed, and in fear of those who were arrayed against them. "Believe me, The Mórrígan is content with her life. Force her to enter this argument, and she will destroy you.

"My advice is to accept this lesson. Rule the Land of Immensity as you wish—whether as dictators or fair kings and queens is not our concern. It is your domain. The portals will remain closed to the Womb-Born. Do not retaliate against those standing before you or their families.

"Sadly, your bruised self-esteem says you likely will. In which case, we will destroy you as we did Áine. Enjoy what time the Goddess has allotted to you and pray she does not curtail your duration." At a nod from Mongfhionn, Brianag cloaked her friends, and they were gone from the chamber.

✳✳✳

"Shite!" gasped the Leader.

"This happened under your leadership," snarled Daghdha. Several siblings agreed and the War of the Womb-Born began.

CHAPTER 44

Dùn Brion

"Remind me never to get on the wrong side of Grandma," said Brianag as she tore into a filet of beef that had barely tasted the flames of the cooking pit. Those seated around the table—a round one—in Dùn Brion banged their cups on the table in agreement. "What comes next, Grandma?"

"I hope the Womb-Born see sense, but I am not optimistic. We prepare for battle and wait for their first move. In the meantime, we celebrate with our friends."

Mongfhionn raised her cup and shouted, "*Sláinte Mhaith!*"

***

"What's the matter, Ma?" asked Brianag. "You appear subdued this evening and not enjoying the company of our friends and family. The millstone of A 'Bhanrigh Fuil is no longer a burden. Are you missing Amodocus? Grandma says his wounds are healing well and we will be in Càrn Liath in a half-cycle of the moon." A moment of anxiety made Brianag bite her lip. "Is it something I did or said?"

Gràinne smiled, hugged her daughter, and shook her head. "My mood has nothing to do with you. Recently, I have thought a lot about the past and the future." Brianag's brow furrowed, not knowing whether to be happy or sad. Still, she sensed deep turmoil in her ma.

"Over a decade ago, you and I arrived in Northern Albu seeking answers. The dreams we came to fulfil became nightmares. I almost lost you. Your father was killed, as were many of our friends." Gràinne choked and her voice trailed off. It seemed as if she were far away.

"Spit it out, Ma. What are you trying to say?"

"I am tired of all the wars and death, Brianag. I think I would like to return to Gaul and the friends I left behind. Sorchae, Niall, and Giosail can govern the Eastern Tribes; Cassán and Eimhir are well-established in the Lowlands."

"What about Seonag?"

Gràinne looked across the room at Seonag. In the middle of the festivities, she laughed and talked, but everything about her demeanour screamed of loneliness. "Her choice of partners, and in this I include your father, have continually let Seonag down. The evil that lurked in her tribe ripped her heart open. Can she be the bhanrigh? Yes. Does she want to be queen of the Forest People? I am not convinced."

Brianag looked across the table to Seonag and saw her smile. It was the only time that evening. She followed the object of Seonag's pleasure to Sorchae. "I think she may have a love, Ma."

Gràinne dipped her head. "I hope so and am happy for her, Brianag, but Sorchae cannot give her an heir… and a queen needs an heir."

"Drostan had an heir, and it did not do much good," said Brianag.

"True, but that points only to Seonag's lack of ruthlessness to seize and hold the throne. Perhaps with Cè at her side, things will be different. Perhaps she will relinquish the throne in his favour."

Brianag's lip trembled. "What about me, Ma? Where do I fit in?"

"You do not fit in, Brianag." Brianag was crestfallen until

Gràinne continued. "You belong." Gràinne looked to Brianag with an anxious face. "Wherever I go, I want you to come with me, Amodocus and your brother and sisters. Will you?"

The glow of delight on Brianag's face gave Gràinne her answer. She laughed. "Luag is going to be surprised at this news, but after Malmhìn's death, he, too, needs a new start. And Dolidh can visit us anytime she wants."

The End

BACKGROUND

This is by way of foreshadowing. It is thought that the Irish author Bram Stoker may have got inspiration for Dracula from his knowledge of Irish mythology. Vampirism, blood drinking, and cannibalism were quite popular in Celtic mythology and the latter in real life. There are two main vampires in Irish folklore: *Abhartach* and *An Dearg Due*.

Abhartach was an evil chieftain who was reportedly small or dwarf-like and known to practice the dark arts. Supposedly, he fell to his death trying to catch his wife in the act of infidelity. He was buried the next day with all the honours of a noble but to the consternation of his people, he kept coming back demanding fresh blood to drink. Eventually he was killed by a sword made from the Yew tree which stabbed him in the heart. Shades of Dracula!

However, the most interesting and likely impossible to resist for an author is *An Dearg Due* (the Red Thirst or Red Bloodsucker) who is mentioned in this story by Brianag, albeit in jest when she hints at preserving Luag's life.

The story of the Dearg Due is the tragedy of a young woman who was beautiful both physically and in personality. Forced into an arranged marriage with a cruel husband and failed by her lover, she wasted away and died. Due to an oversight in her burial, she rose from the dead. However, she arose a female demon that seduced men and then drained them of their blood.

Can I resist this character? You will have to read my future novels!

GLOSSARY

Tribes

Aes Sídhe	Demigods
Cinn Péinteáilte	The "Painted Ones"; early Picts
Clann Ui Flaithimh	Sorchae's original tribe
Connachta	Irish tribe
Na Daoine Tùrsach	Gràinne's tribe
Na Daoine Cait	The Cait People's tribe
Na Mèadaidh	Cassán's tribe

Words & Phrases

(IG = Irish Gaelic; SG = Scottish Gaelic)

A 'Bhanrigh Fuil (SG)	The Blood Queen
Anas (IG)	Anus
Àrd-bhanrigh (SG)	High Queen
Àrd Comhairle (SG)	High Council
Bana-bhuidseach (SG)	Witch
Bana-phrionnsa (SG)	Princess
Bean-sídhe (IG)/Bean-sìth (SG)	Banshee, harbinger of death
Bi 'nad thost (SG)	Be silent
Bidse (SG)	Bitch
Bitseach (IG)	Bitch
Bodhrán (IG)	Drum
Brat/Brait (IG)	Blanket(s); cloak(s)
Brillín (IG)	Clitoris

Broch (SG)   Stone tower
Brògan (SG)   Boots, shoes
Cailleach (IG & SG)   Witch, hag
Caomhnóirí (IG)   Personal guard
Ceannard ceud (SG)   Leader of one hundred
Ceannard mìle (SG)   Leader of one thousand
Craic (IG)   Fun; chat
Crannag (SG)   Crannog, artificial island on a lake
Cret (IG)   Basket, also the basket of a chariot
Crúibín (IG)   Pig's foot (cooked)
Diallait (IG)   Thick horse blanket
Ionsaí (IG)/Ionnsaigh (SG)   Charge
Léine (IG/Lèine (SG)   Tunic, shirt, dress
Lincse (IG)/Lince -ean (SG)   Lynx/lynxes
Meadhan-latha (SG)   Midday
Mná-sídhe (IG)   Plural of banshee
Pit (IG)   Vagina
Rí Ruirech (IG)   King over kings
Rígan (IG)   Queen
Righ (SG)   King
Scíath an Fhithich (IG)   Wings of the raven (battle
formation)
Seanchaithe (IG)   Storytellers
Sgiath (SG)   Shield
Sláinte Mhaith (IG)   Good health
Sleagh/Sleaghan (SG)   Spear(s)
Strìopach/Strìopaichean (SG)   Whore(s)
Tá Ár Lá Tagtha (IG)   Our day has come
Tòn (SG)   Ass/bottom
Triubhas (IG)/Triubhsair (SG)   Trousers, pants
Tuili/Tuilithe (IG)   Bastard

DRAMATIS PERSONÆ

Ardghal Sgiathdubh (Sorchae's Shield-man)

Brianag Ni Brion (Daughter of Brion and Gràinne)

Brion Ó Cathasaigh (Father of Brianag and Cassán)

Caoimhe (Princess of the Cait Sìth)

Cassán Mac Brion (Half-brother of Brianag; King of the Na Mèadaidh)

Conall Mac Gabhann (Leader of Clann Ui Flaithimh)

Fearghal Ruadh (Neamhain's father and Mongfhionn's partner)

Íar Mc Dedad (Father of Sorchae)

Íde (Cait Sìth)

Éile (Cait Sìth and Íde's daughter)

Neamhain Ni Fearghal (Queen of the Cait Sìth; also, Tuatha Dé)

Sorchae Ni Íar (Queen of the Ravens and Hand of the Goddess)

Torcán Ó Dubhgall (Mòrag's partner)

SCOTTISH GAELIC NAMES:

Beira (Forest People)

Cè Mac Drostan (Seonag's brother; pretender to the Forest People's
throne)

Conn (Cè's shield-man)

Dolidh (Forest People; Brianag's friend and conscience)

Drostan Ruad (Late king of the Forest People; Cè, Fionn and Seonag's father)

Earc (Seonag's shield-man)

Eimhir Nic Finnean (Cassán's partner and Queen of the Na Mèadaidh)

Ealasaid Nic Finnean (Eimhir's late sister)

Finnean Mac Sèitheach (Ealasaid and Eimhir's late father)

Fionn Mac Drostan (Brother of Seonag; pretender to the Forest People's throne)

Giosail (Gràinne's slave; freed to become the Queen of the Smeared)

Gràinne Ni Fearghal (The Blood Queen; High Queen of the Eastern Tribes; Brianag's mother)

Luag (Forest People veteran; Brianag's lover)

Malmhìn (Forest People veteran; friend of Brianag and Luag)

Mòrag Nic Artair (Queen of the Ravens)

Mùirne Nic Amodocus (Daughter of Amodocus and Gràinne)

Niall (Ravens' leader; abdicates in favour of Sorchae)

Ròs Nic Cassán (Cassán and Eimhir's daughter)

Seonag Nic Drostan (Rightful Queen of the Forest People)

Teàrlag (Mother of Seonag; Drostan's widow)

NON-GAELIC NAMES:

Áine (Womb-born Tuatha Dé; demigod)

Amodocus (Thracian; Gràinne's partner)

Cu Sídhe (Ancient abomination)

Daghdha (Womb-Born Tuatha Dé; demigod)

Draighean (Aes Sídhe; demigod)

Fate (God)

Heilasa (Thracian; daughter of Amodocus and Gràinne)

Leannán- Sídhe (Aes Sídhe; demigod)

Medb (Aes Sídhe; demigod)

Mongfhionn (Aes Sídhe; demigod; mother of Gràinne)

Oghma ((Womb-Born Tuatha Dé; demigod)

Pytheas (Greek merchant)

Sidheag (Aes Sídhe; demigod; blood-drinker)

Serendipity (God)

The Goddess (God)

The Mórrígan (Womb-Born Tuatha Dé; demigod)

Thrax (Thracian; Son of Amodocus and Gràinne)

LOCATIONS

AFTERLIFE
Mag Mell (Warrior heaven)
The Otherworld (Hell)
Tir na nÓg (Land of Youth)
Tir Tairngire (Land of Promise)

EUROPE
Curraghatoor (Íar Mac Dedad's ancestral home, Ireland)
Ériu (Ireland)
Gaul (France)
Lugudunon (Conall's capital; France)
The Great Sea (The Mediterranean)

NORTHERN ALBU (SCOTLAND)
A 'Chrìon Làraich (Seonag's stronghold)
Abhainn Dubh (Forth River near Dùn Brion)
Càrn Liath (Raven's stronghold)
Clota (River and estuary)
Dùn Brion (Cassán's fort; ancient site of Stirling Castle)
Dùn Athad (Cassán's fort)
Loch Eireachd (Fionn's headquarters; lake in the Highlands)
Loch Nan Clàr (Gràinne's stronghold; lake in the Highlands)
The Sleagh (Mountain range in the Lowlands close to Dùn Brion)

TUATHA DÉ

Land of Immensity (Home of the Tuatha Dé)
Coria (City in the Land of Immensity)
Muria (City in the Land of Immensity)
Oileán Dubh (Black Island; place of Leannán's exile)

ABOUT THE AUTHOR

Author David H. Millar is an award-winning author who was born in Belfast, Northern Ireland. He settled in Houston, Texas, in 2011 and is the founder, owner, and author-in-residence of A Wee Publishing Company.

David writes historical and urban fantasy influenced by Celtic mythology. He is the author of the five-volume, *Conall Series*, and the series spin-offs: *The Dog Roses Series* and *The Blood Queen Chronicles*.

An avid reader, armchair sportsman, and Liverpool Football Club fan, Millar lives with his family, and two recent family members, tuxedo cats Beau and Stiletto.

Contact me:

Website:	www.aweepublishingco.com
Email:	davidm@aweepublishingco.com
Facebook:	facebook.com/aweepubco
Instagram:	@author.davidhmillar
Twitter (X):	@DavidHMillar